Adam gave Sophia a speculative look.

"I was just thinking that opportunities for privacy are so few that we should perhaps take advantage of them when they come," he said.

Sophia's eyes widened. "Do you mean what I think you mean?"

"What do you think I mean?" he teased.

"Here . . . now . . . ?" Sophia looked around the tiny space. "But it's broad daylight . . . It's not decent." Her eyes glinted with mischief.

"By the law according to whom?" inquired Adam with a raised eyebrow, drawing her against him so that her head rested on his shoulder.

"You are a shameless rake, Count."

His head bent, his lips pressed against the soft curves of her mouth . . .

SILVER NIGHTS

JANE FEATHER

AVON BOOKS ⬥ NEW YORK

AVON BOOKS
A division of
The Hearst Corporation
105 Madison Avenue
New York, New York 10016

Copyright © 1989 by Jane Feather
Published by arrangement with the author
Library of Congress Catalog Card Number: 88-92121
ISBN: 0-380-75569-6

First Avon Books Printing: March 1989

AVON TRADEMARK REG. U.S. PAT. OFF. AND IN OTHER COUNTRIES, MARCA
REGISTRADA, HECHO EN U.S.A.

Printed in the U.S.A.

K-R 10 9 8 7 6 5 4 3 2 1

Prologue

July 1764

The piercing wail of the newborn taking hold on life occurred simultaneously with the last breath of the woman who had given her that life.

The man standing by the bed, holding the child between his hands, gave a great cry of sorrow; that she should die, his Sophia in all her delicate beauty, here in this squalid chamber where rats scuttled across the earthen floor, and the light and warmth of the bright summer day outside failed to penetrate the tiny unglazed aperture that went by the name of window.

The old babushka who had attended the birthing was now attending to the dead, closing those once ravishing dark eyes, cleansing the slim, fragile body of the woman who a short time before had graced the glittering palaces of St. Petersburg and Moscow, only to die in blood-soaked agony in a wretched hovel.

"The soldiers were not more than half a day behind us. They will be here within the hour, Prince." A voice spoke with barely concealed anxiety from the low doorway of this one-roomed roadside posting house. A bearded giant of a man in rough homespuns crouched beneath the stone lintel, massive shoulders hunched, eyes worried.

Prince Alexis Golitskov turned, the babe still in his arms. His eyes were blank as if he no longer looked upon the corporeal world. "I must bury my wife," he said.

1

Boris Mikhailov regarded his master sorrowfully as he spoke the simple truth. "If you stay, Prince, you will be arrested."

"And if we had not run, my Sophie would still live," replied the prince. "She would not have died such a death in St. Petersburg."

"If you had stayed, the princess would have given birth in the Fortress of St. Peter and St. Paul," said the other with stubborn truth. "She also was implicated in the plan to deliver Ivan from imprisonment and have him proclaimed rightful emperor in the czarina's stead. Her Imperial Majesty will not be merciful; the evidence gathered against you is at present irrefutable." He spoke urgently in this chamber where the stench of blood and death hung heavy. "There has been one execution, six men sentenced to run the gauntlet ten times between a thousand of their strongest comrades. You know these truths, Prince. If you are found within the borders of this land, you will be arrested. If you maintain your freedom, you will have at least the chance to defend yourself."

Alexis shook his head. "Why should I wish to defend myself now, Boris? When the one thing that gave my life meaning has been taken from me. No, I will bury my wife; but have no fear, old friend, Prince Dmitriev's soldiers will not take me here." The shadows in his eyes deepened. "It is a puzzle, is it not, Boris, why the man Sophia Ivanova and I called friend, to whom we opened our hearts and our house, should be the instrument of the empress's justice?"

"It is to be assumed Prince Dmitriev must obey imperial orders like anyone else," Boris Mikhailov responded. "He is a colonel in the Imperial Guard." The statement was accurate enough, but the muzhik's tone had an ironic edge.

If the prince heard it, he ignored it and simply shrugged as if dismissing the puzzle as an irrelevancy. He held out the child. "Take the babe to Berkholzskoye. The unborn cannot be held responsible for their parents' crimes—real or manufactured." A faint, cynical smile twisted the sculpted lips. "What could she know of assassinated emperors and hasty words, private enemies and whispered lies? My father will care for her. Tell him she is to be called Sophia.''

"Sophia Alexeyevna," said Boris, giving the child her patronymic as he took the scrap of humanity who had ceased wailing and stared up at him with her mother's dark eyes—a little princess of the great house of Golitskov, born in a dark, flea-ridden hovel to a desperate couple fleeing the consequences of a deadly intrigue at the court of the czarina Catherine, Empress of all the Russias.

When Prince Paul Dmitriev and his pursuing soldiers arrived at the post house, they found the old babushka with a tale of birth and death, a newly dug grave, and the body of Prince Alexis Golitskov, his hand in a death grip around the revolver that had shattered his skull.

Chapter 1

The ancient caravan route connecting the Wild Lands—the savage steppes of the Russian empire—with the west ran from Kiev. Berkholzskoye, the Golitskov estate, bordered the River Dnieper, some fifty versts from Kiev. Sophia Alexeyevna had no memory of a place outside Berkholzskoye; no memory of a guardian other than her grandfather, Prince Golitskov; no knowledge of a world where the great Golitskov family had been once embedded in the fabric of society. The intrigue of the imperial palaces in Moscow or St. Petersburg meant nothing to a girl for whom the haunting, fearsome beauty of the steppes had always been a playground; for whom the romance of the caravan route leading to the civilized glories of Austria and Poland was the material of dreams; for whom the Cossacks, Kirghiz, and Kalmuks, the horsemen of the steppes with their long hair and wild laughter, were the princes of her reveries as the girl became woman.

She was a child of the steppes who, if she ever looked beyond them, looked west, never east into the center of her homeland.

Old Prince Golitskov, from his embittered soul, had taught his granddaughter to keep her eyes turned away from the east and the court of the czarina Catherine. He had taught her that that court and that rule had destroyed her parents, and she should ignore its very existence. And while he taught her these things, he said nothing about his own fears that the heiress to the mighty fortune of the Golitskovs would not be left forever in the obscurity of the Wild Lands that she loved,

4

under the unorthodox guardianship of an irascible old aristocrat who had early eschewed the duties and pleasures of the imperial court.

Such bitter thoughts, such prescient fears, did not plague Sophia Alexeyevna. On her twenty-first birthday, the day she attained her majority, she was told she was heiress to some seventy thousand souls scattered over estates comprising thousands of versts in this vast empire, but she had interest only in Berkholzskoye. Such immense wealth had no meaning for one who saw no need for it. She took for granted the sprawling mansion, the army of serfs, the magnificent horses, the well-stocked library. Her customary dress was a riding habit with a divided skirt, enabling her to ride astride. She had no reason to develop an interest in her wardrobe, since society did not abound in the steppes, and her grandfather was not one to encourage or welcome passing travelers beyond the obligatory courtesies.

Had she been asked, Princess Sophia Alexeyevna Golitskova would have declared herself utterly content with her life; she had horses, books, the companionship of her adored grandfather, and the freedom of the steppes. The vague yearnings that occasionally disturbed the customary tranquillity of her sleep she put down to the extra glass of wine or the second helping of pashka at supper.

The ice on the River Neva was breaking at long last, great cracks resounding in the springlike air as the splits appeared, widened; the separated blocks drifted, growing smaller under the feeble rays of the sun.

The czarina Catherine stood at the window of her study in the Winter Palace in St. Petersburg, looking down at the river. In a week or two, the city would be open once more to shipping; the winter isolation would be over and the outside world could again enter Catherine's frozen empire.

"It is quite alarming to think she has attained her majority already. How life gallops away with one, *mon ami.*" She turned back to the room, giving her toothless smile to its other occupant, a giant of a man in his mid-forties, long-haired and one-eyed, no concessionary eye patch over the empty socket—a veritable cyclops dressed as a courtier.

Prince Potemkin returned the smile. "You do not bear the marks of a galloping life, Madame." It was no obsequious flattery. He did not see a fat, toothless little lady of fifty-seven; he still saw his wonderfully sensual lover of eight years ago, and he saw the vigor, the boundless energy, the vast intelligence of the most powerful and fascinating woman in the civilized world.

Catherine did not question the compliment. Why should she? The young lovers who nightly brought their firm flesh and fresh skin to her bed reinforced her belief in her own sexual attraction.

"The latest report from our agent at Berkholzskoye indicates a somewhat ungovernable young woman," she said thoughtfully. "From all accounts the old prince has allowed her to run wild. His own misanthropy has kept her from any outside influences." She moved restlessly around the room, her loose caftan of violet silk swishing with every step. "I should have removed her years ago, placed her in the Smolny Institute, where she would have received the education befitting a girl of her rank."

"I think your decision to leave her with her grandfather while keeping her under surveillance throughout her growing was both wise and humane," Potemkin said firmly. "The story of her parents' death and the events leading up to it is well known, and to subject an orphan, torn from the only home and guardian she knows, to the taunts and whispers of the other pupils at the institute would have been cruel. She is a woman now, but still young enough for bad habits to be broken."

"General Prince Dmitriev does not seem overly concerned about the prospect of acquiring a wife with bad habits," mused the empress. "But then the prospect of acquiring such a fortune would compensate for much." She laughed with the easy acceptance predominating at this worldly court. "His loyalty to us over the years has certainly earned him a reward, and if the hand and fortune of the Golitskova is his choice then it will serve our own purposes to perfection. He will make a steadying husband for her. The old prince has apparently seen to her schooling with exemplary attention, even if she has not been taught to accept the burdens and responsibilities of a princess of the house of Golitskov. Prince Dmitriev will be able to teach her that, and she will enter Petersburg society as the wife of a wealthy nobleman of the first rank. The circumstances of her birth and upbringing will be subsumed.''

Potemkin gnawed a fingernail already bitten red and raw to the quick. ''It seems curiously fitting that one so closely involved in her parents' disgrace should take on the responsibility of the innocent's social redemption.''

''We do not wish to be reminded of that dreadful business.'' Catherine was suddenly empress. ''It was a tragic waste of two young lives. They had no reason to flee in that manner. If the accusations were mistaken then we would have discovered it. But that was many years ago; the matter is finished.''

Potemkin bowed his acceptance of the imperial wish, while he wondered whether his empress remembered the cold, ruthless ferocity with which she had punished all those connected with the ill-conceived plan to release the deposed Ivan VI from the fortress of Schlusselburg—a plan that had led to the young man's most convenient assassination by his guards. Many people whispered that Catherine herself had instigated the attempt to release him. Such an attempt ensured that certain imperial secret instructions would be put into effect: the deposed czar was to be killed rather than allowed to escape. To squash any such implication, she had shown no mercy to those who were part of the plan for his deliverance—a plan that was said to have been hatched in the palace of the young Prince and Princess Golitskov.

Smoothly, he returned to the original subject. ''It is a pity that General Prince Dmitriev was obliged to return to the Crimea to deal with the insurrection. He could otherwise have gone to Kiev to fetch Sophia Alexeyevna in person.''

Catherine's smile indicated a happy resolution to the problem. "Count Danilevski has asked for leave to visit his family estates in Mogilev. The journey from there to Kiev is not so very great. I have it in mind to charge him with the escort of Princess Sophia. He is, after all, Prince Dmitriev's aide-de-camp. It seems appropriate enough that he should undertake the task."

"Adam is not a man to be moved by protests or feminine tears, either," murmured Potemkin. "Should his charge prove resistant—"

"I do not see why she should," Catherine interrupted briskly. "She cannot wish to spend her life languishing in the steppes as wife to some drunken minor landlord of mediocre breeding, little education, and no manners." Her tone managed to convey the impression that a picture such as she had painted was an inconceivable future for a Golitskov. And Prince Potemkin could only agree.

"Of course," Catherine continued, "the old prince might have some objections; he was always of an awkward turn of mind. But he cannot fail to see the advantages for his granddaughter in such a move. However, you are right. Adam combines a persuasive charm with a resolution of purpose, and he is not in the least susceptible to feminine wiles."

"Not since that appalling affair with his wife," agreed Potemkin. "No one seems to know the truth of her death."

"I was under the impression it was a riding accident," the czarina said. "But more important, everyone is agreed that she was carrying another man's child at the time of her death. The count had been campaigning in the Crimea for the previous ten months."

"The Poles are a proud race," Potemkin said. "They don't take kindly to smirched honor. Adam never refers to the woman; it is as if he had never been married. But he makes no attempt to hide his contempt for the weaker sex."

The czarina, who did not consider herself to be a true member of the weaker sex, took no exception to Potemkin's use of the term. Women were in general whining, feeble, and frivolous. It was merely inconvenient in her own case that the mind of a conquering male should be housed in a body that had the needs and impulses of a weak woman.

"We will send for him at once, and set this matter in motion," the empress declared briskly. "It is past time we executed our responsibilities toward Sophia Alexeyevna. It is time she took her place as a grown woman in the world to which she was born."

Six weeks later, on a glorious April morning, Count Adam Danilevski set off from his own estates in what had once been part of Poland, before the first partition of that country—the collective rape, as it had been called—by Austria, Russia, and Prussia twelve years earlier. The territory was now known as White Russia, its inhabitants no longer under Polish sovereignty but beneath the imperial yoke of Russia.

He was on his journey to the Golitskov estates outside Kiev, accompanied by the troop of twelve soldiers who had been with him since leaving St. Petersburg; every one of the twelve knew better than to intrude on their colonel's musings. His face was as stone, the gray eyes hard, the set of his shoulders forbidding.

Visiting his family estates always depressed him, reminding him as it did of his lost nationality, of the humbling of his once proud country. After the partition, he had been taken as a boy of sixteen with other scions of the most important Polish families to St. Petersburg, there to continue his education in the Russian manner as a cornet in the prestigious Preobrazhensky regiment of the Imperial Guard. They were treated with all the honor due such young noblemen, but they were hostages for the good behavior of their annexed homeland. Twelve years of Russian sovereignty had ensured acceptance, and Adam Danilevski often was unable to separate the strands of his Polish self from his Russian self. But when he went back to Mogilev he was Polish, the head of a Polish family, the owner of Polish lands and Polish serfs. And this was the first time he had been back since Eva's death a year ago.

He had read pity for the deceived husband in every face,

heard it in every silence. His sisters' constant inane chatter considerately ensured that the subject was never referred to; his mother had alternately wept with joy at the presence of her only, beloved son, and wrung her hands in silent yet articulate unhappiness at the dismal certainty that he would never again venture into matrimony, and there would be no heir of this line to the Danilevski name and fortune.

Now, burdened with his resurrected Polishness, his mother's silent reproaches, the vision of a contemptuous compassion for one who could not keep a faithful wife, he was required to journey across this vast plain, lying mute and somber under the spring sun, to winkle out from exiled obscurity a young woman who knew nothing beyond the wilderness, and carry her back to St. Petersburg to become the wife of General, Prince Paul Dmitriev—a man thirty years her senior, who had buried three wives already.

It did not strike Count Danilevski in his present jaundiced frame of mind as appropriate work for a colonel in the Imperial Guard, aide-de-camp to the prospective bridegroom or no. But one did not protest an imperial command, even one presented as a logical request. He could hear the czarina's smooth, friendly tones explaining how convenient it was that the count desired to visit his home at this time. It was not such a great distance from Kiev, and she was certain he would be able to accomplish such a potentially tricky mission with all the diplomacy for which he was justly admired.

The memory of imperial compliments did little to soften him as he and his party followed the Dnieper to Kiev. From there they turned south, into the long waving grass of the steppes over which so many battles had been fought, so many frontiers won and lost, where man pursued his fellow in the primitive combat of hunter and prey—outlaw struggling with outlaw for the crumbs of existence in a place where stalked the ghosts of Tatar, Cossack, and Turk amid the substantive rivalries of brigand and robber.

Although not one member of this troop of the Imperial Guard would have admitted it, they were all relieved that their destination was but fifty versts from Kiev—thirty-three miles that could be accomplished in one day's hard riding across the Wild Lands. The reed-thatched houses of the village surrounding the mansion of Berkholzskoye was a welcome sight in the distance as the sun dipped over a horizon that seemed limitless across the silent flatness.

Adam, frowningly contemplating how best to make his approach to Prince Golitskov, at first did not hear the pounding hooves until a wild yell broke the brooding silence of the terrain. One of the troop exclaimed behind him. A sword scraped as it was unsheathed. Bearing down upon them was a magnificent Cossack stallion, astride it a figure with hair streaming in the wind, a flintlock pistol flourished in one upraised hand.

Adam's first instinct was to reach for his own pistol; then the amazing truth dawned that if this was a brigand attempting a suicidal attack on thirteen armed soldiers it was a female one in flowing skirts. He gave the order to draw rein and waited with some interest for the horsewoman to reach them.

"I beg your pardon for shouting at you like that." Breathlessly the rider began talking as soon as she was in earshot. "But you are heading toward that gully." She gestured toward a thick screen of bush and grass in front of them. "You cannot see it yet. There is a rogue wolf holed up in the gully. He has brought down two horses in the last three days, and I suspect he is rabid."

The woman was speaking in Russian, and Adam used the same language. "Why has it not been shot?" he demanded, struggling to regain his bearings, thrown off course by this extraordinary fellow traveler.

"I am about to do it." She gestured with the pistol. "The villagers are too frightened of the rabies." She smiled at him in friendly fashion. "You can skirt the gully by going about half a mile to the east. Or if you prefer, I will deal with the wolf, then you may continue straight through."

There was a moment of stunned silence while Adam stared at the young woman, absently absorbing the impression of a pair of large, glowing dark eyes set in a suntanned face. No conventional beauty, he thought vaguely, but an arresting countenance. Eyebrows a little too thick and pronounced, nose very straight and definite, teeth white but slightly crooked, giving her smile a rather quizzical twist. A firm chin, with a deep cleft beneath a wide, generous mouth, very dark brown hair tumbling in a windswept tangle around a pair of slim shoulders. Her unorthodox riding costume was shabby and as thick with dust as if she had been riding for hours across the plain; she sat astride her majestic mount as easily as if it were a pony, her carriage erect, the reins held loosely in one hand; and she held the pistol with which she was so kindly offering to clear their path in the manner of an experienced marksman.

"While that is most kind of you . . . uh—" He looked a question mark.

"Sophia Alexeyevna Golitskova," she supplied cheerfully. "And pray do not mention it. It will not be above fifteen minutes. I know exactly where he is to be found."

She turned her horse, and Adam, momentarily taken aback by this fortuitous meeting, returned to his senses. She could not seriously imagine a troop of the Imperial Guard would sit in safety while a slip of a girl faced a rabid wolf. But it seemed that she did. Urgently, he leaned over, seizing her bridle.

"Let go!" Her riding crop flashed, stinging across his hand. "How dare you!" The friendly, smiling young woman had vanished to be replaced by a towering Fury, the eyes no longer soft and glowing but almost black with outrage. She raised the crop again, and instinctively he flung his hand up to catch it as it came down, wrenching it from her grasp.

"Just a minute—," he began in explanation, but she had turned her horse with the merest nudge of her knees and was galloping in the direction of the gully before he could assemble the words. In stupefaction, he looked at his hand where the weals stood out on the palm and across his knuckles. It had perhaps been a bit high-handed to grab her bridle in that fashion, but what an amazing reaction! He became aware of the men around him, all staring at the flying figure.

"Perhaps we *will* wait while Princess Sophia removes the wolf from our path," he said with a calm that did not deceive his companions. Count Danilevski was very put out.

In no more than ten minutes a shot rang out through the gloaming. There was only one shot. The princess clearly knew what she was about when it came to marksmanship, Adam reflected. She did not reappear, so he assumed she had continued on her way through the gully. Since her way was also theirs, he gave the signal to ride toward the gully. They came upon the lean, gray shape of the wolf lying in the long, wavy grass. Curious, Adam dismounted, examining the beast. There was one wound, to the heart. It would have been a clean, instantaneous death.

Thoughtfully, he remounted and they continued on their way to Berkholzskoye. He had not known what to expect of the young woman who was to be his charge for the month it would take them to reach St. Petersburg. He had assumed she would be of the usual kind, simpering and silly, or paralyzed with shyness, either way with no conversation and, inevitably, appallingly countrified. He had expected to be plagued with whining complaints about the length and inevitable discomfort of the journey. He had *not* expected a fiercely independent, hard-riding, fast-shooting Cossack woman with the devil of a temper. And just how was that contretemps going to affect the task ahead of him? It was by imperial command that he would remove the princess from the guardianship of her grandfather, but he had no desire to enforce the command. He had hoped that charm and diplomacy would achieve success. Now, he was not so sure.

Sophie had reached home before her outrage at that insufferable check on her bridle by a complete stranger had subsided sufficiently for her to wonder what a troop of soldiers was doing in the area.

Leaving her horse in the stable, she strode energetically into the house, her booted feet clicking on the flagged floors, her long divided skirt swishing at her heels. Prince Golitskov was to be found in his library at the rear of the house; it took but one appraising look at his granddaughter's flushed cheeks, the angry sparkle in her eyes, to tell him that Princess Sophie was not pleased.

"Did you find the wolf?" he asked.

"He was where I expected him to be, lurking in the long grass beside the path." She placed the pistol on a side table. "Khan was steady as a rock, even when the wolf reared up in the shadows."

"And when you fired?" asked the old man, whose interest in the breaking and schooling of horses matched his grand-daughter's.

"He did not flinch."

"Then what has happened to anger you, Sophie?" He leaned back in his chair, smiling at her. She was one of the few people who could induce a smile from the crusty mis-anthropist.

Sophie told him in few words, pacing restlessly around the book-lined room with her customary long stride.

"What uniform were they wearing?" Prince Golitskov frowned into the empty hearth. Soldiers in the region of Ber-kholzskoye did not augur well. They would not be so far from the beaten track by accident.

Sophie struggled with errant memory. "Dark green tunics with red facings," she said slowly. "And black sword knots."

"The Preobrazhensky regiment of the Imperial Guard. Ah. . ." A bleak look crossed her grandfather's face. The presence of such an elite could only mean that the imperial eye had been turned in the direction of Berkholzskoye. The czarina could have no interest in an old man of seventy. For a moment his gaze rested sadly on his granddaughter, who seemed to be waiting for an explanation.

He was about to attempt one when the library door opened without ceremony. Old Anna, the housekeeper, stood wring-ing her hands in the doorway. "Soldiers . . . at the door. . . ." she stammered. "Here to see Your Highness." Her rheumy old eyes were filled with fright at such a visitation, and she continued to wring her gnarled, work-roughened hands in alarm.

"Soldiers!" Sophie's cheeks warmed with a resurgence of annoyance. "The same ones?" She looked at her grandfather, who nodded.

"There cannot be more than one such troop in these parts," he said dryly. "Show them in, Anna."

"I will not receive them," Sophie declared, moving to the door.

The prince sighed. "You must! Remain here!"

The peremptory tone brought her to a stop at the door; she turned back to him in surprise. "Why must I?"

"They are not here to see me," he told her bluntly. He did not add that he had been expecting this, just had not known when it would happen. But then he had not told her of the imperial secret agents who had visited the estate during the last ten years, sometimes as travelers, sometimes as itinerant workmen. The prince knew the type of old and had little difficulty identifying them. He had not challenged them. What would have been the point?

The pink in her cheeks ebbed, and questions flashed in her dark eyes, but there was no time for them. The crisp voice of earlier in the evening came from the passage, the sharp click of booted feet, the ring of spurs. She stepped away from the door, moving instinctively into the shadow of a wood-paneled corner.

"Prince Golitskov." Count Danilevski bowed in the door. "Colonel, Count Adam Danilevski of the Imperial Guard at your service." He spoke in French, the language of the court and the aristocracy.

The old prince rose from his chair. "Are you, indeed?" he murmured in the same language. "At my service? Somehow, I doubt that. Pray come in." He gestured toward the center of the room. "I imagine you and your men will be my guests for a while." He looked past the count to where Anna still stood, wringing her hands in the doorway. "There is no cause for alarm, woman," he said testily, switching to Russian. "You look as if you are about to mount the scaffold. Get about your business and see to the needs of our guests."

Anna scuttled off, somewhat reassured by her master's customary irascible tone. Sophie drew farther into the shadows but her grandfather beckoned her forward. "You have met my granddaughter, I understand, Count."

"Yes, I have had that . . . uh . . . pleasure," replied the count. "I was not able to introduce myself, unfortunately." He held her riding crop between his hands, and now presented it to her with an ironic bow. "I must ensure that if we ride together in the future, Princess, I am wearing gloves."

"I cannot imagine such an event," Sophie countered, taking back her property. "If you will excuse me, Count, there are matters to which I must attend if we are to provide hospitality for thirteen guests."

A *most* inauspicious beginning, reflected Adam, uncertain what he could have done to alter the course once it had been set. He became aware of the prince's eyes upon him. They contained a suspiciously malicious gleam.

"My granddaughter is an unusual young woman, Count."

"Yes, I have received that impression." He picked up the flintlock pistol on the side table. "An accomplished shot, in addition to being a remarkable horsewoman."

"She has grown up on the steppes, not at court," the prince said gently. "It is not a land to roam freely if one is not able to take care of oneself."

"It is perhaps not a land for a young woman to be permitted to roam freely," suggested the count, equally as gently.

Golitskov shrugged. "I fail to see why not." He walked with rheumatic stiffness to the sideboard. "Vodka, Count?"

"Thank you."

There was a moment of silence as the drink of hospitality was swallowed in one gulp. Then, the formalities out of the way, the prince refilled their glasses and said, "So, Her Imperial Majesty has decided to reinstate my son's family and name."

Adam was conscious of relief. The old man at least was

not going to prove difficult. "General, Prince Paul Dmitriev has asked for your granddaughter's hand. I am here as emissary."

A sardonic smile flickered over the hereditary sculpted lips of the Golitskov. "Emissary?"

"And escort," Adam said, dispensing with euphemism. There was clearly no point in the niceties of diplomacy with this blunt old man.

"I have not been at court for forty years," Golitskov now said. "I know the family, of course. Quite unexceptionable. But I am not acquainted with Prince Paul."

Thankfully, Adam drew from his pocket a document under the imperial seal. He would not be required to give his own opinion of Paul Dmitriev, or describe the prince's somewhat checkered marital history. Catherine in her own hand had written warmly to Prince Golitskov, endorsing Dmitriev's suit in glowing terms and promising her close personal attention to the welfare of Sophia Alexeyevna.

Prince Golitskov perused the document in silence. He was under no illusions that his sovereign's easy missive was the request it purported to be. Sophia Alexeyevna was ordered to St. Petersburg, where she would wed this mature paragon of health and good nature, a general in the army with a catalog of military deeds to his credit, who would ensure that she was established in her rightful place in court society. Golitskov wondered cynically what particular service the general had performed for his empress in order to be rewarded with such an heiress. Presumably it had not been in the bedchamber, since Her Imperial Majesty's tastes and appetites required the rejuvenating freshness and boundless energy of the young.

There was little point in such speculation. The empress's power over her subjects was as complete as that of a man over his serfs—the human chattel who guaranteed his prosperity. The master of serfs, unlike the czarina, did not have the legal power to inflict the death sentence on his property, but he could marry them to whom he pleased, sell them, flog them, send them into battle; and the Empress of all the Russias could demand of any subject, be they free or serf, anything she wished for whatever reason, and their obedience must be unquestioning.

He looked across at Count Danilevski, the malicious gleam in his eye growing more pronounced. "I suggest you broach the issue with the princess after supper, Count. . . . A stroll in the garden will provide the perfect opportunity for you to accomplish your emissary's task."

Adam permitted not a flicker of annoyance or dismay to cross his expression. The old man was playing with him. He knew perfectly well it was up to himself to present the situation, demand—and enforce, if necessary—his granddaughter's obedience. The count's task as escort would be arduous enough with a willing charge; with such a one as Sophia Alexeyevna in recalcitrant mood it would be pure hell.

"I have need of your assistance, Prince," he said smoothly, as if Golitskov did not know this. "Would it be too painful for you to explain the situation to the princess yourself? I would be most happy to be in attendance, to provide any further information that Sophia Alexeyevna might require. But I cannot help feeling that the initial approach should come from one whom she knows and trusts." His eye drifted to the pistol on the side table, and the weals on his hand throbbed anew.

The gleam in Golitskov's eye became full-fledged. "Yes," he said with due consideration. "I think perhaps you will have need of my assistance."

Chapter 2

Sophie left the library, fighting the urge to run to the stables, saddle up, and take to the steppes in search of the calm that would come from the elemental wilderness and her place within it. Ever since she was little, such an escape had soothed her nerves, calmed her temper, cleared her head. And she was now in more need of soothing, calming, and clarification than she could remember being for a very long time. But for some reason she was certain that if she disappeared at this time her grandfather would be very angry. She had not experienced his anger on many occasions, but it was a painful ordeal, not one she had any desire to repeat.

What were the count and his soldiers doing here? What had her grandfather meant by saying that they had not come to see *him*? The questions tumbled unresolved in her head as she consulted with Anna as to the disposition of thirteen guests and the supper that must be put before them. The count would obviously share his host's table. Could his soldiers eat with the household in the kitchen? Probably not, she decided. They must be given their own quarters.

Sophie had been running the household since she was sixteen, and supervising these domestic matters brought her a measure of calm, but it was short-lived, as she realized when she returned after an hour to the library to bid the gentlemen to the dining room for supper. It had not occurred to her to change her dress or even tidy herself, and a flush of embarrassment crept into her cheeks as she saw that the count was out of uniform, dressed with plain elegance in coat and britches of gray broadcloth, lace ruffles at neck and wrists. Even her grandfather had changed his coat and cravat as a gesture of courtesy to their guest—for all that the visitor was uninvited and on what Sophie was convinced was a sinister errand.

"You must excuse my granddaughter's informality, Count," said the prince smoothly. "We are not accustomed to standing upon ceremony in this house." He raised an eyebrow at Sophie. "I am certain supper will wait for a few minutes, Sophie."

She left without a word, blushing in furious discomfort at having been caught at such a mortifying disadvantage before the count. She now felt like a rebuked child, all the advantage she had gained at their previous meeting quite dissipated. Why it was necessary to keep the upper hand in her dealings with this tall, lean aristocrat of the wide, intelligent forehead and deep-set gray eyes, she did not know; but she knew that it was.

Her scanty wardrobe produced a blue woolen skirt, a full-sleeved, white linen blouse, and a sleeveless jacket of gray velvet. The outfit was at least clean, if not elegant. She washed her hands and face and tied her hair back with a ribbon. A critical look in the glass showed her a country girl in country dress. She shrugged defensively. That was what she was, when all was said and done, and it had never troubled her before.

Adam, having decided that he must do something to improve matters between them, greeted her return with a low bow, raising her slim brown hand to his lips. She was taller than average, with a lissom, willowy figure accentuated by her simple attire, yet he was conscious of a muscular strength, the suppleness that was bred from physical exercise, that went with the pleasure he knew himself was to be derived from an active life and the peak performance of those activities.

Adam Danilevski had never met a woman like Sophia Alexeyevna, and he was certain that neither had Paul Dmitriev. He smiled at her.

It was a smile that transformed the stern composition of

his face, set the gray eyes dancing, laugh lines crinkling around those eyes and at the corners of what Sophie recognized with a shock as a most beautiful mouth. Involuntarily, she returned the smile and he saw again the friendly, glowing creature he had first met on the steppes. He discovered a great desire to renew acquaintance with that young woman, and with quiet deliberation brought the full force of the well-known Danilevski charm to bear. He could not offer customary compliments on her dress or coiffure, since they would be hypocritical and he rather suspected that Princess Sophie would have no truck with hypocrisy. At the risk of exacerbating old sores, he spoke of what he could genuinely admire.

"I must congratulate you on your marksmanship, Princess," he said, as they crossed the square hall into the dining room. "I saw the wolf. You had placed your shot impeccably."

Her face radiated all the transparent pleasure a debutante at the court of St. Petersburg would have shown at a compliment on her dress or her dancing. No, not beautiful, Adam thought again, but most arresting. Amazing eyelashes, pure sable and thick as a paintbrush.

"It was not difficult, Count, since I was prepared for him," she said, smiling her thanks as he held her chair for her. "He had followed the same pattern of attack in the past few days, you understand. I had the advantage of knowing the pattern."

"Of course," he murmured. "Unfortunately, I had no inkling of your skill, or of your knowledge, hence my chivalrous anxiety to forestall you in a matter that I so mistakenly considered to be more my province than yours."

Sophie regarded him with a hint of suspicion, but the face bent upon her exhibited only candor and a smile that seemed to invite her to turn the ridiculous squabble into a shared jest. "I do not tolerate having my bridle caught, Count," she said carefully. "But I have a rather hasty temper, and I am afraid that I may have overreacted."

"Perhaps we should agree to forget the matter," he suggested.

"With pleasure," agreed Sophia Alexeyevna. "Will you try a little of the braised pike, Count? It is caught in our own rivers."

Supper passed thus, in pleasant conversation and apposite compliments, while Prince Golitskov ate with the sparse appetite of the elderly and watched and listened in sardonic amusement as Count Danilevski set out to win the confidence of the princess. Golitskov was well aware that Sophie, although she responded with more than simple courtesy to their guest's conversational sallies, was wary, was waiting for an explanation that she knew concerned her. But it suited the old prince to keep her in suspense for a while longer. He was interested to see how she bore up under the strain, whether the cool head that served her so well in the physical arena operated as well when the tensions were social and emotional. If it did, he would fear less for her when she was lost to him, swallowed in the political mire that had destroyed her parents.

But Alexis had been naive, his father thought with the old stab of sorrow. He had trusted, had embraced causes with enthusiastic conviction, had seen none of the dangers inherent in this place and time for those indulging in intellectual and emotional commitment to people or ideas. Why else would a man of thirty put himself in an ambivalent political position, flee without thought, then kill himself because his wife died in childbed? For the old pragmatist, it defied understanding, now as always.

With the benefit of hindsight Golitskov had brought up his granddaughter in a different way than he had her father. He had taught her to trust only in her own strengths, to believe only in the facts of her physical environment. Now he watched the girl, sensing her control, the way she weighed her words, never allowing herself the luxury of an ill-considered response. She was behaving as if she were astride a half-broken stallion whose next move must be anticipated. With an unholy glee, Prince Golitskov could also sense the puzzlement of his guest, confronted by this apparently country-bred young woman who spoke impeccable French, as if she were in one of the salons of Petersburg or Moscow, yet clearly fitted no conventional mold.

How would the unknown General, Prince Paul Dmitriev react to his chosen bride and reward? The prince's amusement died rapidly. It was one thing to take pleasure in observing his granddaughter's behavior with a man who, apart from the briefest involvement, would have no say in her life; quite another to contemplate that behavior with a man he did not know, whose wife, and therefore chattel, she would become. Perhaps he should accompany her to St. Petersburg. . . . But he was old and stiff and tired and he had not been to court for forty years. What help could he be to a young woman starting out on her life?

"Are you quite well, *Grandpère*? Something seems to be disturbing you." Sophie spoke directly across the table, its polished wood glowing, the silver gleaming in the soft yellow puddles of light from the oil lamps. The sudden bleakness of her grandfather's expression had brought the prickles of apprehension into full bloom, and she asked the question without thought.

Prince Golitskov sighed and pushed back his chair. "Let us return to the library. It is time to have done with this, I think." It was the count he was looking at, and Sophie's own eyes went to the figure beside her.

"There seems little point in procrastination," agreed Danilevski, meeting the prince's gaze before turning to Sophie, the gray eyes calm yet with a hint of something swimming beneath the calm. Was it compassion . . . regret?

Sophie shivered, heard her voice as if from a distance, weak and almost pleading. "I don't understand."

"Let us go into the library," repeated the prince, moving with habitual stiffness away from the table.

Spring nights on the steppes were chilly; a fire had been kindled in the hearth, and oil lamps lit, curtains drawn. Sophie looked around the room in all its familiar warmth and comfort, and the cold shaft of premonition entered her soul.

"I think you had better read the letter for yourself," the

prince said, handing her the document under the imperial
seal.

Sophie turned it over in her hands, studying the seal, for a
moment not realizing what it was. She looked at her grandfather in confusion. He told her with slight impatience to
open it and read the contents. She did so, but at first the
words made no sense, seemed to deepen her confusion. The
ticking of the pedestal clock was as loud as a church bell in
the quiet room; the crackle of flame, a slipping log, as violently obtrusive as a forest fire. The words danced on the
paper, as if they would elude her eyes as their meaning eluded
her comprehension. She was aware that her hands were shaking, and she began to walk around the room as she read and
reread the script. Activity always calmed her, and as the full
import of the document finally became clear, a deep stillness
filled her.

"I am not going," she said quietly, folding the document,
holding it out to her grandfather. "It is quite absurd. I am
not a piece of property, to be moved, given away. I have
never come across anything so ridiculous." She looked at the
prince for confirmation of her words, but what she saw on
his face pierced her calm confidence. "You . . . you understand, *Grandpère*. You understand why I cannot go?" she
said with sudden hesitation.

"I understand only why you *must* go," he answered. "Perhaps Count Danilevski would explain the realities to you."

"He?" Sophie turned on the count with undisguised contempt. "Why should he explain anything to me? He is a mere
errand boy, but this is one errand he will fail to accomplish."

"My errand, Princess, is to take charge of you and deliver
you in good health to the czarina in St. Petersburg." Her
angry contempt did not annoy him, since he was all too well
aware of the truth of their relative positions. "I would, of
course, prefer to do that with your agreement."

Sophie paled at the unmistakable implication in the flat,
unemotional statement. She looked again at the prince. "I
am staying here with you. Tell him, *Grandpère*."

The old man shook his head. "You are a subject of Her

Imperial Majesty, the empress Catherine," he said briskly, knowing that the slightest indication of his own sorrow and fear for her would do her the greatest disservice. "That document is an imperial command. You must obey it."

She looked at him as one would look upon a Judas. "No . . . no, you cannot mean that."

"But I do," he said. "This summons was bound to come one day—"

"But you have always said that the court is a place of intrigue and betrayal, that it destroyed my parents, that—"

"Yes, I have said all those things." He interrupted her in his own turn. "And they are the truth. If you remember those truths, then you will be better able to deal with that world than was your father. No, let me finish." He held up his hand imperatively as she opened her mouth. "No one means you any harm. This marriage that has been arranged for you is intended for your good and the good of the Golitskov. It will reinstate the family, something that I am too old to do. You must have children, Sophie. The family will die with you otherwise; and you must have those children with a man of equal rank. It is time for you to enter the world. Her Majesty makes it clear that when you leave my house she will take personal responsibility for you until you pass under your husband's roof. It is a great honor."

"It is no honor!" she spat. "It is tyranny, as you know. You would betray me and everything you believe in!" She swung on the count. "I will not go with you, sir." The door banged violently on her departure; the fire hissed in the draft; the lamp flickered.

Prince Golitskov sighed, trimming the wick until the flame steadied. "I expected nothing less. It is up to you now, Count."

Adam looked aghast. "You are not suggesting I take her away from here a prisoner? You can surely persuade her into acceptance. Or, at the least, use your authority to insist on her compliance."

The prince smiled. *"My* authority, Count Danilevski? I was under the impression that Sophia Alexeyevna is now under the authority of the empress, and *you* are the imperial representative."

"For God's sake, man! What good is this going to do your granddaughter? If you have the slightest affection for her, you will make her see the reality of her situation."

"Do not question my affection for my granddaughter," said the old man very quietly. "I have done all I can, and I will not hinder you in any way. You forget, perhaps, that I know Sophie rather well. Nothing will be gained by my repeating myself. She must come to see these things for herself. She will do so eventually, because she is a remarkably intelligent young woman. But I do not know how long it will take. If you have the time to remain here for a few weeks, then I am sure you and I together will succeed in persuading her to accept her destiny with good grace. But if you are in a hurry . . ." He shrugged, and walked to the door. "I am an old man, Count, and seek my bed early. I will see you at breakfast."

Adam looked in some disbelief at the closed door. Of all the stubborn, malicious, awkward old bastards! He could not possibly cool his heels in this wilderness trying to cajole that hot-tempered creature to come quietly. But he knew how she felt, had felt the same way himself twelve years ago when, under military escort, he had left his own home and all that was familiar for an unknown destiny in a place of which he had heard only stories to alarm. And Sophia Alexeyevna was going to become the wife of General, Prince Paul Dmitriev.

The image of his general rose in his mind's eye. Prince Dmitriev was a martinet, feared and loathed by those under his command. A man who exercised his power without compunction, and who heard no one's voice but his own. Yet he won battles, and so long as he did so no one questioned the gratuitous waste of life, the methods he used to send terrified troops into certain death. But Sophia Alexeyevna was to be Dmitriev's wife, Adam reminded himself, not a member of his army. He quashed the uneasy thought that the general seemed to lose wives, *rich* wives, as indifferently as he lost soldiers in the interests of glory.

The vodka bottle remained on the side table, and he helped himself, certain that sleep would not come easy this night. He was a soldier under orders. It was not a soldier's right to question those orders. This princess of the house of Golitskov was going to St. Petersburg under his escort. Apart from any other considerations, it was manifestly absurd that such as she should spend her life in this forgotten outpost of the civilized world. Once she took her rightful place in the imperial circle, she would forget quickly enough the uncivilized steppes. She would discover there were other pleasures to take the place of riding half-broken Cossack stallions and shooting rabid wolves.

He drew aside the curtain over the long French window looking out onto the garden. Was it really possible for dancing, gossip, obsession with one's wardrobe, the inevitable round of salon visiting, for these city pleasures to supersede the elemental glories of . . .

His musing was abruptly shattered. A figure was hastening across the dark garden, a mere shadow, yet an unmistakable shadow with that long stride, the flowing hair. Where was she going? To the stables, of course. Once astride that horse, there was no knowing where she would go.

He struggled with the bolts of the French window, cursing as his fingers slipped in his haste and bolts that had clearly not been drawn throughout the frozen winter months refused to budge. Giving up, he ran from the library and crossed the hall to wrestle with bar and bolts at the great front door. How the hell had Sophie got out of this fortress? Why were there no serfs to help? Surely they were not all permitted to retire, leaving none awake to attend to whatever needs or whims their masters might have in the night?

No one came to his assistance, but he managed to unbar and unbolt the door eventually. The night was cold and still as he stepped outside. He stood listening. A wolf howled, the wind rustled in the long grass of the steppes, a rhythmic swishing sound that was curiously menacing. It was near as bright as day under the canopy of a silver sky, so pure and bright that for a moment it took his breath away and he forgot the urgency of his errand. Then he was running again, reaching the stables as the clatter of hooves on the cobbles signaled the departure of his quarry.

"Your pardon, lord. Can I help you?"

Adam found himself facing a giant of a man dressed in a peasant's fur-lined skin jacket and baggy linen trousers, wearing the long hair and beard of a muzhik, yet carrying himself with the power and authority of a master.

"Saddle me a horse," Adam said shortly. "One to match the speed of that Cossack stallion."

"We do not have another such, lord," the giant said stolidly. "Khan is one of a kind."

Adam faced the man squarely. The gray hair and beard were belied by the powerful physique and the sharp black eyes; the peasant dress and manner by the assured speech and the intelligence in the broad planes of his face. Adam recognized the type of man with whom he was dealing. They were a rare species, the servant who had been treated as friend, singled out for honorary membership in the ruling class. And the loyalty they gave in return was of an awesome tenacity that not even the knout or the strappado could break.

Adam spoke quietly in the clear, silent night. "If you would do service to the princess, you will find me a mount that might afford me at least the chance of coming up with her. I mean her no harm. But her world is changing and she cannot run from it."

Boris Mikhailov examined the courtier in his lace and broadcloth, and saw the soldier. He looked into the deep-set gray eyes and saw calm purpose and no deception. He thought of the babe he had brought to Berkholzskoye, to whom he had given the allegiance he had given her father. He knew the world from which this gray-eyed man came, and he knew, as did the entire household, why he was here. Boris Mikhailov knew that his princess's destiny was not to be evaded, as he knew that until she accepted that fact only misery would lie before her.

"I will saddle Petrushka for you." He turned to the stables. "If you'll heed the advice of one who knows, you'll let the princess run herself out before you talk with her. The wind and the steppes have a rare calming influence." He chuckled to himself, leading from a stable a diminutive horse that Adam recognized as one of the swift, hardy mountain horses indigenous to the Polish province of Cracow. "She's got more of her grandfather in her than of her father."

Adam was not sure what conclusions he was supposed to draw from that piece of information, but he swung himself astride the mountain horse with a word of thanks, wondering which direction he should take across the limitless expanse of wilderness.

"Follow the north star," the giant said over his shoulder, as he walked back to the stables. "The princess always goes north at night, to the Novgorod Rise."

Always! Holy Mother, how often did she take to the steppes in the middle of the night? He was not dressed for riding, and it was only when he found himself alone in the majestic silence of the barren landscape that he remembered he was unarmed. It was a near-suicidal risk he was taking, to ride the Wild Lands at night without so much as a knife at his side, but having started he would not turn back.

He followed the north star for an hour, hearing the sough of the wind in the long grass, the sudden rustle of man or beast slithering out of his path, but there was no sign of the magnificent stallion and his long-haired rider until he saw in the shimmering silver light of the night sky a small hillock ahead, breaking the unrelieved flatness. Outlined against the horizon stood the Cossack horse, head lifted to the wind; motionless upon his back sat Sophia Alexeyevna, looking to the west and the Polish frontier.

His wiry mount ate up the distance between them, but as he approached, Sophie turned, grim determination etched upon her face. She held her pistol, aimed unwavering at his heart. "Do not come any closer."

Adam drew rein. "I cannot believe that if the prince taught you to shoot he did not also teach you that one does not draw upon an unarmed man." With quiet deliberation, he urged his horse forward again, his eyes holding hers in a silent battle of wills.

Slowly, Sophie lowered the pistol and turned away from him, again looking out across the plain toward the west. "It is foolish to be out on the steppes unarmed," she said, almost indifferently. "What are you doing here?"

"I might ask the same of you," he returned quietly. "I wished to be certain that you intended returning at some point tonight."

That brought her head around sharply. "It is no business of yours." The dark eyes flashed in the starlight, and he sensed the rising of that alarming temper. However, he could not allow himself to be intimidated by it.

"It *is* my business, I am afraid. Until we reach St. Petersburg, you are my responsibility. I must ensure that you come to no harm, and that you take no wild notions of escape into your head." He was deliberately blunt, knowing that the confrontation had to come, and the sooner it was over the better.

She drew in her breath sharply, then, without warning, flicked her rein. Khan turned instantly, gathering himself for flight. Risking an ignominious tumble, Adam leaned sideways, seized the stallion's bridle above the bit with one hand, and caught the wrist of Sophie's whip hand with the other. He clung to both with grim determination, concentrating on asserting mastery over the horse, who, if he decided to take off, was far too strong to be physically hindered by a man's hand on his bridle. In such an instance, Adam would be hauled from his own mount.

The great beast trembled in the cold night air, ripples of tension running across the sinewy neck, arched and powerful. Then, as he sensed his rider's confusion and the force of the other's will, he became quite still, lowering his head to stand patiently waiting for whatever was happening to be resolved.

The swiftness of Adam's restraining movements had indeed confused Sophie, taking her off guard for the precious moment she needed to confirm her own mastery over Khan. The fingers circling her wrist were constricting—not painful, but she could feel the force that would so easily surpass her own.

"Let go!" she said in a fierce whisper. "Damn you, let me go!" The muscles of her arm tensed as she pulled at her captive wrist; his fingers tightened over the fine bones and the pulse beat fast against his thumb.

"Peace," he said with quiet insistence. "Be still, now. I am not enjoying this any more than you are. But we are going to be in each other's close company for upward of four weeks. I do not *wish* to be your jailer, Sophia Alexeyevna." He waited for his words to sink in, the words that permitted no possibility of negotiation. She had no choice, and it was pointless to enter a discussion that might imply otherwise.

A tremor ran through her, reminding him of some wild animal of the steppes recognizing the inexorable approach of captivity. Then she faced him, the dark eyes inscrutable. "I imagine, Colonel, Count Danilevski, that you will obey your orders and perform your duty like the good, mindless soldier you are." Scorn laced her voice. *"I* am not mindless, sir, and I do not easily yield up the right to direct my own affairs."

The count silently cursed Prince Golitskov and his unorthodox methods of child rearing. Controlling his impatience and irritation with her stubborn refusal to accept the impossibility of the odds, he said neutrally, "Then we are going to have a very uncomfortable time of it, Princess."

"So be it," she said, her voice cold and flat.

"Are you ready to return to the house now?" he asked politely, as if she had not spoken. "Or do you wish to commune with nature a little longer?"

"I would be alone," she said.

"In the seclusion of your bedchamber, you will be so," he replied with the same neutral courtesy.

That tremor ran through her again, but Sophie had herself well in hand now. She was not going to be rid of him this night except behind her own door. She would bow to the inevitable for the present. She would renew her attack on her grandfather in the morning. It was inconceivable that he was really prepared to sacrifice her upon the altar of family and imperial duty.

"If you would be so kind as to loose my horse and take your hand off mine, Count, I might be able to achieve that seclusion."

"I do not wish to spend the night chasing you across the steppe," he said carefully.

She gave a sharp, derisive crack of laughter. "Do you really think you could catch Khan?"

"No," Adam said simply. "I do not. But I could keep him in sight. It strikes me as a tedious way to pass the night." With a little shrug, as if to repeat her own "so be it," he took his hands away.

"My thanks," murmured Sophie, softly ironic. "So very kind of you, Count." She swung Khan to the south, pressed gently with her heels, and the magnificent creature broke into a gallop.

Adam set Petrushka to follow, intent on keeping them in sight across the flat landscape, although he was fairly certain that Berkholzskoye was her destination. He reached the stable yard just as Boris Mikhailov had returned Khan to his stable.

"You found her, then?" he said laconically, taking Petrushka.

"I did, but I am not sure I achieved much." Adam frowned.

"The princess doesn't take kindly to another hand on her bridle," Boris said over his shoulder, as he led the horse away.

"Literally or figuratively?" asked Adam, following him into the warm, lamplit gloom, redolent with the rich scents of hay and horseflesh.

"Both," replied the muzhik, chuckling. "You'll get nowhere with her if you go head to head."

But just what choice had she left him? Adam mused irritably as he made his way back to the house. *She* had declared war, not he. He lifted the latch on the front door. It would not budge. Disbelieving, he shook it and felt the resistance of the heavy internal bar. Who the devil would have relocked the door? Even if a servant had happened to come into the hall and discovered the open door, he or she would surely have made the logical assumption that whoever had opened it was still without. Suspicion grew, became certainty. It could only have been Sophia Alexeyevna.

All the anger and frustration he had kept tight-reined since his meeting with her that afternoon finally broke free. Of all the childish, spiteful tricks! A piece of typical female malice, secret and underhanded. The sort of trick that Eva would have played him . . . He hammered on the door knocker with all the force of pent-up resentment, outrage, and the absolute knowledge of the misery in store for him until this abominable mission was accomplished.

"Who is it?" A familiar voice from above broke into the trance induced by his furious thoughts and his rhythmic, remedial hammering.

He looked up and saw Sophia Alexeyevna's face, pale in the starlight, framed in the long brown hair falling forward as she leaned out of a casement. "Come down here and open this door, at once!" he demanded with a parade ground crackle that she found herself obeying without thought.

Sophie flew down the stairs, wondering what disaster could have struck. She wrestled with the bars, but they were too heavy even for her wiry strength. "I cannot," she called. "Just a minute."

A couple of minutes later she appeared from around the side of the house, huddled into a thin wrapper over her nightgown, her feet thrust into a pair of skimpy slippers. "Whatever is the matter?" She pushed her hair away from her face, tossing it over her shoulders, her eyes showing him a mixture of indignation, anxiety, and bewilderment. "You will wake the entire household, and it is not just. They rise much earlier than we do."

His jaw dropped. What on earth was she talking about? "How dare you lock me out!" he spat out furiously. "A piece of childish spitefulness—"

"Lock you out!" Sophie exclaimed. "Why would I do such a thing?" The candid dark eyes stared in shocked confusion. "The front door is always kept locked from sundown. There are brigands on the steppes."

"I left it open," he said, but uncertainly now.

"Then Gregory would have locked it again," she replied. "He is the night watchman. He checks the doors every hour."

Adam sensed the shadow of his inevitable discomfiture. "How did you enter?"

"Through the side door. That stays open until Boris Mikhailov comes in. It is a small door, not easily seen. Did you not ask Boris Mikhailov to let you in?" She shivered as a gust of wind tipped with the cold of the flatlands whistled around the corner of the house.

"No, I did not," Adam said, feeling foolish. "You will catch cold in your nightgown."

"You did not give me time to put my clothes on," she said with utter truth, still standing on the gravel path, regarding him gravely in the milky starlight. "Did you really imagine I would serve you such a stupid, pointless trick?"

He wished with all his heart that he could deny it. Not only did he feel foolish, he was overwhelmed with guilt, as if he had committed some appalling solecism. Indeed, he knew that he had. What little he knew of Sophia Alexeyevna should have told him that she was incapable of such a mean-spirited act.

"I ask your pardon," he said a little stiffly. "I cannot imagine what I was thinking of. But you must go inside now, before I have your sickness on my conscience in addition to my injustice."

Sophie looked at him steadily for a minute. "I want no part of your world," she said, before swinging on her heel and walking away from him.

Adam followed, recognizing that he had done his cause yet further disservice. The thought that had been nibbling uncomfortably on the edges of his mind crystallized. He did not doubt his ability to deliver up Sophia Alexeyevna to the czarina, and thus to Prince Paul Dmitriev. But if she had not achieved at least resignation when he did so she faced a bleak future. Prince Dmitriev did not tolerate opposition or the unconventional. He would permit neither in a wife—particularly one thirty years his junior. And if she did not fit his mold, there was no reason to believe that the methods he would use to reshape her would be gentle.

Chapter 3

Sophie slept little until dawn, when she fell into a heavy slumber disturbed by a confused dream tangle of flight and pursuit. A pair of deep-set gray eyes drew her inexorably toward a tall man with a wide, intelligent forehead dominating a lean, aristocratic face, a beautiful mouth now set in stern purpose as he plucked her from the freedom she knew lay beyond her, drew her body backward even as her soul strained ahead; then she was looking into a pair of yellow wolf's eyes, bared fangs, a spare gray body gathered to spring. She woke, her nightgown clinging damply to her skin, when Tanya Feodorovna, bustling in with hot water, drew back the curtains to let in the spring sunshine.

"It's a beautiful day, Princess," declared the peasant woman who had been Sophie's constant attendant since Boris Mikhailov brought the infant princess to Berkholzskoye. The young mother of a newborn son, Tanya had cheerfully accepted another babe at her breast, where the milk flowed plentifully, and when her own child died she had transferred all her maternal energies to her nursling, caressing and scolding through childhood hurts, scrapes, and temper tantrums, steering her through adolescent confusions with her own brand of practical, no-nonsense wisdom. It was the latter with which Tanya was armed this April morning.

"By all the saints!" she exclaimed, examining the heavy-eyed Sophia. "You'd best not show such a long face to your husband on your wedding morning! A man likes to feel he's pleasured his wife, not subjected her to the torments of the

36

fiery kingdom!" She bustled over to the armoire, saying over her shoulder, "Of course, a woman's chances of being pleasured are not very high, but a man still likes to feel he's succeeded."

"If they were made aware of the fact that they hadn't, then perhaps they would try harder." Sophie found herself responding in usual fashion, despite her wretchedness. "Anyway, Tanya Feodorovna, I am not getting married."

"That's not what I heard," said Tanya, shaking out the folds of a flowered muslin dress. "The sooner you stop fighting it, Sophia Alexeyevna, the happier you'll be." She laid the gown on the bed. "Hurry up now. The prince is waiting for you in the library. You've slept right through breakfast." She poured water into the washbasin. "What clothes do you want to take with you? I'm sure I don't know that you've anything suitable for St. Petersburg. I haven't, either . . . nor Boris Mikhailov . . ."

"What are you talking about?" Sophie swung herself out of bed, standing groggily in a patch of sunlight. "You and Boris—"

"Why, we're to come with you," Tanya said cheerfully. "Bless your heart, you didn't think the prince would let you go off all that way without us?"

Sophie closed her eyes on a nagging thump behind her temples and a welter of confusion. A great many matters seemed to have been decided in the few short hours she had been asleep. "I am not going to St. Petersburg, Tanya."

Tanya humphed. "Hurry with your dressing. I'll fetch you up some coffee and biscuits." The heavy door closed with the emphatic snap that generally expressed the opinion that her erstwhile nursling had better stop talking nonsense and gather herself together with all due speed.

Sophie began to have the frightening sense that events were moving too fast for her to grasp them. She had parted with her grandfather the previous evening stating that she would not comply with the imperial command. But it seemed as if he was proceeding without paying any attention to her statement; as if there was no question of discussion. If Tanya

Feodorovna believed that the princess was about to depart for St. Petersburg and a husband, then the entire household would believe it. The first shaft of genuine panic loomed. Until now she had not truly believed that this could happen. Her grandfather would see her position—he had to. Of course, he would support her. Now a niggle of misgiving rippled across the surface of certainty, threatening to develop into a full-blown storm of doubt. Could it be that no one was on her side?

Tanya brought her coffee and sweet biscuits to compensate for her missed breakfast. She drank the coffee, made as strong as Tanya knew she liked it, hoping that the powerful concoction would haul her clearheaded into the waking world. It helped a little, but she was still heavy-eyed and pale when she went downstairs to the library.

Prince Golitskov was with his lawyer and Count Danilevski, conferring around the leather-topped desk. He looked up as his granddaughter came in, subjecting her to a grave appraisal that missed nothing. "You do not look as if you slept well, Sophie."

"I did not," she replied. "Tanya Feodorovna said you wished to see me." She nodded to the lawyer, whom she knew well, and offered a cool good morning to the count, who had risen at her entrance. He was in uniform once more, his black hair confined in a neat queue at the nape of his neck. The gray eyes held hers for a long moment, the inexorable eyes of her dream, and the spectre of the wolf slid confusingly into her internal vision. Why were the two somehow inextricable? There was nothing remotely wolflike about Count Adam Danilevski.

He was bowing, smiling as he drew forward a chair for her. "I am sorry you passed a bad night, Princess."

Sophie dismissed the polite platitude with an impatient gesture. He was perfectly aware that he was more than partly responsible for her troubled sleep. Disdaining the chair, she walked over to the French window to stand in a patch of warming sunshine. The light accentuated her pallor and the smudges under her eyes, even as it brought out the rich chestnut highlights in the dark hair massed on her shoulders.

Adam's lips tightened at this clear discourtesy. He had hoped to make amends for his error of the previous evening, but obviously Princess Sophie was having none of his conciliatory smiles and friendly expressions.

The old prince came straight to the point. "We are drawing up the marriage settlements, Sophie. I wish you to hear what dispositions I have made."

There *was* to be no escape, she thought in dull despair. They were going to take her off to St. Petersburg and marry her to some complete stranger; only death offered reprieve. It was inconceivable, and yet she knew that it was not. It was the way such matters were conducted. She opened her mouth to repeat her point-blank refusal to go to St. Petersburg, then changed her mind. What was the point? She could only refuse to participate willingly in this selling of her body, soul, and fortune.

"I am not interested," she said, walking back to the door. "I do not consent to any part of this."

"Sophia Alexeyevna!" Her grandfather spoke with the sharp authority that he rarely used with her. "I insist that you remain here and listen to what I have to say."

With a little shrug, she obeyed, but remained standing with her back to the room, her hand on the door latch.

Adam groaned inwardly again at the thought of how he was to manage her on a month-long journey of discomfort bordering upon hardship and immeasurable tedium. Clearly, he was not going to be able to trust her out of his sight, and that prospect filled him with gloom and trepidation. If there was no trust between them, how could he hope to help her achieve the acceptance of her lot that would, in turn, ease that lot?

Prince Golitskov was speaking in the quiet room. He was telling her that she would leave under the count's escort the following morning, that she would take Boris Mikhailov and Tanya Feodorovna with her as personal attendants. They were deeded to her as part of the marriage settlement. Her inheritance would pass into the control of her husband, with the exception of Berkholzskoye, which on her grandfather's death would belong solely to her and her heirs. Thus would she retain some measure of independence.

He fell silent, waiting for a response from the motionless figure. There was nothing, until Sophie raised the latch on the door and left the room.

Golitskov looked at the count with that same slightly malicious gleam in his eye. "I have done my part, Count. Take her to St. Petersburg. Let her wed this Prince Dmitriev. But she will always have a home here, married or no." He went to a rolltop secretaire and took out a heavy metal strongbox. "I would give this into Sophie's charge, but I do not think it will make your task any easier if she has the financial means to evade your escort." A sardonic smile flickered at the corners of his mouth. "I did say I would not hinder you, did I not?" He handed Adam two weighty leather pouches and a sheaf of bills. "She will need wedding clothes . . . other things, too. Ensure that she receives this when she reaches St. Petersburg."

Adam took the money. "I will write you a receipt, Prince."

"That will not be necessary," Golitskov said. "She will take Khan with her, also. Boris Mikhailov will have charge of him."

That thought brought to mind a major concern. Grimly, Adam broached the subject that had been uppermost of his worries since he followed Sophie onto the steppe the previous night.

Golitskov heard him out. "I suppose if you feel you must, then you must," he said slowly. "But I wish you would reconsider. She will be quite wretched."

"Show me an alternative." Adam decided that he had had enough of the old prince's games. On the one hand, with that uncomfortable gleam in his eye, Golitskov would tell him that he must now manage the affair himself; then, when the unpleasant aspects of that management were brought home to him, he implied that Adam was as callous as the harshest jailer.

The old prince shook his head, and for a moment the deep sorrow he felt at the prospect of his loss showed on his face.

He looked a tired old man, shorn of the power of decision and the armor of wit. "Do what you must," he said, and shuffled wearily from the room.

The lawyer cleared his throat, reminding Adam of his presence. "I will draw up the documents, Count, and give them into your charge before you leave in the morning."

Adam nodded. "We leave at cock-crow." He strode from the room, going in search of the sergeant of his troop of soldiers. Sergeant Ilya Passek was to be found in the sunny courtyard at the rear of the house, smoking a pipe and engaged in light dalliance with a chubby-faced young kitchen maid. He came smartly to attention at the approach of his colonel, and it was clear from his nervous expression that he was unsure whether his off-duty demeanor was about to draw censure.

"Playtime is over, Sergeant," Count Danilevski said dryly. He flicked a dismissive hand at the young maidservant, who took herself off with a cheeky grin at her swain.

"Beg your pardon, Colonel, but we hadn't any orders—" began the soldier.

"Now you have," interrupted Adam. "You will post the men in the house and around the estate to ensure that Princess Sophia does not leave the immediate boundaries of the estate between now and tomorrow morning. If she wishes to go farther afield, you will prevent her with all courtesy, before escorting her to me."

Sergeant Passek saluted and marched off, leaving a moody Count Danilevski to wander through the gardens, absently noting the efficient husbandry that produced flourishing currant bushes and vegetable plots, and well-pruned fruit trees in the orchards. The steppes did not provide the most hospitable soil for such fruitfulness, so it was to be presumed someone was a skilled gardener.

He came across Sophia Alexeyevna, in gloves and apron, pruning shears in hand, on her knees in a rose garden. She did not seem to be aware of him, and he hesitated, unwilling to disturb her absorption, yet drawn toward that lissom figure almost without volition. Maybe he could produce some softening of her intransigence, something that would make unnecessary what he must otherwise insist upon during their journey.

"I was thinking that someone around here must have a great love of gardening," he said pleasantly, stepping toward her along the narrow path between the rosebushes.

"Were you?" She did not so much as turn her head.

It was not encouraging. He tried again. "I am surprised in such arid soil you are able to produce so much."

"Are you?" The shears clicked and a green sprouting offshoot fell to the earth, separated from the thick gray stem from which it would otherwise have drawn away strength and sap.

Stubborn, arrogant bitch! he thought with a surge of fury. Well, if that was the way she wanted it, on her own head be it. "Your pardon for disturbing you, Princess." He saluted, spun on his heel, and returned to the house.

Sophie sat back on her heels, dashing the back of her hand across her eyes. Why did she have this feeling that in any other circumstance she would enjoy the count's company very much? And why was she bothering with this pruning of roses that she would not be here to see flower? Why was she doing anything today? Every sight, sound, action of the daily life so familiar to her was another turn of the knife, and she was bleeding enough.

Rising to her feet, she made her way back to the house, to be met by old Anna, wailing over the loss of a dish of pirozhkis prepared for dinner and ready for the pot. One of the dogs had stolen both dish and contents from the kitchen table.

Sophie could summon up no interest in the fate of meat dumplings, or in that of the guilty dog whimpering pitifully in the corner of the courtyard after Anna had wielded her broomstick to good purpose.

"Well, what are we to have instead?" demanded the housekeeper, flinging up her hands. "There's dinner to be made for the dining room, dinner for the soldiers, dinner for the kitchen . . . and no pirozhkis!"

After tomorrow, Anna would have to deal with such matters without guidance, Sophie reflected. But then there would only be the old prince to care for. . . . Tears stung her eyes and she ran from the kitchen, leaving Anna muttering and shaking her head.

"Sophie!" Prince Golitskov appeared in the library door. "I must talk with you, *ma petite*."

She showed him her tear-wet face, and he held out his arms to her. They clung together in the doorway, then he drew her into the room, closing the door quietly.

"You think me harsh, I know," he said. "But, in truth, *ma chère*, you must go. If this prospective husband does not please you, you must talk to the empress. In many ways, she is an enlightened despot." He smiled with a tinge of irony. "It is said that she rules with a scale of justice in one hand, a knout in the other. I do not know how true that may be when it comes to personal matters, but I do not believe her to be utterly tyrannical. I do not think she will force you into a marriage you find repugnant."

"Then why must I go at all?"

"Because you are the last Golitskov. You cannot remain in obscurity. I have always known it, and the empress has been watching you from your earliest years." Seeing her puzzlement, he told her of the secret agents and their surveillance.

"Why would you say nothing of this before?" Sophie, in her bewilderment, saw only betrayal. "You made no attempt to prepare me for—"

"No, I did not wish to spoil your pleasure in the life you led," he said sadly. "I was perhaps in error, but I did it for the best." He went to the secretaire and drew out the strongbox again. "I will not send you into that world without some armor. You will have Boris Mikhailov. If you are in distress, or have need of anything, you will send him to me with a message. He understands that. He will serve you, not your husband." Sophie listened, feeling some measure of comfort. "Here are the Golitskov jewels. They also belong solely to you." The prince laid upon the desk a silver casket, inlaid with mother-of-pearl. "If you have need of money once you are married, these will supply you, and you have my permission to use them however and whenever you feel the need."

She knew what the casket contained—gems worth some three hundred thousand rubles. They had been in the Golitskov family for generations, and this extraordinary blanket permission to use the inheritance as she saw fit destroyed her moment of comfort as it somehow underscored her own unfocused terror. She looked at her grandfather in blank distress.

"Lastly," he said quietly, "as I said to you this morning, Berkholzskoye will be yours. And it will always be here for you. But first you must go and try this new life, a world in which you should have a part."

"How does a wife leave her husband?" Sophie asked. "You tell me I have this option, but I do not know how it could be exercised."

"If you should find yourself in such desperate straits that that action should be necessary, you are resourceful enough to find the way with the tools that I have given you," said the prince. "I have taught you to be resourceful, to look after yourself. Apply the rules of the Wild Lands to the imperial court, *ma chère*, and you will not go far wrong."

Sophie took up the casket. Her grandfather had given her all he could; the rest was up to her. As she walked to the door, he offered one last piece of advice. "Do not engage battle with Adam Danilevski, Sophie."

She did not turn, but replied simply, "I do not go willingly and I will not pretend that I do."

Prince Golitskov sighed. He had done his best. The two of them must fight it out. In fair combat, they would probably be evenly matched, but this was hardly fair combat.

Sophie became aware of the soldier of the Imperial Guard as she crossed the hall for the stairs. He was standing beside the front door, his posture that of a sentry. Frowning, still clutching the casket, she went around the house. At every outside door stood a sentry. She went back into the hall. "Excuse me." With a half smile, she pushed open the door, stepping out onto the gravel driveway. She was not prevented, and the sentry did not move from his post. But as she walked toward the stables, another soldier appeared, keeping pace behind her.

She swung around on him. "Are you following me?"

"Your pardon, Princess, but the colonel's orders," replied the guardsman impassively.

Sophie stood still, feeling the sun warm on her back, the vast expanse of the steppes stretching on all sides, offering their freedom. Clutching a casket containing a not-so-small fortune, wearing a thin muslin gown, she was hardly equipped to taste that freedom and to challenge the man who would curtail it. She returned to the house.

The great gong sounded from the courtyard, signaling the dinner hour over the entire estate. Craftsmen and laborers downed tools and went to their homes or the kitchens of communal houses; the domestic serfs gathered in the big kitchen of the mansion, the soldiers congregated in the parlor set aside for their use; Count Danilevski and Prince Golitskov came together in the dining room.

"Where is Sophia Alexeyevna?" the prince asked Anna, who was placing a dish of sliced pork upon the table.

The housekeeper sniffed. "Couldn't say, lord. There's borscht and salted cucumbers on the sideboard. The pirozhki went to the dog."

"What the devil are you talking about, woman?" snapped the prince.

"One of the dogs stole the dumplings from the kitchen." Sophie spoke distinctly from the door. "I beg you will excuse me from joining you, gentlemen. I find I have no appetite and would prefer to ride."

Both men turned in some surprise. She was wearing her riding habit, her hair twisted into a knot at the nape of her neck. She gave Adam a look of ineffable distaste. "Which one of your soldiers is deputed to follow me, Count? I will alert him to my departure."

The count's gray eyes sparked sharp anger at her look and tone. "Excuse me, Prince." He bowed to his host, then stalked past Sophie into the hall.

"Soldier!" He beckoned the sentry at the door. "Take Princess Sophia to the stables. If Boris Mikhailov is available to accompany her on her ride, then you may wait there until her return, when you will accompany her back to the house. If Boris Mikhailov is not available, you will escort Her Highness to me without delay." He marched back into the dining room. "In such a circumstance, I will make some other arrangement to accommodate you, Princess." He gave her a mocking bow.

"You are too kind, Count. I am overwhelmed by your consideration." She bobbed a curtsy, her lip curling. "I suppose I should be flattered that you consider twelve men necessary to guard me. I had not thought myself so fearsomely dangerous, I must confess. In general, I only shoot rabid wolves." She whisked herself from the room.

With a furious exclamation, Adam took a step after her, then turned back to the table. The old prince appeared unperturbed by the manner of his granddaughter's entrance and exit. "I cannot help feeling, Prince, that you have sadly neglected your duties where Sophia Alexeyevna is concerned," the count declared savagely.

"Quite possibly," agreed Golitskov with a placid smile. "She does have a mind of her own, doesn't she? Allow me to pass you the pork."

Chapter 4

The first jubilant, bragging crow of the farmyard cock was quickly answered by his fellows from farms for miles around. The hens began their gossipy gabble and the new day dawned.

Sophie had been dressed for an hour. She sat on the window seat of her bedchamber, watching as Tanya fussed over the portmanteau, putting garments in, then taking them out again, grumbling to herself. The maid had long since given up expecting any decisions or assistance from Sophia Alexeyevna, and contented herself with this scolding mutter that made no impression whatsoever on its intended recipient.

The awaited knock came at the door. Sophie, still determined that she would show no indication of consent to this forcible removal, had refused to present herself downstairs of her own accord. Tanya opened the door to Prince Golitskov.

"It is time," he said quietly. "Do not make it any harder upon either of us than it must be."

They had said their farewells the previous evening, and Sophie had cried all the tears she had to cry. Now, she rose and went past him, down the stairs to the hall, where the household was gathered in an atmosphere both solemn and excited. Sophia Alexeyevna was going to St. Petersburg, to the czarina. She would meet Russia's "little mother," and she would marry a great prince. Such a glorious prospect brought vicarious exaltation to all those who had cared for the princess and been a part of her growing.

Sophie bade them farewell amid their kisses and their tears.

Her own well of sorrow was dried up and she was able to keep her composure until she went out onto the gravel sweep before the house.

The twelve men of the Preobrazhensky regiment were mounted, drawn up in front of the door. Their colonel was on foot, his horse held by a guardsman. Boris Mikhailov was astride one of his little mountain horses, and he held the unsaddled Khan on a leading rein. A closed carriage, drawn by six horses from the Golitskov stables, stood awaiting its passengers.

Count Danilevski bowed formally to the princess before moving to the carriage. "If you would be pleased to enter, Princess." His face was expressionless, his voice even.

Sophie went the color of milk, the dark eyes becoming even larger in the smooth oval of her face. "I will not ride in the carriage," she said in stifled tones. "I cannot . . . you cannot insist. . ."

"I am desolated to cause you discomfort, Princess, but I must insist," he said in the same even tones. "Would you please ascend? Your maid will travel with you."

"But . . . but you do not understand." Her eyes were wide with distress now. "I must ride. I become sick with the motion of a carriage. I cannot travel shut up in that manner." She looked beseechingly at her grandfather, but although his heart was in his eyes, he had no help to offer. He had known since yesterday that this was the count's intention, and realistically he could not blame him.

"I cannot permit you to ride that horse," Adam said. "You have made it clear that you come with me only under compulsion. I cannot put into your hands the means of flight." He gestured to the carriage. "Please get in. We have many miles to cover today."

Still she stood on the sweep, making no move. She reminded him again of some small wild animal of the steppes, anguished in a manmade trap. The image was so painful, reflected so poorly on his own role in this abduction, which was what she was making it with her obstinacy, that he welcomed anger to his aid. He strode toward her, his voice harsh. "Must I put you in?"

With a horrified exclamation, Prince Golitskov stepped between them, and Sophie seemed to come out of her trance. She touched her grandfather lightly on the arm, then walked past him to climb into the carriage. Tanya, laden with baskets and packages, scrambled up behind her. The door closed.

"God damn it, man!" Golitskov had lost all his calm, the ironic veneer wiped away as if it had never been. "She cannot bear confined spaces, and she becomes travel sick in a carriage."

Adam bowed, clicking his heels together so that his spurs rang in the cool morning air. "I did not choose this, Prince. I must bid you farewell, and thank you for your hospitality." The polite phrases tripped off his tongue in his haste to have done with this agonizing scene. The longer they stood here, the worse it would be for both the princess and Golitskov. He turned, swung onto his horse, raised his hand in a signal that they should move out, and the cavalcade set off.

Sophie sat huddled in the corner, unable to bring herself to look out of the window for one last sight of her beloved home, of the man who had been all and everything to her since she could remember. She did not know that he stood in the doorway until the carriage had passed out of sight at the bottom of the poplar-lined drive.

"Cheer up, now," Tanya said, patting Sophie's knee, offering cheerful peasant wisdom. "Don't think of what you're leaving, think of what you're going to."

"I am trying *not* to think of that," Sophie said, then gave up. How could she explain how she felt to Tanya, who from the moment of birth had never expected to have any say in what happened to her? Tanya was another man's property, his to do with as he pleased. She counted her blessings daily that her master was a kind and just man. She had never felt the lash, never gone hungry. What greater happiness could there be for a serf? And now she was going to St. Petersburg with a mistress who was about to take her place in the wonderful world of the court. Tanya could see only joy and magnificence ahead.

The interminable morning wore on. The carriage swayed and jolted over the ill-paved road that was the main highway to Kiev. By the end of the first hour Sophie felt the tightening around her scalp that heralded the violent headache and the wretched nausea of the motion sickness she could never escape when traveling for any distance in this manner. She slumped despairingly into the corner.

An hour later, Tanya leaned out of the carriage window, calling to the coachman. He pulled in his horses and Tanya helped Sophie's hunched figure to the ground. Sophie stumbled behind the feeble privacy afforded by a scrawny bush. Tanya bent over her, rubbing her back as she vomited miserably, the pounding in her head increasing to near-unbearable pain.

"What the devil is the matter?" Adam rode up to the halted carriage.

"The princess, Your Honor, isn't feeling well," responded the Golitskov coachman stolidly. "Can't abide carriages . . . never has been able to."

Adam cursed with soft fluency. Of all the damnably ludicrous things: that that strong, fast-shooting, hard-riding Cossack woman should suffer from travel sickness! He waited until the two reappeared, and his heart sank at Sophie's deathly pallor. "For God's sake, is there nothing you can give her?" he demanded of Tanya. "You must know what to do."

"Not much to be done, lord," said Tanya, clucking soothingly at Sophie as she encouraged her back into the carriage. "She'll be right as rain as soon as we stop moving."

They stopped moving with dreadful frequency throughout the rest of the day, and Adam began to despair of covering the fifty versts to Kiev in the next two days. He had hoped to cover almost half the distance, some fifteen miles, by nightfall, but he was appalled by his charge's distress, even as he had no idea what he could do to relieve it. He could not allow her to ride Khan. Even with a leading rein, the mighty horse would be unstoppable.

By mid-afternoon, Adam knew they could go no farther that day. Sophie seemed to be shrinking before his eyes, a wan shadow of that glowing, vibrant creature to which he had become accustomed in all her infuriating vigor.

They reached a respectable-sized posting house, where he called a halt, going inside to inspect the accommodations. The postman was able to offer a private chamber at the rear of the house. It was not pristine, but it was a great deal less primitive than many they would experience on this journey, as Adam well knew.

He went back to the carriage, opened the door, and stepped onto the footstep. Sophie, still huddled in her corner, did not seem to be aware of her surroundings. Her eyes were lack-luster and sunken in her ashen face. "Come," he said gently. "You will be better in bed." When she showed no inclination to move, he twisted awkwardly in the confined space, slip-ping his arms beneath her to lift her against him. She was no lightweight, for all her slimness and present fragility, he re-flected absently, stepping backward to the ground, where he was able to adjust his burden so that she lay in his arms.

The long sable eyelashes fluttered. "I do beg your par-don," she said in a thread of a voice. "It is feeble, I know, but I cannot seem to help it."

"I did not imagine you could," he observed on a dry note. "We all have our weaknesses." He carried her into the post-ing house, laying her upon the cot in the bedchamber. "The postman's wife will help you with whatever you need," he said to Tanya as he left the room.

"Oh, don't you worry, now, Your Honor," Tanya said comfortably, bustling over to the baggage piled in the corner of the room. "I'll make the princess a tisane, and she'll sleep for a little, then she'll be ready for her dinner, I don't doubt."

Adam stared. The idea that one who had been painfully spewing up her guts every twenty minutes throughout the day, and was now collapsed in a state of complete exhaustion, could possibly be ready for her dinner any time within the week struck him as pure fantasy. He went outside to see to the disposition of his troop and wrestle with the problem of the morrow. A month of days like today would fell an ox, and Sophia Alexeyevna, for all her wiry strength, was not of that breed.

He returned to the posting house two hours later, when the savory smells of cooking filled the air. In the one living room, already sitting at the plank table, he found Sophia, pale, certainly, but composed.

"I am famished," she stated matter-of-factly, cutting into a loaf of black bread and helping herself to a dish of salted pickles. "The stew smells wonderful, does it not?"

Adam sat down opposite her. "Wonderful," he agreed, bemused by this astonishing transformation. "Oh, thank you." He took the slice of bread she offered him on the point of her knife. "You are feeling better, it seems."

"Oh, yes," she said cheerfully. "I am not such a milksop that I cannot recover once the motion stops."

"Clearly not. I cannot imagine how I could have thought otherwise," he murmured, reaching for the pickles.

"It is a chicken stew," Sophie informed him through a mouthful of bread. "The postman's wife killed it in your honor. I am not in general in favor of fresh-killed chicken, myself. I think the flavor is better, the flesh more tender, when the bird is allowed to cool before plucking. But I gather the good woman did not have anything else she considered suitable to put before such an important soldier." Her voice was utterly innocent, yet he could have sworn that there was a glimmer of mischief in the dark eyes, which seemed amazingly to have recovered their glow.

"I am honored," he said. "But I shall be more so if I can find something to drink." He looked around the room.

"There is klukva." Sophie passed him a jug of cranberry liqueur. "The postman's wife makes it. It is really quite tolerable. But she said that if it is too strong for you, you may have kvass, instead."

"Thank you, but I do not care for weak beer," Adam

replied. "You, however, should not be drinking liqueur. It cannot possibly be good for your stomach."

"It is very warming," she declared blithely. "Do not tell me, Count, that I am not even to decide what I may eat or drink on this journey."

The arrival of the postman's wife bearing the chicken stew saved him from response, and throughout the remainder of their meal his companion offered him no further provocation, except that she drank klukva as if she had hollow legs. It appeared to have no effect on her whatsoever, and he decided this version could not be as strong as some he had tasted. Either that, or Sophia Alexeyevna had been taught to hold her drink with the same ease with which she held a pistol. Knowing Prince Golitskov, Adam wryly suspected the latter to be the case.

She led the conversation in the manner of an experienced hostess, asking him the inoffensive social questions about himself and his family, never intrusive, yet giving the appearance of genuine interest. There was not a trace of the bitter anger, the obstinate refusal to accept her situation, to which he had become accustomed, and he was at pains to discover what had produced this change of mood. Perhaps her wretched day had caused the softening effect.

It seemed as if that was the case. When she rose from the table, she yawned delicately, saying, "You will excuse me if I retire, Count. I find myself somewhat fatigued."

"Of course," he said, rising politely. "I am sorry, but we must leave again at dawn. I would like to reach Kiev by nightfall, if it is at all possible."

"I expect it will be, Count." Not a flicker crossed her face, not a hesitation in the equable tone. "I am not made of porcelain." She curtsied, and he found himself looking for a hint of irony in the remark as he bowed in response. But he could detect nothing, and her fatigue could hardly be feigned after such a day.

As she disappeared through the rear door into the chamber beyond, he went outside into the now chilly evening. His own choice of resting place was limited. The one bedchamber having been appropriated for the sole use of the princess and her maid, the postman had been able to offer his distinguished guest a cot in the living room, unless he would prefer to share the family's accommodations in the living quarters behind the kitchen. Or, of course, there was the hayloft over the stables, where the troop, the coachman, and Boris Mikhailov were already installed. Adam had opted for the cot in the living room, but found himself unwilling to seek his rest until the rich aromas of chicken stew and klukva had dissipated somewhat.

Sophie found Tanya snoring resonantly on the mattress in the corner of the chamber. A day that began at sunup and ended at sundown seemed perfectly fitting to Tanya Feodorovna. But Sophie knew that her own fatigue and tension had gone beyond sleep. She was accustomed to vigorous exercise and the bracing refreshment of the open air. Instead, she had spent a day of torment shut up in a dark, airless carriage interior, with the prospect of another such day ahead of her . . . and another such . . . and another such . . . until the city walls would enclose her, and the bars of a marriage . . .

She could not endure it. It was the stark truth, and she knew that, without conscious planning, she had been doing all in her power this evening to encourage her escort to drop his guard. Now, she went to the tiny window, looking out into the dusk, thinking rapidly. She could not return to Berkholzskoye . . . not yet. But she had the Golitskov gems; her grandfather had not intended that they should be put to use so soon, but they had been an unconditional gift. She had her pistol, and she had Khan, the unbeatable Khan. Once on his back, she could outstrip all pursuit, cross the border into Poland . . . and from there into Austria. A world where the czarina's imperial will did not hold sway. What would a fugitive do there?

Not a useful question at this point, decided Sophie. She moved silently around the little chamber, gathering up the few things she considered necessary. The gems, her pistol, a change of clothes; boots, hooded cloak, and gloves would provide protection against the night chills. The thought of the fresh night air, of the sensation as it whistled past her ears, of the sound of Khan's hooves pounding across the steppes, eating up the miles that lay between her and freedom, was so heady that for a second she felt almost dizzy.

There was a profound silence in the posting house. The postman and his family would also follow the sun in their daily routine. Where was the count? That was the all-important question. The bedchamber opened directly onto the living room, and clearly she could not risk leaving by that route. It would have to be the window. She looked doubtfully at the tiny aperture. It appeared barely big enough for an adult, even a tiny one, to squeeze through. But at least she was tall rather than stout. Resolutely, she dropped her possessions through the window, hearing the soft thud as they hit the earth beneath. Swinging herself onto the stone sill, she managed with an elaborate contortion to get her legs through the window. Leaning backward, so that her head was clear of the top of the window, she slithered forward until most of her was hanging in space. Then she dropped, ducking her head, to land intact and relatively quietly beside her bundle.

She paused, listening to the night noises of the steppe. They were the usual noises, the sough of the wind, the howl of a wolf, nothing to alarm . . . no human sounds. Picking up her bundle, she crept around the corner of the house, clinging to the shadows of the walls, wishing the sky were less clear. The stars were so bright, it could almost have been day.

The low stable building loomed ahead, but she had to cross open ground to reach it. Again, she paused, motionless, straining every nerve and fiber to sense another human presence. But again there was nothing, just the lightless building at her back, the white streak of the dusty road, a screen of trees on the other side of that road, and her goal in front of her. Crouching low, she ran across the open ground.

Adam broke from the trees just as she reached the stable door. For a moment, he wasn't sure whether he had really seen that unmistakable figure, whether it was not a trick of the strange light. Then he was running across the road. Stealthily, he slipped into the pitch darkness of the stable behind her. Straw rustled beneath the nighttime stirrings of the beasts in their stalls, but there was no way in the blackness to tell which horse was where. She would have to traverse the entire length of the building, he thought, in order to identify Khan, and he skinned his eyes into the darkness. But he could see no shadow separate from any of the others, could hear no sound of movement other than the horses. Then came a soft clicking sound that was definitely human. It was answered by a low whicker, indicating that Khan and his mistress had their own form of communication.

The sound had come from Adam's right, and he padded on tiptoe toward it. A shape solidified out of the shadows, reaching up to unlatch the gate to a stall.

He pounced; so fast Sophie had no time to register his advent before he had grasped her around the waist with an iron arm, his other hand clamped to her mouth. "You are incorrigible, Sophie!" he hissed against her ear. "Now, don't make a sound or you'll bring the entire troop down from the loft."

In her shock, Sophie offered no resistance; yet despite the painful pounding of her heart, she noticed that for the first time he had used her familiar name. She was hustled, still clutching her bundle, out of the concealing darkness, back into the night brightness.

"Just what have you got there?" Adam demanded. He had one arm still around her waist, but he held out his free hand imperatively for her burden.

Once he saw its contents, she would have no chance of persuading him that she had simply wished to take a nighttime ride after her day of enforced idleness. Never again would he be careless enough to afford her such an opportunity for flight. Sophie looked defeat squarely in the eye. She was going to St. Petersburg with the escort of Count Adam Danilevski, and there was no point fighting the fact any longer. Without a word, she yielded up the bundle.

Adam went through it in silence, whistling soundlessly at

the contents of the gem casket. He thrust her pistol into his belt, placing the rest of her possessions upon the ground before turning her to face him. "What am I going to do with you, Sophia Alexeyevna?"

The oval face, upturned in the starlight, had regained its earlier healthy bloom, he thought with shocking irrelevance. The dark eyes were luminous, that generous mouth opened slightly as if she searched for an answer to his question.

The answer came from nowhere, an impulse he could do nothing to prevent. His head lowered with infinite slowness and his mouth took hers. A violent tremor ran through her body, and she leaped against him as if she had been struck by lightning. The pressure of his lips increased while for a second she struggled to evade an invasion that seemed to go far beyond her mouth. The arm binding her tightened, and with an almost searing thoroughness, he forced her lips apart so that she was opened to receive the deep exploration of his thrusting tongue. There was a moment when she thought wildly that this was some demonic form of punishment; then, in the crimson-shot blackness of her closed eyes, came the absolute realization that nothing so wondrously pleasurable could be punitive. A slow, spreading warmth filled her; her body melted with exquisite languor against the hardness of the one that held her; her mouth softened in welcome.

As if in response, the arm holding her relaxed, became a firm, warm presence on her body. His hand flattened against the curve of her hip as he drew her closer to him and the tip of his tongue played sweetly in the corner of her mouth. Her head fell back, offering the slender, vulnerable arch of her throat. His lips moved down, nuzzled against the pulse point that beat like a bird's wing against his mouth as he slipped his free hand into the opening of her jacket, cupping the soft roundness of one breast in his palm, feeling the heated skin, the sudden hardness of her nipple pressing against the fine lawn of her shirt.

The lean suppleness of the body between his hands delighted him as she moved against him, almost unconsciously wanton in the candid expression of desire. He was aware of the fragrance of her hair and skin, redolent with the freshness of the steppes, and the blood pounded in his veins, his hands moving urgently over her as she reached against him.

Then the dream shattered with the violence of a cannonade. She was destined to be another man's bride! He was behaving with her as some man had behaved with Eva. . . . He was betraying every trust ever invested in him. He jumped back from her, taking his hands away from that warm, giving flesh as if she were a burning brand.

Sophie looked up at him, shock and dismay at this abrupt cessation of contact stark on her face. "What is it? What has happened?"

Adam took himself in hand, fighting the anger that wanted to wound her as the cause, albeit unwitting, of this appalling bolt from the blue. "If you have a grain of common sense, you will forget that ever happened," he said, his voice grating in the stillness. "As far as I am concerned, it did not." Bending, he picked up her bundle. "We are going back to the house. Now, march!" He kept a hand on the small of her back, propelling her in front of him, but the physical contact bore no resemblance to the loving touch of a minute earlier, and Sophie, stunned, bewildered by the onrush of feelings that were unlike any she had ever before experienced, stumbled ahead of him.

A lamp burned dimly in the corner of the living room. He marched his charge across the room, flinging open the bedchamber door. It crashed against the stone wall, and Tanya Feodorovna sat up with a cry of alarm. "Wh . . . wh . . . what has happened?" She tugged at her nightcap, askew on the graying hair. "Why, Sophia Alexeyevna, why aren't you in bed?"

"The princess had other ideas about the way to spend the night," said the count caustically. "You will put her to bed, please, and bring out here, apart from her nightgown, every stitch of clothing she possesses."

"No!" Sophie gasped at such a humiliating instruction. "You cannot take away my clothes!"

"On the contrary, Princess," he said. "I can and I am

going to. I fail to see why I should deprive one of my men of his well-earned rest just to guard that window. And I have no intention of standing guard myself. I do not think even you will venture far in your nightgown.''

The door slammed shut behind him, leaving Sophie standing in the middle of the grimy little chamber, overwhelmed by the events of the evening and by this extraordinary volte-face—the man who could arouse such wondrous sensations with those skilled and tender caresses was suddenly become severe warden, transfigured into this other persona without any apparent provocation and without drawing breath, it seemed. She was bereft, hurt, and utterly confused.

''When will you ever learn?'' grumbled Tanya, rising from her mattress. ''I've never heard of such a fuss. Hurry up, now.'' Scolding vigorously, she got her erstwhile nursling out of her clothes and into her nightgown. ''I'll brush your hair.'' She reached for the hairbrush, but with a furious exclamation Sophie pushed her away and thumped into bed.

''Just leave me alone, Tanya! How can you possibly talk about hairbrushing in such a place, and at such a time?'' This absurd domestic preoccupation did strike her as utterly ridiculous, even as she recognized that for Tanya Feodorovna their present situation was not at all strange. What God and the masters decreed could never be strange. One just accepted it. She lay watching in fulminating silence as Tanya gathered up her discarded clothes, folded them neatly, and took them, together with the portmanteau, out into the living room.

''There you are, lord,'' she said, as placidly as if it were the most ordinary instruction she had received.

''Thank you.'' Adam was rummaging in his own belongings. He pulled out a bottle of vodka, glancing moodily at the woman as he unscrewed the top. ''You may fetch them in the morning.'' Raising the bottle to his lips, he drank deeply.

Tanya shrugged, recognizing the familiar look of a man who was going to be dipping deep into the fiery spirit throughout the night. It was the male prerogative, and a woman could count herself fortunate if the indulgence didn't lead to raised fists. Her own man had been a terrifying devil in the drink. But somehow she didn't think this one would be; depressed and silent, most likely. Not violent, despite provocation. He'd been gentle enough with Sophia Alexeyevna in her sickness that afternoon. But she'd clearly upset him powerfully now. Shaking her head, Tanya returned to her mattress.

Sophie lay looking into the darkness. What had happened? What did it mean? Why did she feel as if some part of herself, hitherto dormant, had come to vibrant life? She had wanted that wonderful moment to last for eternity . . . had wanted most passionately for the next, inevitable step . . . for his hands on her body, for hers on his. What would a man's skin feel like? Wide-eyed, she stared up at the low, beamed ceiling. That was something to be discovered in the marriage bed, something she *would* discover. She ran her hands over her body, trying to imagine what she would feel like to someone else. Would she be pleasing? Such a thought had never occurred to her before, but now it took on the sharp edge of reality. At the end of this journey loomed a husband, not one of her choosing, but unless he exhibited some hideous vice or disfigurement she would not find it easy to refuse him, or imperial command. Indeed, why should she? It was not as if she had an alternative to offer. It was not as if the only man who had ever kissed her could possibly be a candidate. One kiss did not constitute a marriage proposal.

A mere wall away, Adam Danilevski drank vodka and wondered what in Hades had happened to him. He hadn't kissed a woman since the last time he had kissed Eva. He had no truck with women who expected kisses. The only women who interested him these days were those who, for a certain price, could satisfy his basic needs. A purely commercial relationship allowed no emotional ties, and without those ties there was no possibility of the entanglements that led to betrayal. But he had been on the verge of an act of betrayal himself. The betrayal of his orders, of his position in the Imperial Guard, and the betrayal of a man who was owed, in addition to the good faith one gentleman was entitled to expect from another in a matter such as this, his unswerving loyalty by virtue of his being Adam's commanding officer.

Adam looked into the vodka bottle and contemplated the prospect of four weeks in the company of Sophia Alexeyevna, opposing him at every turn. At least if she fought him it would be possible to keep his distance, hide behind the harsh facade of jailer.

Sophie fell asleep finally, the events of the day taking their toll. She had achieved some measure of resignation, as her grandfather had known she would eventually, when she stopped striving against perceived injustice and allowed common sense to reign.

She awoke to bright sunshine. "I thought we were to leave at dawn." She sat up, blinking, taking the bowl of coffee that Tanya was holding out.

"The count said you needed your sleep," Tanya informed her with a serene smile. She did not add her own opinion that the count had needed time to clear his head. "Your clothes are ready. And the count says we'll be leaving as soon as you're dressed."

Sophie put on her clothes, trying to fight the dread of what she knew the day would bring. All thoughts of the previous evening's glory and confusion, and her subsequent conclusions, were subsumed under the sick knowledge of the wretchedness in store for her. With an effort, she straightened her shoulders, put up her chin, and walked outside into the fresh brilliance of early morning.

Adam was not deceived by the erect posture. Her eyes held the haunted fear of a torture victim looking upon the instruments that had broken her once and that she knew were about to do so again. He walked over to her as she reached the carriage.

"If you prefer, you may ride my horse on a leading rein, and I will ride Khan," he said.

There was a moment's silence as she looked toward the now-saddled Khan, his rein loosely held by Boris Mikhailov. Then to his amazement she shook her head. "Khan has never been ridden by any but me, since the Kalmuk who first taught him to take the saddle. I cannot allow anyone else to ride him. It is a Cossack rule, if you would have the absolute trust of such an animal.''

''You have only the two alternatives,'' he said, softly insistent, unable to bear the idea of her suffering in the carriage again, yet knowing that if she gave him no choice he would have to insist.

She looked up at him, her eyes clear, that crooked smile quivering quizzically. ''I think I have a third choice, Count. I will ride Khan, but I will make no attempt to flee your escort.''

Not for the barest instant did it occur to him to doubt her. A great weight rolled from his shoulders. He smiled at her, even as he remembered that without the pretext of the role of jailer he would find it much harder to maintain a distance between them.

''Boris Mikhailov will help you mount,'' he said, catching himself as he was about to offer to perform the service himself.

''There is no need.'' Moving with that long, energetic stride, she went to Khan, rubbing his nose, resting her face against his, whispering to him for a minute, before grasping the reins handed to her by Boris Mikhailov and springing with muscular agility into the saddle.

''Took your time coming around, didn't you?'' said Boris, checking the girth. ''You'll not best that one, I'll tell you that for nothing.''

''Your opinion is sage as always, Boris,'' Sophie said sweetly. ''I had come to that determination myself.'' She settled into the saddle, lifting her face to the sun and the wind, inhaling deeply.

Adam looked at her, thinking that, once more in her own element, she had again acquired that air of power and unquestioning self-confidence. He still had her pistol, though, and on the whole he thought he would keep it until they reached St. Petersburg. What Prince Dmitriev would decide to do with a pistol-carrying bride was no concern of his aide-de-camp. . . . Was it?

Chapter 5

General, Prince Paul Dmitriev, hands clasped behind his back, marched the length of the gallery running the width of his fine stone palace on the bank of the River Neva. Long windows opened onto the river that was now dotted with small craft, schooners gay with the identifying flags of their affluent owners, and rowboats, their oars plied by men in multicolored jackets. The water sparkled under the mid-May sunshine, the merry traffic on the river and crowding the many canals linking the various parts of this city carved out of a swamp augmented the prince's sense of satisfaction; indeed, the whole cheerful scene seemed to have been arranged especially for him.

The prize was almost in his grasp. The runner who had just arrived, breathless and exhausted after a day-and-night ride, had said that they would now be just over a day's journey from St. Petersburg. In the morning, the prince would ride out to meet them, to greet his bride with all due courtesy and consideration, and escort her himself to the Winter Palace, where she was to be lodged until after the wedding.

Was she as beautiful as her mother? Paul wondered. It would be almost too much to hope for—beauty *and* such a fortune. The czarina had laughingly warned him that the princess had had an unconventional upbringing and might not be as docile as she should be. But docility could be taught, as the prince well knew. There were tried-and-true methods at which he was expert for achieving the mastery of spirited creatures, as well as the ordained submission of wives. His

previous three wives had all come sweetly to hand after a
short period of schooling. However, he would show the Golitskova only smiles and indulgence until she was legally his.
The czarina would not force her into the marriage, as Dmitriev knew well. Autocrat though Catherine undoubtedly was,
she was also intelligent and enlightened, considered herself
humane and caring. If Sophia Alexeyevna exhibited genuine
distress at the arrangements made for her, the empress would
make others.

That must not happen. A deep frown buckled Prince Dmitriev's forehead. He had been denied the mother; he would
not be denied the daughter.

Sophia Ivanova had shown only contempt for the heart and
devotion the young Prince Paul had laid at her feet; she had
had eyes only for Alexis Golitskov, the two of them as love-
sick as a pair of turtle doves. The prince's lip curled at the
humiliating memory that still corroded like acid. He had
made a fool of himself, and the whole of St. Petersburg had
laughed. He had followed her around like a spaniel pup, his
adoration there for all to see, and she had spurned him publicly to marry Alexis Golitskov with great trumpeting. And
afterward, the married couple had treated him with such condescending kindness. Alexis, the softhearted fool, had offered him friendship, the freedom of his house, the galling
sympathy of the victor. Sophia had smiled upon him, had
welcomed him to her salon, and had remained as unattainable
as the Holy Mother.

His jealous hatred for Alexis Golitskov had become a monster, many-tentacled, growing daily more hideous, in direct
proportion with his ever-increasing lusting obsession for Sophia Ivanova. In the hatred he had found the salve for hurt
pride, in lust's obsession the cure for love. As he had smiled
and played the game of willing loser, charming friend, in-
souciant companion to both husband and wife, he had waited
for the opportunity that was bound to come. Sophia's pregnancy had rocked him to the core, this overt evidence of
another's man's enjoyment of her. And they had been so

happy, billing and cooing in nauseating self-congratulation, as if no one had ever conceived a child before.

As he paced the gallery, he could feel again the power of his loathing and jealousy. Every time he had seen her, her fruitful belly concealed beneath the loose Russian gowns that the empress had made popular again, violent images had filled his head, setting his heart to pound, sweat to mist his palms.

Then had arisen that whole ridiculous business of Prisoner Number One. In 1741, Peter the Great's daughter Elizabeth had taken advantage of Russia's disaffection with the Germanic influence embodied by Anne of Brunswick, who ruled the country as regent for her infant son, Ivan VI. Elizabeth had carried out a coup d'etat and made herself empress. The mother and child were imprisoned, and the little deposed czar had been known as Prisoner Number One ever since. The young man had grown up an idiot, never allowed to see the light of day, receiving no education, yet his continued existence posed a vague threat to the succession of subsequent imperial rulers whose legitimate right to rule could be challenged by one who had been unlawfully deposed. Elizabeth had been troubled by him; her successor, Peter III, during his brief reign, had been uneasy about him; and the czarina Catherine, having deposed her husband, Peter III, and turned a blind eye to his assassination, had been alert to the possible danger of Prisoner Number One.

His timely demise could only have been a relief, but for one whose husband had recently died a violent death also to her benefit, it was a grave embarrassment, viewed with shock by the courts and governments whose good opinions were a matter of policy and pride—those of Austria, Prussia, France, and England. Catherine had acted promptly and harshly to defeat the rumors that the rebellion leading to his death was incited by herself; visiting exemplary punishment upon any persons implicated in the plan—and incautious words had been spoken in the Golitskov salon.

They had not amounted to much—a statement that Ivan VI had received less than justice in his short life, the reminder that he had once been designated czar and his overthrow had been conducted in a haste and secrecy that bespoke conspiracy. But in the anxious climate of the time those words could be magnified, presented as the beginnings of the plot to deliver the "rightful" czar from imprisonment. The czarina had ordered the arrest of the Golitskovs. They had taken flight in panic, and their good friend, Prince Dmitriev, had taken charge of the pursuit. Under imperial orders, of course, and with the utmost reluctance, but a man must obey his sovereign.

He had intended to be the soul of understanding and compassion when he escorted them back to St. Petersburg and imprisonment in the great fortress of St. Peter and St. Paul—the ominous gray building that he could see now on the opposite bank across the busy, sparkling river. He had intended to promise to intercede with the empress so that Sophia Ivanova could be released to give birth in freedom. And he had intended to ensure that Alexis Golitskov did not leave the fortress alive. The widow, weak from childbirth, sorrow, and fear for her own safety, would be an easy conquest when one she trusted offered his strength and support.

It had been a neat and pleasing plan. But when he had reached that filthy hovel, rank with the stench of blood and death, he had found the plan in ruins.

Nearly twenty-two years later, he was now looking upon a neat tidying of loose ends. He would have under his control the vast Golitskov fortune that had made Alexis so confident, so sure of his place at the top of the court dunghill. And he would have in his bed the daughter of Sophia Ivanova.

It was quite perfect, Prince Dmitriev reflected. He would enjoy his own private satisfaction at this curious revenge, while providing himself with the heirs that none of his other wives had managed to bear. They had gone childless to their graves, but surely this fresh young virgin could not also be barren?

He rubbed his hands together with anticipatory pleasure. Tomorrow he would meet Sophia Alexeyevna Golitskova, and she would meet a graying, distinguished general, anxious to please his young bride-to-be, bearing gifts suitable for a shy,

unsophisticated virgin from the uncivilized steppes, and ready
to offer her the calm advice, the mature strength, the experienced wisdom that would steer her through the intricacies
of her first weeks at court. Thus would he ensure her de-
pendency and allay any fears.

Adam glanced sideways at his companion. It was a surreptitious glance, of a kind he had become adept at taking over
the last weeks. Just looking at her gave him inordinate pleasure, yet he could not allow her to divine this, any more than
he could allow himself to dwell upon the fact. He had fought
against acknowledging it for a long time, but eventually he
could not help but admit to himself that never had he enjoyed
another's company as much as he enjoyed that of this bright,
bold woman, whose mind was as alert as her body. She held
herself as if poised for the discovery and enjoyment of some
new experience, even as she took such clear pleasure in the
simple, customary things such as a ride in the sunshine, the
flight of a hawk, the joyous magnificence of a nightjar, crusty
black bread and mead when one was hungry and thirsty, the
benediction of sleep after a day of physical exertion in the
open air. She was untroubled by discomfort. Indeed, the previous night she had slept wrapped in her cloak upon a table
to escape the vermin in the miserable hovel that was all they
could find as shelter. And she had laughed at his own apol-
ogetic annoyance, dazzling him with those dark eyes, sparkling with fun, and the quizzical, crooked smile that so
entranced him, while she ate rancid cheese and stale bread
as eagerly as if they were delicacies from the imperial kitchens.

Sophie felt his eyes upon her, as she always did, although,
obeying instinct, she was careful not to meet his gaze. She
did not know why he looked at her so secretively, she only
knew that it gave her a little thrill of pleasure. There would
be no repetition of that kiss. She had come to accept that,
just as she had come to accept the inescapability of her present journey. They both behaved as if that glimpse of heaven
had never happened, because, of course, such a thing could

not have taken place between a young woman on her way to
her husband-to-be and the man charged with the trust and
responsibility of escorting her. But the ease she felt in his
company could be enjoyed with a clear conscience, surely;
with the deep pleasure that came from the friendship and
companionship of a like-minded soul. Yet the one subject
they both avoided was General, Prince Paul Dmitriev. Which
was strange, Sophie reflected. Why did she not want to ask
Adam about his general, the man who was to play such a
large part in her own life? And why did he never volunteer
any information or description?

The road they were taking wound across the Novgorod
plain, stretching flat and immense on either side, the occasional gleam of sun on water indicating a river or lake, with
which the plain was dotted. Khan raised his head and sniffed
the wind.

"Adam?"

"Mmmm?" He smiled at her, the laugh lines crinkling
around his eyes and the corners of his mouth.

"May we gallop?"

"So you can have the satisfaction of leaving me swallowing
your dust, I suppose."

"But of course," she agreed sweetly. "What other reason
could I have?"

"A nature that can't sit still for a minute," he retorted.
"You are not at all a restful traveling companion, Sophie."

She laughed. Taking the statement as permission for the
gallop, she clicked her tongue against her teeth at Khan, who
immediately gathered his great front legs and sprang forward. She turned him off the road and onto the grassy sweep
of the plain. Adam made no attempt to follow; it would be
pointless. She would come back when she had shaken the
fidgets from her spirit.

He peered up the winding dusty strip of white road ahead.
A cloud of dust rose in the distance, drifting toward him,
indicating fellow travelers presumably coming from St. Petersburg. They were no more than half a day's ride from the

capital, even at the relatively slow pace set by the carriage in which Tanya Feodorovna traveled in solitary state.

The dust cloud drew nearer, and Adam stiffened suddenly at a premonitory flash. It would be both natural and appropriate for Dmitriev, as befitted an eager groom, to come to meet them. His runner had reached them the day before yesterday, and had stayed for no more than a change of horse before taking the news of their position back to St. Petersburg.

The Dmitriev livery on the front riders at last became clear, and Adam could make out the tall, erect figure of his general, commanding in his uniform, the silver of buttons and sword hilt glimmering in the sunlight. He was come to meet his bride. But where the hell was she?

Adam scanned the flat plain for a sign, but she had disappeared long since behind a screen of brush, leaving her escort in the awkward position of having to explain to his commanding officer, who also happened to be her anxious bridegroom-to-be, the unescorted absence in uncharted territory of a princess of the house of Golitskov.

Adam had given Sophie back her pistol several weeks ago, so *he* was not concerned for her safety, but how could he possibly explain such a situation to Dmitriev? The prince would have to see Sophia Alexeyevna and judge for himself. It was time for Adam Danilevski to bow out. His lips twisted in a cynical smile at the reflection that the prospect of bowing out of Sophie's life somehow did not bring the sigh of relief he should have expected. This irksome escort's task that he had assumed with such annoyed reluctance had taken on a different complexion. And gnawing constantly at the pleasure he took in her company was the knowledge that what he found delightful about Sophia Alexeyevna her designated husband would find objectionable.

When the two parties met up, the general saluted his aide-de-camp with impeccable formality, the martinet's eye sharply inspecting the deportment and uniforms of the guardsmen, who had all come to attention in the saddle. The dullness of buttons, the wrinkles in jackets, the grubby linen were all noted.

"It is a long and uncomfortable journey from Kiev, General," Adam said quietly. "Water, polish, and shoe blacking are not easy to come by in some of the places where we have been obliged to spend our nights."

The general simply nodded. His eyes went to the carriage, which had come to a halt in the rear. "Princess Sophia has not endured too much discomfort, I trust?"

Adam swallowed. "She is remarkably resilient, General."

Dmitriev looked at him in surprise, thinking what an odd choice of word that was. He urged his mount forward to the coach and Adam spoke hastily.

"Sophia Alexeyevna is not traveling in the carriage, sir. She suffers acutely from motion sickness."

The general stopped in his tracks. His eyes swept the column of twelve men, the carriage with its coachman, Boris Mikhailov stolidly astride his mountain horse. He looked at Count Danilevski, not bothering to articulate the question.

Adam scanned the plain, then saw to his relief a figure emerging from the brush. "Here she comes now, General. Perhaps we should ride and meet her." Without looking to see what response his statement and suggestion received, he set off himself.

Sophie saw the two riders coming toward her, both in the dark green tunics with red facings of the Preobrazhensky regiment. But she saw immediately that Adam's companion was not one of his guardsmen; as the distance lessened, she saw that he was a lot older than Adam, distinguished, with graying hair and the erect posture of the career soldier. Then, with a sudden jolt in the pit of her stomach, she realized who he must be.

She drew rein and sat, waiting for them to reach her.

"Princess." Adam spoke almost distantly. "Permit me to introduce General, Prince Paul Dmitriev."

Dmitriev looked in stupefaction. He had noticed first that she was riding astride, then the quality of her mount. Now he absorbed the divided skirt of her shabby, dust-coated riding habit, the wind-whipped tangle of her hair, the candid gaze of her dark eyes meeting his in fearless appraisal. He became aware of the energy that seemed to radiate from her, the restless vigor of some wild creature of her native steppes; he took in the sun-browned health of her complexion, the lean muscularity of her body. And he was filled with a great rage. This was no Sophia Ivanova of an exquisite, delicate beauty; this was no fragile daughter of the naive, trusting, softhearted Alexis. This was a woman to be reckoned with, one not easily broken to his will.

He bowed. "I have been awaiting this moment with the utmost eagerness, Sophia Alexeyevna."

"I also have been curious, Prince," she replied bluntly. She took in his immaculate dress and smiled her crooked, quizzical smile. "I trust you will excuse my untidiness, but we have been long upon the road."

"That will soon be remedied," replied Dmitriev with another bow, impervious to the charm of that smile. "We are but four hours from the gates of St. Petersburg. Her Imperial Majesty is most anxious to welcome you."

Sophie felt a tremor run through her. Instinctively she looked toward Adam for some sign of comfort. There was none forthcoming, however. He seemed to have withdrawn from the scene, his eyes cool and distant. "We should perhaps rejoin the troop, Princess," he said.

So she was to be "Sophie" no longer, she realized with a desolate stab. His task of escort now completed, he would withdraw, having handed her over to her prospective husband. Would he not even stand her friend? A panicky shiver prickled along her spine. She was to go friendless into this new world? Then she stiffened her shoulders, lifted her chin. "Yes, indeed, Count. I would be done with this wearisome traveling."

"I see you carry a pistol, Sophia Alexeyevna," commented the prince, his tone neutral, hiding his shock and outrage at this scruffy hoyden he was to make his wife.

She shrugged. "I am accustomed to doing so, Prince. My

grandfather taught me to be an excellent shot, so you need have no fears of an accident.''

"You will not find it necessary to go armed around the imperial court," he pointed out, thinking acidly of the elegant fans, the dainty tortoiseshell combs, the lace-edged handkerchiefs, the embroidered gloves he had provided as appropriate welcoming gifts for an unsophisticated young woman from her eager, considerate fiancé.

"Of course not," she replied, hiding in her turn the apprehensive quiver at the thought that perhaps he was neither impressed nor reassured by her declaration of prowess with a firearm.

There was nothing further he could do for her, Adam thought. He had brought her to accept the card fate had dealt her, and the acceptance would ease matters considerably. Why should he imagine that she would not eagerly embrace the life ahead of her once the initial unfamiliarity dissipated? It was to be a life of pleasure, and if she behaved herself Dmitriev would have no cause for complaint. There was no reason why she should not conform; Sophia Alexeyevna was no fool. In that single realization lay his only comfort.

The evening sun caught the gilded cupolas of the cathedral of Kazan, shone gently golden off the flat waters of the River Neva as Sophie and her escort entered the city of St. Petersburg. All apprehension was vanquished as she gazed, fascinated, at this enormous, bustling place. Her only knowledge of cities was based on a visit to Kiev two years earlier. She had thought that city overwhelming in its noisy magnificence, but it was nothing compared to the majesty of this capital. They rode down the straight, paved thoroughfare of the Nevsky Prospect, and she stared, openmouthed, at the grandeur of the stone houses lining the road on either side. Did everyone live in a palace?

"Do you have a mansion in this city, Prince?" She turned toward him with the question and was surprised when he laughed.

This first indication of rustic innocence pleased him. "But of course, Sophia," he told her. "My palace is on the river. When you have recovered from your journey, you shall visit it and tell me how you would wish your apartments decorated.''

There it was, Sophie thought; the plain statement that accepted as fact what she had known was going to happen ever since the night Adam had forestalled her escape. She did not wish to think of the events of that night. The memory seemed to create the most unwelcome disturbances in mind and body. No, wisdom lay in making the best of the inevitable.

"Oh, I will not need to recover, Prince,'' she said, in tacit acceptance of the invitation. "I am not at all wearied. Riding does not tire me in the least. Perhaps I could see it tomorrow.''

He swallowed his annoyance at this additional evidence of her unmaidenly attributes, concentrating instead on the fact that she appeared to have no misgivings about the plans made for her. If he did not have to woo her, then matters could move much faster; and the sooner he had her under his roof, subject to the husband's authority, the sooner he could set about eradicating those displeasing attributes.

"I will leave you here, General.'' Adam spoke suddenly, gesturing toward a great gray building on their left. "We are at the barracks.''

"Ah, no, the empress wishes to see you,'' Dmitriev said. "Your mission is not accomplished until you release Sophia Alexeyevna into Her Imperial Majesty's charge.'' He smiled at Sophie. "I am not yet permitted the inestimable pleasure of assuming charge of you myself.''

He had a meagre smile, Sophie reflected, but the statement was clearly intended to be flatteringly warm. He could not help having been born with thin lips and those very pale blue eyes, she decided with resolute kindness. He was not at all an unprepossessing figure. So she told herself, quashing the apprehensive prickle that she could not identify because she did not know what it was about the prince that disturbed her.

Then she had no time for reflection of any kind. They had reached a quay beside the river; a vast square lay before them, and beyond that the Italianate structure of the Winter Palace, with its great outside staircase. They were surrounded by

servants and grooms, one of whom took Khan's bridle.
"No," she said abruptly. "Boris Mikhailov will care for
him." She swung unaided from the great height of the Cossack horse just as Prince Dmitriev moved to assist her. "Only
Boris knows how to handle him," she said with a worried
frown. "Will you make sure that these people understand
that, please, Prince?"

Paul Dmitriev met the steady gaze of a giant muzhik in
homespuns. "Do I not know you?"

Boris Mikhailov bowed low, hiding the flash of uneasy
recognition in his eyes. He had been hoping so fervently, and
so secretly, that the Dmitriev name was simply a coinci-
dence. But nothing would be gained by telling an old story,
or sharing what had to be an unfounded unease, with Sophia
Alexeyevna. "I served Prince Alexis Golitskov, lord."

"And he has served me ever since," Sophie explained.
"He and Tanya Feodorovna, who was my nurse, have been
deeded to me by my grandfather as part of the settlements."
She colored slightly. "This is not the time to talk of such
things, I beg your pardon. But I am anxious for Khan."

The horse would have to go, decided the prince dispas-
sionately. No lady could be seen riding him, even if he could
be ridden sidesaddle. The muzhik and the nurse would have
to go, also. The less she had to remind her of her past life,
the easier it would be to make an amenable wife of her. But
time enough for that when they were all under his roof and
authority.

"Show this man where to stable the horse," he instructed
one of the grooms. "He and the coachman are to receive the
empress's hospitality, so you will see to it. And you . . ."
He beckoned to one of the servants. "The princess's maid is
in the carriage. Have her escorted to the apartments made
ready for Princess Sophia."

"Oh, thank you." Sophie smiled up at him, radiant with
relief and gratitude. "I would not know how to look after
these things myself."

"You could hardly be expected to, Princess." Adam spoke,

just a hint of impatience in his voice. Did she have to look at Dmitriev like a child who has just been given a sweet?

Sophie heard the impatience. She looked at him in puzzled indignation, but he had turned and was striding toward the staircase.

"Come," said the prince. "You must make your curtsy to the empress."

"Should I not tidy myself, first?" asked Sophie, laying her hand on the proffered arm.

"Her Majesty's orders were that you were to be brought to her the minute you arrived," he said, although the thought of presenting this tomboy scruff to the fastidious czarina was not a pleasant one. Then he bethought himself of the pistol and shuddered at the horrifying idea that he might have forgotten. "Give your pistol to Boris Mikhailov," he said with sudden, urgent sharpness. "Her Imperial Majesty would not take kindly to such a thing on your person."

Within ten minutes, Sophia Alexeyevna Golitskova was curtsying to a corpulent woman in a loose caftan of gray silk. A plump, white hand was presented for her to kiss, then she was bidden to rise. A pair of clear, untroubled eyes examined her with friendly interest. The czarina's hair was lightly powdered, drawn back from her face to accentuate a broad, high forehead. She gave Sophia a toothless smile.

"I see you enjoy riding astride, Sophia Alexeyevna. It is one of my great pleasures, also. But it is a pleasure to be taken with discretion."

Sophie glanced down at her divided skirt. "I would have changed my dress, Your Majesty, but—"

"No, no." The czarina waved a dismissive hand. "I was not censuring you, *ma chère*, merely offering a piece of advice. But Prince Dmitriev will be able to offer you all the advice you might need in such matters, I know." She smiled upon the prince, then turned to Count Danilevski.

"We owe you our thanks, Adam. I trust you found all well with your family." She drew him to one side.

"Sophia Alexeyevna."

Sophie turned and found herself face-to-face with a tall,

heavy, robust man with unruly black hair. He had only one eye, and that one eye was gleaming at her with fiery warmth.

"Prince Potemkin." He introduced himself with a smile that showed brilliant white teeth slashing the brown face. "I am delighted to make your acquaintance, my dear."

She found herself responding instantly and unconsciously to that gleam in his eye, fluttering her sable eyelashes as she curtsied, murmuring her pleasure in the meeting.

The empress looked indulgently at her one-eyed lion. He had always had a taste for the young when it came to satisfying his tremendous physical appetites, and he had no scruples whatsoever about where he chose to gratify those appetites. His own nieces had all succumbed readily enough to the avuncular seducer once they reached puberty. However, Sophia Alexeyevna was not destined to receive that tutelage, gentle and pleasurable though it might be.

"*Ma chère*, you and I must have a private talk," she said, gliding in stately fashion toward a door at the rear of the salon. "Gentlemen, you will excuse us."

In the quiet privacy of the czarina's bedchamber, Sophie was subjected to a skillful examination that convinced the czarina that, for all her odd appearance and unpolished manners, the princess was intelligent, well-educated, and evinced a pragmatic acceptance of the destiny the empress had chosen for her subject.

"Prince Dmitriev is a worthy husband for a Golitskova," Catherine said at the close of the interview. "He is able to ensure your position at court, to provide you materially with everything you could either want or need. He will also bring you the wisdom of maturity, *ma chère*, and the experience of a longtime courtier. You will have need of such a counselor and mentor as you take your place in this world that is rightfully yours. You could not remain forever at Berkholzskoye, and, indeed, you have a duty to your family name."

Sophie curtsied without comment. The empress's statement did not invite anything but agreement.

"You must have a new wardrobe, of course," Catherine was now saying with brisk decision. "I understood just now from Count Danilevski that your grandfather has drawn up marriage settlements and provided you with money for your clothes and other necessities. However''—she smiled with warm generosity—''your betrothal and wedding gowns shall be my gift, *ma chère Sophia.*''

Sophie managed to say the expected things at this most distinguishing largesse, indicating as it did the empress's personal involvement in the affair. She began to feel that she was riding a floodtide. She could do nothing to alter the speed or direction of her progress, but could only wait until the wave spent itself upon some quiet shore. Then she would be able to take both stock and charge of her life again.

The feeling intensified over the next weeks. The intricacies of court etiquette at first bewildered then irritated her, but the Grand Mistress of the court, Countess Shuvalova, took her education in hand personally so that Sophie began to feel she could not make a move without the approval of that grande dame. Of Adam she saw almost nothing. He was occasionally present at some of the court functions, when he danced with her once or twice. But he treated her with unbending formality, and she was not to know that he saw her bewilderment, felt her irritation, and ached for her as she was prodded and patted into some semblance of the correct mold. At times, he wanted to stand up, shout his protest at what they were trying to do to this bold, brave, untamed Cossack woman; then he would catch a glint in her eyes, a stiffening of the lissom body, a muscular ripple, and he knew that they were not succeeding.

Sophie was submitting with apparent compliance to the transformation demanded of her, but in essence she was unchanged. At some point, when the bright illumination of her novelty had faded, she could be herself again; she would endure patiently until that time. Meanwhile, Prince Dmitriev paid her assiduous court, was always charming, courteous, and attentive to her every wish. Such a husband was not a dreadful prospect, she had to admit, given that choosing her own was not an available option. It was not an option any girl of family and fortune seemed to have, as she realized

from her discussions with the maidens and young matrons of
the court; if her eyes were frequently searching for the deep-
set gray orbs and the tall, lean, aristocratic figure of Count
Adam Danilevski, it was only because she found it comforting when he was in the same room. He had been her friend,
after all, the only link with her past life.

At the end of June the betrothal took place between Sophia
Alexeyevna Golitskova and General, Prince Paul Dmitriev.
The czarina herself, in front of the entire court, slipped onto
the fingers of the betrothed couple the rings blessed by the
archbishop, and the dinner and ball that followed the ceremony went on until dawn. Sophie continued to ride the floodtide, anxious now for the wedding that would deliver her from
her court apartments to the freedom of her own house. Once
the wedding was over, and a short period of honeymoon, then
she would ask her husband—husband, it was still a strange
concept—she would ask Prince Dmitriev for permission to
visit her grandfather before the winter set in and made traveling impossible. He would not deny her, she was sure. He
showed her so much consideration, it was almost as if he
cherished for her more than the conventional feelings a man
had for a convenient bride.

Fixing all her thoughts on this plan, she did what was required of her, smiled whenever she was in company, spoke
in platitudes, and waited for her soul's imprisonment to come
to an end.

Three weeks after the betrothal, Adam Danilevski, together with all of Petersburg society, was present in the cathedral of Kazan when the tall, slender figure, richly dressed
in a ceremonial robe of heavy ivory brocade embroidered
with silver rosebuds and edged with silver lace, became the
wife of Prince Dmitriev. The rich, dark brown curls had been
powdered and she wore the diamond tiara of the Dmitrievs.
It was as if the young woman who rode Cossack horses
astride, shot rabid wolves, and lost a too-hasty temper with
lamentable frequency had disappeared off the face of the
earth, Adam thought in confused regret, resentment, and a
bone-deep sense of loss.

His eyes moved toward the groom. Prince Dmitriev, also dressed in rich ceremonial robes, allowed just the hint of satisfaction to dwell upon his face as Prince Potemkin held the traditional crowns over the couple's heads. Adam felt a surge of revulsion. By what right would this callous soldier, this rigid disciplinarian who had buried three wives already, enjoy that fresh, lithe body in his bed, have that bright, inquisitive mind and lively spirit to partner him through the years? While he, Adam Danilevski, the widower of a deceiving slut, faced the empty years ahead in the absolute knowledge that never again would he trust a woman enough to share more than a brief burst of pleasurable, necessary release.

Sophie did not seem to inhabit her body, instead seemed to be watching herself from somewhere above as she performed the ritual movements, made the ritual responses. The heavy cloying scent of incense, the fickering candles in front of the icons, the voices raised in mystical chant, all added to the sense of unreality in this gilt-encrusted universe, where all was kneeling and genuflection and cryptic reverence.

The sense of unreality endured throughout the carriage ride to the Dmitriev palace, where the reception was to take place with all the lavish hospitality befitting a bridegroom of the stature and affluence of a prince who had just augmented his own fortune with his young bride's vast inheritance.

The czarina smiled benignly on the couple presiding over the great banqueting table under a gilded canopy. She tapped her foot, beaming with satisfaction as the bride and groom opened the ball. Princess Dmitrievna was a credit to Her Imperial Majesty's careful and benevolent planning. Her installation in the imperial circle meant the reinstatement of the Golitskovs, and Catherine could feel that if there had been any hint of injustice in that tragedy all those years ago, amends were now made.

At ten o'clock, the empress rose, still smiling, to announce that it was time to put the bride and groom to bed, a ceremony over which she intended to preside. It was a great honor, but Sophie was unaware of the distinction as she came back with a jolt to a sense of herself in her body. Her surroundings focused.

Her husband's pale blue eyes were resting on her face, and they contained a look she had not seen there before. The gleam of anticipatory complacence, the unmistakable look of a man about to consummate a long-held, long-planned vengeance, shocked her with the force of an electric current. It was the look of the wolf, prepared to spring. Her eyes darted around the room in sudden panic; the smiling faces, the flickering candle flames, the carved and gilded decorations of the ballroom seemed to run together in a haze. Then she encountered the steady gaze of Adam Danilevski. His face was graven, not a flicker of expression in his eyes, not a movement on that beautiful mouth. Blindly, thoughtlessly, she took a step toward him. He turned away from her and pushed his way through the chattering, laughing throng, out of the house.

"Come, *ma chère Sophia*." The czarina's hand touched her elbow. "Your bridegroom is most anxious." This she said with a conspiratorial smile at the bridegroom, the smile of one who knew well the pleasures of the bedchamber.

Sophie found herself in the middle of a laughing throng, chattering gleefully like so many magpies as they escorted the bridal pair up to the nuptial apartments. At the door to his bedchamber, Prince Dmitriev withdrew to his dressing room to change his clothes in the company of his groomsmen. Sophie, with the empress, the Grand Mistress, and several young matrons of the court who had befriended her, found herself in an enormous chamber hung with emerald silk, lit with branched candelabra, and dominated by a carved four-poster bed with gold velvet curtains, a gold satin coverlet, and the Dmitriev shield surmounting the tester and embroidered on the pillows.

She had been shown weeks ago what would be her private apartments and had been bidden to choose their decorations, but this vast, echoing, opulent chamber had not been decorated with the tastes of the bride in mind. This was the general's bedchamber, and if anything was required to intimidate her, it was to be found in this room.

She was undressed, put into her nightgown, the czarina herself removing the tiara and unpinning the luxuriant pow-

dered curls. Then the door was opened; the room filled with
wedding guests of both sexes come to offer the bride their
congratulation and blessing. All the while, Sophie knew herself to be the target of every gaze, of every whispered comment, be it lewd, bantering, compassionate, curious, or
amused, as she stood in her nightgown beside the bed.

Thanks to Tanya Feodorovna, she knew in principle what
to expect of the night, and in this respect was luckier than
many a bride, although Tanya's experiences had not been of
a kind to reassure. The memory of a night in a posting house
on the road to Kiev intruded with shocking vividness—a night
when she had contemplated the experience she was about to
. . . enjoy? . . . endure? On that night, with her lips still
tingling from a kiss of passion, she had thought only of a
glorious enjoyment. But now . . .

The covers were drawn back on the bed; amidst laughing
applause and encouragement, Sophie put herself between the
sheets. The image of the wolf intruded again, and with it the
face of Adam Danilevski. Once before she had had the fantasy,
when the two images became intertwined and she had not known
why. Now she knew that it was not Adam who reminded her of
the beast. She lay in the bed, staked out like a lamb to attract
that wolf, and the surrounding faces blurred again.

There came the sound of commotion from the corridor
outside; the door was flung wide to admit the bridegroom
with his escort. His gaze rested for a second on the bed and
its occupant; again that complacent smile flickered in his eyes.
Then, with laughing good humor, he turned to answer the
banter of the wedding guests, even as he encouraged them
from the room.

They were alone. Paul Dmitriev closed the double doors
and turned slowly to face the bed. The clock ticked loudly
in a silence that felt to Sophie as if the world were holding
its breath. Her husband untied the girdle of his robe, crossing
over to the bed, the pale eyes coldly appraising.

"What a great disappointment it is that you do not have
your mother's looks," he said. "It is hard to believe that you
are her daughter."

Chapter 6

The silence in the lofty dining room was oppressive—part of the heavy mantle of apprehension and gloom that cloaked the entire mansion. Sophie sat at her place at the massive, elaborately carved mahogany table, a footman behind her chair. There were three place settings, and behind each chair stood a powdered footman. The butler, a napkin draped over one arm, was poised at attention, ready at the door, his eyes darting anxiously from the table to the footmen to the clock, which showed the second hand approaching the hour of two o'clock.

Precisely at two o'clock, the sharp click of boots on the tiled floor of the hall was heard. Sophie's stomach tightened involuntarily in the now-familiar reaction to the approach of her husband.

Prince Paul Dmitriev strode into the dining room. His gaze swept the room in close examination, and the butler trembled. However, it seemed that the prince found nothing out of order. He walked to his place at the head of the table.

"Good afternoon, Sophia." He took the carved armchair pulled out for him by the footman, who settled a heavy, cream-colored linen napkin on the master's lap.

"Good afternoon, Paul."

Sophie sometimes thought she was losing the power of speech, she spoke to so few people these days, sweltering in the hot dimness of this city palace. All of St. Petersburg society had left for their summer palaces along the Gulf of Finland—all but the Dmitrievs. The prince had said he preferred to spend the summer in seclusion with his bride. The time he spent with her, however, was limited to the hour at the dinner table and the nightly visits he made to her bed-chamber, where, with the conscientiousness he brought to all necessary activities, be they pleasurable or no, he set about the task of fathering his heir.

"I had understood that Count Danilevski would be joining us for dinner," she said, taking a tiny sip of wine, praying he could not detect in her voice the great black wave of disappointment washing over her at the aide-de-camp's absence.

"I imagine he was delayed," Paul said indifferently. "There were some important regimental matters to be attended to this morning."

"I see." Silence fell again, broken only by the buzz of a fly, the soft-shoe whisper of a servant moving about the room, the tiny scrape of cutlery on china, the murmur of pouring wine.

Paul observed his young wife in covert satisfaction. The last two months had wrought some considerable transformation. No longer did she meet his eye with that bold, glowing gaze of fearless candor; no longer did she stride around the house with restless energy and vigor. No, she moved slowly, keeping in the shadows almost, her eyes lowered. She spoke in hesitant murmurs, then only to respond if he chose to make some remark to her, or to beg him for some small favor that in general he refused, surprising her just occasionally by granting it. It had not been as difficult as he had feared to achieve this docility, although it had taken longer than it had with his previous wives. But then they had been bred from a more conventional mold and were half-broken by the time they had come to him.

He had not been entirely successful with Anna Kyrilovna, of course, the prince mused, twirling the stem of his wine-glass between his fingers. She had become quite impossible with her endless tears, her silent reproaches. In the end he had had to have her cloistered. Had she not been barren, of course, he might have been able to endure her.

He looked at Sophia Alexeyevna again. He did not think

this one would suffer a nervous collapse, for all that she had lost her previous ebullience, the self-confidence of one secure in her place in the world. By the time society returned to the city in a week or two, he would feel confident in permitting her to attend court occasionally, to participate a little in the round of social visiting. His training was secure enough now to withstand exposure to the outside world.

The sound of voices from the hall shattered the brooding silence of the dining room. Sophie kept her eyes on her plate, even as her heart leaped in her breast, and her fingers trembled.

"My apologies, General." Count Danilevski stood in the doorway. He saluted his general, then bowed to Sophie. "Princess, pray excuse my tardiness. I was obliged to wait for the arrival of a dispatch from Moscow."

"Do not apologize, Count," Sophie said, raising her eyes to look at him for the first time since he had come in. Her face was expressionless, her smile purely perfunctory. "Please join us." She gestured to the third place.

Adam sat down. He knew the effort it was costing Sophie to maintain that cool indifference because he was paying the same price. But if Dmitriev were to catch the faintest inkling of the powerful current flowing between his wife and his aide-de-camp it would be catastrophic for Sophie.

She had lapsed into submissive silence again, while the general questioned his aide-de-camp about matters that the husband would not expect to interest his wife. But Adam was aware that the meek posture, the lowered eyes, the mute respect concealed a volcano of rage and rebellion. What it would take for that volcano to erupt, Adam did not know.

Sophie did not know, either. She only knew that protest, complaint, even tears would meet with cold reprisals. When Paul had told her in the second week of their marriage that he was sending Tanya Feodorovna to his estates in the country because she was not suitably trained as a lady's maid, Sophie had exploded in outrage, violently protesting that he had no right to dispose of her serfs. He had demonstrated her powerlessness by showing her how it was possible for a husband to assume whatever rights he chose. Tanya Feodorovna had disappeared overnight, to be replaced by a dour, silent woman who watched her mistress with sharp little eyes, who listened with ears pricked, and who, Sophie knew, reported every detail of her mistress's behavior to the prince.

She had wept with anger when her protests met only the blank wall of callous indifference, and the prince had sent for the physician. They had forced laudanum down her throat for her "excitation of the nerves," and for a week she had been kept in a state of semisedation. She had learned the lesson well, now playing the part her husband would have her play, while she waited. For the moment, in virtual imprisonment in this gloomy mansion in the deserted city, she had no redress. But at some point, this enforced seclusion would come to an end. When the court returned from the country her husband could not continue to keep her away from human contact. Until then, she would continue to draw her lifeblood from the times she was in Adam Danilevski's presence.

Even when she dared not look at him, when not a word beyond the formalities passed between them, she was infused with his strength and spirit. It had been so from the first time he had entered this mansion to greet her as his general's wife. One all-encompassing look had seemed to tell him every detail of the unforeseen ordeals that had left her fearful, disillusioned sometimes to the point of desperation as she searched for some indication that this present reality was only a temporary condition, that there was some possibility of escape, of relief, of change. The unexpectedness of her husband's behavior, the complete switch in his personality, once he had her secure under his roof, had shattered her composure more effectively than the subtle cruelty itself.

What she did not know was that Adam, who could have prepared her, saw himself as culpable. As she thrashed blindly in the morass of bewilderment and frustration, seeking a reason why her husband should want as his wife a person other than the one she was, the count was consumed with compassion, with the overpowering need to help and support her.

Whenever she was in his company, Sophie felt the unspoken power of this need, and drew from it the strength to hold on to herself, to conceal her rage under the required meek demeanor, to control the urge to rebel. For as long as her husband believed he had the upper hand and she knew he had not, then she was still whole. Somehow, she knew that Adam saw this, and was willing her to stay strong.

Prince Paul did not consider it necessary to include his aide-de-camp in the proscription on society requisite to this training of his wife. The colonel was simply a soldier, a senior member of Dmitriev's regiment, whose duties involved his frequent visits to the Dmitriev palace. If the count happened to meet Princess Dmitrievna on one of these business calls, it was a matter of indifference to the general. There was nothing social in the visits, and even dining together as they were now doing was simply an occasion for the discussion of regimental matters. The princess was as excluded as if she had not been in the room. The prince did not know that as she sat, ignored in her silence, she was more vibrantly alive than ever. He did not know that the count was aware of her every move, however infinitesimal, was aware of every breath she took.

The meal came to an end. Sophie, following old Russian custom, curtsied to her husband as the head of the family, thanking him for her dinner. It was yet another example of the protocol to which the general/prince was addicted. Every aspect of life in the Dmitriev household was regulated by protocol. Failure to adhere to the rules brought instant punishment, and rarely a day passed without screams shrilling from the courtyard at the back of the palace as a serf suffered beneath the cane or the knout. Sophie had learned to close her ears. She was powerless to intervene, as the servants all knew. The household ran without her supervision, in an atmosphere of dread and mistrust. It was an atmosphere that accompanied General, Prince Paul Dmitriev wherever he held sway.

Now he nodded with the appearance of approval as his wife duly performed the ritual. Emboldened, although without much hope of success, Sophie asked if she might go for a ride that afternoon.

The prince frowned but spoke with apparent solicitude. "I do not wish you to run any risks, my dear. It is far too hot, and I am afraid you will get the headache. No, you must rest quietly in the shade."

Sophie knew why she was not to run any risks. Her husband lived in the continual hope that she had conceived. Her failure to do so, so far, meant increased restrictions on her physical activities; implicit in these restraints lay the paradoxical message that should she become pregnant, much more freedom would be permitted. As if, Sophie thought bitterly, she had any control over the matter. Her husband was certainly doing his part, and if passive submission was all that was required of the female in these affairs, then his wife was doing hers.

She was too accustomed to disappointment these days, and too adept at hiding her feelings from her husband to allow him the satisfaction of seeing so much as a revealing flicker enliven her bland expression. "I am sure you know best, Paul." The tone was as neutral as her expression. "If you would excuse me . . . Count." Another little curtsy in the vague direction of the count, and she left the dining room.

As she brushed past him, Adam caught her scent, felt her vibrant warmth, and the urge to take hold of her stunned him with its power. But he was helpless—as helpless to ease her lot, except with his mute understanding and support, as he was to fulfill the need to hold her, to feel again those lips opening sweetly beneath his. She was another man's wife, and he would not do to another, however much he despised that other, what had been done to him. Sometimes he thought that if he could avoid seeing her he would do so, but he knew that even though he could not help her practically, he had to know what was happening with her.

Dmitriev caused her no crude physical injury, except insofar as the enforced inactivity, the confinement within the house would hurt such an active individual for whom the freedom of the Wild Lands had been necessary for happiness and the soul's peace. No, the injuries were to the spirit, a subtle erosion of the person she had been, the fragmenting of her integrity so that she would cease to believe in herself. He had seen his general use similar tactics within the regiment when he identified a square peg. The nonconformist would be humiliated, derided, deprived of the things that gave meaning to himself and what he considered his place in the world. When he had lost those self-defining factors, had lost his self-respect, then he could be rounded to fit the hole in the general's pegboard.

Adam knew that he had to prevent that from happening to Sophie, and he sensed that she drew strength from his presence, for all that they barely exchanged two words most of the time; so he continued to expose himself to the torment of her company, to the abysmal frustrations of helplessness and deprivation. Once the court returned to St. Petersburg, Dmitriev would have to widen the bars somewhat. She would be expected to take her place in society, and her failure to appear would draw remark. If she could hold out until then, survive this diabolical honeymoon, matters would have to ease for her, and he could cease this self-martyrdom, request a mission outside St. Petersburg, return to the self hardened by disillusion, retreat into his carapace again, become whole again. So Adam told himself, struggling to believe it, as he watched her and tried to guess how close she was to breaking.

"I will go to the barracks and see to this matter myself," the prince was saying, unnoticing of his colonel's preoccupation. "There has clearly been an error in the dispatch." He marched into the hall, calling for his sword, hat, and cane. "Would you, Colonel, go through the copies of the dispatches sent to Moscow last month? You will find them in the bureau in my study. I must ensure that the error did not originate with us."

Adam wondered if he had heard aright. The general was going to leave him in the house with Sophia Alexeyevna. But then Dmitriev believed his colonel to be an embittered misogynist, in addition, of course, to being a loyal officer of the

Imperial Guard whose only interest could be in regimental affairs; in short, one quite safe to be permitted under the same roof as a cowed wife. "As you command, sir." He offered a smart salute, waiting until the general had left the house before turning toward the stairs leading to Dmitriev's study on the second floor.

The door to a small parlor stood open, inviting his questing eyes. She was standing at the window, looking out, her appearance as forlorn and despairing as that of a caged bird. He stepped into the parlor, unable to help himself.

Sophie did not know how she knew it was Adam, but she had no need to turn to identify her companion. "I am dying," she said dully. "Inch by inch, minute by minute—"

"Do not talk such maudlin nonsense!" The lowness of his voice in no way detracted from the fierceness of his tone. He closed the door. "What would your grandfather say to hear you talk such defeatist rubbish?"

"Then I shall kill him," she said simply. "Only he has taken away my pistol." Her shoulders sagged again. "I cannot abide knives; I never have been able to."

Adam covered the distance between them in two long strides. Catching her by the shoulders, he spun her to face him. To touch her after so many weeks of holding himself away from her with a restraint that clenched his muscles, knotted his belly, was like laying hands upon the Holy Grail. The pale oval of her face was upturned, no longer brown with health, the dark eyes seeming larger than ever in its wan thinness, but as he stared into them, a shadow of the former glow shimmered in their depths. Her lips parted. Was it in invitation or surprise?

It was a question of supreme irrelevance, he found, as he kissed her, felt her shudder against him as she had done before, sensed the hunger that matched his own. And this time, augmenting the hunger, was a fierce desperation, a shared desperation. Then she was fighting against the arms that held her, the mouth that caressed her. He drew back and read the fear in her eyes.

"No . . . no," she gasped, pulling away from him, one

hand pressed to her warmed, tingling lips, her eyes darting
in panic around the room as if in search of a spy. "If we are
discovered . . ."

"Your husband would kill me," Adam said with a calm
that surprised him. "If I did not kill him first." That look of
abject terror upon her face filled him with an icy rage greater
than any he had ever felt. "He has gone to the barracks,
Sophie."

"Yes, but Maria . . ." Again her gaze swept the room,
fell upon the closed door.

"Maria?" He frowned, taking her hands. They quivered,
cold despite the warmth of the late September day.

"When he sent away Tanya Feodorovna," she explained,
"Maria came in her stead. She is a spy." It was a flat statement. "Everything I do or say is reported to Paul." She took
her hands out of his. "It is no secret. I am supposed to know
of it. Paul repeats things to me at night, when . . . when he
comes to my room." She wrapped her arms around herself,
facing him with a small, bleak smile. "He is a frequent visitor."

She was another man's wife. His mind filled with the distasteful images conjured by her statement. Adam drew away,
burned by the unpalatable truth that he was honor bound to
respect. How a man chose to manage his wife was no one
else's concern. He was her lord, under God and the laws of
the land, and he could make whatever dispositions he thought
necessary or convenient. Yet, even as he recognized these
truths, Adam could not accept their implications, not when
applied to Sophia Alexeyevna.

"I will see if I cannot contrive for you to ride Khan," he
said, moving swiftly to the door, his step agitated, rapid as
if he could not get away from her fast enough. "I will do
what I can." Then he was gone.

Sophie stood by the window. The imprint of his lips upon
hers, of his arms around her, maintained the impact of reality. Yet, true reality was composed of other lips and arms.
Not that her husband ever kissed her; the softness of caresses
was no part of the reproductive act, although she assumed he

was fulfilling some other need while he tried to father a child upon her body. The coupling certainly seemed to give him some strange pleasure, and it always brought that gleam of satisfaction to his pale eyes as he looked at her, lying beneath him, spread to receive the assault of his manhood. But somehow she felt that it was not herself he was seeing in her subjection. Curiously, this feeling made it easier to bear, made it easier to separate herself from her body until he left her, returning to his own chamber without a word or a touch.

The contrast between a gray-eyed Polish count with a beautiful mouth that could give such exquisite pleasure, and the cold disdain, hard pale eyes, and thin lips of the man to whom she was wedded made the present even harder to endure. What could have been if fate had taken a different turn was as hopelessly unattainable as a return to the past, when a young woman had ridden the steppes without a care, secure and strong in her own world.

Sophie turned to the door. She could at least visit Khan, even if she was not permitted to ride him. Her husband had not forbidden her to visit the stables. And in the company of Boris Mikhailov she could gain some comfort, although, after the removal of Tanya, they were both careful not to be seen in conclave.

It was a week before Adam was able to fulfill his promise to arrange for Sophie to ride Khan. In the planning and execution of an elaborate deception, he found the pleasure of action overcoming the torments of his helplessness. It was not much he was doing for her, yet it would give her inordinate joy. He had to arrange for the absence of the prince, a stable yard deserted of all but Boris Mikhailov, and some way of getting a message to Sophie, explaining his plan.

As it happened, fortune intervened to ease matters for him. A messenger arrived from Czarskoye Selo, the empress's summer palace outside St. Petersburg, requesting information on the present disposition of the Preobrazhensky regiment. It took little persuasion from his colonel for the general to agree that he should answer the imperial summons in person.

All Adam had to do was ensure that the general was obliged to stay at Czarskoye Selo overnight. Sophie could then ride before dawn, before the household was up and about, and be back in her chamber with no one except Boris any the wiser.

Alerting Boris was a simple enough matter. The muzhik, as befitted his previous privileged position with the Golitskov family, was as literate as he was intelligent. He did not blink an eye when the count, riding into the Dmitriev stable yard one afternoon, slipped a folded piece of paper into his palm as he gave his horse into Boris's charge.

Adam strode into the mansion with the attitude of one on an important errand. He asked for the general, although he was well aware that Dmitriev was attending a brigade review. "Then, perhaps I might beg the favor of a word with Princess Dmitrievna," he said, when informed of the prince's absence. "She could convey my message to the prince. It is of some importance, as it relates to his journey tomorrow."

It was quite clear from the butler's expression that he was uncertain how to respond. The princess did not receive visitors; it was an unspoken rule. Yet Count Danilevski was not an ordinary visitor. He was the prince's aide-de-camp, frequently in the house, and frequently in her presence, although always in her husband's company.

"I am not sure where the princess is, Count," he said hesitantly. "Perhaps I could convey your message to His Highness?"

Adam had been afraid of this, knowing that he could not insist upon seeing Sophie if she was not there by chance. He was about to accept defeat and give his fictitious message to the butler when his quarry came into the hall.

"Count Danilevski," she said on just the right note of surprise and indifference. "My husband is not here, I am afraid."

"No, your butler was just telling me so. I have a message for him. Perhaps you would be good enough to convey it for me." He held out his hand in polite greeting.

Sophie curtsied, took his hand, felt the crumpled ball of paper against her palm. There was not so much as a flicker in her eyes as her fingers closed over the ball, her hand dropped to her side. "What is your message, Count?"

"Why simply that the papers he wishes to take to Her Imperial Majesty tomorrow morning have had to be recopied. However, even if the clerks must work all night, they will be ready for him when he comes to the barracks in the morning."

A somewhat unnecessary message, Sophie thought, but it did not seem to strike the butler as such. He still stood sentinel in the hall. "Nikolai, you will ensure that His Highness receives the message," she said with studied indifference. "Good day to you, Count." A polite smile touched her lips before she turned, walking slowly toward the stairs.

Adam remembered that long-legged stride, the way her skirts swished around her ankles, the crispness of her step, and he contemplated the slow death of General, Prince Paul Dmitriev.

In the privacy of her chamber, Sophie uncrumpled the scrap of paper. *Your husband will not return from Czarskoye Selo tomorrow. If you wish to ride, Khan will be saddled and waiting for you two hours before dawn on the following day. Ride to the north gate of the city. I will meet you outside the gate.*

How did he know Paul would not return the next evening, as was his declared intention? But that did not matter. Her heart lifted in her breast, the blood began to dance through her veins, bringing warmth and a resurgence of the quickness of life. She had not ridden Khan for two months. On the very few occasions she had been permitted to ride, it had been in her husband's company, sidesaddle on a mild-mannered mare. Boris told her that he had been instructed to exercise the stallion regularly on a leading rein, and to give him the best of care. It was the muzhik's somewhat caustic opinion that the prince knew a fine and valuable animal when he saw one, but hadn't yet decided how best to capitalize on this unusual beast.

But now she was going to ride Khan . . . ride like the wind through the night freshness, through the false dawn, see the sun rise. . . . And she was going to share this ecstasy with Adam Danilevski. To be raised from the despondent depths of hopeless acceptance to such dizzying heights filled her with a joy so powerful that she felt almost sick with it.

Joy notwithstanding, she still kept her head, ripping the message into tiny shreds until it resembled confetti. When Maria came into the chamber to help her mistress dress for supper, the maid saw only the neutral expression to which she was accustomed, heard only the flat, resigned tones of a prisoner who has given up all hope of regaining her freedom.

When the prince left her bed that night, he told her that he would depart at dawn and would return in the evening. "You need not wait supper for me," he said, retying the girdle of his robe. "If I am unable to leave Czarskoye Selo until late in the afternoon, I will not return before ten o'clock. But I will come to you when I have supped."

"I look forward to it," Sophie heard herself whisper, insolently sardonic. She froze, praying he had not heard her.

"I beg your pardon, Sophia?" her husband said, frowning.

"I wish you a safe journey, Paul," she said, closing her eyes, lest he should see the gleam she knew they contained.

"You will remain within doors during my absence," he told her crisply. "I do not wish to be anxious for your safety, my dear, and will only be easy in my mind knowing that you are protected by my people." A thin smile touched his lips as he offered this considerate order for imprisonment. Protection meant surveillance, as Sophie well knew, but never did her husband acknowledge the true facts of her existence. Every restraint was presented as an indication of his care for her. He had to be the most caring and considerate husband in St. Petersburg, Sophie reflected ironically as the door closed on his departure. She was quite sure that that was how his constant watchfulness would be interpreted by others once he considered her sufficiently submissive to be permitted to venture forth into society.

Gingerly, she got off the bed, going to the ewer for the cool water that would ease her soreness—the inevitable aftermath of these nightly rapes upon an unprepared and unaroused body. At least tomorrow night she would sleep alone, if Adam kept his promise, and then . . . She hugged herself with fierce joy as she looked upon the prospect of such a ride in the exclusive company of Adam Danilevski, away from all eyes.

When General, Prince Dmitriev arrived the following morning at Preobrazhenskoye, the regiment's barracks, it was to be met with chaos. A fire had started in a wastepaper basket in one of the offices. It had been discovered before it had got out of hand, but there had to be an investigation, an examination to see which documents had been destroyed, an exhaustive search for the careless culprit. The general was obliged to set these matters in train before leaving for Czarskoye Selo. His aide-de-camp could have seen to these things himself, but as that aide-de-camp knew well, when it came to issues of discipline the general preferred to deal with them personally.

The culprit would elude discovery, since no one would suspect Count Danilevski of firesetting, but the regiment trembled as the general set off some four hours later than he had intended, promising with customary cold ferocity that the one responsible would pass six times beneath the rods of a hundred of his comrades.

Fervently trusting that a flayed back was not in his stars, Adam continued conducting the pointless investigation started by his general, and reckoned that Dmitriev could not reach his destination until mid-afternoon, even if he did not stop for dinner. His audience with Her Imperial Majesty would be of several hours' duration, then he would have to eat. It would be well past nightfall before he could start for home. He would not bother; there would be no point in exhausting himself and his escort, when they could leave first thing in the morning, after a night's rest. And by the time he returned, Princess Dmitrievna would be safely back in the house with just a little hope in her heart.

Sophie barely closed her eyes all night. Terrified that every sound heralded the return of her husband, she tossed and turned amidst the fiery tangle of sheets until the clock struck three. All her Berkholzskoye clothes, which she had kept as reminders of the past, although they were hopelessly unfashionable and could not possibly be worn in St. Petersburg society, had been burned at her husband's orders. But she had managed to preserve her riding habit from the grasping clutches of Maria. It was bundled at the back of the garderobe. Now she put it on, feeling as if she was putting on her own familiar self again as the divided skirt freed her stride.

The house was silent, corridors dimly lit by occasional candles set in wall sconces. The night watchman would be dozing in the kitchen, Sophie knew. He made his rounds on the half hour, but hopefully he would not notice that the window in the dining room was not properly fastened. Her heart beat uncomfortably fast as she slipped down the stairs, into the dark dining room. The window opened with the smooth ease to be expected in Prince Dmitriev's well-run household. She swung herself onto the sill, remembering with a stab of nostalgia that other window, on another flight, in another life. . . . That flight had brought her into the arms of Adam Danilevski.

And this one . . . ? Not a permissible train of thought. Sophie dropped to the soft earth of the flower bed, reaching up to pull the casement closed behind her. It lay snug against the frame and would pass casual scrutiny, although a touch of the finger would swing it open again. Keeping to the shadows, she hurried to the stable yard, which at first glance appeared deserted, as would be expected at that time of the night. Then the gigantic bulk of Boris Mikhailov emerged from the shadows, Khan stepping at his side.

Sophie ran to her horse, whispering to him, before flinging her arms around the quietly smiling muzhik, hugging him tightly. "I will be back before sunrise."

"Have a care. He's not had a saddle on him for two months," was the only response from Boris, although the gruffness of his tone was belied by the softness in his eyes.

"Do I not know it, Boris?" said Sophie bitterly. But now

was not the time for bitterness, and she put it from her. Gently, she talked to Khan as she took the reins, lifting one foot into the stirrup. The great beast raised his head, snorting at the tug on the saddle, but when her voice continued in soft reassurance he became still. Nimbly, she sprang upward, landing lightly in the saddle. Khan quivered, then at the flick of the rein took off out of the yard as if feeling his freedom as vividly as did his mistress.

The nighttime city streets were deserted, and there was no one to witness the exultant charging progress of a magnificent Cossack stallion and his long-haired rider. The guards at the north gate, in the absence of orders to halt anyone passing through, merely looked in sleepy surprise as Khan galloped by, so fast they could almost have imagined his passing.

About a mile along the dusty, winding road stood a break of poplar trees. In their shadow, astride his own mount, was Adam Danilevski. Watching her coming toward him, he could feel the vitality emanating from the erect figure, her hair streaming in the wind. It was a vitality that he hadn't seen since he'd delivered up his charge to the czarina, and its resurgence under his contriving brought him an immense satisfaction.

"Is it not wonderful?" She drew rein beside him, the dark eyes glowing in the milky starlight, her crooked smile wide with pleasure. "I cannot thank you enough, Adam."

"You already have," he said quietly.

"How so?" Her head tilted to one side. The smile became more quizzical.

"Just by your presence and your pleasure," he heard himself say. "You see, I love you." How slowly were the words of truth dragged from him. Yet he felt a great peace with this final acknowledgment of a fact that he had been trying to deny for longer than he could imagine. The force of his compassion, his overwhelming need to protect and arm her, they were drawn from the well of love, not remorse.

A perceptible quiver shook the slender frame. Her smile faltered, her eyes darkened. "Do not say such a thing," she said in stifled tones. "It can do no good for either of us, and can only increase unhappiness."

"It is the same for you, too?" Despite her plea, he could not help persisting.

There was a long silence. Sophie looked out across the plain bathed in the false radiance of the Nordic night. She saw years stretching ahead of her, a barren eternity of imprisonment under a cold, vengeful tyranny. It was a lot shared by the majority of the empress's twenty million subjects. What right had she to protest? She was not starved, tortured, beaten like many of those others. She was just shriveling away in the arid presence of the ungiving.

"Yes, I love you," Sophie said. Admitting the truth could not worsen the situation, and, indeed, she too discovered that the admission brought a measure of peace. "But what difference does it make?" She looked across at him, her eyes shadowed with the knowledge of futility. "Let us ride." On the words, Khan sprang forward, out onto the plain.

Adam followed, knowing that the purpose of this ride was not social. She would not wait for him, not yet at least. He was content to have it so. Had he not arranged this escape in order for her to do just what she was doing? And in the solitude of his own thoughts, he could savor a shared love, for all that it was an impossible one.

It was half an hour before Sophie drew rein, slowing Khan to a trot, then to a walk. The hooves of Adam's horse pounded the plain behind her; she turned to look over her shoulder as he came up beside her. "Do you think I could ride Khan from here to Austria?"

Adam stared at her, as if trying to determine whether she was serious. He decided that she was more than half so. "No, of course you could not. Not unless you wish for rape and murder at the hands of brigands. Do not talk nonsense, Sophie." The impatience in his voice was feigned, but he could not let her see his own frustrated grief at a wretchedness that could produce such a desperate suggestion.

Sophie did not say that at least it would be a relatively quick end. She did not know how she could endure returning to the prison of her home after this heady taste of freedom, but without Adam's prompting, she turned Khan back the way they had come. The subject of love was not touched upon again. The fact lay open between them, the impossibility of its fulfillment as inexorable as death.

At the break of poplars, they halted. "I want to touch you," Adam said softly, "but I dare not."

Sophie looked at him in bleak acceptance. "No, I do not think I could bear it, either."

"Go!" he ordered, shockingly abrupt. "It will soon be sunrise."

She hesitated. "Adam . . ."

"Go!"

Without another word, Sophie left him beneath the poplars and galloped back toward the north gate of the city.

The stars were fading as she clattered into the stable yard of the Dmitriev palace. In the middle of that yard, his cane beneath his arm, his back erect, pale blue eyes as polished as diamond chips, stood General, Prince Paul Dmitriev.

Chapter 7

There was a moment of complete terror, when Sophie felt the power of thought and movement gone from her. Then she saw Boris Mikhailov standing between two of the prince's attendants. A bloodied weal slashed his cheek. She had seen such a mark many times in her days in this house. Prince Dmitriev used his cane indiscriminately. Fear for herself vanished as if it had never been. She must protect Boris and ensure that not a suspicion could fall upon Adam.

Recognizing instinctively that her position way up atop her Cossack stallion would put her husband at a physical disadvantage, one which would increase the viciousness of his fury, she swung to the ground before reaching him, crossing the yard on foot, her eyes not once meeting those of Boris Mikhailov.

"Who assisted you in this act of flagrant disobedience?" Her husband's voice was hard, clipped, seemingly dispassionate yet somehow imbued with the same ferocity that caused the bravest soldier under his command to tremble.

Sophie knew she must take his anger onto herself by a show of insolent bravado—a show that would negate all her efforts of the past weeks to convince him he had succeeded in driving the spirit of rebellion from her soul. An eyebrow lifted. "Why should you imagine I needed help, Paul? I have been able to saddle my own mount since I could first ride." Her eyes flicked toward Boris, almost indifferently. "You have no reason to hold Boris Mikhailov responsible. Even had I wished for his assistance, I would not have known where to find him in the middle of the night, or how to do so without waking others." She shrugged with seeming insouciance, continuing swiftly, "When you did not come to me last night, I realized that you had not returned home. I had thought to have my ride and be back in the house without anyone knowing that I had left it."

He stared at her with his cold eyes as if he would bore into her skull. She met the stare, armored against fear by the knowledge of those others dependent for their safety upon her ability to see this through. His head jerked toward the attendants, who stepped away from their prisoner. Dmitriev's gaze flickered in disgust over his wife's costume, missing not a speck of dust, not a tangled wisp of her hair.

"Why was that habit not burned with your other clothes?"

It seemed as if the question of Boris had been won by default. "Maria did not find it," Sophie said deliberately, not averse to sacrificing the spy to Paul's wrath, if by so doing she would further deflect that wrath from Boris.

"Then she must be taught to look with greater care," observed the prince in the same cold, dispassionate tone. "And this time you *will* learn, my dear wife, the lesson I had thought already taken." That travesty of a smile touched the thin lips. "Let us go inside." With a gesture of mock courtesy, he bowed slightly, gesturing toward the mansion before laying an apparently considerate, husbandly hand upon her arm.

Sophie only just managed to control her jump of alarm and revulsion. His fingers curled over her forearm, gripping with bruising pressure as she and the prince strolled into the house with all the appearance of a couple in perfect accord.

"First, you will show me how you left the house," he said calmly when they had reached the hall.

In normal circumstances, the household would only just be stirring, but Sophie was conscious of shadowy figures seemingly afraid to show themselves. Servants terrified that they would be implicated in the princess's escape? She had lived in this household long enough to know what they feared. The butler, who had opened the door for them, now stood rigid, his face working.

"I climbed through the dining room window," Sophie said, as calmly as her husband. She felt the anger surge through the powerful frame so close to her at this added reminder of the hoydenish tendencies he had believed eradicated.

He marched into the dining room, maintaining the painful grip on her arm. She showed him the window, still unlatched although drawn closed. "It seems that some members of my household have need to be taught their duties," murmured the prince in the tone of voice that spelled torment for the watchman.

Sophie swallowed. She could do nothing to help the man, could only be sorry that she had caused him suffering, even while she wondered what her own punishment would be.

"After such an energetic night, my dear, I am sure you have need of your bed," said her husband, in the silkily solicitous tone he always used when tightening the bars of her cage.

Sophie fixed her gaze on a whorl embedded in the heavy damask wall hanging. She must not let him see how she feared the thought of a repetition of those dark days, drifting in a drugged trance. "I find I am a little fatigued," she managed to say, hoping to deceive him. "I should welcome the opportunity for a few hours' sleep."

"Then let us go upstairs, my dear Sophia."

In Sophie's bedchamber, a quivering Maria stood beside the empty, tumbled bed. "I had no idea, lord," she stammered. "Her Highness said nothing . . ."

"Why should you imagine she would say anything, you fool!" snapped the prince, whose polite facade did not extend to serfs, errant or otherwise. "In future, you will sleep across the princess's door."

"Yes, lord." Maria bobbed curtsies as if she were on a marionette's string.

"Help Her Highness into bed, and remove that garment which you so signally failed to dispose of earlier," the prince instructed acidly. "For your negligence, you shall have six lashes."

The serf's complexion went gray as putty, but the sentence was lighter than she could have expected. Sophie avoided looking at her, while she waited to hear her own sentence pronounced in the form of a considerate summoning of the physician, but her husband merely offered an ironic bow.

"I will leave you to your rest, my dear. I trust you will feel less fatigued at dinnertime."

So she was not to face the laudanum imprisonment again? If not that, what? After the departure of the tearful though mute Maria, Sophie lay in the darkened bedchamber. Would Adam know by now of the discovery of her escapade? Presumably the general's surprisingly premature return would be known in Preobrazhenskoye, in which case Adam would be in a fever of anxiety.

The morning dragged interminably. Sophie was unable to sleep, despite her largely sleepless night. She lay awash with trepidation, not daring to rise and show herself about the house in case Paul, choosing to interpret such restlessness as a sign of ill health, should act accordingly.

It was just after noon when a timid knock at the door heralded the arrival of a young maidservant whom Sophie did not remember seeing before; not that that was unusual, since the army of serfs staffing the Dmitriev mansion was enormous, and constantly subject to change as serfs were moved, sold, or brought in for training from the country estates.

"If you please, Princess, I'm here to help you dress for dinner." The girl bobbed a curtsy.

"Where is Maria?" Sophie sat up, pushing aside the bedcovers, unable to hide her relief at this end to bed rest.

The girl turned away, burying her face in the armoire. "She's in the servants' quarters, Princess. She'll be keeping to her bed for a day or two."

Sophie said nothing. She should have known better than to ask. Sentences in the Dmitriev household were always summarily executed. Except, she thought, for her own in this instance. That had not even been pronounced yet.

Nor was the matter referred to throughout dinner, which was undertaken in customary formality and with the minimum of conversation. Sophie forced herself to eat, to drink, to ask a polite question about her husband's visit to Czarskoye Selo, even to listen to the answer. And all the while she felt as she had when waiting for the rabid wolf to show himself in the long grass, poised to spring for the jugular. Now, as then, she must be prepared for any eventuality, must keep her mind's eye free of the images that would create the fear that would impede clear thinking and the smooth reactions on which her safety and that of others depended.

The meal ended as always at precisely three o'clock. Punctiliously, Sophie performed the ritual of thanks, receiving a cool bow in return.

"Why do you not visit the stables, my dear Sophia?" suggested the prince. "It is a most pleasant afternoon, and I expect you would enjoy being out of doors after your quiet morning."

The wolf had shown himself. She knew it with absolute certainty as she looked into her husband's pale eyes, where swam a shark of complacent anticipation—anticipation of another's pain.

Was it Boris? No, she must not speculate; if she did so she would be unable to conceal her dread, and Paul would read it on her face. He must not have that satisfaction.

"What a considerate suggestion, Paul," she said, smiling blandly. "I would, indeed, enjoy a walk in the sunshine."

"I have certain matters to go through with Colonel, Count Danilevski in my study this afternoon. However, I will be escorting you to Countess Narishkina's soirée this evening." A smile flickered over his lips, but the smile in his eyes was far from pleasant. "The Narishkins returned to the city last week. I received their invitation yesterday and had thought it would be a pleasant surprise for you . . . a little social diversion." The thin-lipped smile vanished. "I do trust it is not unwise of me to permit this diversion, Sophia. Her Imperial Majesty will be in residence again in the Winter Palace at the beginning of next week, I understand, so there will be other invitations during the winter season. It would be a great pity if your behavior necessitated your withdrawal from society."

"I cannot withdraw from something which I have not yet entered, Paul," Sophie pointed out quietly. The certainty that he had taken reprisals—reprisals that she was about to discover—for her nighttime ride, somehow made arousing his anger with a further show of spirit unimportant. Indeed, it gave her some satisfaction as she felt a resurgence of the Sophia Alexeyevna of Berkholszkoye—one who did not easily yield up control of her destiny. The meek facade behind which that Sophia had been concealed suddenly appeared a cowardly deceit, an abnegation of her true self.

She met the stab of cold fury in his eyes with a steady gaze, then curtsied deliberately. "If you will excuse me, Paul, I will take my walk to the stables."

Dmitriev watched her walk away from him, her head high, carriage erect, just as she had used to walk before her wedding night. Had he miscalculated? Obviously, to some extent he had. He had believed her spirit broken, but the belief was clearly premature. However, she was about to be reminded that acts of independence and disobedience would meet with exemplary and appropriate penalties.

He stood, frowning, massaging the palm of one hand with his thumb. For some reason, he was deriving much less than the expected satisfaction from his possession of Sophia Ivanova's daughter. He had thought that this possession would compensate for the loss of the other, that in the subjugation to his will of a Golitskova he would experience the satisfaction of a neat revenge for the humiliations and frustrations of the past. But she lay like a stone beneath him, eyes staring blankly at the ceiling, as he spilled his seed. While her lack of pleasure did not concern him, the complete indifference she evinced was almost insulting . . . condescending in some way. And she had not conceived. An heir would make up for everything, but add barrenness to her other faults and it would appear that, with the exception of her fortune, he had made a poor bargain. However, he *could* ensure her submission, and he would do so. It would not be difficult to make her life even less pleasant than it was at present if she continued to show herself intractable. On that comforting determination, Prince Paul Dmitriev went upstairs to his study to await the arrival of his aide-de-camp.

As Sophie walked through the mansion she became conscious of something strange, something not quite right about the household. It took her a minute to realize that even in this usually depressing atmosphere she would generally encounter a murmured greeting, a half smile from the domestic serfs as she went about the house. Now, eyes slid away from her, bodies shrank into the shadows at her approach, as if at the approach of a pariah. Of course, two quite innocent people had been flogged as a result of her activities. It was obviously considered safer to keep away from the mistress's purview as far as possible.

A despondent wave washed through her, adding to the sum of her unhappiness. She was friendless, apart from Adam and Boris, whose feelings toward her, however powerful they might be, could not be made manifest, and therefore could do her no good.

But what of Boris now? Her step quickened anxiously at that thought. What would she find in the stables? Would she pass through the courtyard to find Boris Mikhailov hanging by his hands from the scaffold, his back in bloody tatters from the great knout? The image brought a nut of nausea to lodge in her throat; she had difficulty keeping to a walking pace, her eyes darting from side to side in dread of what they might fall upon. But the courtyard was deserted; only the freshly scrubbed condition of the paving at the base of the scaffold, gleaming white beneath the heedless afternoon sun, offered mute witness to the blood-spattered torments of the night watchman.

Boris was drawing water from the well in the stable yard as she hurried in. When he straightened, looking toward her, she knew that something dreadful had happened. The giant muzhik appeared to stoop, and the usually piercing black eyes were dulled with sadness; quite suddenly the gray hair and beard seemed accurate reflections of his years instead of the incongruous indications of a man past his prime.

"What is it? What has happened?" The questions emerged through stiff lips, a throat of sand, as she hurried toward him, for once not caring that they would be seen by the stable hands and grooms to be talking privately.

His face twisted with sorrow. He took her hands in his, grasping strongly. "It is Khan, Princess."

"Khan!" Black dots swam before her eyes. "Dead? Has he

had him shot?'' It was the worst she could think of, but the muzhik shook his head.

"It would be better so. The prince has sold him."

"Sold him?" She stared, aghast. Khan could not serve another master, could not be tended by other than Boris Mikhailov, who had just spoken the truth. The stallion would be better shot than broken to another will. Because he would have to be broken; he could not be bought by kindness, and he was far too mighty a creature to be mastered by the puny strength of a mere man. "Sold him?" she repeated in a whisper. "To whom, Boris?"

Despair darkened his features. "To a horse trader, for three imperials."

Thirty rubles! He had sold that priceless animal for a mere thirty rubles to a horse trader, one of the notorious breed who would not care what he had bought for such a miserable sum, would care only about reselling him. And to do that, Khan would have to be beaten and starved into submission, for no one would pay good money for the wild beast he would appear to be in unfamiliar hands.

"No . . . no, it cannot be!" Sophie shook her head in disbelief. "You must be mistaken, Boris Mikhailov."

"I wish I were," the muzhik said gently. "But I was present at the sale. Holy Mother forgive me, but I handed Khan over to him."

"You cannot blame yourself for that," she said dully. "I know you would have had no choice." She turned away from the pain in his eyes. So this was what her husband had been so anxious she should hear. He would have known, also, how much it would hurt Boris to be the one to tell her.

Abruptly, she was engulfed with rage, a blind fury welling up from the depths of her soul to vanquish all thoughts of caution, all fear of the man who controlled her existence. The temper that she had struggled so strenuously to contain in the last weeks burst its restraints, and she was running toward the house, catching up her skirts to free her stride. She ran through the house, taking the stairs two at a time, heedless of the amazed stares, the forest fire of astonished whispers she left in her wake. Without ceremony, she burst into Prince Dmitriev's study.

Adam, swinging around from the window, recognized the Sophia Alexeyevna he had first met, the fiery creature who had turned into a Fury when he caught her bridle.

Paul Dmitriev saw a woman he had not seen before. The dark eyes were almost black in their outrage, glaring in her whitened face, her mouth drawn back in a grimace of rage.

"How dare you!" The door crashed against the wall as she flung it from her. "How dare you sell Khan? How could you condemn such a beautiful creature to a slow death? What has *he* done that he should deserve such a fate? You had as well sell *me* to a horse trader as a Cossack stallion. I cannot imagine a more *stupid* vengeance . . . mindless to sacrifice such a beast—"

"Be silent!" thundered Prince Dmitriev, recovering from the shock of this incredible outburst. "You forget yourself." His voice had dropped to an icy, dangerous calm. "If you imagine I will tolerate such a disgraceful public outburst from my wife, Sophia Alexeyevna, you are much mistaken."

Sophie's eyes darted toward Adam, who stood like a graven image beside the window, his expression completely impassive. "If you will excuse me," he said now, bowing to his general. "I am *de trop*." Without another word, he left the study, abandoning Sophie to Dmitriev's anger even as she took an involuntary half step toward him.

"You will go to your bedchamber and calm yourself," the prince now said with the same icy calm.

The anger ran from her, to be replaced by a bleak hopelessness. "Khan belonged to me," she said in a low voice. "You had no right—"

"You will not talk to me about my rights," he snapped. "You are my wife, and you may count as yours only those possessions I permit. I will dispose of any others as I see fit. Now, go to your bedchamber. Quite clearly, you are too overwrought to attend the countess's soirée this evening. You will keep to your bed until I consider you have fully recovered from this extraordinary outburst. If you oblige me to summon the physician, I shall have no hesitation in doing so.''

Sophie turned and left without another word. In the Wild Lands, she had learned the wisdom of accepting defeat. It did not mean that one could not fight again, and her grandfather had told her to apply the rules of the Wild Lands to her new life. Her grandfather . . . She had not wanted to worry him with her tale of woe, had wanted to see this through herself, but he had told her that he would not send her without armor into this new world; if she had need of him she had only to send Boris Mikhailov with a message. Now she knew that she would fall back on that weapon in her armory. She would appeal to the old prince, who would be outraged by such an inhumane and pointless act as had been perpetrated this day.

But she could not put the plan into effect for the moment. She must keep to her bed as ordered, endure her grief, mourn in silence for the loss of a part of herself, show her husband the face of submission and docility until she was released from the imprisonment of her room.

Adam, hardly able to contain his own rage at the senseless violence of Dmitriev's revenge, left the general's palace, haunted by the knowledge of Sophie's pain. He found Boris Mikhailov in the stable yard and hailed him, credibly imperious. ''A word with you, fellow!''

Boris touched his forelock. ''Yes, lord.'' He hastened over to the count, bowing. There was nothing in either the summons or the demeanor of the count or the muzhik to draw remark from the other serfs in the yard, who, after a casual look at their master's aide-de-camp, continued with their own tasks.

''What do you know of this horse trader?'' Adam asked softly.

''From Georgia,'' Boris replied as softly. ''Said he was taking the road to Smolensk this afternoon with a string of horses. Seemed mighty pleased with himself.'' The black eyes hardened. ''Had good reason to be, with such a buy as Khan for three imperials.''

''Three imperials!'' Adam was betrayed into a gasp. Then he recovered himself. ''The road to Smolensk?''

Boris nodded, glancing up at the sun. "Left about four hours ago, lord. A fast horse would catch him in half that; a string of horses, some of 'em half-broke, isn't easy to manage at speed."

"What do I need to know to manage Khan on a leading rein?" The question was clipped, businesslike, and received a similar response.

"Keep him on the left side. He's inclined to shy at sudden movements." Boris tapped out the factors on his forefinger. "He doesn't like a strange hand on his bridle, so he'll probably put you to the test. Keep the rein short. When he shies don't tug him, just hold him and pray. If he's going to take off, there's nothing you can do to stop him, anyway." Boris frowned, thinking. "Oh, and Sophia Alexeyevna always talks to him. Swears it calms him." He shrugged, smiling slightly. "I don't know if another voice would work as well, though."

"My talent for mimicry is somewhat underdeveloped," observed Adam dryly. "Let us hope I am not required to attempt it."

"And the princess . . . ?" Boris asked hesitantly.

"Knows nothing of this, yet. She has fallen foul of her husband and I cannot help her in any other way, Boris Mikhailov." Frustration scudded across the lean, aristocratic features. "A man's wife is his own." Except that that rule had not applied to his own wife—the faithless Eva and her unknown lover. Why the devil should he adhere to . . . No! He would not repeat the wrongs that had been done to him. But the reiterated decision seemed to have lost some of its force under his fury at Dmitriev's senseless viciousness, under Adam's overpowering need to help Sophie in whatever way he could, under the memory of their shared declaration in the hour before dawn.

"I will keep Khan in my own stables," he said now. "If you have the opportunity, tell Sophia Alexeyevna that I *will* succeed in this. I will redeem Khan from the trader; he will be quite safe with me."

Not for one minute did it occur to Boris Mikhailov to doubt the count's statement. If this man set out to do something, he would succeed. "I'll tell her, lord. For all her fortitude, such cruelty will have pierced deep."

Adam, thinking of the virago who had confronted Dmitriev, smiled despite his bleakness. "It will take more than the general to break her, Boris."

"Let's hope you're right," the muzhik replied somberly. "Anyone can be broken with sufficient time. His Highness has all the time he needs, seems to me."

Adam, who could find no words of comforting contradiction, left immediately, taking the road to Smolensk in pursuit of the horse trader.

Boris Mikhailov stood frowning in the stable yard. He had not confided his suspicion that the general had some reason of his own, some reason from the dark past, for his treatment of Sophia Alexeyevna. What could be gained by revealing his unsubstantiated hunch either to Sophia Alexeyevna or to the count?

Prince Dmitriev went alone to Countess Narishkina's soirée, offering a bland excuse for his wife's absence with a severe migraine. He stayed for an hour, was charming, accepting renewed congratulations on his wedding with soft-spoken thanks, smiled gratefully when he was told by various prominent ladies that they would call upon his wife in the next week, murmured how pleased Sophia Alexeyevna would be, and how grateful he would be for their interest in his young and inexperienced wife, who was in need of much guidance. Then, like the most uxorious husband, he pleaded his sick wife's bedside and left.

Once home, he went to his own apartments, where he prepared himself for the night. Then, clad in his dressing gown, he entered his wife's bedchamber without ceremony. The room was in semidarkness, only a night light burning on the table, the curtains drawn tight around the bed. Twitching aside the bed curtains, he looked upon the pale, drawn face of the Princess Dmitrievna.

"You look like a sick cat," he commented coldly, untying the girdle of his robe. "It would appear that I was not altogether guilty of untruth when I said a headache had kept you from this evening's dissipations."

"As it happens, I am not well," Sophie murmured, looking at him through half-closed eyes. "The time of the month . . ."

Dmitriev's face darkened with annoyance. He retied his girdle with ominous deliberation. "Clearly we must try harder, my dear. And you must strive for a little more composure. These violent outbursts cannot be good for you." He left the chamber, and Sophie heard the key grate in the lock of her door.

She turned her face into her pillow, fighting the tears, the despairing hopelessness that could only worsen this living death, the desperate longing for Adam. How she ached to be held again in love and tenderness, to feel again the wondrous blossoming deep in her body beneath the sweet caress of his lips. What would it be like to share with Adam this cold, hurtful act in which she participated with her husband? There could be no comparison. But she would never find out. The tears flowed despite her efforts, tears for herself, for her grandfather, lonely at Berkholzskoye, so many tears for Khan, tears for Adam and for a love that could only wither unnurtured.

The door was not unlocked until noon of the following day. She did not bother to ring the bell for the little maidservant, being fairly confident that for as long as her door remained locked, any summons would be unanswered. The mortification of being ignored by the servants, even though they would be doing so on her husband's orders, was more than she could bear. She would pretend to be asleep, lost in peaceful oblivion. No one, least of all her husband, should have the satisfaction of thinking she might be suffering from this neglect.

When the key sounded again in the lock, she propped herself up against the pillows, schooling her expression to one evincing an anxious desire to please. "Good day, Paul." She greeted him with the hesitant smile she had perfected over the weeks, as if the circumstances were quite ordinary.

He fitted the key in the inside lock again, before approaching the bed. "You had better summon your maid to help you dress for dinner. I am expecting guests."

"Guests!" She could not control the surprised exclamation. "Count Danilevski, you mean?"

"I do not consider my aide-de-camp to be a guest," her husband informed her. "When he dines here it is simply because we have work to do."

Sophie, afraid that she had been on the verge of betraying herself by that incautious question, dropped her eyes to the coverlet, murmuring meekly, "Yes, I do see that, Paul. How foolish of me."

He regarded her with a degree of suspicion. Until yesterday, he would not have doubted the sincerity of her meek demeanor, but now he was unsure. However, she had suffered some severe blows since then: the loss of her horse, denial of a social visit for which she must have longed after the long period of isolation, then the mortification of this imprisonment of which she must have known the servants were aware.

He decided to give her the benefit of the doubt. "As it happens, my guests are regimental colleagues newly returned from an expedition to Kazan. Count Danilevski will also be joining us. I trust the role of hostess will not be beyond you." He raised a sardonic eyebrow. "You will not be required to participate in the conversation beyond the formalities, and you will leave the table as soon as the meal is over."

Rebellious fury welled anew at these insulting instructions better suited to a child at an adult's table or a poor relation dependent upon charity. She kept her eyes down, stilling the angry trembling of her fingers, concentrating on the singing thought that Adam would be present throughout the interminable tedium. Perhaps they could steal a glance, exchange a comment that would carry a meaning apparent only to the two of them.

"You will be in the drawing room to greet my guests at a quarter to two," Paul informed her, marching to the door. "You will not dress yourself too elaborately—a morning gown will be sufficient for the modest part I wish you to play."

"Yes, Paul," Sophie dutifully murmured; then, as the door closed behind him, she picked up the brass candlestick beside the bed and hurled it at the paneling. There was a splintering crash, and she waited with bated breath to see if it would bring him back into the room. But the door remained closed. The violent gesture had so relieved her feelings that she could almost laugh at the thought of how she was to explain a bent candlestick and splintered paneling to her maid. At least it wouldn't be

Maria for a while longer, and the timid little girl presently allocated to her didn't seem to have the makings of a spy.

She pulled the bell rope with a surge of energy and flung open the door to her armoire. Maybe she had been forbidden to dress with any ceremony, but there was some pleasure in the thought that she was to lay eyes upon representatives of the outside world, and they would have to respond to her in some small way, just as a matter of simple courtesy.

A smile played over her lips as she dressed in a gown of apple green cambric over a very small hoop. She was remembering the first evening with Adam, when, in customary careless fashion, she had presented herself for supper in her dusty riding habit and boots, hair still wind-whipped. In the few weeks at court before her wedding, she had discovered some of the pleasures to be found in an elaborate wardrobe and the sophistication of ceremonial dress. Her present gown was elegant in its simplicity. The color brought out the deep highlights in the rich brown hair coiled heavily around her head to frame her oval face. A lace fichu at the neck of the gown bespoke modesty, but it exactly matched the froth of lace foaming at the edge of the elbow-length sleeves. Her forearms seemed to curve nicely, Sophie thought, examining them for the first time in her life with a frown of interest. She turned them this way and that, admiring the daintiness of her wrist, the smooth creaminess of her skin.

Her lip curled in sudden distaste. What was the point of admiring her so-called charms when they were laid to waste night after night beneath an indifferent husband? What did Adam think of her arms? Perhaps they were a little too muscular for true elegance. . . . Oh, stop it! She scolded herself vigorously for such pointless, potentially hurtful musings, as she slipped into the deep pocket of her decorative apron the letter to her grandfather she had written during her imprisonment the previous evening. It was possible she would be able to slip away to the stables, and she must be prepared to seize whatever opportunities arose. Armored with the decision, she went downstairs to the drawing room.

When Sophie appeared in the drawing room, curtsying politely to her husband and the two senior officers of the Semeonovsky regiment of the Imperial Guard, Adam covertly, carefully, scrutinized her. There was nothing out of the ordinary in her demeanor, no indication that she had suffered unusual hurt as a result of her outburst over Khan. There was one moment when those dark eyes met his inspection. In their depths he read a glimmer of complicity, a glow of warmth, instantly extinguished when she turned from him to murmur some meek assent to a comment from General Arkcheyev.

She was not going to break, Adam decided. If anything, he thought he could sense a resurgence of the old Sophie, as if, instead of crushing her further with his cruelty over Khan, Dmitriev had had the opposite effect. She had gone beyond his power to hurt.

She did not yet know that Khan was safe and sound in Adam's stables. Boris had said the princess had not appeared since the previous afternoon. When she had that knowledge, it would augment her will to resist. But he could not stifle the slow burn of rage at Dmitriev's manner, which, by effectively excluding his wife from the conversation, implied that her presence was simply a necessary nuisance.

Sophie retreated into herself—a trick she had taught herself in the last two months. The pompous voices, the laughter growing louder, more immoderate, as the wine and vodka passed back and forth, drifted, unheeded, over her head. She was vaguely conscious that her husband had imbibed much more than was his custom, or, at least, his custom at this dinner table; what he did when he was with his friends was a different matter. A flush had appeared on his sallow cheeks, and his movements were not as precise. A knife clattered against a plate, wine spilled over the lip of his glass. His voice became, if not slurred, then a trifle thick. But this condition was shared by his two friends.

Adam, alone, remained as cool and distant as ever. Sophie's eyes slid across the smooth, polished surface of the table, around the heavy silver serving dishes, over the delicate delftware, the cut glass goblets, to lift in a secret whisper of a glance to his face. His lips moved fractionally, yet she felt the kiss they gave as a vital force, as real as if it had been planted upon her mouth, now tingling in response. Desire, invincible, swelled within her, filling every corner of her body. There was a moment when it shone, naked, from her eyes, glowing now as they looked openly at him, meeting a hunger to match her own. Then sharp warning sparked in his eyes, dousing passion, and she lowered her gaze to her plate.

Filled with a secret joy, Sophie left the dining room the minute she could decently do so. The drinking was continuing, and three of the four seemed set fair for an afternoon that would vanish into the mists of bibulous unremembering. The jubilant memory of that clandestine look and promise buoyed her as she made her way to the stables, intent on sharing a moment of silent memory with Boris Mikhailov, before telling him he must depart for Berkholzskoye to explain to Prince Golitskov the full wretchedness of her situation. But when she saw Boris, saw his shining eyes, the radiance of his expression, she gathered up the soft cambric of her skirts and ran across the cobbles toward him.

"Hush!" he cautioned in a whisper as she reached him. "You are too impulsive, Sophia Alexeyevna! There are eyes and ears everywhere."

"I forgot for a minute," she said with a return to somberness. "You looked as if you had good news."

"I have. Khan is safe with Count Danilevski. . . . No, control yourself!" he said sharply as tears suddenly filled her eyes and her face shone with wonder and joy. "If I can slip away from this place this evening, I will go and check on him, but the count says he is calm, eating well—"

"Listen, Boris," Sophie interrupted in an urgent whisper, controlling her joy and relief until the time when she could savor them. "I have decided that my grandfather must know of these things. He will know how to help. You must go to Berkholzskoye."

Boris nodded slowly. "The prince told me what I should do if you felt the need. He gave me money for a horse and for the journey. Have you a letter?"

Sophie turned her back on the yard, beginning to saunter toward the gate, stealthily drawing out the paper from the pocket of her apron, holding it at her side, concealed in a fold of her skirt. "It explains everything . . . about Tanya Feodorovna, Khan . . . and . . . oh, so many other things." Things Boris knew nothing about, all the hurts and humiliations that she could not bring herself to talk about, although writing about them had put a distance between herself and the wounding memories.

Her lips barely moved as she spoke; the muzhik's hand covered hers for the barest second, and the document changed owners. Without another word or glance, Sophie strolled from the yard, fighting to keep the skip out of her step. Khan was safe. Adam had saved Khan. Boris would reach Berkholzskoye in two, maybe three, weeks of hard riding, and Prince Golitskov would not ignore her plea. What he could do, Sophie did not know; but she knew that he would do something. The bars of her prison seemed to be widening, offering a glimpse of a possible future other than the drear withering of her soul beneath the tyrant's yoke.

She reentered the house, finding it as dark and oppressive as ever, yet, for once, the atmosphere did not deaden her uplifted spirits. There was a distinct spring in her step as she passed the dining room, from whence came the muffled sounds of voices, a low rumble of laughter. She would go up to the long gallery and look over the river. At least there was to be found light and airiness. The river symbolized freedom, a highway to the outside world.

She turned a shadowy corner at the head of the stairs. "Adam!" Her urgent, joyful cry was a little too loud for caution, but her heart had speeded at the sight of the tall figure striding down the tapestry-hung corridor ahead of her. He turned, and she ran into his arms. "You saved Khan!" With blind recklessness, she flung her arms around his neck, reaching up to embrace him, initiating a passionate kiss that for a moment he could not help but respond to, so sweet were her lips upon his, the eager darting of her tongue as she took possession of his mouth, the lithe slenderness of her body molded to his, the fragrance of her skin and hair.

"Sophie! This is madness!" At last he drew away, pulling her arms from around his neck.

"They are all drunk," Sophie declared with a dismissive

gesture, a gay laugh. "I wish to kiss you, because you saved Khan and because I love you!" Smilingly importunate, she raised her arms again.

Adam could not prevent his own delighted laugh at her words, but he caught her hands. "At least let us get out of the corridor, you foolhardy creature!"

"I do not care anymore!" Sophie declared, although she allowed him to pull her into the gloom of a small, rarely used parlor.

"You *must* care enough to take reasonable precaution," Adam chided, pushing the door half shut behind them. "Do you wish to spend the rest of your life in the cloister?"

Sophie paled. "He would not do such a thing."

"His second wife died in the Convent of Suzdal," Adam informed her bluntly. "He forced her to take the veil and she died five years later. It is a man's prerogative with an unsatisfactory wife."

"One who is barren and looks upon another man," Sophie said slowly, hugging herself in a fierce gesture of self-protection. "*Grandpère* would not allow him—"

"Prince Golitskov has not the right to prevent him," Adam interrupted with harsh truth.

"He will do something," Sophie declared with intense conviction. "I have given Boris Mikhailov a letter, telling him of . . . of the way things are, here. He *will* do something."

Adam looked down at the pale oval face, the dark, glowing eyes where lurked a glimmer of hope, and he could not bring himself to stifle that hope. "How is Boris to leave here?"

"I do not know," she replied. "But he has promised that he will. I do not know when he will find the opportunity, but he will keep his promise. *Grandpère* gave him money for a horse and travel expenses in case . . ." Her voice faded, the light dimmed in her eyes. "It is a long way to Berkholzskoye, I know."

Adam, unable to bear the resurgence of despondency, took her in his arms, smoothing a loose strand of hair from her forehead. "Sweetheart—"

The sound of footsteps in the corridor outside stopped his

words. Sophie went rigid, her eyes darting wildly around the room. "Behind the tapestry," Adam whispered, pushing her roughly toward the far wall, where hung a Gobelin tapestry. She slipped behind it, holding her breath, sucking in her stomach, trying to flatten herself against the wall.

"Count Danilevski, is there something you wish for?" It was the butler's measured tones, although the surprise he clearly felt at the count's presence in this dim little chamber was apparent in his voice.

"No, nothing, thank you, Nikolai," responded Adam smoothly. "I was passing this parlor and heard a scrabbling in the wainscoting. I think you may find a mouse. It would be as well to inspect the woodwork, I think. One mouse usually means more. They have such prolific breeding habits." He smiled, gently benign, and strolled past Nikolai, whose expression exhibited great alarm at the prospect of such a disorderly infestation in Prince Dmitriev's regimented household.

Sophie waited, breathless behind the tapestry, until she was sure that Nikolai had left, presumably to bring reinforcements to attack the mice. Despite the heart-thumping danger of the last minutes, she could not help a little chuckle at Adam's improvisation. The idea would have the servants in an uproar, turning this forgotten parlor upside down in search of something that wasn't there.

Slipping out of the room, she continued innocently on her way to the long gallery, there to spend the afternoon gazing out at the sparkling river, now coming to life again as society returned to the capital, and to daydream of what might have been . . . of what might yet be. . . .

Chapter 8

"Disappeared! What the devil do you mean, Boris Mikhailov has disappeared?" Prince Dmitriev brought his cane down in a vicious swipe across the top of his desk, although his voice did not rise above a normal pitch.

The head groom trembled, flinching, knowing that his shoulders could well be the next target. "Sometime in the night, lord," he stammered. "It must have been . . . when he went."

"It is now the middle of the afternoon," announced the prince with deadly calm. "How is it that no one has noticed his absence until now?"

"Your pardon, lord, but he keeps to himself, that one, and since that great horse was sold he's kept apart even more. Just goes about his business. You don't notice he's there most of the time." The man subsided, miserably aware of the inadequacy of his explanation.

"You realize that he has had perhaps a twelve-hour start, don't you?" inquired the prince pleasantly, caressing the smooth oak of the heavy cane.

The groom swallowed, taking a step backward. "Yes, lord."

"Then I suggest you find him and bring him back." The prince smiled his meagre smile. "By tomorrow morning. If you fail, then you shall pay his penalty for him—the penalty of a runaway serf." The smile stretched thinner. "You understand me?"

"Yes, lord." The groom backed to the door, bowing until his nose reached his knees.

"Take six of your strongest fellows with you," the prince instructed. "He's to be brought back in chains."

The door closed on the still-bowing groom. Dmitriev slammed the cane across the desk again. Did Sophia Alexeyevna know of this? In principle, Boris Mikhailov belonged to her, although in practice, as they would both discover to their cost, he belonged to Dmitriev, the man under whose roof he slept, whose food he ate, whose tasks he performed. The muzhik would be trying to return to Berkholzskoye; it was the only rational destination. He would seek the protection of Golitskov, and it would not be denied him because in theory he was still Golitskov property.

He had to be found and brought back to suffer publicly the fate of a runaway. Were such a flight to succeed, there was no knowing what precedents it might set. Dmitriev was well aware that he ruled his vast households with the scourge of terror. For such a rule to remain impregnable, there must be no perceived cracks in the system; one successful uprising, however insignificant, could lead to wholesale mutiny.

Cold fury filled him. Was this flight made with the connivance of Sophia Alexeyevna? He had prevented her from writing to her grandfather in the last two months by the simple expedient of failing to provide the means by which a letter could be carried. The two letters she had received from Golitskov were locked in her husband's bureau, unopened, and she had given up asking if the carriers had brought anything for her. But had she decided to provide her own messenger? What would she have said? Not that it mattered. Her grandfather had no jurisdiction, no possible right to come between a man and his wife. But Prince Paul Dmitriev did not like his affairs made public.

Leaving his study, he went to his wife's apartments. She was dressing for a reception at the palace, the czarina having returned from the country some three days earlier. Sophia Alexeyevna had been bidden to attend at court this afternoon, and even had he wished to do so, her husband could not refuse the invitation for her. Purely social invitations he could oblige her to accept or refuse as whim took him, but an imperial summons must be obeyed.

Sophie's surprise at this unexpected visit showed for a moment on her face, then disappeared as she smiled. "Do you accompany me to the palace, Paul?"

The cold blue eyes skimmed her expression. "But of course, my dear. You would not imagine that I would expect you to go without a husband's escort."

"No, of course not," murmured Sophie, bending her head slightly as Maria fastened the clasp of an emerald pendant.

"I do not think you should wear the emeralds with that gown, Sophia." His fingers hovered over the contents of the gem casket on her dressing table. "Something a little less flamboyant, I think." He selected a string of pearls. "Allow me." With his usual flat smile, he unfastened the emeralds.

Sophie's skin crept at the brush of his fingers, even as she wondered what lay behind these unusual attentions. She knew that her sole possession of the Golitskov gems infuriated him, but it was one thing he could do nothing about, although he could prevent her from wearing the emeralds if he chose; that did not matter to her in the least. But what was he doing here? He only ever came into this chamber at night, and he left it the minute he had done what he came to do.

"I have just been informed that the muzhik who accompanied you from Berkholzskoye has disappeared," he said now, casually, as he fastened the pearls around her neck, his eyes examining her reflection in the mirror. There was not a flicker of an eyelid, not a quiver of a muscle to betray her—if, indeed, she had anything to betray. He waited for her response with a politely interested expression.

Sophie shrugged, raising one hand to adjust the tortoiseshell comb in her hair. "His only task was to care for Khan." Her eyes met her husband's in the mirror. "I expect he felt he was no longer needed." Behind the mask of indifference her mind was racing. It had been a week since she had given Boris the letter, and she had been waiting in ever-growing impatience to hear that he had made his escape. He would have planned it with meticulous care, she knew; but the knowledge could not mitigate the dreadful anxiety for his safety, now that the waiting was over.

His hands slipped to her shoulders, rising in soft ivory from the low neck of her gown. Fingers curled like spines as he continued to smile at her in the mirror. "My dear wife, it is not for a serf to decide where and when he is needed. He will be brought back. And when he is, he will suffer the punishment of a runaway." Did he imagine that minute tremor in the skin beneath his fingers?

Make no response, Sophie told herself. There was no reason to suppose they would catch Boris, and she must show only the most casual interest in the affair. Were her hands trembling? She smoothed down the skirt of her turquoise taffeta gown, lowering her head as if to concentrate on the task. When would he take his hands from her creeping flesh?

"If you are to accompany me, Paul, had you not better change your dress?" It was unusual for her to make such a definite statement, but she could think of nothing else to do. To her relief, he appeared to show no surprise at such directness.

"Yes, you are right, my dear. We should leave within the half hour." He went to the door. "I will join you in the drawing room at half past four."

The door closed on his departure, but still Sophie must maintain the impassive front before the spy, Maria, who had become both more vigilant and increasingly hostile since her whipping. Sophie could hardly blame the woman, but now, when she wanted to pace the bedchamber, giving vent to the agony of apprehension for Boris, and for herself, she must dab perfume behind her ears, flutter her handkerchief, check the contents of her reticule. At least, at a thronged court reception she could perhaps let her guard relax just a little. Paul could not watch her constantly. She would be able to talk naturally, to laugh, even to dance; and in these ordinary activities she would find momentary surcease from this overpowering apprehension.

Maybe Adam would be there . . . maybe he would dance with her. It would not look strange for him to do so, quite the reverse. And during the dance, words could be exchanged without audience. She rose from the dresser stool. "Thank you, Maria." Her voice was cool, distant. "I do not know how late we shall be, but you will wait up for me." With that slight, but satisfactory exertion of authority, Sophie swept from the room. Maria would wait up for her anyway, just as she would sleep across the door to the corridor, but it still gave Sophie the illusion of control.

All evening, she was on the watch for the tall, lean figure, immaculate in dress uniform, for the deep gray eyes that would rest upon her for a second of warmth and complicity. Her ears strained through the chatter, through the melodious plucking of strings, to identify the light tones, carrying just the faintest hint of accent, yet it was so faint one could hardly call it an accent. It was more of an intonation, more noticeable when he spoke Russian than French. But then, of course, French was the language of the aristocracy in Poland as well as Russia, so he would not have had to learn that language when he had been transplanted to St. Petersburg all those years ago.

These irrelevancies flitted in and out of her head throughout the evening, yet they were not really irrelevancies, because they related to one of the two subjects that absorbed her, body and soul. In Adam's presence, some of her anxiety about Boris would be relieved simply by sharing it.

But he did not come to the Winter Palace that day.

The czarina greeted her former protégée kindly, but the sharp eyes noted the absence of the previous glow and vibrancy. The early days of marriage were a cross all young women had to bear, Catherine reflected. Perhaps the princess was pregnant. That would account for the slight listlessness, the pallor. Her husband, on the contrary, appeared mightily pleased, and kept a most flatteringly close and uxorious eye on his bride. If she were carrying his long-awaited heir, it would certainly explain such care and attention.

Catherine dismissed the question when she dismissed Sophia Alexeyevna with the instruction to enjoy herself amongst the friends she had made at court before her marriage. Before her instruction would be obeyed, however, Prince Dmitriev took his wife home.

Only Prince Potemkin, with the sensitivity drawn from his vast experience of women and their ways, was uneasy. There was something about the lowered eyes, the set of her head, that bespoke trouble. Potemkin knew General, Prince Paul Dmitriev better than did his empress. They were both soldiers, after all, and Dmitriev had served under Potemkin on more than one occasion. Potemkin did not care for Dmitriev's style of command, any more than did Adam Danilevski, but like Adam he was obliged to recognize success. He stood staring with his one eye and scratching his chin; then he shrugged. When all was said and done, a man's wife was his own. Sophia Alexeyevna had shown no reluctance for the marriage, and she had had time enough to become acquainted with her prospective bridegroom. No, it was probably the unfamiliarity of wedded bliss that had disturbed her . . . that and the heat. Whatever had possessed Dmitriev to keep her in St. Petersburg throughout the summer? Shaking his head, Potemkin went in search of vodka.

It was noon of the following day when the nightmare began. Sophie was in the mausoleum of the drawing room, made even darker by the rain scudding from a leaden sky beyond the windows, where, as in all St. Petersburg palaces, mica substituted for glass. She was seeking consolation and distraction from anxiety in her usual fashion. Her husband did not appear to find anything potentially subversive in reading and, indeed, ignored her pursuit of this leisure activity. She was now deeply absorbed in a volume of the letters of Madame de Sévigné when the sounds of disturbance came from the hall. Voices were raised— an unheard-of occurrence in this deadened house. The great front door slammed, footsteps scurried, clattering across the marble floors.

A cold sweat broke out on her forehead, trickled down her back; her hands began to shake uncontrollably; nausea rose in her throat. She knew what was happening even before her husband flung open the drawing room door and stood looking at her, silently, a mixture of rage and triumph in his eyes.

"I have managed to retrieve my property," he said in his customary calm tones. "Unfortunately for him . . . although most fortunately for me . . . he met with some delay on the road so the pursuit was able to catch up with him without difficulty."

The thin lips flickered in a snake's smile. "Come into the hall, my dear. Boris Mikhailov has something to return to you."

Sophie wondered if her legs would bear her weight, if she would manage to swallow the nausea, or if she would collapse upon the rich Persian carpet, vomiting in helpless humiliation as the fear became uncontrollable. But strength came from somewhere. Slowly, tentatively, she rose from her chair. There was no point pretending she did not understand what had happened, that she knew nothing of the letter; and there was no point attempting to conceal her fear, even had she been able to do so. Her legs somehow obeyed the order to move. She walked past her husband, politely holding the door for her, into the hall.

Despite the leg irons and the manacles, Boris Mikhailov held his head high. His lip was swollen, crusted with dried blood. One eye was closed, purpling with a great bruise. His shirt was torn and bloodstained, drenched with the rain that dripped from his hair and beard.

"You have something that belongs to the princess, I understand, Boris Mikhailov," came the silkily smooth tones of Prince Dmitriev. "Return it to her."

Between his manacled hands, Boris grasped the letter. Now, painfully, he extended his hands toward her, holding out the paper. Moving as if through a blanket of fog, she stepped forward, unable to meet his eyes, which held a plea for forgiveness, as if the failure of his mission was entirely to be laid at his door. She took the paper, and for an instant her fingers closed over his.

"Perhaps you would read the letter to me, my dear wife," requested the prince. "Just to refresh your memory."

To be obliged to read aloud the catalog of hurts and mortifications to the one who had visited them upon her was a refinement of cruelty beyond belief, she thought distantly. "Have you not read it yourself already?" she heard herself say. Amazingly, her voice sounded quite steady.

"I would like to hear it from you," he replied, looking at her with that snake smile, reminding her of one of those reptiles, which, having paralyzed its prey with venom, can take its time before delivering the final blow, enjoying the victim's dreadful helplessness, the terror of anticipation.

Slowly, she unfolded the document, quietly began to read it in the hushed hall. She kept her voice as low as she could so that the men guarding Boris would not hear clearly, but the humiliation was still so great she did not know how she managed to endure it.

Adam Danilevski stood in the shadow of the staircase at the rear of the hall. Obeying an ordinary summons from his general, he had entered the house from the rear, having left his horse in the stable. The minute he walked into the building, a breathlessness in the atmosphere had told him that something more than ordinarily unpleasant was happening. Instinctively, he had rejected the escort of an overly nervous Nikolai and had made his way, almost stealthily, to the front of the house. Now he stood concealed in the overhang of the staircase, watching this ghastly scene unfold before his eyes. He could be of no service to Sophie or to Boris by showing himself, could only wait and listen.

Sophie finished reading. She folded the letter again. Blood smeared the back of the paper. Boris Mikhailov's blood. That thought came from a great distance as she stood immobile before her husband, waiting for the next stage of the nightmare to be revealed.

"Chain him in the stables," the prince now said, cool and dispassionate. "He may spend the afternoon in contemplation of the punishment for a runaway—fifty blows of the great knout."

Violently, Sophie was jerked back from her distant plane. A man of Boris's stature and strength could conceivably survive fifty blows of the ordinary knout, but no man could live through such torture from the great scourge. In essence, Boris Mikhailov had just received a sentence of "cruel" death. Paradoxically, a sentence of "simple" death by hanging or beheading was not permitted the master of serfs, but he could condemn to torture, and if it resulted in death then that was simply a misfortune.

"You cannot order such a thing!" she exclaimed, wringing

her hands in horror. "Boris is my serf. He was in my service, obeying my instructions—"

"Then he and you must learn that only *I* give orders in this household, Sophia Alexeyevna. And the only serfs under my roof are *mine*." Dmitriev brought his face very close to hers, so that she could feel his breath on her cheek, was impaled by the ferocious cruelty in his eyes, the invincible power of some hatred that she knew was directed at her, yet she knew not why.

"No . . . no, please, you must not." She was begging now, slipping to her knees on the hard marble floor, heedless of shame. "The offense is mine, not Boris Mikhailov's. It is upon my back your lash should fall—"

"My dear, you are not very clever." Her husband interrupted her coldly, looking down at her as she knelt in front of him, the dark eyes imploring in her upturned face, deathly white. "Do you think I do not realize that you would heed your own punishment less than you would heed his, earned for you?" Contempt laced his voice. "Maybe this last lesson will teach you to understand what it means to be my wife. But believe me, Sophia Alexeyevna, if further lessons are required, you shall have them." He gestured to the guards. "Take him away!" Turning his back on the still-kneeling figure, he marched for the stairs.

Adam kept himself hidden only with the exercise of supreme control. He wanted to run to her where she knelt, head bowed in defeat, skirts heaped around her, sunbright yellow, a shocking, incongruous burst of color in the rain-dark gloom of the hall. But Boris Mikhailov could not be saved if Adam's presence at the scene were revealed. No one must know he had been a witness. Silently, agonizingly, he left her alone in her grief and despair, melting into the shadows as he slipped from the house by a side door.

He sauntered into the stable yard some ten minutes later, when he was sure sufficient time had elapsed for Boris to be chained and the excitement of his recapture had died down a little.

"Do you wish for your horse, lord?" A groom came running as the count entered the yard.

"No, I left something in the saddlebag," Adam responded

easily. "I would prefer to fetch it myself." A note of sharpness in his voice, an eyebrow raised with a hint of derision, and he managed to convey the perfectly reasonable impression that he did not trust anyone in Dmitriev's stables to meddle with his possessions. The man bowed, returning to the tack room.

Adam went into the long, low stable block. The rain beat down upon the roof, which had sprung several leaks so that water splattered noisily into iron buckets set beneath the holes. The floor was wet beneath his feet, the straw soggy, and the stables' occupants hung their heads in the resigned patience of their kind. Boris Mikhailov was in the last stall, an iron collar around his neck fastened to a ring in the wall, shackles on wrists and ankles similarly fastened. Adam barely glanced in his direction as he passed, seemingly in search of his own horse, but the look showed him what he had hoped to find. The keys to the chains hung upon a hook set into the wooden partition of the stall.

"Hey! You, there!" Imperatively, he summoned the only other free occupant of the building, a young lad mucking out a stall across the gangway from him.

"Yes, lord." The lad dropped his spade and came running, tugging his forelock.

"Look at this!" Adam gestured into the stall that held his horse. "Is this the way you treat animals belonging to your master's guests?" He allowed his voice to rise with anger. "It seems to me Prince Dmitriev cannot be aware of such insolent negligence."

All the color drained from the boy's face; he began to stammer wildly. "Please . . . please, Your Honor, I didn't realize. It wasn't my fault, Your Honor. I didn't stable him, I didn't, lord . . . It wasn't me—"

"Fetch fresh hay at once!" snapped the count. "The water in the trough is dirty, and there is nothing but bran dust in the manger!"

The lad scuttled off, fear and bewilderment on his face. He could see nothing wrong in the stable, but it was the master's prerogative to find fault and no right of the serf to disagree.

Adam ran to the stall holding Boris. "I will create some sort of a disturbance in the next few minutes," he whispered, swift and low, fitting the key into the locks on the chains. "I cannot promise to draw attention for long. But try if you can to make your way to my house. Take this." He slipped from his finger an intricately worked signet ring, tucking it into the muzhik's hand, still held against the wall. Boris said nothing, but his fingers curled over the ring. "Show this to my butler and he will take you in." There was no time for further words. The chains were unlocked although still in place; they would pass casual inspection.

Adam was going through his saddlebags when the lad hurried in with a pail of fresh water and an armful of straw. "What the devil . . . !" Adam bellowed, and the lad dropped the pail. "There was a pouch of rubles in here." Adam grabbed the collar of the threadbare shirt. "Who else has been in here?"

The boy began to wail piteously. To be accused of theft was the ultimate terror for a serf. Men boiled into the building as Adam's accusations gathered volume and momentum and the lad's cries of innocence grew more frantic.

"Who is in charge around here?" demanded Count Danilevski, staring around at the stunned circle of heavy peasant faces. "Someone has stolen a pouch of rubles left in my saddlebag."

"No . . . no, lord, no one would have done such a thing." The head groom, whom Adam had last seen guarding Boris, stepped forward, trying to sound calm and strong, but they were all jumpier than usual as a result of Boris's flight, his recapture, and the appalling knowledge of what was to happen to one of their number in the courtyard that evening.

"Outside! All of you!" Adam instructed brusquely. "I can see nothing in here." He hearded them out into the pouring rain, where they stood miserably, turning out their pockets, knees knocking, feet shuffling, fear and dread on every face. And while they did so, Boris Mikhailov slipped loose from his bonds, gritted his teeth as the pain from his fractured ribs stabbed sharply, and inched his great bulk through the window at the rear of the building, melting into the rain to make his way to the house where he had visited Khan.

Adam, in a most credible imitation of his commanding officer, managed to intimidate the group of stable hands to such an extent they no longer seemed to know what day of the week it was. Those gray eyes seemed to see into their very souls, and the questions were barked in an endless stream, allowing no time for reflection, demanding answers whether they had them or no. After five minutes, although the search had turned up nothing, they were all so demoralized, so utterly convinced that they were about to be convicted of theft by this terrifying soldier, that they would be quite unable to reconstruct the events of the last half hour, if asked to do so when the disappearance of the captive serf was discovered.

Adam kept them quaking in the yard until the noon dinner gong rang. Then he dismissed them, confident that they would not think to check on the securely chained prisoner in the stable after the ordeal they had been through, and with the prospect of the main meal of the day cooling on the table. He was unable to quash a guilty stab as he stalked out of the yard, threatening further investigation after he had talked with Prince Dmitriev. But the sacrifice of those poor, petrified souls had been necessary. The image of Sophie, on her knees in front of the cold, brutal bully she had drawn as husband, her softly despairing pleas, the head bowed in submission, would not leave him. Never had he known such a murderous rage, and he did not know how he was to conceal it from Dmitriev. But he had to keep the appointment, had to appear oblivious of anything untoward in the household, had to hope that in the uproar when Boris's escape was discovered Nikolai would not see any relevance in the fact that Count Danilevski had actually been admitted to the house once already. It was not unreasonable to expect Nikolai to have forgotten such an insignificant fact in the extraordinary turmoil. And if nothing more was said about the alleged theft from the count's saddlebags, the stable hands would breathe a sigh of relief. They would not bring it up, praying instead that the incident would remain buried. They would have no reason to draw any connection between a runaway serf and the general's irate aide-de-camp. No one would, except Sophie.

* * *

Sophie sat for hours in her bedchamber, staring sightlessly at the wall. She was as dazed as if she had been felled by a blow to the head. Boris Mikhailov was going to die in slow torment, and she had sent him to that death. Khan would have died if it had not been for Adam. God alone knew what fate had befallen Tanya Feodorovna. She clasped her hands over her breasts, trying to enclose herself, to imprison the badness within her—this rot that led to so much suffering for those who had any affection for her. Why was she afflicted in this way? Why did she have this . . . this unidentifiable fault . . . that made her husband loathe her to such an extent that anyone connected with her must suffer horribly? From now on, she must live quite alone. She must offer no one a smile, a word, lest they too should fall beneath the evil umbrella of her affection.

She did not go downstairs at dinnertime and received no summons. The dark, rainy afternoon trickled past. No one came near her. Untended, the fire in the porcelain stove built into the wall died down. The rawness of mid-October had descended upon the capital with a vengeance; the green-and-gold warmth of September vanished as always with the abrupt onset of winter. But Sophie did not feel the chill, damp air, did not notice that she sat in darkness. She was waiting for the moment when her body would tell her that Boris's long, slow road to death had begun.

The door opened. She looked up with utter indifference into the scared eyes of Maria. "Is it over?" she asked, although she knew it could not be. She had not felt it yet.

Maria shook her head, her eyes darting this way and that, as if she would see something in the shadows.

"I'm sure *you* can speak to me," Sophie said dully. "It is only those for whom I hold any affection who must suffer."

Maria stood gawking at her. "He's escaped," she said, finally. "Disappeared from the stable where he was chained."

Life shot through Sophie like a spurt of flame in a revived fire. "When?" was all she said, remembering she was in the presence of a spy.

"No one knows," Maria told her, bustling over to draw the curtains against the night. "Sometime during dinner, it's thought. Didn't see no need to put a guard on him, chained up as he was." For once, she was talking to Sophia Alexeyevna instead of performing her duties in sullen watchfulness. But the habits of caution were now entrenched, and Sophie was not to be seduced, despite her almost disbelieving joy and her need to know every detail the maid might have to offer.

She did not have to pretend to be indifferent to Boris's fate, since the truth would be known throughout the household, but she did not have to give the maid any clues as to the depth of her present feelings. "How did he escape?" she asked, in the same dull tone.

Kneeling in front of the stove, Maria opened the door and began shoving fresh logs onto the embers. "Fire's almost out," she muttered. "Cold as death in here. No one seems to know how." She got to her feet, smoothing down her apron. "His Highness bids you sup with him. What gown will you wear?"

"I really do not care, Maria," Sophie said, wondering how she was to break bread with her husband after the shame of this morning. Then she remembered that the miracle had occurred. Her shame was as nothing compared with Boris's reprieve. Her head went up. "The rose silk, I think. And I will wear the rubies."

Prince Dmitriev, locked in an icy fury, balked of his revenge, greeted his wife's arrival in the drawing room with stony silence. There was no possibility that she had been implicated in the muzhik's escape. Maria had been guarding the princess's door from the moment she reached her bedchamber only minutes after Boris Mikhailov was taken off. But if it had not been Sophia Alexeyevna, who could have provided the necessary assistance?

An afternoon of interrogation had produced nothing but the confused tales of the terror-struck, all trying to escape blame. Now, as he looked at his wife, he sensed that he was losing. There had been a moment of supreme gratification that morning when he had brought her to her knees, a supplicant whose prayer he had denied. Now she seemed to have regained some core of strength. She curtsied as meekly as ever, her eyes lowered, her voice soft, but there was a vibrancy about her now, a rich luster to match the Golitskov rubies clasped with such defiant insolence around the slender throat.

Sophie felt the impotence of his rage and reveled in her private rejoicing. She knew now what she must do. In the decision to take action, desperate though that action was, she found herself again. No longer the passive, bewildered recipient of inexplicable hurts, she was again capable of implementing change.

She was going to appeal to the czarina. Annulment by imperial manifesto was not unheard of. Surely, when Catherine learned of the full catalog of the prince's enormities, she could not fail to grant her subject permission to return to obscurity. Dmitriev would still hold title to her fortune, and he would be free to find another wife.

And Adam? Thoughts of Adam followed the previous thoughts as naturally, as inevitably, as day follows night. What part had he played in this? How could she be so certain that he had had a hand in it? But she *was* certain. The current that flowed between them told her so, even when he was not with her.

For the same reason the sound of his voice in the hall came as no surprise, although Prince Dmitriev frowned. A visit from his aide-de-camp at this time of day could only mean regimental business, and he had thought they had dealt with everything earlier in the day.

"Colonel, Count Danilevski, Highness." Nikolai bowed in the door, and Adam stepped through.

"Your pardon for disturbing you, General, but I thought you would wish to see this dispatch from the Crimea immediately. Princess, pray forgive this intrusion." He bowed toward Sophie, who remained seated.

"Please do not mention it, Count," she said softly. Her eyes looked the question. He nodded fractionally, but it was enough. Boris Mikhailov was safe with Adam, that was all she needed to know. And it was to tell her that, that he had come here this evening.

Dmitriev looked up from the dispatch. "There appears no special urgency, Colonel, but I commend your diligence in bringing it to me on such a night. Let us have supper." He glanced coldly at Sophie. "I suggest you sup abovestairs, madame. Your presence can add nothing to our discussion."

"As you command, Paul," she murmured, rising immediately. "Count, I bid you good-night."

With a soft rustle of rose silk she had gone, brushing so close beside him that her special fragrance—one that always reminded him of spring flowers—lingered in the air he breathed. The warmth of her skin burnished his own. A smile riveted to his lips, murder in his eyes, Adam turned toward his general.

Chapter 9

It was four weeks later, on the night that the first snow of the winter fell upon St. Petersburg, when Sophie finally had her opportunity to seek private audience with the empress.

Soon after the disappearance of Boris Mikhailov the winter season had fallen into full swing. Catherine laid down a strict program for court life, functions taking place each day according to schedule. Russian and French theater productions, comedy, tragedy, or opera were all assigned a place in the weekly calendar, as were balls and the official, ceremonial "court" on Sunday evenings. In addition to these formal requirements, the salons of St. Petersburg hummed as hostesses vied to provide the most innovative entertainment, the most distinguished guests, access to the most scurrilous morsels of gossip.

Prince Paul permitted his wife to attend the Sunday court, where appearance was *de rigueur.* It was a cumbersome, tedious affair, regulated by ritual and the rules of etiquette as decreed and enforced by the Grand Mistress. The czarina rarely graced the occasion for more than an hour or two, and Sophie found it impossible to approach her in private. Infrequently, Paul would accompany her to the Hermitage for some theatrical performance, but Sophie was aware that these outings were carefully chosen, and not for their entertainment value. Her presence on the grandest occasions was designed to give the impression that Princess Dmitrievna was very much an active participant in court life, when, in fact, she remained immured in her palace for the most part. She received some calls, paid a few to the most sedate matrons, the arbiters of St. Petersburg society, but friends she had none.

On this snowy afternoon at the end of November, the occasion was a little different. The czarina herself had bade Sophie attend a private gathering in the Hermitage, where the empress liked to amuse herself in the company of close friends playing cards, literary parlor games, or impromptu charades. It also provided the opportunity for Catherine to cast a kindly eye on members of her court in whom she took a special interest.

Sophie was, for once, without her husband's escort because Paul was attending a regimental function. Much as he would have wished otherwise, refusal of the empress's invitation was unthinkable, so Sophie, wrapped in sable, was alone in the traveling carriage taking her through the increasingly heavy snow to the Hermitage. She used the short period of solitude to rehearse the speech she had had planned for the last weeks, awaiting the opportunity for delivery. She had lived on her plan, drawing nourishment for the soul from the prospect of taking action. It had enabled her to withstand Paul's icy anger, which led him to humiliate her in front of the servants whenever the opportunity arose, and it had enabled her to bear Adam's absence. He was in Moscow, and she had no idea when he would return. She could not ask her husband, even supposing he would deign to answer her, because why would she be interested in the movements of his aide-de-camp? Prince Dmitriev must never suspect for one minute that such a question held an all-absorbing fascination for his wife.

Catherine had built the Hermitage as a place for retreat and as an intimate theater. Sophie, still huddled in her sable against the bitter cold, walked quickly along the covered passageway connecting the empress's retreat with the Winter Palace. In her anxiety, she stepped out as if she were striding through the halls of Berkholzskoye, remembering to moderate her step to one more suited to court decorum only as she was announced at the door of the gracious, velvet-hung chamber where Catherine was entertaining her select group, very much in the domestic manner of any lady at her own fireside.

"Sophia Alexeyevna, come by the fire, *ma chère*." She held out her hand as Sophie crossed the rich Astrakhan carpet. "It is not the weather for venturing forth. I am deeply complimented by my dear friends who have shown themselves willing to honor me with their company." She smiled with warm friendliness around the group, drawing Sophie to the fire's warmth. "Are you acquainted with the French ambassador who has just come amongst us—Comte Louis Philippe de Ségur?" She beamed as she made the introduction, and it was clear to Sophie that the count had found favor in the empress's eyes.

"Good evening, Comte." She curtsied, smiling, and received from the worldly, charming, thirty-two-year-old diplomat a smile and a most careful appraisal in return.

"*Enchanté*, Princess." He raised her hand to his lips, looking deep into her eyes, and Sophie understood exactly why the ambassador had found favor with the empress.

She turned to greet Prince Potemkin, whose one eye looked fondly upon her, and then paid due reverence to a beautiful young officer of the guard, Alexander Mamonov, who presently graced the favorite's apartments adjoining the imperial bedchamber.

"Come, Monsieur Redcoat," Catherine said playfully to her youthful lover, "you are challenged to compose a quatrain for us."

As the evening progressed in laughter and the exercise of wit during various literary parlor games, Sophie began to wonder whether she would find the opportunity to request a private audience with the empress. But if she did not do so this evening, there was no knowing when another chance would be given her. As they moved into the supper room, she took her courage in both hands.

"Madame, I wonder if you would grant me a few minutes in private?"

Catherine looked startled, and just a little disapproving. The young woman had an overly serious expression suddenly, the dark eyes intense, her mouth set with anxious determination. It spelled trouble, and Catherine did not like the intrusion of unpleasantness on these domestic evenings. "Must it be tonight, Sophia?"

Nervously, Sophie moistened her lips. How could she explain publicly that if it weren't tonight, there was no knowing when she would again succeed in evading her husband's surveillance? "If you please, Madame," she answered, her voice low but nonetheless firm.

Catherine frowned. "Very well. Before you return home, then." That promised, the empress dismissed the disturbing matter from her mind for the remainder of the evening.

Sophie found it much harder to do so, but she forced herself to behave as if she had nothing on her mind beyond the need to keep her wits sharp in this cultivated, amusing company. At last, however, everyone but the empress, Mamonov, and Sophie had gone in great good humor out into the bitter, snowy night.

"Now, what is it that is so urgent and so private, Sophia Alexeyevna?" Catherine spoke briskly, implying that she considered her guest's importunate request to be out of place, a faux pas on such an occasion.

Sophie looked desperately toward the guards officer, in his red uniform, lounging on a sofa while eating bonbons with apparent absorption. She could not say what she had to in front of that beautiful young man, even if the empress, deluded as always by passion, considered his presence indispensable at all times.

Alexander Mamonov looked up as if he felt Sophie's anguished glance. The appeal in those dark eyes was unmistakable. He rose from the sofa. "I think I'll go to my apartments," he said, taking his mistress's hand, raising it to his lips. "Do not be long."

Catherine smiled joyfully. "I will come to you soon, my love."

Even in her distress, Sophie could not help wondering how that virile young man could possibly sacrifice himself night after night upon the altar of that corpulent, wrinkled, sagging body. It was amazing what people would do for power and money—both of which were inevitable concomitants of inhabiting the favorite's apartments. Yet Catherine, lost in a self-delusion bordering on the irrational, actually believed the love was shared. It was an amazing delusion for such a brilliant woman to harbor.

The door closed on the favorite. "Well, Sophia?" Catherine reposed herself in a silk-covered armchair.

In the absence of an invitation to seat herself, Sophie remained standing to tell her tale and make her extraordinary request. Her voice was strong, the tone unemotional, but even as she talked she could feel her heart sinking. The empress looked utterly dumbfounded, and not in the least encouraging.

Catherine was incredulous. This young woman was asking for an annulment of her marriage—a marriage promoted by the empress with the most benevolent intentions, a marriage celebrated a mere four months previously under imperial auspices with the greatest ceremony and distinction. And she was asking for this amazing thing simply because her husband was not treating her exactly as she would like. That was really what all this talk of serfs and horses came down to. What on earth did Sophia Alexeyevna expect? She was a Russian woman married to a Russian man.

Since her arrival in Russia at the age of fourteen, Catherine had made herself Russian. She had adopted the country, its people, its language, and its customs to such an extent that she was as at home ruling this land as if, indeed, she had been born to it. But occasionally the purely Germanic heritage of a princess of Anhalt-Zerbst would raise its head, and she would find herself contemplating the paradoxes and peculiarities of her adopted country with the objective dispassion of an outsider. She was doing so now, listening to this young woman who was asking for the impossible while denying the truth. They were a strange race: revering motherhood, they beat their wives as a matter of course, without thought or compunction; detesting war, they fought with demonic courage; indolent in the extreme, they worked like dogs. They certainly did not make considerate husbands, as Catherine, after eighteen wretched years of her own marriage, would contest without a qualm. But that was a woman's lot—a Russian woman's lot.

"My dear Sophia Alexeyevna," she said, when Sophie had fallen silent. "I will do you the kindness of forgetting the request you have just made. You must realize how impossible such a thing would be. Your life is not endangered. You are merely not completely happy. I will give you some advice: One must be cheerful. That is the only way to overcome and endure everything. I, too, had much to endure from my husband. Why, he kept his mistress in his apartments in the palace and lost no opportunity to humiliate me, even threatening to have my head shaved in a convent!"

And all the while you were enduring so cheerfully, you were plotting and planning, until the moment came when you overthrew him and had him assassinated, Sophie thought bitterly. Could the czarina not hear her own hypocrisy? Or did she simply consider that there was one rule for women and one for the empress?

"Do not look so dejected, *ma chère*." Catherine leaned forward to pat Sophie's hand. "Marriage always comes as something of a shock, and you have led such a sheltered life. It is only understandable that you should find certain . . ." —she looked for the delicate way of putting this—"certain aspects of marriage strange . . . distasteful, even. It is often the way at the beginning." She smiled her toothless smile. "In time, you will become accustomed to these things. Now, I think you should go home and have a good night's sleep. Things always look better in the morning. And remember: Be cheerful. I am sure Prince Dmitriev does not enjoy such a long face around the house all the time. It must annoy him. Why do you not try to smile a little, Sophia?"

And that was that. Only now did Sophie truly realize how much she had relied upon this meeting, how every hope had been fixed upon it. Now, that hope shattered, she felt as empty as a hollowed-out gourd, scraped clean of all expectancy, all trust, all aspiration; a hollowed-out shell, she would

grow sere in her hopelessness, unnourished by the rich mois-
ture of possibility. Long ago—oh, so very long ago—her
grandfather had said that if she had to leave her husband, she
was resourceful enough to find a way. But she could not even
leave the house undetected. The servants were her enemies,
forced into that position by the prince and the savage reprisals
he had taken after her ride. She should have gone, then.
Astride Khan, she could have ridden to the frontier. What
dangers could she have faced worse than the deadliness of
her present existence?

All she could do now was curtsy, thank the empress for
listening to her, apologize for the unseemliness of her request, and go home, back to the connubial attentions of her
husband, who would be waiting for her.

Catherine, her equanimity annoyingly disturbed, frowned
as the door closed on Sophia Alexeyevna's departure. The
princess did look somewhat peaky. Potemkin had commented
on it, also. But when innocence was violated, as it inevitably
was in the nuptial bedchamber, there was always some shock.
Somehow, though, she had thought the Golitskova to be made
of sterner stuff than the usual. The empress rose from her
chair, still frowning. She liked Princess Dmitrievna and had
no desire to see her unhappy. Perhaps a tactful word in her
husband's ear would help. Men never saw what was in front
of their eyes. A mild suggestion that he treat his bride with
a little more gentleness would not come amiss.

On this happy resolution, Catherine went off to enjoy her
own night in the arms of Monsieur Redcoat.

Two days later, General, Prince Paul Dmitriev, in answer
to an imperial summons, stood in the czarina's study rigid
with mortification, rage, and shocked disbelief. Sophia Alexeyevna had complained to the empress of his treatment,
and the empress was now taking him to task! Admittedly, she
was doing so following her oft-repeated maxim that while
she praised loudly, she scolded in a whisper, but to be up-
braided, even in this soft manner, was insupportable.

"She is so much younger than you, Prince," Catherine

finished with an agreeable smile. "And she has had a some-what unusual upbringing. I am sure, now you understand the situation, you will be able to put matters between you to rights."

"I trust so, Your Majesty." The prince bowed low, hiding behind drooping lids the savage fury blazing in his eyes. His thin smile flickered. "I am most grateful to Your Majesty for pointing out to me Sophia Alexeyevna's grievances."

"Oh, that is too strong a word," protested the empress. She had not deemed it necessary or wise to mention Sophia's wish for an annulment. "I think she is a little confused, that is all. You have so much more experience of the world than she; it is all too easy to assume that knowledge is shared. It is a very common error," she added with a kindly smile.

"I shall endeavor to ensure that Princess Dmitrievna fully understands things from now on." Again the prince bowed low, his voice bland. Sophia Alexeyevna was most definitely going to understand. She was going to understand how a man disposed of an unsatisfactory, barren, deceitful wife who went behind her husband's back!

He left the imperial presence, and Catherine had no inkling of the ferocious need for vengeance now seething beneath his cool exterior. He had had enough of a woman who defied him with every step she took, although he could not pinpoint how or why he knew she was doing so; enough of a barren woman who lay beneath him like a corpse, somehow denying him any vestige of satisfaction in an act that should have salved so many past injuries; enough of a woman who did not understand what it was to be a wife—*his* wife.

Prince Dmitriev drew his sheepskin hat over his ears. If she did not care for marriage, then he would return her to Berkholzskoye. But he would do so in such a fashion that her chances of arriving would be minuscule. The cold was be-coming ferocious, and snow now lay thick upon the ground. A sleigh, drawn by four horses, harnesses jingling, slipped past as he crossed a bridge over one of the canals intersecting the city. The water beneath was frozen, and in a few weeks the River Neva itself would be icebound. The conditions were hardly ideal for traveling, although they could be mitigated. Princess Dmitrievna, however, would make the month-long journey without the comforts vital to health and security.

The revenge pleased him with its neatness. He would simply be giving her what she desired. The empress would applaud his consideration. To permit Sophia Alexeyevna to spend the winter with her grandfather was a kindly act; it would be granting her a respite in which to come to terms with her marriage. Only her husband would know the conditions under which she made the journey. And when she did not arrive at Berkholzskoye, he would be horror-struck, the very epitome of a bereaved husband.

Pleasure and satisfaction gleamed coldly in the pale blue eyes as he entered his house. "Where is Princess Dmitrievna?"

Nikolai bowed. "In the gallery, I believe, lord."

Paul went up the stairs in leisurely fashion. Sophie was to be found looking out on the snowy city, over the now-deserted river. She turned as her husband came into the gallery. "Good morning, Paul."

Rage burned within him at the submissive curtsy, the lowered eyes. He still could not fully grasp the horrendous depths of her deceit, the magnitude of his own blindness. Not a tongue of fire from the conflagration blazing within him showed on his face, however. "Good morning, Sophia Alexeyevna. There is to be a concert at Prince Stroganov's palace this evening. We have both been invited. I am unable to attend, but perhaps you might care to."

Sophie could not hide her surprise, both at the unusual courtesy of his tone and at the suggestion. She was to go forth into society without his escort, accepting an invitation to a function that he would ordinarily have refused without even mentioning it to her. "Thank you, Paul," she responded meekly, offering a hesitant, grateful smile. "I should enjoy it above all things."

"Then you shall go, my dear." He smiled. "I will see you at dinner."

During dinner, her husband became again the charming,

attentive man of her betrothal. Sophie was at a loss. She responded in like manner, even as she was filled with mistrust, an apprehension that had no sticking point, but that would not be eased. His eyes were flat, expressionless, his voice pleasant, his smile flickering as always; so why did she feel he was regarding her rather as one would regard an exhibit at a fair, contemplating the performance it would eventually give?

He appeared in her bedchamber as she was dressing for the concert, sitting in front of the mirror in her peignoir while Maria did her hair. "Why do you not wear the aquamarines, my dear?" He selected the necklace from her gem casket. "They will go beautifully with the ivory satin gown."

"I had thought to wear the amber velvet," Sophie demurred. "It is such a cold night."

"Nonsense. The ivory compliments your coloring," he declared, touching her cheek. She shuddered at the extraordinary caress. He felt the repulsion and smiled. "There will be a brazier in the sleigh, and it will not be cold within doors."

"No . . . no, I am sure you are right, Paul," Sophie managed. She had wanted to wear velvet and diamonds. Instead, she must wear satin and aquamarines. It was a small enough concession in the light of Paul's amazing behavior. The aquamarines were not particularly fine stones, though. Of all the contents of the gem casket, they were the least valuable. But then ostentation was hardly attractive. With that reflection, she submitted to her husband's attentions as he fastened her necklace, watched Maria help her into the dress he had selected, and then put around her shoulders the lynx-lined velvet cloak. He escorted her downstairs and into the waiting sleigh.

Dmitriev watched the elegant, richly furbished conveyance leave the courtyard before beginning to give instructions that were obeyed unquestioningly. Yet comprehending looks were exchanged among the servants hurrying to fulfill their orders. The two serfs designated to undertake the journey from which they did not expect to return accepted their lot with dumb resignation. It was a better fate than torment on the scaffold, and no worse than being ordered to give their lives in some obscure battle for their lord. Besides, there was always the possibility that the Holy Mother was watching over them and death at the hands of brigands or the elements was not in their stars. In such fashion was comfort drawn from the peasants' contradictory yet interlocking beliefs in religion and inescapable destiny.

Any enjoyment Sophie might have gained from her evening was counteracted by her sense of puzzled apprehension. Something had occurred to bring about Paul's abrupt volte-face, and she had learned enough in the months since her wedding to distrust any out-of-character behavior. She now knew what constituted *in*-character behavior: polite conversation, encouragement to attend social functions alone, and concern over her dress were not components of it. If Adam were at least in the city, she would feel less vulnerable. He was her only prop, and she needed him . . . oh, how she needed him. Just to feel his eyes resting upon her occasionally, the firm grip of his fingers when he took her hand, the current that flowed between them, swift and strong—a vital force that was strengthened, if anything, by the facade they must maintain, so that every clandestine look, every apparently accidental touch, assumed the importance and passion of the most ardent embrace.

It was nearly eleven o'clock when she returned home, wrapped in furs, hands buried in her lynx muff, feet warmed by the little brazier in the corner of the sleigh. The sleigh came to a halt in the courtyard at the rear of the Dmitriev palace. Sophie descended, shivering at the icy blast sweeping in from the river, freezing the tip of her nose, solidifying her breath.

Her husband, in fur pelisse, hat, and boots, stood in the doorway. In front of that door stood a mean, black-painted sleigh of the kind and condition used by serfs on their masters' business. It was drawn by two scrawny horses, each one ridden by a well-wrapped muzhik.

"I understand from our most gracious czarina that you do

not care for your position as my wife," Prince Dmitriev declared with frigid dispassion as she came to the door. "Therefore, my dear wife, you shall return to your grandfather." He indicated the black sleigh. "Your conveyance awaits you. Pray ascend."

Sophie was speechless, struggling to make sense of this. The empress had betrayed her—that was the first thought. She was going back to Berkholzskoye—that was the second thought, one that filled her with a dizzy joy. Then came the realization that he was sending her now, in the middle of a freezing night, clad only in a satin evening dress, her only protection the lynx-lined velvet cloak. She stared up at her husband, uncomprehending.

"Now?"

"Yes, my dear Sophia Alexeyevna. Now," he replied, smiling. "You wished to leave, so there seems little point in delay." He gestured toward the black sleigh.

"But my clothes . . . luggage . . ." she stammered, still unable to grasp that he really meant what he had said.

"You are not naked," he answered. "And you have the aquamarines to furnish you with whatever you might require on the journey."

The significance of his earlier involvement in her dress and ornament stood out, etched in clarity. Her only financial resources on this hideous journey were to be the stones around her neck. The other gems, even more precious, would remain here, in her husband's keeping. If she could not turn the necklace into currency through some jeweler in the city, and at this time of night such a thing was impossible, she would be obliged to expend it, stone by stone, on a night's lodging, a crust of bread, a mug of mead. It would be the most profligate waste.

"My maid?" She asked the question, although she had already guessed the answer.

"You will manage without an attendant," her husband told her. "I am becoming a trifle cold, debating issues with you, Sophia Alexeyevna." Taking her arm, he pushed her toward the waiting sleigh. "Pray give my regards to your grandfather.'' His voice dripped sarcasm. ''You may express my regret that you have proved so unsatisfactory a wife that I am obliged to return you in disgrace.''

The interior of the sleigh was dark and bare. There was no brazier, only a wooden bench and a ragged fur to offer comfort and protection. She was to journey four hundred leagues at the onset of winter in a satin evening gown, with no money, no provisions, her only escort two illiterate muzhiks with pistols. What defense could they put up against brigands? Her husband's imagination when it came to disguised death sentences was remarkable, Sophie reflected with brutal irony.

She climbed into the sleigh. There was nothing she could do at this point except obey. There was no one she could turn to; never had she felt so alone, so overpoweringly conscious of her friendlessness, of the isolation so carefully, so purposefully, created by her husband. But she had been brought up to rely upon herself, and maybe inspiration would come to her on the road, although persuading the prince's serfs to deviate from their orders would be a forlorn hope. They were too much afraid of their lord's long arm, which they would be convinced would reach as far as necessary to pluck out an unruly weed.

General, Prince Paul Dmitriev closed the door of the sleigh with a crisp finality, confident that he had just looked his last upon his objectionable wife. He had possessed her and in the doing had almost been able to imagine he was possessing Sophia Ivanova; he had the Golitskov fortune, the Golitskov gems. But as he turned back to the house, he could not extract the right degree of satisfaction from these benefits. He had not broken her to his will. Never before had he failed in such a task. The failure left a sour taste to spoil his complacence.

In the musty, frigid darkness, Sophie tried to keep from panicking. Standing in the courtyard had chilled her badly, and she had no way of replacing the lost warmth. She pulled the hood of her cloak way down over her face, so that her breath was trapped, warm and moist to keep her face from freezing. The ragged fur she used to wrap her feet. Her cloak she pulled tightly around her. Then she buried her hands in her muff and settled down to pray for morning. It would be a little warmer then, and at least she would not be in darkness.

The city gate was closed, a winter precaution against wolves, who, becoming more intrepid when snow and ice cut down on their food supply, had a tendency to prowl within the city walls. The sleigh halted so that papers could be inspected, but Sophie made no attempt to look out and risk losing one iota of warmth. A troop of soldiers from the Preobrazhensky regiment, wrapped to their ears in fur, on their way back from Moscow, was also at the gate, their colonel engaged in discussion with the commanding officer at the sentry post. They all looked curiously at the black conveyance, and one or two of them felt a graveyard shudder. It was a gloomy vehicle with the air of death about it.

"Who was that?" Colonel, Count Danilevski inquired casually as the sleigh was waved through.

The officer shrugged. "Papers issued by General Dmitriev. On their way to Kiev, poor devils. But you know what the general's like."

Adam quivered with a dreadful premonition, but he could show not the slightest sign. No connection must ever be made between the general's aide-de-camp and the general's domestic affairs. Hastily, he bid the guards officer farewell and signaled to his troop. They entered the city gladly, heading for the warmth and comfort of the barracks.

"I am going to report to the general," Adam told his second-in-command. "Take over, Major."

"Yes, sir." The major saluted. It did not strike him as at all extraordinary that the colonel chose not to wait until morning to make his report to the general. Such diligence was expected by General Dmitriev.

At the Dmitriev palace, Adam was received and escorted to the general's study, where, despite the lateness of the hour, its occupant was perusing reports.

"Ah, Colonel, you made good time." Dmitriev looked up. "I was not expecting you until tomorrow."

"It is too cold for dawdling along the road, sir," Adam said lightly. "Winter's come early and with a vengeance. Do you wish to hear my report now or in the morning?"

"Since you are here, I will hear it now." The general pulled the bell rope. "You look in need of food and vodka, Colonel."

Adam, in a fever of anxiety and impatience, was obliged to accept the hospitality, to answer all his general's searching questions, and it was not until nearly three o'clock in the morning that he was able to make a move to the door. "I trust Princess Dmitrievna is keeping well."

There was an infinitesimal silence, then the general replied casually, "She expressed a wish to visit her grandfather. She will leave later this morning."

No, Adam thought with cold certainty. She has already gone . . . in haste and secrecy in the middle of the night, traveling in that wretched sleigh. It was obvious why Dmitriev had lied to him. No man in his right mind would send his wife off in the middle of a snowy November night, so it had to be given out that she had left at a civilized hour.

Clicking his heels smartly, Adam saluted and left his general. With the greatest difficulty, he forced himself to think before chasing off in pursuit. He could not depart St. Petersburg without permission from the empress, and he could not get that until daybreak. An urgent message of distress from Mogilev, delivered during his absence in Moscow, should provide excuse. He was planning with military precision now as he considered the proper preparation for such a journey. Boris Mikhailov, whose injuries, sustained during his recapture, were now healed, would accompany him, and Khan, of course, although it would be too cold for Sophie to ride the stallion. Extra furs could not come amiss. What had she taken with her? What might she lack?

They were questions impossible to answer, so he decided to take as much extra protection as he and Boris could manage to carry. They would need weapons, plenty of ammunition; in addition to the usual hazard posed by brigands, there would be wolves to contend with.

The remainder of the night passed in a fever of preparation, and at seven o'clock the czarina, working in her dressing room in the quiet of early morning, was informed that Count Danilevski desired audience most urgently. Reflecting that it must indeed be urgent if the count could not wait until nine, when she gave audience to those with problems, the czarina received him in her bedroom. One look at his face was sufficient to convince her that some tragedy had occurred.

"Why, Adam, you look positively distraught, *mon ami*," she said, rustling across the room toward him in her white silk taffeta dressing gown. "How can I help you?"

It was not difficult to appear distraught, Adam discovered, since it was an accurate reflection of how he felt. Every minute that Sophie traveled without properly armed escort, with every verst drawing her farther from the capital and into the wilds, the danger increased. Riding hard on good mounts, he and Boris could catch up with the sleigh without difficulty, but it would still take at least half a day.

"Madame, I have received most disturbing news from home," he lied smoothly. "My mother is ill, at death's door, if my sister is to be believed."

"Then you must go to her immediately," cried the empress, whose soft heart, while it could never be allowed to rule her political head, frequently governed her personal actions. "Go at once, and we will not expect you to return until the spring." She waved him away as if his urgency were her own. "Hurry now. You must not lose a minute. It is a very sad thing when one cannot attend the sickbed of one's parents." A shadow crossed her face as she remembered how she had been prevented by the czarina Elizabeth from attending her own father's funeral, let alone his sickbed. No one should accuse Catherine of such inhumanity. She saw the grateful colonel from her bedroom and returned to her work, well pleased that she should have begun the day with an act of kindness.

Chapter 10

Sophie had lost track of time. There was little sensation of movement in the sleigh, sliding slowly over the snow, drawn by its sluggish horses. The sky was so leaden, the light so gray, it was hard to believe it was daylight. Indeed, so little outside light penetrated the grimy windows of the icebox in which she shivered, it might just as well have been night.

She supposed she ought to tell her escort to halt at the next post house they came to, but she felt neither hunger nor thirst and knew that the muzhiks had their own food with them. When she had needed to leave the sleigh just after daybreak, they were eating raw onions and black bread, and the smell of vodka hung around them.

She could no longer feel her feet, and it was too much trouble to keep her eyes open. At one point, during the dreadful reaches of the night, she had begun to cry. The tears had frozen on her cheeks and to her horror she had felt her eyes freezing, icicles forming in her nose. The sleighs at Berkholzskoye were equipped with braziers, stoves, chamberpots. Couches piled high with furs kept the traveler as warm as within doors, and she had always loved winter excursions across the virgin snow of the steppes, where the white ground merged with the white sky so that they voyaged within a dazzling, shining capsule of absolute purity. If she kept her eyes closed she could be there, now, warmed by her grandfather's smile, hearing his voice as she snuggled into her furs. She was perfectly warm, and so deliciously sleepy . . .

The sound of shots barely penetrated her trance. The sleigh

lurched to a halt; there was confused shouting. Her eyes opened for a second, then closed again. What did it matter if it was brigands? She was too sleepy to care, and that wonderful white world beckoned . . .

"Holy Mother!" Flinging open the door, Adam stared in horror. Sophie, no longer tightly wrapped in her cloak, lay back on the wooden bench, her eyes closed, hair tumbling loose from her hood, her cloak hanging open, revealing the thin satin of her gown. "Sophie!" He climbed into the freezing interior, pulling her up. "Sophie! Wake up! Wake *up*, damn you!" He shook her vigorously. Her eyelids fluttered, and the force of his relief set his knees trembling.

"What is it?" Boris's head appeared in the doorway. Then he, too, swore as he took in the sight and its implications. "Got to get the blood moving, Count."

"I know!" Adam said between his teeth. "Sophie!" He shook her again. This time her eyes opened fully, but there was no recognition, no awareness in them.

"Leave me alone," she mumbled. "Want to go to sleep."

"You are not going to sleep." Taking her wrists in one hand, he jerked her up into a sitting position, then, with carefully judged force, he slowly and deliberately slapped her face with his gloved hand until her eyes focused, and he read anger behind the sleepy bewilderment.

"Adam?" She stared at him. "How . . . ? What . . . ?" Then the anger blazed, pure and clear. She touched her smarting cheeks. "You struck me! How *dare* you?"

"That's better." With a great sigh of relief, he spoke over his shoulder. "Bring me the pelisse and the boots."

"Got 'em already," said the imperturbable Boris, handing the required articles through the door.

"Put these on." Kneeling, Adam pulled off her thin evening shoes and began to rub her feet vigorously between his hands. "Can you feel anything?"

Sophie shook her head, slumping back against the bench, her eyes closing. Another stinging slap brought her upright with a cry of fury. "That's going to happen every time you close your eyes," Adam told her with the ferocity of desperation. "You *cannot* go to sleep, Sophie. If you do, you will never wake up. Do you understand me?" His eyes raked her face. "I am not going to lose you . . . not now."

The gray eyes pierced the white world that beckoned her into oblivion, sent it scurrying backward into the shadows from whence it came. His words, spoken with such savage intensity, seemed to take on shape and solidity, to form the reality to which she was now returning. She had no idea how he had got here, or even where here was, but such issues were supremely unimportant.

"I do not want to be lost," she said, managing to twist numb lips into the tiniest of smiles.

"Then cooperate." He kissed her hard, until warmth and life came back to her mouth, before resuming his rubbing of her feet.

As life returned to her body, she began to shiver uncontrollably, her teeth chattering. "It's so cold suddenly."

"It has always been cold," Adam told her, his tone short with worry. "You had just reached the point where you could not feel it any longer." He pushed her feet into the deerskin boots lined with Siberian fur, and muttered, "How long did that murdering savage expect you to survive?"

"Not l . . . l . . . long!" Sophie agreed through the frantic clattering of her teeth. "I have never been so cold."

"Put this on." He pushed her arms into the heavy pelisse, buttoning it securely. A thick fur hat with attached earmuffs went over her head, mittens on her hands, so that she was cocooned in fur. Adam inspected his parcel with a critical frown. "I do not see any gaps," he pronounced eventually. "Now you are going to run."

"R . . . run!" Sophie exclaimed. "I am not!"

"Oh, yes, you are." He stood up. "Come along." Hauling her to her feet, he stepped backward out of the sleigh, lifting her down beside him.

Sophie stood, weak-kneed, blinking in the snow's dazzle, shaking and chattering her teeth. The two serfs who had formed her escort lay in the snow, their bodies at strange angles that seemed not to resemble a human position. Her eyes went to Adam. "It could not be helped," he said curtly. "They could not be allowed to take this tale back to Dmitriev." Sophie shuddered at the implication, and the complexity of this turmoil swam into her head with sudden clarity. Adam's tone softened. "They fired to kill, Sophie."

Obeying their master's orders, Sophie thought. And there were always casualties in battle. If they had not met their deaths, she would have met hers. Then a wave of lightheadedness banished the moment of clarity. "I want to sit down. . . . Please, Adam, my legs feel strange." She looked at him in appeal.

"You have to get the blood moving in your body again," he said. "I am sorry, sweetheart, but you are going to run. He drew her over to his horse. "Trust me." With a swift movement, almost as if he hoped she would not notice what he was doing, he fastened her right wrist to his stirrup with his scarf.

Sophie, mute with disbelief, looked at him, then at her wrist. She tugged it, shaking her head. "What are you doing?" Her voice sounded frightened in its confusion.

Adam cupped her face and kissed her. "I know what I am doing, sweetheart." He swung onto his horse, shook the reins and the animal started forward.

Sophie stumbled with the surprise she should not have felt, but her ability to connect actions with consequences seemed to have become shaky, like the rest of her. Of course, she thought numbly, if one is tied to a horse and it starts to move one is going to move with it. The recognition brought another surge of anger, as her pace increased perforce to keep up with Adam's mount. "You are detestable," she yelled from her furry cocoon, running through the snow. "I loathe you!"

Adam chuckled. "No, you don't. You love me."

Sophie gasped, then closed her mouth rapidly as the air lacerated her lungs. Amazingly, she could feel the warmth returning to her body, reaching the extremities, setting her toes to tingling in a painful but blissfully reassuring fashion. Her stride lengthened as her sluggish blood resumed its customary speed and flow.

After ten minutes, Adam drew rein. He dismounted and
swiftly released her wrist. "If we cannot contrive some form
of heat for the sleigh, you must become accustomed to running every hour. Even in the furs, you will become chilled
to the bone."

Sophie did not immediately respond. For the first time,
she realized that they were not alone. While she had been
running, the sleigh had been following, driven by . . .

"Boris Mikhailov!" Her voice rang joyfully across the deserted, snowy landscape. "Why did I not know you were
here, also?"

"Didn't know anything at all," Boris said gruffly. "Not
in the state you were in. See who else is here." He gestured
to the back of the sleigh.

Sophie looked, then she was running again, plowing
through the snow. "Khan!" The stallion, tethered to the rear
of the sleigh, snorted his own pleasure and recognition, tossing his head in the needle-sharp air. "Where is his saddle? I
will ride him." She turned eagerly to Adam, yet keeping her
hand cupped over Khan's velvety nose.

Regretfully, he shook his head. "It is too cold for riding,
Sophie."

"But you are!" she exclaimed indignantly, huddling into
the stallion's warmth.

"Boris Mikhailov and I will share the driving, with hourly
changes," Adam said. "The other horses will be tethered to
the sleigh. It is imperative that they keep moving, and that
we keep as warm as we can." He was hustling her toward
the sleigh as he spoke. "In you get."

Sophie found herself bundled inside. Adam followed in a
few seconds with an armful of furs. "When did you last
eat?" Sitting beside her on the unyielding bench, he piled
furs over both of them, drawing her against him.

"Yesterday sometime," Sophie murmured, snuggling, as
a wave of peace washed blissfully over her. "But I'm not
hungry!" The last was a wail, because Adam was moving
away from her.

"I know it was impossible, but I wish we had been able

to carry a samovar," he muttered, jumping to the ground again. He was back within a few minutes with a hamper. As he opened it, the sleigh began to move forward. "Red currant syrup." He handed Sophie a bottle.

She wrinkled her nose. "I would rather have vodka."

"Not on an empty belly. Drink the syrup. The sugar will be good for you."

"There's sugar in vodka," Sophie persisted, peering into the hamper. "Look, you have some there." She reached for the bottle.

Adam sat back, watching as she took a deep draught of the fiery liquid. There had been times in the last months when he had feared that Sophia Alexeyevna Golitskova was vanquished and vanished, Paul Dmitriev's puppet permanently in her place. But the woman sitting beside him now was the woman he had first known. He was filled with an overpowering joy.

She wiped her mouth with the back of her hand and looked laughingly at him. "That is much better. Red currant syrup is for milksops."

"Maybe so," he replied, laughing back, relishing his moment of secret delight. "But at present it is still better for you than vodka."

Sophie drank again, then passed him the bottle. The glow was back in her eyes, even a hint of mischief as she asked, "May I go to sleep now?"

Adam returned the vodka to the hamper before drawing her across his knees, holding her tightly beneath the nest of furs. "You may." He kissed the tip of her nose, the only feature readily available.

Contentedly, Sophie allowed her eyes to close, her mind to drift. Vodka curled warmly in her stomach. Even through the layers of clothing she could feel the steady thump of Adam's heart against her cheek, his arms enfolding her. The night terror had exhausted her spiritual resources as the fearsome cold had exhausted her body. How or why this miraculous rescue had occurred somehow did not seem to be of any interest. Only the fact was of importance. She was awash with contentment, with peace, with utter languor, secure in the absolute certainty that her present position, locked in love, had been ordained from the first. There had just been a rather irritating delay in the inevitable . . .

"No . . . no, don't go! Where are you going!" Deprivation broke into the blissful world where she drifted, half in sleep, half lost in daydream. The arms were moving away from her, a cold space replacing the vibrant strength of the body supporting her.

"Boris Mikhailov must come inside," Adam told her, smiling at her sleepy indignation. "He has been driving the sleigh for over an hour."

"But if you go, I shall freeze again." She sat up, shaking the bemusement from her head.

"Then you will have to run, won't you?" Adam said cheerfully, tucking the fur around her. "Give Boris the vodka and make sure he wraps up well. He'll be very cold."

Sophie instantly forgot her selfish preoccupation with Adam's presence. It had come from the mists of sleep and had no place in present reality. "Yes, of course." Reaching for the hamper, she took out the vodka. "I hope this is not the only bottle. It has a miraculous effect on the body's temperature." She raised the bottle to her lips.

"I always knew you had hollow legs." Adam jumped to the ground. "There is plenty, but just make sure you do not drink so much that you do not know what you are doing." The gray eyes burned suddenly; the laughter left his voice. "The time is not far off now, Sophia Alexeyevna, when I will want to be certain you know exactly what is happening, when all your senses are at their sharpest."

Sophie shivered, but not with cold this time. Although that declaration of intent had been understood between them, the time to which he referred, the sense of hovering on the edge of a commitment, the consequences of which could not be computed, was suddenly terrifying. Love was a terrifying emotion. Her dark eyes lifted to his face, outlined against the gray-white horizon.

"I love you," she said quietly. "You need have no fears I will lose sight of that in the vodka bottle."

Slowly, Adam smiled. "I am reassured, Sophia Alexeyevna." He turned from her, finding Boris Mikhailov standing behind him. The muzhik was regarding him gravely, as if not a nuance of that exchange had escaped him. Then Boris nodded, a fractional movement of his head, but it was clear to Adam that he had just been given permission. Which was just as well, he thought, grinning ruefully to himself as he swung onto the lead horse. If Boris Mikhailov chose to interpose himself between a man and Sophie, only death would remove him.

He flicked the reins, and the sleigh moved forward slowly, the wooden blades whispering across the snow. Steel blades, of course, would have increased the pace considerably, but then Paul Dmitriev had not been interested in expediting his wife's journey. That reminder brought a resurgence of the fierce hatred Adam bore the barbarous Dmitriev. It was not a constructive emotion at the moment, however. He was more interested in the other side of the coin of passion—in love, and the expression of that love in passion's form.

Within the sleigh, Sophie anxiously ministered to the half-frozen Boris, piling furs upon him, holding the vodka to his numbed lips until he protested this care, gruffly insisting that it was not the mistress's place to tend the serf. Sophie's scornful laugh cracked in the dry, icy air. "It is not like you to talk nonsense, Boris Mikhailov. Now, unless you wish to sleep, will you tell me how the count rescued you from the stable?"

When Boris changed places with Adam, Adam made Sophie run beside the sleigh for ten minutes. This time, though, he took her hand and ran with her, needing the exercise to force his own slowed blood to quicken again. Just before nightfall, they came across a ruined farmhouse, behind it a barn with walls and roof intact. Boris drove the sleigh with the riderless horses tethered behind it into the building, and dismounted. "We'll get a fire going in no time. Rub down the horses, feed 'em, and stand them by the fire. They'll be as good as new by morning.'' Muttering, he set about tending the animals, always his primary concern.

Sophie herself took charge of Khan, while Adam gathered kindling and lit a fire in a circle of stones in the middle of the barn. He watched her tending the horse, whispering to him constantly, involved in some private communication with the great beast on which not even the power of a human love could intrude. Holy Mother! He was not jealous of a stallion, was he? His lips twitched at the absurdity of the notion as he began to unpack the carefully provisioned saddlebags.

''Is that food?'' Sophie came over to the small but strong blaze, peering hungrily at the neatly wrapped packages Adam was laying upon the ground.

''It is. . . . Sophie, if you touch that vodka again before you have eaten anything, you and I are going to have a falling out.''

''That would never do,'' she said peaceably, taking her mittened hand from the bottle. ''It is just that this is a rather superior vodka.'' Squatting before the fire, she drew off her mittens, stretching her hands to the flickering flames. ''Have you not noticed how creamy the really fine vodkas are?''

''Like velvet,'' he agreed, the solemnity of his tone belied by his dancing eyes. ''In the saddlebag behind you I think there is a saucepan and a skillet.''

Sophie rummaged, found the required utensils, and passed them to him. ''Are we going to cook?''

''In a primitive fashion.'' Taking the saucepan, he got to his feet. ''I'm going to fetch snow for tea.''

That made her laugh. ''But you said we do not have a samovar.''

His eyebrows lifted in mock reproof. ''Have you never heard of improvisation, Sophia Alexeyevna?''

''It is something at which I have become a master,'' she said quietly, looking up at him as she sat on her heels, warming her hands at the fire.

''We both have.'' His eyes held hers for a long moment. ''And the need for it is not disappeared.''

"No," she agreed. "But it is less immediate, is it not? We can begin a time free of deception?"

Adam inclined his head in silent acknowledgment, and the truth flowed between them. For the moment they were free, free to give reign to the hungers so long tamped down, free to explore the glorious implications of the current of love that charged them both.

Sophie looked around the barn, where the shapes of horses emerged from the shadows, lit only by the dim glow of a single oil lamp and the flickering flames of the fire. There was one small circle of warmth, beyond it the fierce cold. She smiled, an unconsciously seductive smile. "I think that perhaps we *will* have to improvise."

Desire leaped, a naked blade, into the gray eyes at that smile, the softly suggestive tone. Slowly, he put down the saucepan, dropping to his heels beside her, gently cupping her face in his hands.

"I am frightened," Sophie whispered. "Frightened of the power of our love. It is devouring me, melting me down so that I will have no form . . . no shape of my own."

"There is nothing to fear, my love," he replied gently, tracing her mouth with his thumb. "Not when the feeling is shared. We are both in thrall to the power." He kissed the thin, blue-veined eyelids, feeling the rapid pulsing of her eyes beneath his lips, the flutter of those sable lashes against his cheek. Slowly, his lips annointed the high cheekbones as his thumb traced the fine line of her jaw, and he felt her suspended beneath the caress, her breath paused as if she was savoring every nuance of sensation with her whole body.

Quietly, Boris Mikhailov picked up the saucepan and went outside to fetch snow for the tea.

"I want to hold you," Adam said. "Hold you for the first time without the restraints of guilt and fear." He ran his hands over her shoulders, feeling the sharp delineation of her collarbone. She was thinner than the first time he had held her. He thought how then he had jumped back from her as he realized what was happening, realized how close he was to betraying the trust imposed upon him. But Dmitriev had forfeited all rights to that trust. . . . Had Eva's lover considered that the absent husband had forfeited his rights? The acid skewer of disillusion twisted in his entrails. He saw her at the head of the stairs, her belly, swollen with another man's child, pushing against her skirt. . . .

"What is it?" whispered Sophie, chilled by the strange hardening of the face that a minute before had been dissolved in tenderness. "What are you seeing?"

His eyes focused. "A moment in the past." That was where it belonged. It must not sour this present, must not prevent his giving and receiving the wonder of love with a woman who looked the world straight between the eyes; one who he would swear had not a dishonest bone in her body.

"A bad moment?" She touched his face, the gesture expressive of both compassion and distress.

"Yes." He would not lie to her. "But it is gone now."

"I do not really know anything about you," Sophie said, on a note of amazement. "Yet, I feel as if I know everything important about you."

Adam smiled. "My love, you do." He kissed her quickly, then stood up, deliberately dispelling the tension of uncertainty and of a fearful passion yet to be consummated. "I cannot help feeling that Boris Mikhailov has spent long enough away from the fire."

Sophie, stricken, looked anxiously into the shadows. "How could we have been so selfish? Boris Mikhailov!" she called into the murky gloom outside the charmed circle.

"Princess?" The muzhik materialized, calm and collected, the saucepan in his hands. "I was just filling the pot."

Sophie peered suspiciously at him, but could read nothing untoward in the familiar face. "Come and warm yourself." She shifted sideways, giving him access to the fire. "What are we going to eat?" Seeking distance in domesticity, she began to unwrap the packages Adam had laid out. "I am famished."

"You have not eaten since yesterday evening," Adam observed in the same ordinary manner.

"Yesterday?" Sophie sat back on her heels, shaking her

head in a measure of disbelief. "Was it only yesterday at the Stroganovs'? It seems a lifetime away." Still shaking her head, she began to slice sausage, tossing the slices into the skillet, which she handed wordlessly to Boris. Accepting his task, he held the pan over the fire, turning the sizzling pieces. Adam, in similar fashion, found himself in possession of a knife and a loaf of bread. He cut the loaf, smiling to himself as he watched Sophie, a critical frown drawing those pronounced eyebrows together, setting out what else she considered necessary for this supper, before turning her attention to the complicated process of making tea in a saucepan of melted snow.

After a half hour of almost complete silence, broken only by the occasional scrape of knife against platter, Sophie sighed with contentment. "I have never tasted anything so good. And the tea . . . elixir from heaven!"

"Better than vodka?" teased Adam, smiling at her over the rim of his cup.

"There's a time and a place for everything," Sophie declared haughtily, gathering up the dishes and knives. "If you fetch some more snow, Boris Mikhailov, we can wash these."

"They can wait until the morning." Adam spoke decisively. "It is too cold to make unnecessary journeys outside." He stood up. "We are all going to have to make one necessary journey. Boris and I will go first, Sophie. Then I will escort you."

"I do not need an escort." Sophie flushed slightly.

"I do not wish to offend your delicate sensibilities, Sophia Alexeyevna, but you will present a very vulnerable target for any prowling beast."

Sophie shrugged, recognizing that it was the colonel who was speaking, briskly authoritative as he assumed command of this expedition.

"With any luck, we'll find a post house for tomorrow night," Adam comforted.

Sophie chuckled. "Do you really think such a hospice will provide much luxury? Vermin, certainly."

"I daresay you are right." Laughing, Adam primed his

pistol, then he and Boris went out into the night, leaving Sophie contemplating her own trip into the snow with the glum reflection that the male sex had some most unfair advantages in certain matters.

She managed, somehow, with Adam at a discreet distance, pistol in hand, peering into the darkness, watching for the yellow eyes, the bared fangs of a hungry predator. "This is madness." Sophie came running up to him, rubbing her mittened hands together, her breath freezing in the air. "Will we make it to Berkholzskoye, Adam?" She leaned into him for a minute, unable to pretend that the question had been asked purely in jest.

"You have my word on it," he said with ineffable reassurance. "If we can purchase a chamberpot and a brazier for the sleigh, it will ease things considerably. Come now, inside quickly before we both become stalagmites."

In the stable, they discovered that Boris had been busy in their absence. He had prepared a bed of straw and furs amongst the horses for himself, close enough to the fire that he could tend it easily throughout the night. Within the sleigh, furs were piled in thick profusion. "Found an old iron bucket," he informed them in customary laconic fashion. "Knocked some holes in it, filled it from the fire; makes a passable brazier for the sleigh."

Sophie peered into the vehicle and was instantly struck by the warmth thrown off into the small space by Boris's contraption. "It's almost cozy," she said in awe. "Boris, you are a miracle worker."

The muzhik grunted. "Nothing to it. I'll bid you both good-night, then."

They returned the valediction, then stood for a second, suddenly, unaccountably awkward. Sophie stared into the fire. She knew what was going to happen; she wanted what was going to happen with an all-consuming desire, had wanted it for so long; so why on earth should she feel as trembly and apprehensive as a virgin on her wedding night? Then it occurred to her that the analogy was not absurd. In matters of loving, she was still a virgin. Slowly, she raised her eyes. Adam was looking at her with quiet comprehension.

"I am going to love you, sweetheart. There is no need for fear." Taking her hand, he drew her toward the sleigh. Within its shadowed warmth, he pulled the door shut, closing them into this tiny chamber of fur lit only by minute pinpricks of red glowing through the holes in the makeshift brazier. So- phie, kneeling on the fur bed, waited trustfully, opening her arms to him as he came down on the bed beside her.

"We are going to have to learn each other without eyes," Adam whispered against her ear, caressing her face with his open palm, rubbing his knuckles against her cheekbone. "It is too cold, even with the brazier, for visible nakedness."

A shiver quivered through the body beneath his hands at the words. "Do not be afraid." His hand slipped down to her throat, exploring the soft contours of that slender column.

"I am not," she replied truthfully. "Unless it be fear that I may not please you."

His lips took hers in answer, his thumb resting against the pulse at the base of her throat, his other hand palming her scalp in firm support. Gently, playfully, he nibbled on her lower lip, and her mouth curved in a smile of pleasure at the sensual little game. Her tongue darted into the corner of his mouth, and their breath mingled, sweet and warm in this moist, silken conversation of lips. Boldly, she pushed her tongue into the velvet recess, exploring the hollows of his cheeks, the con- trasting texture of his teeth. The pulse beneath his thumb quickened. Her body strained against his as for the first time she could give fearless expression to the rushing desires she could not have put into words.

His hands moved down her body, holding her against him as he took over the kiss, his tongue joining with hers in danc- ing delight. There was a moment when he opened his eyes and met the wondrous glow in the dark ones facing him. Slowly he drew back, placing his hands on her shoulders, leaning away from her as he explored her face, a shadowy oval in the dimness. "Let us get beneath the covers, sweet- heart." His voice was a husky murmur as he drew back the top layer of furs. ''I have to have more of you than your mouth.''

''I also.'' She stretched out between the layers, her arms circling him as he lay beside her. For a few minutes they lay alongside each other, savoring the freedom bestowed by the long, uninterrupted hours ahead, falling in with the other's breathing rhythm, allowing the passion to build between them with each breath, until the warmth of their bodies filled the nest.

Adam shifted slightly, leaning up on one elbow without disturbing the tightness of the wrappings. ''I am going to undress you,'' he said in the whispering darkness. ''If I do not let any air under here, you will not be cold.''

''I could not imagine being cold,'' Sophie said, touching his face. ''Not now.''

Smiling, he turned his mouth into her palm. ''I shall develop eyes in every finger,'' he murmured. ''Even though I cannot see you, I shall know you in every facet before this night is done.''

A tremor ran through her again. She lay utterly still, poised on the brink of she knew not what, feeling his hands moving over her, drawing aside the pelisse, unfastening the cloak beneath, spreading aside the layers of material until he could sculpt the shape of her beneath the satin gown, and his hands could play upon the rise of her breasts swelling at the low neckline.

Sophie stirred beneath the touch, felt her nipples peak, hard and burning. She moved her own hands to close over his. ''I am filling with wonder,'' she murmured.

Taking her hands, he pressed kisses into the palms, before lifting her against him so that he could reach the hooks at the back of her gown. Deftly, as if indeed he had eyes in his fingertips, the hooks flew apart. He drew the satin forward over her shoulders, pushing it down to her waist before letting her fall back upon the furs. The little pearl buttons at the front of her chemise slid undone with sensuous ease, and Sophie felt the warm air on her breasts, the kiss of fur against her nipples as he leaned over her, exploring the soft contours with the delicate tip of a finger before taking each nipple in his mouth, nibbling the rosy crests, his tongue painting fire over the smooth hillocks.

Sophie was cast adrift, floating on a warm, viscous sea that bore her up as if she were weightless. A flat palm slipped inside the layers of clothing gathered at her waist, slipped into the cambric pantalettes beneath her bottom, lifting her so that the wadded material could be pushed down her body. The shocking intimacy of the touch brought a startled gasp to her lips. Paul would grip her hips occasionally with bruising pressure as he expended himself, but it was merely a vessel he touched; the spirit inhabiting that vessel was on some other plane. Not now, though. It was her self touched by the hands of Adam Danilevski, touched in a hungry passion that acknowledged her own.

Her thighs parted involuntarily for the magical quest for her essence. His lips nuzzled her belly so that she stirred and whimpered in pleasure, her body tightening in response. His tongue dipped into the tight bloom of her navel and she was lost in this dark, warm enclosure where delight visited her blind, naked body in ways unimagined, and she could do nothing but lie beneath the pleasure bringer, breathless for the next touch, the next whispering breath.

With sudden urgency, Adam slipped out from the covers. "I have to take off my own clothes, sweetheart. I cannot do so under the covers without letting in the cold." Swiftly, he shed his garments, while Sophie lay watching him, then the pale shadow of his body came down to her again. His skin was chilled even by that short exposure to the air, and she drew him fiercely against her, imparting her own warmth. Instinctively, she rolled on top of him, pressing her heated body upon his, murmuring with delight at the joining of their skins, the hard thighs beneath her own, the muscular concavity of the belly that seemed made to receive the softness of her own. His hands ran down her back, molding her to him; his heart beat swiftly against her breasts, flattened against his chest; her lips took his with fierce joy as the wanton hunger demanded satisfaction and he rose in hard, throbbing promise against her thigh.

His hands spanning her narrow back, Adam rolled over, reversing their positions. "Another time, we'll love in that way, sweet." She could not see his smile, but she could hear it in his voice. "This way, you will stay warm."

He was inside her, a part of her, filling her with his presence, reaching to her core, and she was taking him, consuming him, as he possessed her. Inextricable, inseparable, minds and bodies meshed, they rose in bliss, hung in ecstasy, fell in joy. And Sophie wept with the wonder of it.

Chapter 11

Sophie woke, naked and alone beneath the furs. She lay still, eyes closed, as reality reestablished itself. Slowly, she opened her eyes and sat up, holding the covers securely to her neck. It was daylight, judging by the grimy square of mica in the window aperture of the sleigh. The brazier was still alight. Someone must have replenished it at some point in the hours she had been asleep.

A tiny smile played over her lips. So that was what it was really like? The journey begun on that star-filled night when Adam had first kissed her had reached its goal. Now there was a new journey to make from this fresh beginning. With a smug chuckle, she snuggled down under the furs again, allowing her hands to roam over her warm, soft flesh. In a curious way, she felt as if she had been reborn. As if during those dark days and hurtful nights in the Dmitriev palace she had been serving a species of apprenticeship, a preparation for the moment when, like the butterfly, she could emerge fully fledged from her chrysalis. She was whole, knew herself capable of arousing passion and of fulfilling her own; of inspiring love and of being inspired by it. Womanhood was hers, with all its magical rewards, its obligations and its penalties, and she looked upon the world with the clear sight of one who was finally wide awake.

"Sophia Alexeyevna, you are a shameless slugabed! It is an hour past daybreak." Adam spoke in laughing reproof as he opened the door of the sleigh. "If we are to reach Berkholzskoye this year, we cannot lie around in barns."

"I would have got dressed, but I do not know where my clothes are," Sophie declared with an attempt at lofty dignity. The covers were pulled up to her nose, the dark eyes, glowing with love and the wondrous memories of passion, laughed at him, even as they invited.

It was irresistible. Adam, conscious of the time and his own frailty of will in certain matters, had determined to remain outside the sleigh until Sophie was once more clothed and beyond temptation. Instead, he found himself kneeling on the fur bed, the door closed firmly behind him.

"Your clothes are where you left them last night," he announced solemnly, removing his gloves before sliding a hand beneath the covers. "Somewhere in here."

Sophie squeaked in mock dismay as his questing hand found what it sought. It was not seeking her clothes. "Shame on you, Colonel! To take advantage of an innocent maid in such fashion."

"Innocent maid, my foot!" scoffed Adam. "You are lying on your chemise. Lift up." The hand assisted her to comply with the instruction and Sophie wriggled seductively against the flat palm. Lust, brilliant in its purity, sparked in the gray eyes. "Damn it, Sophie," he groaned, moving his hand abruptly. "We do not have time for this. Boris Mikhailov is preparing the horses and you must have coffee and breakfast. Get dressed quickly, now." He shuffled backward, reaching behind him to swing open the door, but his eyes remained riveted to her face.

"When will we have time?" Sophie asked matter-of-factly, aware of her own arousal, enjoying it even as she lamented the impossibility of its satisfaction at this point.

"It depends what the day brings," Adam replied, jumping down. "Hurry, now."

Smiling, Sophie scrabbled under the covers until she had located her various articles of clothing. Putting them on without exposing herself unduly to the air was a cumbersome procedure, but she succeeded eventually and stood up, buttoning the fur pelisse thankfully over what she knew must be the most crumpled muddle beneath.

"Adam, if I am going to spend a month in the same clothes, I am not going to be at all nice to know." She spoke as she emerged into the frigid gray light of the barn, where a fire still burned, Adam squatting in front of it. "We cannot even wash."

He stood up from the fire, holding a mug. "Coffee." He handed her the steaming mug. "I think cleanliness is the least of our problems, Sophie. We cannot afford the luxury of such refined concerns."

Sophie sipped her coffee, wondering why she felt as if she had been rebuked. She glanced at him over the rim of the mug and saw that his mouth was drawn, his face set, anxiety in the gray eyes. "What is troubling you?"

"The weather," he said shortly. "Boris says he can smell a blizzard, and the sky does not look at all inviting."

"Perhaps we should stay here today, then," she suggested, both practically and hopefully. For all its lack of creature comforts, the barn did provide dry shelter and a measure of warmth.

Adam shook his head almost impatiently. "If we do not move whenever there is the possibility of ugly weather, we will never get anywhere. We cannot spend forever on this journey, and the weather will not improve before the spring."

Sophie shrugged, draining her mug. "Then let us start. There seems little to be gained by standing around fretting."

Adam's laugh cracked in the dry air, chasing the worry from his eyes. "That's my indomitable Sophie! There's bread and honey for your breakfast. Eat quickly while Boris and I harness the horses."

Sophie munched on bread and honey while ensuring the saddlebags were securely packed, shaking out the furs from the sleigh and replacing them. She refilled the brazier with the last of the fire. It was certainly going to be an improvement on the previous day's journeying.

She remembered that cheerful thought later that morning, and the memory brought a hollow laugh. By ten o'clock the sky was as dark as a starless night. Adam's expression became more grim by the moment as he looked anxiously through the window, rubbing at the dirt with a sleeve as if it would improve the visibility.

"I don't think it's the dirt," Sophie commented from her cocoon of furs. "Boris has always been able to smell a blizzard."

Adam merely grunted, continuing his anxious watch until, abruptly, they were enveloped, blinded by an impenetrable yet constantly moving wall of snow. The temperature dropped even further, and the already feeble warmth emitted by the makeshift brazier ceased to penetrate a cold that was almost solid. Sophie found herself struggling for breath.

"Get on the floor!" Adam's voice came, harsh, cracked with effort through the darkness. His hands on her shoulder forced her to the floor. "Pull the furs over your head."

"But you—"

"Don't argue with me!"

Sophie decided that perhaps she would not. She huddled on the floor, completely covered by furs. It was easier to breathe the trapped air warmed by her body as she crouched, hugging herself. The sleigh was moving so slowly now that when it came to a stop, at first she barely noticed the cessation of movement.

"Don't you move!" Adam's sharp instruction reached her just as a blast of fearsome cold stabbed into her nest. She realized that he must have opened the door, then it banged closed and she was left with the residue of that rapier thrust.

In the minute or so since the sleigh had halted, the snow had drifted above the level of the wooden blades. Adam struggled blindly to the horses, making out the great bulk of Boris Mikhailov astride the lead horse. Shielding his mouth with his arm, the count bellowed up at the muzhik.

Boris's reply was snatched away in the snow, but Adam had realized the problem for himself. The horse that Boris was not riding was turning to ice as the snow froze on contact with his coat. The animal was wracked with violent spasms as it stood, yielding itself to death.

Adam mounted it, grabbing the frozen reins. The metal of the bit was so cold it burned like the heart of a furnace. It took every vestige of skill for him to get the beast to move, but at last he took a step. Boris's mount moved forward also, and the sleigh inched out of the rapidly icing drift around the blades. Adam, as he knew Boris would be, was obsessed with worry for the other horses, tethered to the rear of the sleigh; Khan, in particular. They had to keep moving, however slowly, just so that the blood would not freeze in the animals' veins.

It was impossible to tell whether they were still on the route. Whirling snow blanked out the landscape so that they moved without direction, without purpose, it seemed. Then Adam became aware of a movement in the veiling whiteness, coming up beside him. Stiffly, he turned his deadened body. A white heat of fury sent the blood shooting through his veins. Sophie, crouched low over Khan's neck, the two other horses on leading reins to either side, was forcing the beasts through the snow, pushing them to increase their speed. Adam bawled at her to get back inside, but the cold froze his lungs, and she ignored him anyway. He could do nothing without stopping, but to stop even for a second would spell disaster. Seething with fury, fueled by terror, he was obliged to accept her presence, knowing, as his own body succumbed to the disembodied sensation of extreme cold, that she must be in the same condition.

For a terrifying half hour, the three of them rode side by side through the storm, until Boris, with supreme effort, raised his arm, pointing with his whip into the white darkness. A shape loomed. Roofed, walled, it was the lifeline without which death was a certainty.

There was a chimney, smoke curling, melting into the snow; outbuildings solidifying, all evidence of a post house. Adam forced himself from his horse; reaching up, he pried Sophie loose from her death grip on Khan's neck, hauling her to the ground. Boris leaned sideways, grabbed the three reins, and drove the sleigh toward the outbuildings, the three horses obeying blindly.

The door of the post house crashed open under the force of Adam's shoulder. He stumbled inside, Sophie, whose legs would not work, held against him. They found themselves in a room warmed by a vast potbellied stove set into the wall and a fire blazing in the hearth. Adam shoved Sophie so close to the fire she was almost inside it, then he took stock. Faces—a whole crowd of faces—stared at him through a smoky haze; children, men, women, two ancients rocking beside the stove. The earthen floor swarmed with dogs, cats, chickens, and a goat. They had fallen upon a post house of the most primitive kind, but its one room, although fetid, was warm.

He forced his lips to move. "My servant needs help with the horses." His hand plunged into his pocket, pulling out a leathern pouch. Stiffly, fingers fumbling, he extracted a coin, handing it to a brawny lad. "There'll be another when the job's done."

The lad touched his forelock, pocketed the coin, and grabbed a wolfskin from a wooden settle by the hearth.

" 'Tis a powerful blizzard, lord." An elderly man was the first person, apart from Adam, to speak, and there was awe in his voice. "Not fit for man nor beast."

"No," agreed Adam shortly. "Bring me vodka." He turned to one of the women. "What can you give us in the way of hot food?"

The woman shook her head in its greasy cap as if trying to dispel hallucination. "Cabbage soup, lord."

"Then see to it. I want some privacy around this fire. Have you a screen?"

The idea seemed extraordinary, but the memory of that pouch of coins, the richness of the travelers' furs, the authoritative tone could produce a near miracle. Sophie, thawing painfully, shivering violently as sensation returned to her body, suddenly found herself enclosed in a tent of sheets draped from hooks in the ceiling. The strings of onions and garlic also hanging from the hooks added the strangest decorative touch to a scene so bizarre that she began to laugh weakly.

"Get out of those clothes!" Adam spoke in French, ensuring that they could not be understood by any curious ears beyond their tent. He held the vodka to her lips. "Never, ever have I seen such a piece of crass, mindless stupidity. Half an hour more and you would have been beyond salvation! What did you hope to achieve with that nonsensical act of martyrdom?" He tipped the bottle vigorously, his hand shaking. Sophie choked, the spirits trickling down her chin.

"I expected to achieve what I succeeded in achieving," she replied in the same language, through chattering teeth. "Don't bawl at me, Adam. You didn't expect me to leave Khan to suffer?"

"As it happens, I did," he said dryly, taking a deep revivifying draught of the vodka. "Foolish of me. Now get out of those clothes. They are frozen stiff."

Gradually, the point of the tent penetrated her numbed brain. Sophie stared at him. "Here, in the middle of this room? With all those people . . . ?" She gestured vaguely to the grimy curtains. A chicken, clucking cheerfully, pushed beneath one of the sheets to enter the makeshift chamber.

"Shoo!" Adam toed the bird back the way it had come. "Yes, here, Sophie. Now, this minute. You may not realize it, but your clothes are frozen to your body." He was beginning to unfasten his own pelisse, his fingers tingling painfully as life returned.

"I can't stay stark naked," protested Sophie. Then she became suddenly aware of a puddle at her feet as the fire melted the frozen snow from her clothes. An icy wetness seemed plastered to her skin, and she realized the truth of what Adam had said. Fingers fumbling, she began to strip off her clothes, finally standing in her cold-reddened skin.

"Come here." Adam, as naked as she, began to scour her with a harsh scrap of toweling. "I have to say this was not the way I had envisaged my first sight of you," he murmured, turning her around, scrubbing vigorously the length of her back and legs. "It is just about the least erotic moment imaginable."

"You're scraping all my skin off," Sophie complained. "I'll be as raw as a peeled potato!"

"See what I mean? Not at all erotic," Adam said, with a mock sigh. "Apart from tuberlike, how does that feel now?"

"Alive and warm," she said. "But what now?"

"Maybe we can beg a blanket."

"It'll be flea-ridden, Adam! I'll be eaten alive." She huddled into the hearth, scorching one side of her with the blaze, hugging her arms across her breasts. "I feel so exposed."

"Count?" It was Boris Mikhailov from outside the tent. "Thought you might like your cloak-bag."

"You thought well, Boris." Adam stretched a bare arm through a gap in the sheets. "You'd best get out of your own clothes."

"Just doing so," responded the muzhik. "Is Sophia Alexeyevna all right?"

"Quite well, Boris." Sophie answered for herself.

"Don't deserve to be," declared Boris. "Such craziness!"

"I could not permit Khan to freeze!" Agitated in her defense, Sophie stepped away from the blissful scorching heat of the fire, her arms dropping away from her breasts.

Adam, rummaging through his valise, glanced up and drew in his breath sharply, seeing her now for the first time: clean-limbed, high-breasted, the soft curve of hip, elegant length of leg. She was too thin, but the lithe muscularity he had first noticed appeared little diminished by her imprisonment in St. Petersburg. . . .

"Adam!" Sophie choked with laughter. "What are you thinking?" Her eyes gazed with unashamed satisfaction at the very obvious physical expression of his thoughts.

"Put this on, for pity's sake." He handed her a brocaded silk dressing gown. "This is the most absurd situation." He began to dress himself rapidly, conscious of the teeming room beyond the tent.

"This is the most absurd garment," Sophie declared, hitching up the skirt into the girdle so it would not drag upon the earth floor. "Silk brocade in this place!"

"If you prefer your bare skin, the choice is yours," he retorted, restored to himself in dry britches, shirt, and jacket. "Were the horses well provided for, Boris Mikhailov?" He pushed through the curtains, his tone brisk as he spoke once more in Russian, reassuming the dignified mien of a colonel in the Preobrazhensky regiment of the Imperial Guard.

Sophie, undeceived, chuckled to herself as she spread out their wet clothes in front of the fire, where they would gently steam until morning. The sheets were taken from the hooks and the room given back once more in its entirety to the postman and his family. Boris Mikhailov, for whom the need for privacy was unfelt, had changed his clothing by the stove under the indifferent eye of an old babushka stirring cabbage soup.

The soup, heavy black bread, salted cucumbers, and raw onions appeared on the stained plank table. A communal cup of kvass passed around the table, refilled when empty from the beer barrel in the corner of the room. Sophie, who shared Adam's dislike of the weak beer, settled for the occasional gulp of vodka, but fatigue swooped down upon her like a hawk on an unwary sparrow. One minute she was sitting upright on the long bench, her belly filled with soup and bread, the next her eyes had closed and she had slumped against Adam's shoulder. Voices, cackling chickens, snapping dogs squabbling over scraps, whining children—she heard none of them. When Adam carried her over to the settle beside the fire, she curled onto the hard wood as if it were the softest feather bed. He covered her with one of the furs from the sleigh, sparing a rueful thought for the denial he had imposed upon them both that morning. Maybe, in future, it would be sensible to take advantage of opportunities when they offered themselves.

He found himself a corner of the room where everyone slept in a higgledy-piggledy confusion of cradles, cots, and mattresses, the oldest and youngest closest to the sources of heat. Fleas hopped, chickens pecked, dogs scratched. Adam finally slept.

Sophie awoke at daybreak. She awoke with a surge of vitality, unlike anything she had felt since she first arrived in St. Petersburg. Pushing aside the fur, she sat up on her hard bed, swinging her legs to the floor. A cat twined itself around her calves; something tugged at the hem of Adam's dressing gown. A pair of solemn brown eyes peered up at her from a dirt-encrusted face. Smiling, she bent to scoop up the soggy baby who hungrily stuck his fist into his mouth. Around them, bodies began to stir, making reluctant waking noises. Holding the babe on one hip, she went to the tiny, snow-encrusted window. It was impossible to see out, so she stepped over animals and still-recumbent bodies to the door, gingerly lifting the crossbar.

Outside, the sun sprang off the snow with blinding brightness. All traces of the storm had vanished, although it was still bitterly cold. She closed the door swiftly. A child was feeding kindling into the sinking fire; another was doing the same for the potbellied stove. The babushka yawned toothlessly and took the baby from Sophie, thrusting a milk-soaked rag into the roundly opened mouth. Dogs were sent outside with the encouragement of booted feet; Boris Mikhailov opened up the saddlebags, and soon the aroma of coffee filled the hovel.

Sophie brushed at the wet patch on the silken robe at her hip where the babe had been perched. Looking up, she saw Adam smiling sleepily at her from his corner. Crossing the room, she held out her hands to him. He grasped them firmly and pulled himself upright.

"Good morrow, sweetheart." He kissed the tip of her nose. "What's the weather doing?"

"It's beautiful. Freezing, but bright sunshine. I have to go to the outhouse, but I must get dressed first." She gestured expressively around the busy room.

"Quite frankly, I don't think anyone is going to show the slightest interest," Adam said. "Unless it be an inquisitive babe or a chicken." Retrieving her dried, warmed clothes from the fireplace, he brought them back to the corner. "The less fuss you make, the less anyone's going to notice." He planted himself, foursquare, across the corner.

Her crooked, quizzical smile quirked before she turned her back on the tumbling scene, pulling on stockings and pantalettes beneath the robe. Modesty beyond that stage seemed singularly pointless. Dropping the robe, she scrambled into the rest of her clothing behind the screen of Adam's back. The satin gown was a sad sight, water-stained, crumpled, a seam split from yesterday's ride. Her hair, uncombed for over two days, hung bedraggled to her shoulders. Dirt clung beneath her fingernails. The image of General, Prince Paul Dmitriev rose unbidden, unwanted, in her mind's eye. Quite suddenly, she burst out laughing.

Adam swung around. "Whatever has amused you, love?"

"I was thinking of Paul," she said, then saw his face close. "Only in terms of what a spectacle I must present and how he would react," she explained, hesitant, tentative beneath his abruptly forbidding countenance.

"He tried to kill you," Adam said flatly. "I do not find anything amusing in that thought, or in any other to do with your husband." He turned from her, striding across the room to the door. It swung open, letting in an ice-tipped finger of air, a brilliant shaft of sunlight, then closed.

Adam marched to the stable. How could Sophie possibly be amused by thoughts of her husband? Had she no understanding of the situation in which she . . . they found themselves? Her husband was eventually going to find out that against all odds she had survived this journey, but he must not discover Adam Danilevski's part in it. Boris Mikhailov could have made an opportune reappearance to explain her safety. At Berkholzskoye, the muzhik would be beyond Dmitriev's vengeful hand. The thoughts, plans, explanations ran through his head as he checked on the horses. The one thought he could not evade was that Sophia Alexeyevna was another man's wife and would remain so until death broke the contract. And he, Adam Danilevski, a man of stern moral rectitude, one who had sworn never to become entangled with a woman again, was playing a part in the same sort of triangle that had destroyed his own marriage—except that this time he was playing the guilty role.

He could hear Eva's scornful laugh as she accused him of prudery, of ignoring, of hiding from, the realities of the world they inhabited; standing at the head of the stairs, her belly, swollen with another man's child, pushing against her skirt . . .

"Something bothering you, Count?" The calm tones of Boris Mikhailov shattered the corrosive images.

"Not at all," he denied, turning toward the muzhik, aware, even through the denial, that his mouth was set, his eyes hostile with memory. "I was just looking at the horses. They seem not to have suffered any serious ill effects."

Boris looked at him with the wise eyes of one who has seen and learned much. "Best to be honest with her," he said. "Sophia Alexeyevna can deal with most things, but she can't abide confusion and lies."

"And you think I am about to confuse her with lies, Boris?" Adam's eyebrows lifted sardonically. "What have I done to deserve such a judgment?"

But Boris was not to be intimidated. He simply shrugged. "You know your own business best, lord." Bending, he began to run knowing hands down Khan's hocks, feeling for the heat that would warn of a strained tendon.

Adam left the stable. He had not told Sophie of his marriage; there had seemed no point. He could not talk about it without bitterness, a bitterness he knew would become directed toward his audience. And now, enmeshed in this tangle of love, it would be even more difficult. The parallels were too clear, too agonizingly obvious.

Sophie was just coming out of the post house as he emerged into the dazzling morning. She was wrapped tightly in her pelisse, the pale oval of her face framed in the fur hood. Her hand lifted in salute, but she did not wait for him, simply turned toward the noisome outhouse at the rear of the inn.

Had he hurt her? Adam swore softly. Of course, he had. Pacing up and down in the snow, he waited until she emerged; she came hurrying toward him, her boots scrunching across the crisp ground, one hand shielding her eyes from the sun's dazzle. "Are we ready to leave?"

"In a minute," he said quietly, taking her mittened hands. "I am a bear in the morning, Sophie, particularly when I have spent the night fighting off fleas." He smiled. "Forgive me."

Her candid dark eyes regarded him gravely, as if reading his soul. Then she shrugged. "There is nothing to forgive, Adam. You do not wish to talk of Paul. I cannot blame you. We will not do so again."

"I hurt you," he said, squeezing her hands.

She smiled with a hint of resignation. "I have had my head bitten off before, love. There is no damage done."

With that, he was obliged to be satisfied. They resumed their journey with Boris Mikhailov driving, but a constraint hung over the occupants of the sleigh. Sophie seemed distant, although she smiled and responded whenever Adam attempted to initiate a conversation. But it was clearly an effort for her, so eventually he fell silent, leaving her to draw pictures in the dirt on the window as she peered out at the landscape that today sped by, the blades of the sleigh cutting through the crisp snow.

By mid-afternoon, Adam decided he had had enough of this unrelieved tedium. He could not accuse Sophie of sulking—indeed, such behavior would be foreign to her nature—but there was more to her introspection than a simple desire to be alone with her thoughts. Action was definitely required. He gathered up a handful of sticks from the pile in the corner of the sleigh and replenished the brazier, giving Sophie a speculative look.

"What is it?" Suddenly, vividly aware of the look that penetrated her not-very-pleasant reverie, she gazed back at him, puzzled yet with a prickle of anticipation.

Stroking his chin thoughtfully, Adam remarked, "I was just thinking that opportunities for privacy are so few and far between, we should perhaps take advantage of them when they come."

Sophie's eyes widened. "Do you mean what I think you mean?"

"What do you think I mean?" he teased.

"Here . . . now . . . ?" Sophie looked around the tiny space. "But it's broad daylight." The prickle was blossoming into full-blown awareness, sending tingles up her spine, creeping across her scalp, creating a hollowness in her belly.

"So it is," agreed Adam solemnly.

"It is not decent," Sophie said, her dark eyes glinting with mischief.

"By the law according to whom?" inquired Adam with a raised eyebrow, drawing her against him so that her head rested on his shoulder. He smiled down at her, and she wrinkled her nose wryly.

"You are a shameless rake, Count."

His head bent, his lips pressed against the soft curve of her mouth, a finger brushing in a stroking caress over the planes of her face, before trailing down to the mounded curve of her breast. The slow, sweet spread of longing annointed her. Her body moved into the caress as his fingers deftly unfastened the buttons of the pelisse and her nipples lifted into his molding palm. Without loosing her mouth, Adam spread the fur over them both before he pulled down the low neckline of her much-abused gown and released her breasts from the confinement of the chemise.

Sophie's sighing pleasure rustled against his lips, all discontent, the vague niggling unhappiness left over from the morning, subsumed now under the touch of lust, the affirmation of love. She felt his hand slide from thigh to knee, drawing up her skirt and petticoat, slipping into the waistline of her pantalettes. The garment was pushed down to tangle at her ankles, and the bared flesh of hip and thigh danced beneath the sensuous stroking fingers and the soft brushing warmth of the fur covering. He unfastened his own clothing, wriggling free of his britches with an agile twist, then caught her behind one knee and drew her leg across his hip.

He held her strongly beneath the cover, her body fitted to his, as the sleigh slid across the snow and its whispering progress matched the whispering rise of pleasure within as he allowed an infinity of stillness to pass, when she was conscious only of the throbbing presence filling her body, the only movement that of the sleigh insinuating its gliding rhythm into their joined selves. Slowly, he turned her until her hips rested on the edge of the wooden bench, twisting himself to rise above her smoothly, so there was no loss of contact. Then he added his own movements to the movement of the vehicle, thrusting with gathering tempo, until she was no longer aware of her body as an entity apart from the motion beneath her and within her.

She sank into extinction, sank through layers of delight, drifting down, a cloud speck in the wide blue horizon, until she lay lapped in peace upon the luxuriant verdant carpet of release. Adam looked down at her closed eyes, the sable lashes dark half-moons on the delicately flushed cheeks. She was limp in his hold, but as he moved to withdraw from her, her arms tightened around him in protest.

"How fortunate the movement of a sleigh does not have the same effect upon you as that of a carriage," he observed with a lazy grin. "One day we must try making love across a galloping horse." He was quite unable to help a chuckle, despite his own fulfilled lassitude. "If the simple motion of a sleigh can assist one to such heaven, think what—"

A yell from Boris, the violent cracking of a whip, the sudden surge forward of the sleigh brought an end to this interesting speculation.

"Hell and the devil!" Adam pulled away from her, grabbing his britches, yanking them up his body. He flung open the door of the sleigh, leaning out precariously, despite the rollicking speed of the cumbersome vehicle. Across the white plain, galloping toward the sleigh on fast mountain horses, came a group of riders.

"Can't outrun them!" Boris shouted, cracking the whip again. "I'll try to make for those trees."

"Is it brigands?" Sophie, fumbling desperately with her undergarment, which was hopelessly tangled in the folds of satin, cambric, and fur, gasped out the question, her face pink with her exertions. "Holy Mother! What an invitation to rape I must present."

Adam stared at her in amazement. "If we can't beat them off, that's exactly what will happen, before they trample us to death," he said vigorously.

Sophie looked up. "They're only brigands. Of course we'll beat them off. Do you have a pistol for me?"

This was the woman who shot rabid wolves, Adam remembered with a jolt. Chivalrous concerns were out of place. "Here." He handed her a flintlock pistol. "If we can reach the shelter of the woods before they come up with us, we might stand a chance. Can you prime that?"

The look she gave him told him he shouldn't have asked the question. "Ammunition and the other pistols are in that pack. Get them organized so we may reload swiftly." On that crisp instruction, he left her in the sleigh, swinging himself out and up onto the second horse. Their pursuers were gaining, but the woods were a great deal closer.

"We've plenty of ammunition. Sophia Alexeyevna is preparing it," he told Boris briefly. "There are three of us and four of them. Reasonable odds."

Boris grunted his assent, expertly swinging the sleigh into the cover of the first line of trees. As the conveyance slowed, Sophie sprang down, running to the rear.

"Sophie, what the devil are you doing?" bellowed Adam.

"Releasing Khan," she yelled. "They'll do anything to get their hands on him."

"That goddamned horse!" exploded Adam. "Does she never think of anything else?"

Boris chuckled. "Not often, Count. Although I've noticed her attention's been a bit divided just recently."

Adam shook his head in wonderment. What sort of people were these products of the Wild Lands? Neither the muzhik nor the woman exhibited the slightest fear. Instead, they made jokes. Sophie had swung herself onto the stallion's back. "The ammunition and pistols are laid ready for you on the bench." Then, before he could absorb the implication of her words, she had galloped into the trees.

"Best get inside, Count." Boris released the horses from the traces.

"Sophie—"

"She'll be all right—"

A pistol shot cracking almost in range brought an end to

further discussion. The two men dived into the sleigh, where
four pistols lay ready for them and ammunition was organized for easy reloading. Two pistols were missing. What was
she intending to do with them? But at least she was out of
immediate danger. If her need to save her horse meant she
had saved herself, then he was not going to complain. On
that comforting thought Adam settled into the corner of the
sleigh, pistol cocked, and aimed through the crack of the
door. Boris took up a similar position on the other side.

The brigands, riding low over their horses, made elusive
targets as they charged ferociously at the sleigh. Adam's first
shot whistled past harmlessly as its intended recipient swung
beneath the belly of his horse. Instead of being three to four,
Sophie's defection left them two to four, and one of them was
obliged to reload.

Then a shot rang out; one of the brigands clutched his
shoulder, falling forward over the neck of his mount. Adam,
on the point of squeezing the trigger, looked in disbelief at
Boris. The muzhik was stolidly reloading. "Someone out
there is on our side," Adam said slowly, turning back to the
aperture and taking aim.

"Sophia Alexeyevna," Boris confirmed calmly.

The unexpectedness of their comrade's injury from a shot
that seemed to come from nowhere had thrown the other
three brigands into some confusion. Adam's next shot fell
true, and there were now only two men upright outside.

"We'd best get them all," Adam said grimly. "We can't
afford to leave even one able-bodied."

A shot smacked against the mica window, shattering it,
before burying itself in the floor of the sleigh. "Too close!"
muttered Boris. Then suddenly a wild Cossack yell rang out,
and Khan leaped into the clearing. Both attackers swung
around to face this apparition. Boris's pistol blazed, and one
man toppled to the ground. The other dragged a wicked curving blade from his belt and slashed at the rearing Khan.

Adam aimed but was unable to shoot for fear of hitting
Sophie. His heart in his throat, he watched as the stallion
sidestepped out of the line of fire with extraordinary delicacy

for such a mighty beast. The blade sliced again through the air. Adam fired in the same instant, and the brigand slipped sideways to crumple on the ground.

Clutching her arm, Sophie sat astride Khan, looking down in some disbelief at the blood welling between her fingers. "How did that happen?" she asked in a dazed tone, as Adam pounded up to her.

"Jesus, Mary, and Joseph! Of all the foolhardy . . . ! What did you think you were doing?"

"Creating a diversion," Sophie said in a faint voice. "It worked, did it not?"

"Oh, yes, it worked—"

"Watch her, Count!" Boris Mikhailov interrupted him sharply. "Can't stand the sight of blood. Never could."

"What!" Adam was momentarily speechless, staring up at Sophie, who, without warning, swayed and slumped sideways, tumbling inert from Khan's back.

Adam managed to catch her, then stood looking down at the unconscious figure in his arms. She swooned at the sight of blood, became hideously sick in a closed wheeled carriage, rode like a Cossack, shot with the accuracy of a skilled sniper, withstood the full force of Paul Dmitriev's tortuous, devious plotting to break her . . . Oh, it was unfathomable.

He carried her back to the sleigh; the sable eyelashes fluttered and her eyes opened as he laid her down on the bench. "I do beg your pardon," Sophie said. "I have the strangest weaknesses." She turned her head away as he pushed up the sleeve of the pelisse. "It isn't even as if it were dreadfully painful."

"It is only a flesh wound," he said after a silent, thorough examination. "You may count yourself lucky. Boris, pass me the bandages and the salve, please?"

"I would never make a soldier." Sophie attempted to joke as Adam began to bind up the wound with the medical supplies he had ensured would form part of the provisioning for the journey.

"I would just like to have you under my command for a

week," he declared furiously. "I would teach you a few things about soldiering that you would never forget."

"You are angry," Sophie said in surprise. "Why ever should you be so? I was simply playing my part."

"When I command a military operation," Adam said with studied calm, "I do not tolerate independent flights. In particular those that are not communicated to me beforehand."

The color had returned to Sophie's cheeks. "I do beg your pardon," she said in dulcet tones. "But I had not realized we were engaged in a military operation, or that you were in command. I had thought we were all fighting off brigands. You must make these things clearer in future."

There was a moment's stunned silence. Then Adam began to laugh in rich enjoyment, exclaiming as he had once before, "Oh, Sophia Alexeyevna, what *am* I going to do with you?"

The dark eyes glowed up at him. "Oh, come now, Colonel, Count Danilevski, you do not in general suffer from a failure of imagination."

Chapter 12

It was an icy gray afternoon at the end of December when the reed-thatched roofs of the village of Berkholzskoye appeared across the frozen steppe.

Sophie, who had been glued to the window since they left Kiev, jumped as if the sight were unexpected. Tears filled her eyes, and she kept her gaze averted from Adam in sudden embarrassment at this unstoppable flood of emotion.

Adam was not deceived. Reaching over, he took her jaw between long fingers, turning her face toward him. Tears made tracks down her cheeks, and she sniffed pathetically. "I did not think I would ever see Berkholzskoye again."

He smudged a tear with the flat of his thumb. "You do not want to show such a wan countenance to your grandfather, sweet."

"If he is still alive." Finally, she was able to voice the fear that had haunted her for weeks. "I cannot understand why he never wrote—"

"The fact that you did not receive any letters did not mean that he did not write them," Adam said quietly, watching her face.

For a moment she looked blank, then understanding dawned. Tears dried instantly, in their place the fierce anger that he knew well and now welcomed. "Paul kept them from me. That is what you mean, is it not?"

He nodded. "I do not know it for a fact, but it does not seem unlikely."

"I wish I had been able to kill him!" She flung herself

against the back of the bench with a furious thump. "I would not mind my own death if it brought about his!"

"There are times when you do talk the most extravagant nonsense, Sophia Alexeyevna," Adam observed coolly. He was rewarded by an indignant flash from the dark eyes, then a reluctant gleam of humor.

"And when I do I can always be certain you will pull me up," she said, chuckling, turning back to the window in growing impatience. "Oh, I wish I could ride Khan. We would be home in twenty minutes. This is so slow!" She was clenching and unclenching her hands, twisting them in impossible knots, her feet drumming unmelodiously upon the floor.

Sitting back in the corner, Adam smilingly watched her through half-closed eyes. A two-day halt in Novgorod, the first sizable city after leaving St. Petersburg, had provided her with clothes and other basic necessities, so that, despite the privations of the journey, she no longer had the appearance of a homeless gypsy. But they were all dirty, fatigued with travel, and had almost forgotten what it was like to be properly warm or how it would feel to be without the furs they had worn day and night for a month, to have a bath, to sleep in a proper bed in a warm room, with no need for anything more than a nightshirt. . . . It was a heady prospect. His lips curved in pleasurable anticipation. An entire night of privacy with Sophia Alexeyevna in his arms, naked . . .

The image of Prince Golitskov rose before him. Just what was the irascible old man going to make of this tangle?

"You may leave the explanations to me." Sophie spoke softly, and he realized that at some point in his reverie she had diverted her attention to him.

"How did you know what I was thinking?"

"It was not difficult." She smiled. "*Grandpère* will make no difficulties for us. It is not in his nature."

"I must go to Mogilev," he said slowly. "The empress gave me leave to visit my family. There would be no satisfactory explanation for my failure to do so."

"But not for a while," Sophie said. "There will be no couriers between here and the capital until the spring. Paul will not know of my survival until then, and the empress will not look for you in St. Petersburg before March."

It was quite possible, Adam thought with a seeping joy. In snowbound exile, locked in love, they could, for a short, yet infinitely precious time, share lives, keeping a secret that need never leave the boundaries of Berkholzskoye, and building the memories that would inform and enrich all that came later for both of them. He smiled. "You are right. We will take a few weeks to ourselves."

"An idyll in the Wild Lands." Her eyes sparkled. "Berkholzskoye is a magical place in winter. I will show you all its magic, Adam."

"Embodied in you, my Sophie, there is enough magic for one man's lifetime," he said softly.

A delicate pink touched her cheekbones. "What a lovely thing to say to someone."

"It is but the truth."

The moment hung between them, intense and promise-filled. They had been given a gift; if the gift should prove only to have been a loan, then they would make good use of it for as long as they had it.

The sleigh swished down the long, poplar-lined avenue to the circular sweep in front of the house. Sophie, with impetuous lack of caution, flung herself from the vehicle while it was still moving, catching the hem of her gown on a loose splinter of wood in the door.

"Damnation!" She yanked roughly at the material, rending it heedlessly, before running to the closed front door. The whole house seemed sealed and shuttered on this gray afternoon; an air of desolation hung in the blind windows. She banged with the great brass knocker without pause until Adam came up behind her.

"For pity's sake, Sophie! You will wake the dead." He laid a hand over hers, stilling it. "Give them a chance to answer."

"But suppose they do not." She looked up at him, her

face deathly pale beneath the dark crown of her hair. "I do not think there is anyone here." She raised the knocker again.

"Don't be foolish." He grasped her hand, holding it prisoner within his own. "Give them a chance."

The steady gaze, the firm voice, the calm good sense served to ground her. She took a deep breath, and the sound of bolts rasped in the stillness. Sophie whirled back to the door, her hand still gripped in Adam's.

"What ever is it?" The door swung open. Anna, pale and anxious, her rheumy eyes gazing fearfully, stood in the doorway. When she saw who it was, she grasped the door frame with one hand, crossing herself automatically with the other. "Oh, my goodness me. Is it you, Sophia Alexeyevna? Is it you? Oh my goodness, my heart!" She flapped her hand in front of her face.

"No ghost from the Wild Lands, Anna," Sophie said, her own equilibrium restored under Anna's disarray. She hugged the woman fiercely. "See, I am flesh and blood." She stepped past the housekeeper into the familiar square hall, warmed by a porcelain stove and a great fire in the stone hearth. "Where is *Grandpère*?"

"In his library," Anna fluttered. "Oh, Boris Mikhailov. Is it you?" She held out her hand to the muzhik who came swiftly toward her. "After Tanya Feodorovna told us—"

"Tanya!" Sophie swung around to face the old woman. "Tanya! Here?"

"Yes, bless you, Princess. Been here a month and more. Walked, she did, all the way from Kaluga. The stories she told. The prince hasn't been the same since."

But Sophie was off, running down the corridor to the rear of the house. *"Grandpère!"* Flinging open the library door, she catapulted into the firelit, lamplit, book-lined room.

Prince Golitskov started up from his chair by the fire, the calfbound book upon his lap falling to the floor. "Sophie!" Like Anna, he stared as if at a spectre from the steppes.

Adam, with a muttered exclamation, pushed past Sophie. He had not been able to prevent her impetuous rush, although the dangers of shocking the old man in this way had been at the forefront of his mind. "It is Sophia Alexeyevna, Prince," he affirmed rapidly, crossing the room in three long strides. "Safe and well. Sit down again." Gently, he eased the trembling, suddenly frail figure back into his chair.

"Oh, *Grandpère*, I did not mean to frighten you." Sophie ran across the room, dropping to her knees in front of him, looking anxiously up at him. She took his hands, chafing them. "Oh, you are so cold. Is it because I shocked you?"

The old prince took a deep, shuddering breath, then sat back in his chair. "Let me look at you, *petite*. I was coming to St. Petersburg myself, once the snows melted." He touched her hair wonderingly. "You did not answer my letters—"

"I did not receive them," she broke in swiftly. "And after he sent Tanya Feodorovna away . . . Oh, is she really here?"

"Yes, she is here." Anger burned in the faded eyes, and some of the fragility seemed to leave him. "An amazing journey she made. But she comes of determined stock. She came back to tell me of your . . ." A shadow passed across his face. "Of your husband. You have left him?"

Sophie lifted his hand, rubbing the knuckles across her cheek. "It is a little more complicated than that." She looked up at Adam, who still stood quietly beside the fire, watching the reunion.

Golitskov turned to look at him also. "So," he said, a smile enlivening the sunken countenance. "Having taken her away, you decided to return her, Count."

"You could say that." Adam smiled back. "It has been an arduous journey, and I know Sophie will wish to tell you of it herself. I will leave you." He bowed to the prince, then, very deliberately, bent to kiss the corner of Sophie's mouth. "I shall see if I can charm a bath out of your housekeeper." His eyebrows quirked. "You could do with one yourself."

The door closed quietly on his departure. "So that's the way the land lies," murmured the old prince, stroking his chin.

"Yes, *Grandpère*, that is the way the land lies," Sophie confirmed. "Without Adam I would have died . . . died in spirit many months ago, and in body but a short while since."

She stood up to unbutton her pelisse, not needed in this warm room, then began to tell her tale, leaving nothing out from the moment of her first meeting with Paul Dmitriev.

At story's end, there was silence in the room, save for the hiss and crackle of the fire, the sudden rattling of the casement under the wind blasting off the steppe. Then the prince spoke. "So, Sophia Alexeyevna, what do you intend doing now?"

Sophie looked into the fire. It was right that her grandfather had not assumed charge of the matter, had asked her what plans she had made, instead of describing his own. She was her own woman, and her problems belonged only to her . . . and to Adam, she amended. "I had thought no further than reaching here," she now said. "My husband will assume that I am dead. I must decide whether to leave him in that assumption or inform him of the truth."

"He will discover it for himself soon enough, Sophie. We may live in relative isolation, but it is not complete. When the snows melt, travelers will come and go in usual fashion."

She nodded. "But there is no need to concern ourselves until February. We may stay here with our secret until then." Her eyes met her grandfather's. He knew to what secret she was referring, and he knew she was asking permission, for all that there had been no question mark in her voice.

"I stand much in Adam Danilevski's debt," he said. "I do not know how much wisdom there is in your indulging yourselves with a happiness that can only be ephemeral. But that is a decision you must make for yourselves."

"Should one not grasp happiness when it is offered?" she asked, taking his hand, playing with the gnarled fingers with great concentration. "I have learned since I left here that there is little enough of it, and a great deal of its reverse."

"You and Adam are welcome to live here as man and wife for as long as you choose." The old prince touched her face. "I wondered if I would ever see you again."

"And I you." Her eyes were misty as she kissed his hand. "Boris Mikhailov will be anxious to see you. Shall I send him to you?"

"No, I think I will find him myself." Golitskov pulled himself out of his chair. "Where is my stick? No . . . no, I do not think I have need of it." He pushed the heavy staff away. "I find that I am not as old as I have been feeling lately." He walked to the door with no more than his customary stiffness. "Go you to Tanya Feodorovna, *ma petite*. The count is quite right. You are in sore need of a bath." He chuckled. "Your father and Sophia Ivanova always occupied the apartments in the west wing when they were at Berkholzskoye. They seemed to find them quite satisfactory. I am sure you will also."

Sophie stood in the library for a minute after her grandfather had left, absorbing the familiarity of home; a surge of elation, the most wonderful lightness of heart suffused her. She was back where she belonged, once more in charge of her life with the gates of heaven standing open before her.

She danced from the library, running for the stairs, calling for Tanya Feodorovna at the top of her voice.

"Goodness me, Sophia Alexeyevna, just look at you. What a sight!" Tanya bustled out of Sophie's bedchamber at the insistent repetition of her name. Her face was wreathed in smiles and tears were in her eyes as she hugged the tall figure of her erstwhile nursling. "Gracious, but how thin you have grown!"

"Oh, do not scold, Tanya." Sophie kissed her, laughing and crying together. "I must have a bath, and you and Anna must prepare the apartments in the west wing. I am not going to sleep in my old room."

"Ah . . ." Tanya nodded sagely. "Well, Anna has put the count in the blue room."

"Oh, then I will go and see him. Will you have his things moved as soon as may be?" She pranced down the corridor, throwing open a door onto a blue-painted bedchamber. Adam lay in a large porcelain hip bath in front of a roaring fire. He turned his head as she came in, regarding his energetic visitor with sleepy lethargy and a degree of trepidation. "Do not be unrestful, Sophie. I have not enjoyed myself so much in a very long time."

Sophie pouted in mock annoyance. "That is not at all flattering." Dropping to her knees beside the bath, she kissed him. "I think we had some most enjoyable times." Her hand, wickedly knowing, slipped beneath the water. "You *are* sleepy, aren't you?" she said with a frown. "Ah . . . now that is much better."

"You are less than sweet-smelling, Sophia Alexeyevna!" His hands went around her waist, and before she could guess his intention, he had pulled her down on top of him. "There'll be no games until you are clean and fresh."

Sophie spluttered wetly, pushing against his chest in an effort to right herself. "Look what you have done! I am all wet in front." She squeezed out her skirt in feigned indignation.

"It's a start," he declared, heaving himself, naked and dripping, out of the tub. "Tanya Feodorovna has a bath waiting for you in your own chamber. Why do you not go and put yourself in it?"

Sophie regarded him speculatively. "Shall I dry you?" She stretched out her hand for the towel, but Adam snatched it from her grasp.

"No games!" He hastily rubbed himself down under Sophie's mischievous, desirous stare, the tip of her tongue trailing lazily over her lips. He shrugged into his dressing gown, tying the girdle securely before stepping toward her with clear purpose.

Sophie took a step backward. "Adam . . . Adam, no!" Squealing, she found herself slung unceremoniously over one broad shoulder.

"It's bathtime." Adam strode with his noisy, struggling burden back to Sophie's bedchamber, where a clucking Tanya waited.

"Goodness gracious, lord. Just put her down there."

"Traitor, Tanya!" accused Sophie, set on her feet.

Downstairs, Prince Golitskov smiled to himself as the old house came to life again under Sophie's ringing accents and bubbling laughter. There was a different tone to that laughter, but he could find nothing amiss with it. When a woman was touched with love, it tended to be heard. On this sage reflection, he went down to his cellar in search of a celebratory bottle or two.

On returning to the library, he found Count Danilevski, most elegant in a dark green coat and dove gray britches, the elaborate folds of a starched cravat at his neck.

"Some transformation, Count," observed the prince, going to the sideboard to pour vodka.

"Yes, thanks to Anna's skills," replied the count, taking the proffered glass. "She managed to achieve miracles with the contents of my cloak-bag."

"I trust Sophie will undergo a similar transformation." Golitskov raised his glass in salute.

Adam chuckled, returning the salute. "I left her in the competent hands of Tanya Feodorovna, who was threatening any number of dire consequences if Sophia Alexeyevna did not stop behaving like an overexcited child on her name day."

The prince smiled, a little absently, Adam thought. Then he said, "Tell me of this Dmitriev, Adam. Sophie cannot be objective, understandably enough."

"I am not sure that I can, either," Adam said candidly. "But I have known him for many years. I will tell you what I can."

When he had finished his description, Golitskov said nothing for a minute. He poked the fire, staring into the surging flames. "In your opinion, how will he react to Sophie's safe arrival here?"

Adam frowned. "Dmitriev does not care for his plans to go awry. It is always possible he will repudiate her as his wife and be satisfied with leaving her here in disgrace. But . . ."

Golitskov waited. "But he knows that far from hurting Sophie, such action would afford her the greatest pleasure," Adam finished. "For that reason, I do not think he will take that course."

"She must not . . . Oh, Sophie, there you are, *chère*." Smoothly, the prince broke off at his granddaughter's entrance. "Hardly the first style of elegance, but an infinite improvement," he teased, taking in her white blouse and simple skirt and bodice of amber corduroy.

"They were about the only clothes I could find," Sophie said ruefully. "I brought nothing with me but the two gowns Adam purchased for me in Novgorod, and they have seen better days." She laughed. "I would be glad if you would have an accounting with Adam, *Grandpère*. He disbursed all the charges of the journey and would not permit me to sell the aquamarines to cover my own expenses."

"I will excuse such a nonsensical statement on the grounds of overexcitement," Adam said bluntly. "The matter is not to be referred to again."

"But, Adam, I cannot possibly allow you to—"

"Now, you just listen to me, Sophia Alexeyevna! For the last four weeks you have fought brigands, ridden through blizzards, taken exactly what action suited you at any time, however reckless and unnecessary, and I have barely remonstrated with you. I know you do not tolerate another hand on your bridle, but in this instance you will curb your tongue and respect *my* wishes."

Sophie gulped and began busily smoothing down her apron. Adam had not spoken to her in that tone before, but it was abundantly clear that even if she persisted he would not back down. The ensuing unpleasantness would hardly be consonant with a magical idyll. "I'll just go and see how Anna is managing with supper," she said, beating a prudent and orderly retreat.

"I congratulate you, my dear Count." Golitskov smiled dryly. "I will not echo Sophie's error, but I will express my gratitude."

"Could we have an end to this now, Prince?" There was a note of impatience in his voice. "If I have done anything to merit gratitude, I am amply recompensed by your hospitality."

The old prince bowed and deftly returned to the subject interrupted by Sophie's appearance. "As I was saying, Sophie must not under any circumstances return to her husband.

If he makes such a demand, then I shall send her out of Russia. We have relatives in France; she will be beyond his jurisdiction there.''

"Let us pray it does not come to such a drastic move, Prince." Adam went to the French doors, where he stared somberly out into the night. To be deprived of the right to offer her his own protection ate into him like a snail on a cabbage leaf, yet he had no rights, none whatsoever. He was merely the lover, a parasite of love, living off the host . . .

"Supper is ready." Sophie's voice came cheerfully from the doorway. "There is duck! Just imagine, Adam, duck!"

"I am not sure I can." Resolutely, he put the dark moment from him and turned back to the room. "My palate has been so battered in the last weeks that I doubt it retains the ability to respond to refinement."

"Anna's duck is the ultimate in refinement," Sophie told him earnestly, linking arms with him as they went into the dining room. "It will heal the most maltreated palate." She sat down, shaking out her napkin. "Linen! Amazing!" Her eyes danced across the table at him. "After supper, we will go and skate in the Devil's Punch Bowl."

"We will *what*?" Adam was betrayed into something resembling a yelp.

"Skate," she said in wide-eyed innocence. "You can skate, surely?"

"Yes, of course I can."

"Then I shall show you my favorite place. It is at its best at night, and tonight is full of stars."

"Not tonight, Sophie," Adam said, slicing into his duck.

"But I want—"

"Not tonight, Sophie," he repeated in the same level tone.

Prince Golitskov's shoulders began to shake. Sophie, with her boundless enthusiasm and restless vigor, had always had a passion for sharing her treasures, and very little tolerance for delay in the imparting of these delights.

"But there might not be such a perfect night again for days." Frowning, she sipped her wine. "I said I would show you all the magical places at Berkholzskoye."

"And I said something about magic also," he responded as evenly as before. "Do you not recall?"

Sophie did. That delicate blush that Adam loved crept over the smooth, pale complexion. "If you are fatigued, I daresay it would be better not to skate tonight," she murmured, burying her nose in her goblet.

"Traveling is a somewhat fatiguing business," Adam agreed placidly, catching the old prince's eye. Golitskov was clearly deriving huge enjoyment from the exchange.

Looking up, Sophie intercepted the glance. Her flush deepened, but she only reached for the big bowl of caviar standing in the middle of the table, spooning a generous portion onto her plate. "Adam, will you have some? It is very fine caviar." She passed him the bowl.

They did not linger long in the library after supper. Sophie, her former ebullience somewhat subdued by the checks it had received, made no demur when, her grandfather announcing that he was going to seek his rest, Adam rose too, reaching down his hand to draw her to her feet. His eyes smiled at her with a mixture of amusement and pretended reproof as he slipped his arm around her waist and escorted her up the stairs to the west wing.

"I cannot help feeling, Sophia Alexeyevna, that you need to get your priorities straight," he said, once the door of the large bedchamber, its walls decorated with painted frescoes, was closed behind them. "Skating! In heaven's name! We have a feather bed in a warm chamber, complete privacy, clean skin, no journeying to do on the morrow, and the woman wants to go skating!" He flung his hands up in affected exasperation.

"It was just so exciting to be home," Sophie mumbled. "And I do so want you to love all the things I love." The dark eyes lifted to his face. "But I do see that it was perhaps a little premature."

"Just a little," he agreed, drawing her into his embrace, burying his face in the rich shining hair, the chestnut highlights glinting in the candlelight. "How often I have dreamed of being able to do this," he whispered. "The scent of you used to drive me to the edge of distraction, spring flowers and lavender.''

''Not recently,'' she corrected with a little chuckle, lifting her arms to encircle his neck. ''Kiss me.''

There was silence in the room. The candle flickered in a draft from the window. The wood in the blue-tiled porcelain stove in the wall blazed merrily. ''Love me,'' Sophie whispered, drawing back from him for the barest instant. ''Love me now, Adam.''

Within a week, Sophie's complexion had regained the healthy glow of an outdoor life, and soon her bones began to be a little better covered under the combined influences of an appetite sharpened by exercise and Anna's cooking. She swung through the house with her long stride, carrying the freshness of the steppes with her as she took over the household reins again. Her garden was buried under snow, but she took Adam through it nevertheless, telling him what would be coming up with the first spring thaw.

Such enthusiasm she had, he thought. She threw her heart into whatever interested her, be it the settling of some domestic dispute, an ailing serf on the estate, the choice of paint color for one of the parlors, a litter of puppies, the chess board, or a card game.

To his enormous amusement, Adam had discovered that Sophie was an inveterate cheat when it came to cards. It was such a wonderful paradox that this utterly straightforward individual should stoop to sly little tricks, none of which deceived him for a minute.

''I won again!'' she announced one evening after supper, laying her cards upon the table. ''See, I have an ace.'' She gleefully rubbed her hands together. ''You owe me a fortune, Adam.''

''I owe you nothing,'' he said. ''Do you really think I didn't see you slip that ace onto your lap when you were dealing?''

''I did not!'' she protested, but a telltale pink showed against her cheekbones.

"You are no better at lying than you are at cheating," Adam declared. "Which is why I do not take the reprisals to which simple justice entitles me."

"I'll never make a cardsharp," Sophie said wistfully. "I have often thought what fun it would be to play in the great gambling houses, winning fortunes by tricks."

"You shameless creature!" Adam reached for her hands, pulling her around the table onto his lap. "What a disgraceful ambition."

"Yes, isn't it?" She laughed down at him. "But we are all entitled to our sins." With a burst of vitality, she sprang from his knee. "Let us go and skate at the Devil's Punch Bowl. The stars are wonderful tonight."

Adam looked longingly at the blazing fire, the ruby wine in his glass. "It is so cold, Sophie."

"Oh, but you promised you would come one day." She took his hands, tugging imperatively. "I swear to you it will be worth the cold. You have never seen anything so beautiful . . . never done anything so beautiful. Is it not so, *Grand-père*?"

Prince Golitskov looked up from his book. "I sympathize with you, Adam, but Sophie is right. If you have any feeling for the steppes, then the Devil's Punch Bowl on such a night can only bewitch."

"Then let us go." Adam stood up, stretched lazily. "I know when I am defeated, but you are a shameless bully, Sophia Alexeyevna."

"But I only wish to give you pleasure," she replied in simple truth. "Sometimes one must be led along the paths of pleasure." That crooked smile quirked, and his heart turned over with the power of his love.

"Oh, Sophie" was all he could say.

Outside, where the air was so sharp and dry it seemed it could be shattered like crystal, they took one of the open sleighs, drawn by a high-stepping, powerful-chested gelding. Sophie tossed the curving metal blades that they would strap to their shoes on top of the lynx fur rug. Beside them went two pistols. "Wolves," she explained, as if Adam were in need of explanation. Climbing swiftly into the sleigh, she settled the rug over them and took the reins.

Adam sat back, content to leave this expedition in Sophie's charge. The Nordic sky, black, with the depth and softness of velvet, tactile almost, provided the background for a profusion of stars, each one a separate entity, clear, defined, pouring light upon this glistening whiteness over which they traveled. The night sounds of the steppes were in the air, but they were intrinsic to the scene and could not be separated into their component parts. He turned his head sideways to look at Sophie, her profile etched against the horizon where white met silver and black. She had the air of complete absorption she wore when in her own element, at one with her surroundings.

"What do you see?" she asked into the night, without turning her head.

She was obviously not as absorbed as he had thought. Adam smiled. "You. In your own world."

"Yes, it is mine," Sophie said, quietly matter-of-fact. "I do not think I could bear to leave it again."

And if you have to? But he did not say it; instead, he sat back again and wrestled with the demons of frustration and helplessness. How to reconcile this bone-deep love and its need to protect with the knowledge that in all essentials he was powerless. He could not take her to Mogilev. His family estates were now under Russian hegemony and a declared adulteress could be removed by her husband with the full force of law—moral, religious, and legal. He could not go into exile with her. To do so, he would have to desert from the Russian army, abandon his family and estates, renege upon every duty and responsibility entrenched since he could first stand. He would have to become a different person to do such a thing; and that different person, sullied by betrayal and deceit, could not love and be loved by this bold, brave, honest Cossack woman.

"Here we are." Sophie drew rein. "You have been having sad thoughts, but you must not have them here." She placed her gloved hand over his, her eyes seeking the truth as they raked his face. "For now you must lose yourself in the wonder, Adam. It is not in the nature of idylls that they should last. But they spoil, crumble, if put to reality's test. We have what we have, and it must be sufficient unto the moment." Her eyes held his until she read his acceptance, and he nodded, touching her lip with a caressing fingertip.

Sophie stepped from the sleigh, tethering the horse to a scrawny, bare thorn tree. Adam picked up the skates; she took his hand. "Come. Close your eyes." When he did so in laughing obedience, she led him across the snow, then stopped. "Now you may look."

Adam opened his eyes. He was standing on the brink of a deep basin, snow-covered sides rising steeply from the glistening floor of ice. There was not a mark to scar the smooth virginity of it. It was as if they had stumbled upon a place never before penetrated by the crassness of mankind. For a moment he hesitated, stunned by the beauty, afraid to think of despoiling it. Then he knew he had to become a part of it. "How do we get down?"

Sophie patted his bottom. "Simple."

"How do we get up?"

"Not so simple. Come on." Sitting on the edge, tucking her skirts tightly around her legs, she launched herself, squealing with a mixture of fright and exhilaration, down the slope.

Adam sat down, raised his eyes heavenward, offered a quick prayer, and pushed off, holding the skates on his knees. The snow was so dry it barely clung as he tobogganed, with his body as sleigh, after Sophie. He heard his own involuntary cry, echoing, bell-like, around the basin as his speed increased, the air rushed past him, and he was engulfed in a terrified exultation. The slope ended, but his momentum carried him onto the ice until he came to a gentle stop somewhere in the middle, beside Sophie, who was still sitting upon the ice, gazing about her in wonder.

"Look up," she said, softly insistent, as he slid to a halt.

He did so. They were encapsulated in a bowl of white, lidded with velvet black and silver starshine. There was not a sound. The life of the steppes continued above them, outside their bowl.

"They call it the Devil's Punch Bowl, but I think it has too much of heaven for that," Sophie said. "Perhaps it is to remind Lucifer of the time before he became the fallen angel." She took her skates from his lap. "I told you it was magic."

"Or is it God-given?" He strapped the blades to his boots.

Sophie shrugged easily. "There is enough mystery in the Russian Church to allow for both." She stood up on her skates, drawing in a deep breath of the pure air cutting clean as a knife through her chest. Pushing off with an apparently gentle, gliding movement, she slid away from him. But the power behind the push became clear as he watched her travel on a one-foot glide way to the other side of the lake. He watched, spellbound, as she curved around in a long slow arc, resting on the outside edge of the blade, changing to the inside, carving an elaborate design on the clean surface. She beckoned to him, and he skated across in the silence.

"See if you can make your initials twine with mine." she said, her voice muted as if in deference to the peace.

He looked down at the *S* and *A* inscribed on the ice, frowning with concentration. Then he nodded, seeing how it could be done. The design flowered beneath his whispering blades until he stood to one side, examining his handiwork.

Sophie slipped her arm into his. "See, we have a coat of arms."

"Until the snows melt," he said.

Chapter 13

"I have it in mind to invite Princess Dmitrievna to accompany us on this state visit to the Crimea, Grisha." The czarina finished the line she was penning as she said this. She looked up affectionately at her roaring, one-eyed lion. "You have gone to such pains to ensure that the journey will be an unqualified success, providing pleasure for all. I think it is time the princess enjoyed herself a little. I will appoint her lady-in-waiting."

"A position which will keep her more in your company than in her husband's," observed Prince Potemkin from the couch where he was lounging, nibbling on a dish of salt fish.

"If some estrangement still exists between them after her visit to her grandfather, then this will give them breathing space in which to heal the breach," said Catherine blithely. "It was wise of the general, I think, to send her to Berkholzskoye after that little . . . misunderstanding. But clearly the separation cannot continue; it would imply that Dmitriev has repudiated his wife."

Potemkin regarded his empress thoughtfully. "Are you certain he has not?"

"Why ever should he have done so? Sophia Alexeyevna was guilty only of a little, very natural, dismay at certain . . . certain aspects of marriage."

Potemkin shrugged, lethargically putting his large, heavy body into motion. He stood up. "For which you took the husband to task."

205

"Would you have advised against such a thing, Grisha?" Catherine looked surprised.

"Had I been asked, Madame, yes," responded the prince, with the petulant flash of annoyance that the czarina knew well. Potemkin, in addition to being her most trusted and dearest friend, was her adviser in all matters, including who should be selected to occupy the favorite's apartments. Since Potemkin had first entered the czarina's bed, Russia had had two rulers, and although the fire of carnal passion had died down between them years ago, he continued to govern, albeit unofficially, at her side, and he could become extremely piqued if he considered his opinion had been slighted.

"I did not think the matter of sufficient importance to trouble you with," the empress said placatingly, even as she thought with a quirk of irritation that this sublime politician could behave like a ten-year-old sometimes. It was an oft-recurring thought, but when one was in the presence of genius, and particularly temperamental Slavic genius, one was obliged to accept minor exasperations.

"I am more familiar with General Dmitriev than you, Madame," Potemkin replied with haughty dignity.

"I should have asked your advice." Catherine smiled winningly. "Do not be cross with me, Grisha, and tell me whether you approve of my plan to take Sophia Alexeyevna to the Crimea."

Potemkin smiled, his mood changing with customary abruptness. "Yes, as it happens, I do think it a good idea. Such an educational journey in the close company of such dignitaries as Prince de Ligne, diplomats such as Comte de Ségur, can only have a beneficial influence. She is an unusual and intelligent young woman. If her husband does not appreciate her, there is no reason why others should not."

"Yourself, for instance?" asked the empress with a wicked gleam.

Potemkin laughed with sudden sensual mischief. "I will admit that my thoughts have strayed in that direction. It may well be that an intelligent and experienced lover will complete her education."

"It would certainly appear her husband does not come into that category," mused the czarina. "Yet Dmitriev is no fool, and he has had enough experience in such matters, one would have thought, to know to treat a virgin with a little gentleness and consideration."

"Paul Dmitriev does not have a gentle, considerate bone in his body, Madame," Potemkin informed her with an arid smile. "But he is no different in that regard from the majority of husbands. Gentle consideration is the province of lovers."

Catherine's gaze rested softly on the door to the favorite's apartments, and she smiled. "Yes, how right you are, Grisha." Then she became all briskness. "Well, I shall put this matter in train by telling General Dmitriev of my intention. When we reach Kiev, I will send a messenger to Berkholzskoye, bidding the princess join our suite. You still intend to leave in the morning?"

Potemkin bowed low. "If I am to ensure that only perfection awaits my sovereign on such a magnificent venture, I must leave within the hour."

General, Prince Paul Dmitriev listened to his sovereign's flattering intention to appoint his wife lady-in-waiting for the state visit to the Crimea.

"You do my name great honor, Your Majesty," he said with his thin smile. "Princess Dmitrievna will be overjoyed."

"You will be accompanying Prince Potemkin, I understand," the empress said. "It will be an opportunity for you to become reacquainted with your wife." She smiled benevolently. "In a holiday atmosphere, my dear Prince, I am sure your differences will be resolved."

"I venture to believe that they have already been so," said Dmitriev smoothly. "Before Sophia Alexeyevna went on her visit to her grandfather."

"Oh, that is splendid." The empress's toothless smile widened. "It was wise of you to permit her to make a journey that I know she was most anxious to make. When we reach Kiev, where we must wait out the remainder of the winter before continuing to the Crimea, I will send for Sophia. I am looking forward to seeing her again.'' She inclined her head in graceful dismissal, and the prince left the imperial presence.

Sophia Alexeyevna would not be at Berkholzskoye to receive the imperial summons, the prince thought. She must now be a winter-bleached corpse somewhere under the infinity of snow covering the land. The czarina's messenger would be told that Princess Dmitrievna had never arrived. Since, of course, she had not been expected, news of her failure to appear would not have been transmitted to her husband, who had spent the winter in St. Petersburg, secure, it was to be assumed, in the knowledge that his wife was safe and sound in her childhood home.

It was all most satisfactory, reflected Dmitriev. He would appear the distressed widower and begin to look around him for another wife. At least he now felt purged of his rage and hatred for the Golitskovs. Revenge had brought him peace, in addition, of course, to that vast inheritance. The Golitskovs and all they owned would be subsumed under the Dmitriev name, the family ceasing to exist with the death of the old man. Yes, it was all most satisfactory.

The royal progression set out on the first stage of the journey in a style that would have amazed Sophie, in the light of her own recent travels along the same route. The sleighs resembled little houses on runners, furnished with cushioned seats, carpets, divans, and tables. Six hundred horses awaited for the change at each relay point. Servants boiled samovars in the snow during afternoon halts and moved among the sleighs with cakes and tea. Prince Potemkin, ever the superlative planner, had bonfires lit across the featureless white landscape to mark the route. There were no post houses for this party. Nightly accommodations were to be found in houses specially furnished for the occasion and prepared by the servants who preceded the imperial party to each resting place.

It still took four weeks to accomplish the distance from St.

Petersburg to Kiev, and at the beginning of February the procession entered the city to wait for the ice on the River Dnieper to melt.

The lovers at Berkholzskoye, unaware that their assumptions about winter journeyings were inaccurate, continued in their idyllic isolation. They hunted duck in the freezing dawn, took sleigh rides across the steppe, skated and tobogganed, tumbling in the snow like children. They read aloud before the fire in the evenings, played cards, at which Sophie continued her blatant cheating, and chess and backgammon, at which she could not.

Old Prince Golitskov watched his granddaughter bloom beneath love's nurturing, and his heart ached for the loss she was sure to suffer. He also saw Adam's anguish, the darkness that crossed his face sometimes when Sophie was not looking, and the old prince guessed at its cause. Adam Danilevski was an honorable man, and he was loving another man's wife. To be unable to declare his love openly, unable to stand by that love in the eyes of the world, unable to protect and shelter the object of that love, would destroy such a man eventually. Once this enclosed fairyland was breached, he would have to face these limitations and make the only decision possible. He would return to his regiment, and Sophie . . . That would depend upon her husband's next step.

The dream was broken one snowy afternoon in mid-February. Adam stretched his long legs to the fire's blaze and yawned. "It is very strange, but I have always found restfulness to be one of the most attractive qualities in a woman," he remarked plaintively. "Why I should now find myself in thrall to the most restless creature on this earth I cannot imagine."

"I am not restless," Sophie denied, pausing in her pacing. "It is just that we have not been out all day." She came over to perch on his knee, cajoling. "Come for a walk."

"There is a blizzard blowing, Sophie. Or have you not noticed?" He sat back in his deep chair, holding her hips lightly, laughing up at her. "If you wish, we could go up-stairs for a little indoor exercise."

"It is not a blizzard! Just a few snowflakes."

Adam turned to the window. A white swirling mass was all that was visible. "A few snowflakes," he mused. "Yes, of course. How foolish of me."

"Oh, don't tease! We can wrap up."

"I did just offer you an alternative."

"If you come for a walk first."

"There are some counters with which I will not bargain, Sophia Alexeyevna," he rasped, shockingly harsh. "You do not agree to make love as some kind of bribe or reward."

Sophie looked aghast. "I did not mean that."

"That is how it sounded." His voice was clipped, his face closed, his knees shifted beneath her in unmistakable rejection.

Sophie stood up, as stunned as if he had struck her. "I will go alone then."

The door shut softly. A log slipped in the fire. He recalled Eva's complaining voice, then the note of resignation as he coaxed her, then the hard edge, as, duty done, she demanded some favor. Eva's body had been her bargaining counter in every dispute. But she had given it freely to someone. . . . Or had she bought something with it even then?"

The bile of disillusion and betrayal roiled anew in his belly, made more corrosive by remorse. He had let the past touch Sophie—a woman so different from Eva they could almost belong to different species. And he had smirched her with his bitterness. He jumped to his feet, intending to go after her, but as he reached the hall Gregory was closing the front door.

"Has Sophia Alexeyevna gone out, Gregory?"

"Yes, lord," the watchman replied stolidly. "But she'll not be out long in that."

Adam was not so sure as Gregory, but he returned to the library, reasoning that by the time he had dressed himself for the weather she would have disappeared into the storm and pursuit would be futile.

Sophie, head down, battled against the snow blowing into her face, blinding her, freezing on her eyelashes. It took her no more than five minutes to realize that the impulse had been foolish, yet she kept walking, trying to dissipate against the elements her confused hurt.

Once or twice before, Adam had bitten her head off when she made some flippant remark, but usually it had to do with Dmitriev, and she could understand that, even though it hurt. But what had just happened in the library could not be laid at her husband's door. It seemed somehow part of that darkness she sensed in Adam's soul when the shadows crossed his face and he did not think she had noticed. Delicacy had kept her from probing. If he wished her to share those thoughts, he would have confided in her. That was what one did, after all. Everyone had their secrets—both good and bad. He had confessed to bad memories on one occasion in St. Petersburg, but insisted they belonged to an irrelevant past. She could not possibly pry; it was not in her nature. Yet, on this occasion, she had been in some way responsible for that painful misunderstanding. It had been just a misunderstanding, hadn't it?

Deciding that this walk was impossible, Sophie turned around to retrace her steps. The blasting snow quickly plastered her back, and the force of the gusts almost lifted her off her feet. A horseman, leaning low over the neck of his mount, materialized out of the white blanket as she neared the house. He half fell, half jumped from the horse before the front door. Sophie plowed toward him. "Do you have business at Berkholzskoye?"

"A message from Her Imperial Majesty for Princess Dmitrievna," he mouthed. The words disappeared into the storm, but not before Sophie had heard them. An icy stillness enveloped her.

"I am Princess Dmitrievna," she said. "You may give me your message and take your horse to the stables. The serfs there will care for him and show you to the kitchen."

Relief scudded across the man's expression at these crisp orders promising deliverance from the storm, fires, vodka, and a full belly. Digging into the leather pouch at his waist, he drew forth a letter. "Here you are, Princess." He presented it to her with a bow while the snow swirled around them.

"Hurry along now," she said, taking the letter. "The stables are behind the house. Your horse needs tending."

Her Highness seemed to show disproportionate concern for his horse, thought the messenger, rapidly leading his mount in the direction of the rear of the mansion.

Sophie went around to the side of the house, where the little door was unlocked. She slipped inside. The letter in her hand seemed to burn with a dreadful menace. The imperial seal pressed against her palm. Why was she receiving missives from the empress in the middle of a blizzard?

Presumably Paul had been obliged to account for her disappearance, which would explain why Catherine assumed she was at Berkholzskoye. But why? She turned the letter over in her hand as if she could divine the contents, much as she had done with the other one, way back at the beginning of time it now seemed. That summons had led to misery. Why should the outcome of this one be any different?

"Sophie!" Adam's voice pierced her guesswork. "Oh, look at you! You are the most nonsensical creature, sweetheart."

She realized that she was standing in the hall, snow melting on her eyelashes, running down her cheeks in a freezing stream, pouring off her pelisse to puddle at her feet. "I'll just go upstairs," she said vaguely. "Change my clothes."

"Sophie." He took her hands, gripping them fiercely. "Sweet love, I am sorry for what happened. I had no right to snap at you in that fashion."

All thoughts of that distressing exchange had vanished in the last few minutes, and she looked at him blankly.

Adam could think of no reason for such an expression except that he had wounded her even more deeply than he thought. Guilt and remorse washed through him. He would have to explain it to her, open up those corrosive, shaming memories for another's eye. It was perhaps time, anyway.

"Do not look at me in that fashion, love. I will try to explain—"

"A message has come from the empress," she said as if she had not heard him.

"What?" Adam looked down at the hands he held and realized she was gripping something. That same icy stillness enveloped him. "What does it say?"

"I do not know yet. I have not opened it. I came across the messenger as he arrived. I sent him to the stables immediately. It seemed best, do you not think? His horse was half frozen." The staccato sentences emerged in a distant, abstracted voice; her eyes were still blank as if they did not see him.

"Yes," he agreed quietly. "Quite the best thing to do. Now, let us go upstairs and get you out of those wet clothes. We will open the letter when you are warm and dry." Still holding her hand, he led her to the stairs.

Sophie, her mind wandering through a landscape of dread and the certainty of loss, allowed herself to be delivered to a clucking Tanya, whose scolding went unheard as she undressed, dried, and reclothed her frozen mistress under the concerned eyes of the count.

Adam sat on the long, low window seat, holding the unopened letter. As it had for Sophie, premonition became certainty in his mind. It had been inevitable, he had thought himself armed for it, but foreknowledge provided no shield, no buckler against the pain.

"Open it, Adam." Sophie spoke in her normal voice; her eyes had returned from the sad internal land they had been viewing. She turned from her mirror, where Tanya had been braiding her hair. "I am prepared now."

Silently, he complied.

When he had read the contents, he told her in flat tones, "It seems there is to be a state visit to the Crimea. You are appointed lady-in-waiting to Her Imperial Majesty and bidden to Kiev to join the imperial suite."

Sophie frowned down at her fingernails. "And my husband?"

"According to the empress, he awaits you most eagerly."

Sophie exhaled through her teeth. "What a consummate actor he must be. It is to be hoped he will be able to hide his surprise at seeing me."

Adam sprang to his feet, looking at her in horror. "You are *not* going back to him, Sophie."

She ignored this statement for the moment. "What of you, Adam?"

He sighed, saying with difficulty, "I must go to Mogilev immediately. It is to be assumed my own orders will be delivered there and I must be there to receive them."

"We had best find *Grandpère* and tell him of this." Sophie went to the door, calm and collected, her carriage as erect as ever, her stride as energetic. She knew what she was going to do; indeed, the decision had made itself. In fact, if she really thought about it, it had been made all along; it was just that she had not wished to contaminate the idyll with thoughts of its ending.

Adam followed her to the library, where, without explanation, she handed Golitskov the imperial summons. "Adam must leave straightway for his home," she said briskly, once he had read it. "It is to be assumed he will be bidden to join this journey himself if my husband is to be there in an official capacity."

"You must go into France," the prince said, tapping the letter against his palm. "The empress will be angered, but it cannot be helped—"

"I am not running away," Sophie interrupted. "I am going to Kiev to join the czarina's suite."

"You most certainly are not!" both Adam and the prince exclaimed in the same breath with equal fervency.

Sophie looked from one to the other, and spoke with quiet determination. "Paul cannot harm me anymore. I have moved beyond his power to hurt. Besides, I shall be a member of the czarina's retinue. He cannot keep me prisoner in such circumstances, and I shall ensure that I have nothing and no one about me who could be made to suffer in order that I should suffer with them. I daresay I shall hardly see him, except for the formalities."

"If you believe he cannot hurt you, you do not know him as well as you should," Adam said. "He will find ways. Maybe not on this journey, but what of later, when you will not be under the empress's close observation?"

Sophie shrugged. "Later will take care of itself." She reached for his hands. "Love, listen to me. I cannot bear being away from you. Death would be preferable. I will suffer my husband in order that I may see you sometimes, talk with you sometimes, feel your eyes upon me, be warmed by your smile—"

"Sophie, stop! I cannot endure it!" Adam cried. "You cannot believe that I will be able to tolerate watching you, knowing that night after night you are possessed by that barbarous man, knowing how he is hurting you, unable to touch you, to protect you—"

"But surely a little is better than nothing at all," Sophie interrupted passionately. "I cannot live with nothing; never to see you again. I cannot!"

"So you would have me without honor, living for the moments when I might look upon another man's wife? Scurrying around, hugger-mugger, trying to contrive a word, a kiss, a touch in dark corners, a squalid tumble between soiled sheets?" he said, vicious and bitter. "I'll not play that part, Sophie." He turned from her, hearing Eva's laugh again, mocking the outraged cuckold.

"It would not be like that between us," she whispered, recoiling both from the picture he had painted and from the idea that Adam could possibly depict their love in such language.

"It is *always* like that."

"But . . . but it has not been. Please . . . you know it has not been." Ineffably distressed, she took a step toward him, hand outstretched. "Say it has not been like that, Adam."

"Can you not see the difference between what we have had here, in our own world, and what will happen at court, under the scheming, prurient eyes of gossips?" The gray gaze was cold as the ocean, hard as a pebble beach. "There is no future, Sophie. God knows, I would that there were; but I cannot leave my responsibilities here, not even for love. If you will go into France, then I may contrive to visit you sometime."

Sometime . . . this year, next year, sometime, never. Sophie shook her head at the old adage. "If I leave Russia without the czarina's permission, there will never be hope for us," she said. "I would not be able to return, even if something should happen to remove my husband. I will not separate myself from you. You may do as you please, Adam, but I am going to obey the czarina's summons. *Grandpère*—" Only when she turned to include her grandfather did she realize that he had left them to a discussion that required no intruder.

"You would put me on the rack," Adam declared in soft anguish.

"I will put us both on it, but at least in pain one is aware of life," she replied. "The alternative is the numbness of living death." The dark eyes held his. "I have the courage to live, Adam. I will live without you as lover, but I will not live without your love and your presence."

"I do not know whether you talk of the courage of heroes or of martyrs, Sophie," he said slowly. "But I daresay we shall find out in our pain. Now, I must make my preparations."

He left her alone in the library, where Prince Golitskov found her a few minutes later. "You are set upon this course, Sophie?"

"It is the only choice that provides any hope," she replied.

"And Dmitriev?"

She shrugged. "I am armored against him, *Grandpère*. And I will have the czarina's protection."

"For the moment," he agreed soberly. "But your husband is your lord, Sophie. He may use you as he pleases, and the czarina's eye will not always be upon you."

"I will take my chance."

"Very well." The old prince bowed to the inevitable. Sophia Alexeyevna was a grown woman, entitled to make her own life-defining decisions. He could draw a smidgeon of comfort from the knowledge that she was rarely less than clear-sighted.

But that night, as she lay alone in the bedchamber in the west wing, her last sight of Adam galloping into the snow burned upon her eye, she felt neither grown nor clear-sighted. There had been constraint between them, the farewell abrupt. She knew he was angry at her obstinacy, just as he was fearful for her safety, but underlying those emotions was whatever darkness had caused him to cast that dreadful blemish upon their loving, to use such bitter words. It was the same darkness that had caused him to strike out at her that afternoon, when she had so flippantly insisted upon a walk before lovemaking.

And there had been no time . . . or was it no inclination . . . for a last loving. Turning her head into her pillow, Sophie wept tears of loss and bewilderment, railing against an unjust fate.

A week later she arrived in Kiev. The city was thronged with delegates pouring in from every country and representatives from every part of the vast Russian empire to pay their respects to their empress. Despite her depression, Sophie could not take her eyes from the window of the sleigh drawing her through the streets. There were Cossacks and the horsemen of the steppes, Khirgiz and Kalmuks; bearded merchants rubbing shoulders with nobles; officers, splendid in every kind of regimental uniform, parading beside Tatars and Indian dignitaries.

The sleigh drew up in front of the palace housing Catherine and her retinue. Lackeys ran up to assist this clearly noble personage to alight from the elegant, comfortable equipage. Sophie entered the palace, identified herself to a majordomo, and was swept away without further question into the presence of the Grand Mistress.

Countess Shuvalova smiled graciously at the princess. "We have been expecting you daily, Princess Dmitrievna, since the messenger returned from Berkholzskoye. Your apartments will be in this palace," she said. "As lady-in-waiting, you will be accommodated under the same roof as Her Imperial Majesty throughout the journey."

Sophie curtsied in acknowledgment. "And my husband?" she asked as if it were the most ordinary question in the world.

"Of course, you have not seen him for some time," said the countess. "He will have his own duties beside Prince Potemkin, but whenever he is able to visit you, I am certain he will do so." She looked shrewdly at the young woman, but could see nothing untoward in her expression. The countess, who was in the empress's confidence, was well aware of the czarina's benevolent plan to bring husband and wife together in the relaxed, holiday atmosphere of this magical tour.

"You will be shown to your apartment now," she continued calmly. "You will wish to change your dress before presenting yourself to Her Imperial Majesty." She pulled the bell rope beside the hearth. "General, Prince Dmitriev had your belongings brought from St. Petersburg. And you will find your maid also."

The faithful Maria, Sophie thought sardonically. Well, that servant was going to find some considerable changes in her mistress. Paul must have gone through with the elaborate charade, all the while believing that the clothes and jewels so solicitously brought from the capital would find no real woman to adorn. Just how was he going to react to the living, breathing proof of his failure?

She followed the lackey through a series of passageways and up a flight of stairs onto a broad landing. He flung open a carved oak door. The chamber beyond was hung with velvet and tapestries, richly carpeted, furnished with a large four-poster, a silk-covered divan, a marble-topped dresser, and a huge armoire. In the corner of the chamber stood the obligatory icon, a candle burning before it. Ladies-in-waiting did well for themselves, thought Sophie, nodding her thanks to the lackey. The familiar maid bobbed a curtsy, but it lacked the previous insolence, as if, on this unfamiliar territory, Maria was unsure of her position or that of her mistress.

"Good day, Maria." Sophie's greeting was cold and distant. "Lay out the cream velvet gown." She threw her muff onto the divan, tossed back the sable-lined hood of her cloak, and went to the window. Below flowed the River Dnieper, except that in its present icebound state it could not be said to flow. It was in use as a thoroughfare, however, by skaters and sleighs, the busy scene carrying the same carnival air she had noticed in the streets.

"It seems, my dear wife, that you are to be congratulated on a safe journey. I bid you welcome."

Sophie controlled the instinct to whirl from the window. Instead she turned slowly, drawing off her gloves as her husband softly closed the door behind him. "Why, thank you, Paul. I am most happy to be here."

Chapter 14

Her laugh mocked him. Every toss of her head implied defiance. Every quirk of that crooked smile, every fluid movement invited flirtation, and in the gay, pleasure-oriented court at Kiev her invitations were happily accepted. Sometimes Paul Dmitriev could not contain his rage, and he would have to leave the room to compose himself. The woman who had come back from Berkholzskoye was in essence the woman he had sent to her death, but there was a sureness about her, an impregnable confidence that had not been there before. She now took her place at court as naturally as if she had been bred to it, and she was received with the most flattering attentions from foreign diplomats and courtiers alike. The czarina looked upon her with a fond and pleased eye, congratulating the husband on his wife's blossoming in such a gratifying fashion. And Paul Dmitriev, ungratified, would smile and murmur his own satisfaction, while the black fury built within.

He watched her now across Prince de Ligne's crowded salon. The envoy of the Prussian king, Joseph II, was one of Catherine's favorite ambassadors, one of the most popular of the distinguished members of the select group around the empress. Prince de Ligne found Princess Dmitrievna utterly enchanting. He made no secret of this, and the princess, in response, lived up to the reputation he accorded her of intelligence and vivacity, of an unusual beauty, with that crooked smile and clearly defined features, deep, dark eyes glowing in an oval face radiant with health.

The pale, subdued prisoner had vanished; she made no pretense, even in the private presence of her husband, of submission. Under the umbrella of the court, she was effectively removed from her husband's jurisdiction, and he could visit none of the subtle deprivations with which he had accomplished her appearance of subjection in the past. She rode, took sleigh rides, went to balls and card parties. At times his fingers would curl around his cane and he would toy with images of a cruder form of domination, but she could not appear in public with the marks of brutality upon her. He could only bide his time until life became normal again, when his wife would be returned to the marital roof.

Glancing across the room, Sophie met the cold blue stare, read the loathing it contained, and in spite of the impregnability of her present position, a shiver of fear quivered her spine, crawled across her scalp. Why did he hate her so? He seemed repulsed by her. That first night in Kiev he had come to her bed, and she had lain like stone, untouched because she now knew the glory of loving, and this hideous travesty was not worth suffering over. But he had failed to achieve his own release and had left her with a violent execration, telling her she was unworthy to be his or anyone's wife—cold and barren, she was a disgrace to womanhood. She had said nothing, and her silence had driven him to greater fury, but he had not since touched her with the coldness of his vengeful lust.

"I understand Count Danilevski has arrived in Kiev." The light voice, accompanied by a pleasurable titter, came from a young matron engaged in gossipy conversation with another of her kind in the circle behind Sophie.

Unobtrusively, Sophie took a step backward so that she was half in her own circle and half in the one behind. A smiling, complimentary comment to pretty little Countess Lomonsova and she was a part of the other group.

"I find him so intimidating, do you not?" chattered Natalia Saltykova, the young matron. "He smiles and says just the right things, but you feel as if he is looking right through you." She turned, laughing, to Sophie. "What do you think, Princess?"

"About what?" said Sophie, smiling blandly.

"Why about the count, of course. He is your husband's aide-de-camp. You must see much of him."

"Not really," Sophie said indifferently. "My husband conducts his business in the barracks, in general."

"Oh." Natalia returned her attention to more rewarding conversationalists, dropping her voice confidingly. "It is said that he does not care for women. Ever since that dreadful business with his wife."

Wife! Sophie felt the color drain from her cheeks even as she swallowed the exclamation. She took a glass of champagne from a passing lackey. "I did not know he was married." Was there a squeak in her voice?

"Oh, he is not anymore." Natalia, gratified by this apparent interest from one who had appeared indifferent to such juicy whispers, and not loath to display her own knowledge, spoke eagerly. "She died just over a year ago, I believe. Some say the count was heartbroken, but some say . . ." Her head bent into the circle, and other heads followed, like so many hens pecking in the dust. The words rustled in the enclosed space. "Some say that she was carrying a child at the time, and it could not have been her husband's." She stood up in smiling triumph, examining the faces of her audience for evidence that her whispers had impressed.

"How did she die?" The question came from Countess Lomonsova, sparing Sophie the need to ask.

Natalia looked mysterious. "It was a riding accident, I believe, but no one is certain. It happened in Moscow."

With a smile and a soft word, Sophie moved away from the group. How could he not have told her something so fundamental, so basic in his past? Why had she never asked? Because, in her naïveté, it had not occurred to her to probe. The present was so all-absorbing, nothing else had seemed relevant. She knew he was experienced with women, but that was only to be expected. Of course, he had had lovers. But a wife . . . weddings, honeymoons, shared names, commitment . . . children. Did he have children? Cared for by the mother and sisters he had told her about on the family estates at Mogilev? And what of the child his wife was said to have been bearing?

The fabric of the world she had constructed for herself was disintegrating, crumbling like a skeleton exposed to the air after centuries sealed in the tombs. It was not extraordinary that she had not heard the gossip before. She had been afforded no opportunity for gossipy congress with her peers in St. Petersburg; her husband's isolationist policy had ensured that. But how, in all the weeks she and Adam had spent in the closest contact, had he failed even to refer to such a fact? Such failure had to be deliberate, Sophie thought, moving blindly through the salon, a smile fixed to her mouth, meaningless words of greeting on her lips. If it was not deliberate, an accidental reference would have been inevitable.

"Sophia Alexeyevna. I have not yet had the opportunity to welcome you to my . . . our . . . grand parade." Prince Potemkin, resplendent in full field marshal's uniform, smothered in diamonds and lace, his hair powdered and curled like a nobleman at the court of Versailles, stepped into her path.

Sophie dragged herself back to full awareness of her surroundings. One must not appear lacking in concentration in the prince's company. She curtsied. "Thank you, Prince. I have been looking for you since I arrived in Kiev, but I understood that you had gone into retreat in the Petcherksy monastery."

"So I have, my dear Princess, so I have," said Potemkin, smiling. "At times, I find all this"—he gestured expressively at the glittering, ceremonial throng—"a little too much confectionary for my tastes, and I must replenish myself with plain fare and solitude." His gaze ran appreciatively over her. The dark hair was unpowdered, curling in soft, feathery ringlets to her shoulders. Her gown was of rose-pink taffeta edged with lace, her petticoat sewn with seed pearls. The diamonds at her throat were among the most magnificent the prince had ever seen. Catherine had not been exaggerating the transformation, he decided. His one eye gleamed seductively. His smile slashed the brown face. "You are enjoying yourself, I trust."

"Indeed, I am," Sophie replied. "I am awestruck, Prince, at how much planning and organization this orchestration of splendors must have involved. It is the work of genius."

Potemkin's smile broadened. "I am not averse to flattery, my dear Sophia," he said. "I see you have discovered that."

"There was no flattery," she replied with another curtsy. "It was a statement of fact, Prince."

He looked at her closely, and only an inexperienced babe would have mistaken the message he was transmitting. Prince Potemkin was Paul Dmitriev's superior, Sophie thought. Such a friend would be invaluable when this carnival was done and life had returned to normal. But how to ensure the friendship while refusing this unmistakable invitation to his bed?

She was unaware that the frank speculation in her candid, dark eyes was easily read by her companion, who was hugely amused and not a whit offended. "Will you do me the honor of visiting me in my humble abode tomorrow?" He bowed as he made the request, raising her hand to his lips. "I will show you the plan of the route we will take when the ice melts."

"I should be most interested. At what hour do you receive?"

He chuckled and sighed in mock resignation. "How prudent you are, Princess. I would much prefer to receive you alone, but if you must come with the hordes, then my cell door is open between eleven and noon."

Sophie simply smiled. "Excuse me, Prince. Her Majesty appears to be leaving."

"Until tomorrow then." He watched her move through the crowd to join the czarina's departing retinue. Such energy she had, he mused. It was obvious she had difficulty adapting her pace to the limitations of hoop and high-heeled shoes. Such energy expended between the sheets would be a joy to share. He'd lay odds it was not a joy her husband shared, but somebody had. Potemkin was convinced of it. Sophia Alexeyevna radiated the sensuality of the awakened, something conspicuously absent before her visit to Berkholzskoye.

Sophie spent a wretched night, tormented with doubt and misgiving. Her faith in Adam, the implicit trust she had placed in his integrity, and in the integrity of their love, was cracked, something she had never believed could happen. She had to confront him with her knowledge. It was impossible to forget it, or to pretend to forget it, yet she dreaded what she would hear. What possible acceptable, unhurtful explanation for his silence could there be? And this anxiety was confused by excitement at the thought that he was in Kiev, sleeping somewhere in this city; it was inevitable that they would meet in the next day or so. They would have to meet as cool, indifferent acquaintances, but just to be in the same room had to be joy.

The czarina had smiled knowingly when her young lady-in-waiting asked for leave to attend Prince Potemkin's reception on the morrow. "I trust you will not find him in morose mood, my dear," she had said. "It is often the way that after an evening's enjoyment Prince Potemkin will become gloomy, and those upon whom he smiled in the evening receive only frowns in the morning."

"I will take my chance, Madame," Sophie had replied in the same light tones.

The atmosphere at the monastery was so different from that reigning in the palaces and salons in Kiev that Sophie felt as if she had arrived upon another planet. She was led by a robed monk through hushed stone passageways and shown into an ordinary monastic cell. It was filled with people, officers and dignitaries in court dress, all come to pay their respects to the field marshal. But no one was talking. Indeed, to Sophie the air held not only discomfort but a tinge of fear as these august personages attempted to reconcile the calm, meditative atmosphere of this holy place with the robust frivolity of the court. The man who had created the court at Kiev, who last night had appeared in a diamond glitter of full regalia, now lay sprawled upon a divan in the midst of a circle of officers. He was unshaven and unkempt, his legs bare beneath a half-open pelisse, under which it was clear he wore not even a shirt.

One of the officers standing beside the divan was Colonel, Count Danilevski. For Sophie, the extraordinary tableau lost the hard edge of substance; she saw just that one figure standing out, etched in his own three-dimensional reality. Sophie stepped into the cell.

"Ah, Princess Dmitrievna, I hardly dared hope you would remember your promise." The languid figure extended his hand toward her without moving from his position on the divan. Sophie took the hand and smiled a greeting. Her entire frame seemed to be vibrating as if that silent presence were a tuning fork playing upon the instrument of her body.

"I always keep my promises, Prince." Her voice sounded hoarse, shocking in the surrounding silence.

The prince looked vaguely around the room. "You are acquainted with Count Danilevski, of course. Was he not your first escort from Berkholzskoye?"

"Yes, that is so." Sophie looked up at the count. "How nice to see you again, Count."

The count bowed, but the strain of restraint was revealed in his eyes, in the lines drawn at the corners of that beautiful mouth.

"I have taken the colonel from your husband," the prince informed her idly. "He is now on my personal staff."

"My husband's loss, I am sure," murmured Sophie as she wondered hopelessly how long this could go on. How long could she stand here making these inane polite noises in this artificially silent monk's cell under the burning gray gaze? Adam had been right. It required more than human strength to endure this perverted situation. Every sinew ached with the agony of holding herself away from him, and she knew it was the same for him.

"You promised to show me the route we shall take to the Crimea," she reminded the prince, desperate to create a diversion, to make something happen.

"Ah, so I did." Potemkin yawned profoundly. "I daresay the colonel will show you. The maps are upon the table." He waved in the direction of a simple table against the wall and below the high slit of a window.

A sigh of relief rustled around the cell at this prospect of activity to break the brooding awkwardness. They all turned toward the table, where Adam, his face expressionless, was opening maps. They listened, commented, murmured admiringly at the magnificence of the grand plan laid out before them, explained in the count's calm tones.

Sophie stood as far from Adam as she could on the outskirts of the group. She heard nothing of what he said, but simply

allowed his beloved voice to wash over her, purifying and revivifying. How could she contrive to be alone with him? Or
would he do the contriving? *Scurrying around, hugger-mugger,
trying to contrive a word, a kiss, a touch in dark corners, a
squalid tumble between soiled sheets.* The dreadful word picture
rang again in her ears.

"I must return to the empress," she said, heedless that she
had interrupted an exposition on how the southern sections of
the River Dnieper had been widened for navigation by blowing
up rocks and leveling sandbanks. "It is all most interesting,
Count, but I cannot stay, I fear." She hastily turned toward the
divan, holding out her hand. "Prince, thank you for your hospitality."

"Such as it was," murmured the prince, a sardonic gleam in
his one eye. He heaved himself from the divan, throwing off the
appearance of affected disdain. "You have brightened my morning, Princess Dmitrievna."

"If you are returning to Kiev, perhaps you will accept my
escort, Princess." Adam spoke casually, rolling up the map he
had been using. "I have business at court."

"I should be delighted." The formal exchange, the ritual
words, and it was done. She was sitting in the sleigh, Adam
Danilevski beside her. The door closed, a whip cracked, and
they glided forward over the snow.

Nothing was said. She turned within the circle of his arm,
her lips parted, her glowing dark eyes consuming his countenance. Lifting one hand, she ran her palm over his face in curious wonder, feeling the living warmth of his skin, the firm
moistness of his pressing lips, the silky flutter of his eyelashes.

Gently, with the same wonder, he made his own reexplora-
tion, a fingertip caressing her parted lips, painting the planes of
her face, smoothing over her eyelids.

"Why did you not tell me about your wife?" She had not
meant to ask it so abruptly, had she? But the words had spoken
themselves.

His hand fell to his lap. "I suppose it was inevitable you
would hear of it on some gossip's tongue."

"It does not alter anything," she said. "But I do not understand why you would not have mentioned it."

"It is a piece of the past that had no relevance to the present," he said quietly. "It would have relevance only to the future—the future we do not have, Sophie." He shrugged. "I saw no point in discussing it."

She sat, feeling chilled and empty. It was not unreasonable to say that such a fact had had no importance in the fairyland they had inhabited at Berkholzskoye. Yet the cold dismissal of her perceived right to have been told hurt most dreadfully. "Do you have any children?" She tried to make the inquiry sound simply curious, but the throb of anxiety in her voice could not be disguised. Adam merely shook his head in brusque negative. She swallowed, plunged. "How did your wife die?"

"They did not tell you?" A scornful, acid laugh cracked in the enclosed space. "It was an accident."

And the child she was supposed to have been carrying? But clearly he was not going to mention that. And she could not ask. The words would not form themselves. Whatever the truth of that, it was his to keep. She had transgressed sufficiently with her questions.

She leaned back against the fur-covered seat, closing her eyes against the pain. Her body ached for his, for the conjoining of flesh and spirit, yet they were as far apart in this tiny, private, gliding space as Siberia is from Moscow. Then she felt his breath rustle across her cheeks, his mouth cover hers. Her head fell back, neck arched against the seat back. His hand slid over the vulnerable, opened column, tracing her jaw as his tongue pressed deep within her mouth. She received this kiss; her mouth was the passive receptacle possessed by the conquering, insistent one above. And in the passivity was to be found a blissful yielding of pain, of doubt, of the need to act and to decide. Her hands lay open on the seat at her sides, palms up, fingers curled; her throat arched white above the dark fur of her cloak; her eyelashes spread, sable half-moons against the delicate pink-and-cream complexion.

Adam drew back and her eyelashes fluttered. Her eyes opened, looking into the intent, passion-filled gaze hanging over her. "I do not know how this is to be managed." The usual light tenor of his voice was lost in the deep resonance of desire. "How closely watched are you?"

Her head moved in languid negative against the seat. "Not at all. Paul rarely comes near me, except in public. I do not know if he questions Maria, but I come and go so freely she could never be certain where I was, or with whom."

"Then I will see what I can contrive. Such liaisons are conducted all over the city. I am sure there must be commonly known methods of facilitating them." His tone was neutral, but Sophie could hear his distaste and it shook her out of her languor.

"Adam, love, if you do not wish for this, then we do not have to—"

"Don't be foolish! At least let us be honest in *this*. Being near you, I cannot deprive myself of your sweetness, of your body, of loving your body with mine. I told you the way it would be. I have neither the strength of spirit nor of flesh."

The words of love and passion came out with the angry force of body blows, and Sophie flinched at the implicit accusation. She was responsible for this self-directed derision because she had been too incontinent herself to accept the clean break that would have brought some measure of peace.

The sleigh drew to a halt. Her hand fluttered toward his cheek—in apology, in appeal, Sophie did not know. Adam regarded her gravely for an instant. "I will tell you where to come to me as soon as I have made the necessary arrangements." He swung open the door, sprang lightly to the ground, and reached out his hand courteously to assist her to alight.

"Thank you, Count," she said in a dull tone. How could there be so much anger and resentment where there was an infinity of loving need and surpassing desire? How could he speak so coldly about arrangements for an assignation, when a minute before she had been pierced with his longing for her, awash with her own? He had treated her curiosity about his marriage with the indifferent contempt one accorded an inquisitive gossip, so that *she* felt at fault—not just for asking about it, but for knowing about it. Her interest was considered imper-

tinent and irrelevant because Adam Danilevski's past could only
be of importance to her if she had a future with Adam Danilevski; something that was not to be.

Methodically, and with the cool efficiency he would bring to
preparations for a military exercise, Adam set about organizing
his affair with the wife of General, Prince Paul Dmitriev. A
word or two dropped in the mess elicited an address: A small
hunting cottage on the banks of the river, some three versts from
Kiev, offered a secluded trysting place. Only money was required to ensure that it would be empty whenever he needed it,
fires and refreshment provided by peasant hands—hands that
would disappear at least an hour before the count was expected.

The court calendar being common property, it was a simple
matter to pick an afternoon empty of official engagements, when
Princess Dmitrievna could reasonably be excused attendance
on the empress.

Directions, the day and time of the assignation, were committed to paper. Not once did his blood race at the prospect of
an afternoon of love in a cottage on the banks of the frozen
river. He was as coldly detached as if he were making these
arrangements for some other pair of illicit lovers snatching a
clandestine hour or two for the hasty and imperative satisfaction
of their lust.

He picked the occasion for instructing his mistress with the
same dispassionate care. Catherine was giving audience to pe-
titioners from all over the countryside in one of her open recep-
tions, when she received the most humble muzhiks, accepted
their obeisance as they prostrated themselves before her, then
listened with the utmost attention to the problems of a village,
domestic or agricultural, questioning the peasants in detail about
the dried-up well, the murrain that had destroyed a herd of cat-
tle. There was not an issue, however insignificant, that she did
not accord her full attention.

Sophie was in attendance, as usual, sitting with Prince de
Ligne and Comte de Ségur, who made no attempt to conceal
their fascination with this aspect of the empress and her subjects. ''Is it customary, Princess, for a peasant to call his em-

press, Little Mother?'' The Comte de Ségur raised a questioning eyebrow. ''Such familiarity is extraordinary. In France it would be unheard of.''

Sophie smiled. ''The relationship of the Russian to his sovereign is complex, Comte. He reveres her as a divinity, yet worships her as a mother. You notice that they use the familiar second-person form of address and Her Imperial Majesty responds—oh—'' she broke off. ''Count Danilevski. Are you too come with a petition for Her Majesty?'' She smiled archly, although her heart lurched, and a mist dewed her palms. They had had no speech since the sleigh ride. She had glimpsed him across a salon, a courtyard, heard his voice occasionally, but until now he had never come close enough to acknowledge her presence.

''My message is for you, Princess, as it happens,'' he said easily, bowing as he handed her a folded paper. ''Prince Dmitriev desired me to give you this. He is occupied with a review at present.''

''Oh, yes, he said he would send me some details for tomorrow's procession.'' Sophie slipped the paper into her reticule, wondering at how readily one developed these skills at deception. ''We were just discussing the peculiarities of the Russian's relationship with his sovereign, Count. It is very different in Poland, I understand.''

''Poland as it now exists, Princess, bears little resemblance to the nation of my childhood,'' Adam replied. ''Then it was clear to whom a Pole owed his allegiance.'' He shrugged. ''Now, except for the tiny minority still under the sovereignty of the king of Poland, an Austrian, Russian, or Prussian demands allegiance. Indeed, even in minuscule Poland, the Russian ambassador is the real ruler. Stanislas Poniatowski is a puppet king and has always been so.''

''Those are strong words, Count.'' Prince de Ligne spoke gently, yet with ill-concealed interest.

With a smile and a word, Sophie excused herself. She had known her question would elicit the reaction from Adam that it had. His feelings about the country of his birth and his confused sense of nationality had not been kept from her. She understood that in many ways it was now an intellectual issue for him rather than an emotional one, and the conversational diversion she had presented them gave her the natural opportunity to leave the ambassadors, whose entertainment was her responsibility during the audiences, whilst taking attention away from the message-passing.

The message was terse, no words of love and promise, simply precise directions, a time set for the following afternoon, the curt instruction to come alone and on horseback. Did he really think she would arrive at a lover's hideaway in a sleigh complete with driver?

A prickle of unease, a spurt of misgiving deep in her belly, took the edge off anticipation's delight. Adam didn't want this. He did not want it, but he could not help himself from taking it. Where was the joy in that? Where was love's light touch? Was there only to be the weight of lust? Was this what he had known would happen when he painted that dreadful picture of sordid scrabbling? Or was he determined to fulfill his own prophecy, forcing her participation in the fulfillment?

The following afternoon, these questions about to be answered, Sophie rode along the bank of the river, the instructions engraved on her brain so that she had no need to consult the paper in the pocket of her habit. A little bridge appeared exactly where it was supposed to. She turned her horse to cross over the frozen water. The air was crisp, but the bite of winter had gone from it and the sun's power could be felt. The ice glistened damply as the surface melted, and the snow beneath the horse's hooves had turned to slush. A flock of ducks rose from the marshes lining the far bank; wings outstretched, they swooped low over the river, crying in mournful alarm at Sophie's approach.

Her hand went to the pistol fastened to her saddle. Then she shook her head in annoyance. The action had been the automatic one of an inveterate hunter, but ducks were not her quarry this afternoon.

Adam stood in the doorway of the cottage, looking along the river, waiting for his first sight of her. The peace was profound, not a sign of human occupancy in the sunlit, white, gleaming landscape. It should have brought him a matching peace as he waited for the woman he loved, but he could find no feeling but weary disillusion in his soul. This was no solution—a snatched afternoon in a borrowed cottage. Where had Eva conducted her little adventures? The thought intruded in its ugliness. Of course, in the absence of the husband she would not have had to scurry in corners. Perhaps she took her lovers from the household staff, virile young lackeys and grooms all eager and willing to serve the mistress.

With an exclamation of disgust, Adam swung on his heel, going back into the cottage. Wine, olives, a plate of cakes stood upon the table; the stove glowed warmly; the divan was spread with cashmere shawls. The perfect picture of the perfect love nest. Impatiently, he went outside again. Sophie was cantering toward him on an ordinary-looking mount that did not do her justice. But Khan had been left in safety with Boris Mikhailov at Berkholzskoye.

"Oh, what a pretty place." Laughing, glowing, sparkling, she came up to him, throwing her leg across the saddlebow as she sprang energetically to the ground. "How clever of you, love."

"These things can be arranged, as I told you," he heard himself say almost distantly, when he wanted to laugh with her, take pleasure with her in their surroundings, carry her into the cottage to the soft divan and the stove's warmth.

Uncertainty scudded across Sophie's mobile countenance; hurt swam in the dark eyes. Then, resolutely she smiled again, pulling off her fur hat, tossing back her hair as it tumbled over her shoulders. "Show me inside. If it is half as pretty as the outside, it must be enchanting." She reached for his hand, refusing to be daunted by the lack of response, pulling him to the door. "Oh, it is enchanting! An enchanted cottage!" She turned into his arms, standing on her toes to kiss him, holding his head firmly between her hands.

Slowly, reluctantly almost, his arms banded her waist, his hands flattening on her back, molding her to him as her tongue danced with his and weary disillusion retreated under the hungry onslaught of passion. It was as if an eternity had passed since they had last held each other, an eternity of believing that never again would they embrace each other in this way. The wanting exploded in savage necessity. He was pulling her clothes from her body while she still clung to him as if to move so much as an inch away from him would rend her flesh. His nails scraped her skin under the urgent stripping, but she barely felt it, moving sinuously against him, her mouth adhered to his, their whispering, whimpering breath mingling in the candid words of desire.

Naked, she stood against him, feeling the roughness of his jacket rasping across her nipples as his hands felt her, probed her, his knee pushing apart her legs, the wool of his britches harsh against the inner softness of her thighs. She felt as if she could never have enough of his hands, of the rough possession that confirmed his own desperate urgency as it brought her to frenzied bliss. She bit his mouth, wild in her wanting, and he lifted her, tossing her onto the divan, coming down with her even as he unfastened his britches, kicking them from him. Her thighs fell open to receive him, his hands beneath her buttocks bruised as they lifted her for his plunging entry. Deep, deep he drove into her, his mouth on hers, his clothed body pressing her into the mattress. There was no slow spiral of desire leading them to extinction. Annihilation engulfed them in a heart-stopping moment when the intensity of pleasure could not be believed.

Sophie heard the pounding of her blood, so loud it seemed to fill the room. Her skin was drenched with the sweat of ecstasy, her body, felled by pleasure, sprawled unmoving. Slowly, Adam rolled away from her, falling upon his back, one hand resting heavily on her belly. They lay thus for a long time, until life and strength crept back. Adam turned, propping himself on one elbow to look down at the prone body beside him.

Her lips were swollen with his kisses, her skin reddened by the abrasiveness of his clothes. A long scratch ran down her arm, another across her thigh. "You bear the marks of battle, my love," he said with a soft smile, bending to kiss the mute witnesses to shared passion's satisfaction.

Sophie stretched lethargically, caressing the bent head. "They were earned in a good cause. But it's fortunate Paul no longer visits my bed.''

Adam sat up abruptly. ''Was that necessary?'' The gray eyes had lost their love light. ''Do you think this is some sort of game? In the name of all the saints! Do you think I need that kind of reminder?'' Eva would not have had to worry about such marks of passion upon her body with her husband so conveniently absent. They were an inevitable risk, weren't they, in these tricky triangles? Marks of wantonness to be hidden if excuses could not be found . . . lies constructed . . . husbands deceived . . . The weary disillusion slopped over him again. He got off the bed, going to the table to pour wine. ''You had better get back to the palace. We do not want your absence to be remarked.''

Sophie sat up, trying to gather herself together to confront this stranger in Adam's skin. ''I do not understand why you see things as different between us now, just because we are no longer at Berkholzskoye.''

''Don't you, Sophie?'' He pulled on his britches and crossed to the bed. ''Do you really not see the difference? Does the deceit not touch you in the slightest? The contriving, the conniving, the pretty love nest used by so many others in need of seclusion for their own little adventures?''

Sophie put her hands over her ears. ''I won't hear these things! It is love we share, the grandeur of love, not some sordid carnal need.''

''And what was that, would you say?'' Bitterness laced his voice as he looked down at her, wanton and vulnerable in her nakedness. ''Was that lust or love, Sophie?''

''Both,'' she whispered. ''I would not feel the one without the other.''

''And what do you feel now?''

''Nothing,'' she said in defeat. ''Nothing at all.''

''Then shall I show you the power of lust?'' He sat down on the bed. ''Demonstrate how it is possible to feel the one without the other?'' He pushed her backward on the bed. ''Let me show you what needs such a love nest satisfies, Sophie.'' There was a caressing note in his voice, yet it set her trembling as if at some menace. The gray eyes were cool as he brushed aside the tumbled brown hair, glinting chestnut against the whiteness of her breast. Her skin jumped at the brush of his fingers, burned at the press of his lips, the dewy stroking path of his tongue teasing the proud curves of her breast, flicking the rose-tipped crest. Sophie could not fight the responses of her body, could not prevent the tumultuous beat of her heart, the suffusion of anticipated pleasure.

The muscles of her abdomen grew rigid under the hard pressure of a flat palm. She looked up into the face above her. It was Adam's face, closed in concentration, detached, not a flicker of response as he performed this task he had set himself. Shocked despair drained her of all initiative. She closed her eyes tightly, but tears scalded her eyelids, squeezed beneath them to cluster on the thick sable eyelashes. They were tears of loss, of humiliation, as the inexorable trespass continued and her body rose to meet this pleasure that was being administered as some form of penalty for an offense she did not know she had committed.

Her eyelashes swept up, showing him the drenched dark pools of her eyes. "How could you?" The words were no more than a whisper. "Why would you do this to me? What have I done?"

Adam drew in a long, shuddering breath. Sweat stood out on his forehead. His face was gray. "I cannot do it!" he rasped, suddenly gathering her against him, cradling her in his arms as if she were a hurt baby, smoothing back her hair, kissing her eyelids. "I am tormented by past demons. To be forced to love you in secret is tearing me part. It is not your fault, yet I felt that it was, and I had in some way to brand you for it. Forgive me, sweet love."

Sophie lay warm in his hold, unable to speak for long minutes while he stroked her hair from her forehead, touched her eyes, her lips, with a fingertip, a touch not of passion but of appeal. "You knew this was how you would feel," she finally said. "I did not understand how dreadful it would be for you." She raised her eyes to his face. "I did not understand because I do not know the reason."

There was only one response to the demand in the dark eyes,

to the question in her voice. Adam shifted her on his knee so he held her fast in the crook of his arm. "I come from a race cursed with the most damnable pride, Sophie. We do not lightly accept the humiliation of being deceived."

"Your wife?"

"I loved her," he said softly. "And with the arrogance of youth and the blindness of love I believed that I could kindle the same response in one who spared no pains to demonstrate that it was an emotion she could not feel for me."

"Why did she marry you, then? I do not imagine she was coerced." She reached up to touch his face. "I cannot imagine how it would be possible not to love you if one was loved by you."

Adam looked down at her in wonder at such forgiving generosity. "I love you," he said. "I have never loved anyone before. It is possible to mistake the emotion."

"To mistake love for lust?"

"They are distinct from each other," he said gravely. "But thank God they can coexist."

Sophie snuggled closer, enjoying her nakedness cradled against his strength. The soul's rawness was gone now, almost as if it had never been. Adam had need to exorcise his hurt, and in many ways it was an obligation of love to facilitate the exorcism.

"I do not know why Eva married me," he said now. "Maybe I tired her out with my importuning. I am rich enough, my lineage is impeccable, and . . ."—that bitter smile twisted his lips again—"an army career ensures an absent husband for much of the time. My absences did not appear to distress my wife." He bent to kiss Sophie's upturned face and smiled suddenly. "There, it is told now."

"But you feel, when we are like this, that we are somehow touched . . . soiled . . . by that?" The thick eyebrows drew together in frowning intensity as she put her finger on the core.

"I was feeling that," he agreed. "It is at an end now."

There were still questions: questions about Eva's death, about the child it was whispered she had been carrying. But they were questions she had not been given permission to ask, and they were not relevant to loving with Adam.

"I think," she said thoughtfully, "that this time it would be agreeable if you were to take *your* clothes off as well as mine."

Chapter 15

Cannons boomed, resounding across Kiev, to announce the breakup of the ice on the Dnieper. The city and its population, both indigenous and imported, rejoiced, rejuvenated by the spring as they cast aside the furs, moved away from the stoves, and Potemkin's grand carnival prepared to continue its journey to the Crimea on the water.

Prince Dmitriev, in his wife's apartments, wondered how long he could contain his rage and frustration.

"I wish to know where you were going when you were seen riding out, unescorted, in such disgraceful fashion yesterday afternoon," he demanded in the cold, dispassionate tones always so expressive of his anger.

The chamber was strewn with clothes, open trunks, and portmanteaux. Maria, in the middle of her packing, had been dismissed from the room on the prince's arrival. Sophie idly rolled up a pair of long silk gloves while her mind whirled. She had visited the hunting cottage several times in the last couple of weeks; until yesterday her solitary rides had drawn no remark. But she had been seen by one of her husband's fellow officers, who had presumably carried the tale.

"I have always enjoyed riding, Paul," she said with studied indifference. "It is not a habit that is new to you." She kept her back to him, picking up another pair of gloves from the pile on the bed, examining them critically as if for tears or stains.

"Where were you going?" The question rapped.

239

"Duck hunting," she replied blandly. "Another of my great pleasures."

A hand on her shoulder spun her around with terrifying force. She found herself impaled by the venom in the pale blue eyes. "You are my wife! Much as I may regret that fact, it remains fact." He articulated his words slowly and carefully. "If you think, just because for the moment you are protected by your proximity to the empress, that you may offer me this insolence with impunity you are gravely mistaken, Sophia Alexeyevna. My wife does not ride unescorted. Neither does she hunt unless it be on a court-appointed expedition. The time will come in the not-too-distant future when you will be under my roof once more. Then, my dear wife, you will pay a hundredfold for every act of defiance, every impertinence." The icy gaze held her, mesmerized like a staked goat before the wolf. "You know me well enough, Sophia Alexeyevna, to believe in what I say. In the seclusion of my estate at Kaluga, I shall endeavor once again to make a decent wife of you. It is my duty. And this time I will succeed in that duty."

He took his hands from her with a fastidious grimace, as if she were in some way unclean. Sophie could feel the shaking begin deep in her belly, creep up the back of her neck. She must not show her fear. Silently, she turned back to the bed, praying that the violent tremors would not be visible. He had terrified her with the truth, with the reminder of his power and his hatred when she had thought herself immune, lost in the dreamland of love. The fragility of that dreamland, its temporal nature, now struck her with the force of the knout, and she cringed as if in expectation of another blow.

When the door shut behind him, she sank onto the bed, feeling queasy. She had been a self-indulgent fool to provoke him as carelessly as she had done. At the end of this journey . . .

No, she would not think of endings. The spring lay ahead. Anything could have happened by the time the imperial procession was done. Rubbing her stomach where the nausea still lay heavy, she went to the window. The river was alive with craft now, the seven great galleys that would transport the imperial party rocking at anchor. They were crawling with men like so many ants, laden with provisions, scurrying with paintbrushes, hammers, nails, as they put the finishing touches to the vessels that tomorrow would begin their stately progression down the River Dnieper.

How many of the oarsmen were convicts, riveted to their oars? wondered Sophie. Deep down in the bowels of those magnificent red-and-gold ships, did they have any inkling of the amazing luxury, the staggering extravagance paid for and preserved by their sweat and tears? Did they ever wonder, as they writhed beneath the slavemaster's lash, what it would be like to belong to that other order of being? Probably not, she reflected. Imagination was a luxury, one that ceaseless toil and incessant punishment tended to erode. The greater proportion of the population of this vast land, illiterate and enslaved as they were, bowed to the old proverb: The soul belongs to God, the head to the czar, the back to the lord. It was the established order of things, not to be questioned by a serf.

Such gloomy thoughts! But the bright day and the excitement of tomorrow's journey had been touched by despondency. Sophie turned away from the window, depressed and queasy.

The next morning, however, she could not help but be swept on the tide of joyful exuberance during the embarkation. Her cabin, like all the others on the imperial galley, had an alcove as dressing room, a water supply, a bed, a writing table, and armchairs. There was a music room, a library, and a tent on deck where the passengers could take the air whilst being protected from the sun. Even for those accustomed to the extravagant luxury of Catherine's court, the attention to every detail of comfort and entertainment as directed by Prince Potemkin was staggering.

The first day, the entire party dined together in the special galley that served as dining room. Sophie found Prince Potemkin waiting to assist her as she stepped from one of the rowboats ferrying the guests from their own vessels to the dining galley.

"So, Sophia Alexeyevna, what do you think of my little wonderland?" The grand master of the production was clearly in good form, reveling in the delighted exclamations of the guests, in the bemused admiration of the foreign diplomats, in his empress's serene pleasure as she smiled upon everything, congratulating her roaring one-eyed lion on an achievement that demonstrated to the world the glory and grandeur of her realm.

"I am spellbound, Prince," she replied in truth.

"You will be more so as the journey progresses, I can promise you." He bowed over her hand. "You shall sit at my table. I've a mind for an agreeable countenance and a quick wit as company."

"You do me too much honor." Sophie smiled quizzically. "I am glad my countenance is agreeable to you."

Potemkin's eye sparkled responsively. "You are not a beauty, Sophia Alexeyevna, but in truth, I find I prefer such unusual looks to the milk-and-water conventions."

That brought a deep flush to Sophie's cheeks. Looking for a suitable response, she felt another pair of eyes upon her. Adam had just come on board. He was standing to one side, clearly an audience to the exchange, his gaze holding wicked amusement at Sophie's embarrassment.

"I think Princess Dmitrievna is unaccustomed to compliments, Prince," he observed lightly.

"How am I to answer that, Count?" Sophie had recovered herself, and her tone was a little tart. "I can neither deny it nor agree with it with any grace."

"Yes, indeed, Adam, it was most ungallant," announced Potemkin. "I suggest you take the lady in to dinner and attempt to make reparation."

"Gladly, sir." Bowing, Adam proffered his arm. "I am desolated to have offended you, madame."

There was a playfulness about him, Sophie thought, as she laid her hand on his arm. It was as if he, too, had been affected by the magic of this journey where convention's rituals had been suspended and amusement and wonder were the only acceptable responses.

Her gaze skimmed the brilliant dining room, looking for her husband amongst the seventy chattering, bright-plumed guests. "How strange I do not see my husband, Count."

"I understand he excused himself from attendance this evening. He is responsible for the arrangements for the reception of the Prince of Prussia when we reach Kaidak. It is not a light burden."

"No," agreed Sophie, taking her place at the table. "It will be quite a few days before we reach Kaidak, will it not?" Her tone was innocent, her smile sweet.

"I imagine Prince Dmitriev will be much occupied with details until then," responded Adam gravely.

"My husband is always a stickler for detail, and indefatigable when it comes to duty," said Sophie. "Yes, just a little of the salmon, thank you." She smiled at the footman, standing at her elbow with the silver platter of fish. "No, I will just have water, thank you." She waved away the butler with the wine decanter.

Adam looked at her in surprise. "No wine, Sophie?"

She frowned. "I don't feel like it tonight. Maybe water travel does not suit me any better than carriages."

"It is as smooth as glass," Adam protested, slicing into his salmon. "You will become accustomed soon enough."

"I am sure of it." Sophie shrugged. "I am ravenous, at all events."

All around them conversations buzzed, heads were bent in intimate conclave, laughter rose, sometimes immoderate. Adam and Sophie enjoyed a form of public privacy, drawing no attention in the general hum as they conducted the conversation of intimates in the language of acquaintances.

An orchestra played on deck after dinner, and throughout the spring evening, into the radiant night, the party danced, strolled, laughed, and exclaimed as they sailed through the country of the Cossacks, peaceful under the starry sky.

The czarina, on the arm of Monsieur Redcoat, retired early, but there was no curfew upon her guests or her ladies-in-waiting. It was very late when Sophie was rowed back to the imperial galley to seek the peace of her cabin, where Maria waited to help her into bed.

Once in her peignoir, Sophie dismissed the maid. "I will brush my own hair. Go to bed now. You must be tired."

Maria looked surprised and gratified at this consideration. She bobbed a curtsy, then left to seek her own rest in the servants' quarters below decks.

Sophie drew her brush through the silken cascade of her hair. She had found a semblance of acceptance where Maria was concerned. One could not blame the serf for obeying the orders of such a master as Prince Dmitriev; but the longing for Tanya Feodorovna and her abrasive common sense could not be assuaged.

Slipping off the apricot-colored silk peignoir, she stretched tiredly. It had been an amazing day, promising to be the first of many such. She was unusually fatigued, though. The luxury of a feather mattress enclosed her as she climbed into bed. The porthole was open, filling the chamber with the milky light of a northern night; the rhythmic swish of oars lulled her, the regular slap of water soothed, her eyes closed. . . .

The tapping on the partition wall beside her head melded into the noises of night and motion. Through the delicious languor of half-sleep, she did not separate the sound until it became a rhythm, insistently obtrusive. She was wide awake. That was no accidental rhythm. It was clearly designed to produce a response.

Hesitantly, she tapped back, as laughter at this game, ridiculous yet somehow in keeping with Potemkin's fairyland, bubbled in her throat.

"I thought you were never going to wake up." There was a deep chuckle in the voice whispering to her from behind a bare inch or two of wood.

"Adam!" Sophie sat up, covering her mouth with her hand to stifle her squawk of astonishment. "Where are you?"

"Next door, of course. Where are your wits?"

"Gone begging," she whispered with a choke of laughter. "How did you get there?"

"Simple. The disposition of cabins on this galley was my province."

"Why did you not tell me?"

"I thought you overdue for a surprise."

"Are you coming in?"

"I thought I might."

Sophie curled over her laughter at his solemnly considering tone, burying her face in her pillow, pulling the sheet over her head.

"Hey! What are you doing in that cocoon?" In no more than a minute or two, the sheet was pulled free, Adam's whisper, suffused with his own hilarity, sounding above her. "Turn over!"

Sophie rolled onto her back, showing him pink cheeks glistening with tears of laughter. "I cannot believe you have contrived this," she gasped. "It is not like you."

Adam looked hurt. "I had thought myself grown rather accomplished recently in such matters."

Sophie stiffened slightly but could detect not a trace of the old constraint in his voice or expression. Indolently, she stretched, smiling seductively up at him. "An expert, if the truth be told."

The gray gaze ran slowly down her body. The thin satin nightgown clung to the soft curve of breast and hip, dipped into the concavity of her belly, outlined the pointy hipbones that were one of his greatest delights in this garden of delights laid out in wanton offering.

"Take your nightgown off," he softly commanded.

"You take it off," she returned, running her tongue over her lips, stretching again, deliberately taunting.

Adam shook his head. "Life would be a lot easier if you had ever learned to do as you are told," he murmured plaintively. The plaintive tone, however, was belied by the energy of his action. Swooping down upon her, he lifted her off the bed, setting her firmly on her feet. "Now, do as I tell you."

Sophie's eyes narrowed. She reached for the girdle of his

robe, very slowly untying it, spreading apart the sides as she looked hungrily down his body, thus bared for her desirous gaze. Moving closer, she pressed her lips to his nipples, tantalized with her tongue until the little knobs hardened beneath the moist caress. One hand drifted over his belly, feeling the involuntary contraction of his abdominal muscles under the touch, drifted down to whisper between his thighs.

"Disobedience is not always an offense, is it?" she murmured wickedly, sliding to her knees, holding him between her hands, smiling with sensual mischief up at his transported face as her tongue flicked in an erotic dance that forced a groan from his lips; his hands urgently grasped her head, fingers twining in the luxuriant dark fall.

"Witch!" he declared on a shuddering breath. "Get up, for pity's sake." Catching her beneath the arms, he drew her to her feet again. "Take that damned nightgown off."

"I hear and obey, lord." Sophie laughingly obliged, tossing the garment to the floor. "Now what?" She planted her hands on her hips and threw back her head, more than a hint of challenge in her glowing dark eyes.

The air scintillated as the game took shape. Reaching out his hand, he caught the swirling mass of hair, twisting it around his wrist, pulling her toward him like a fish on a line. "Sophia Alexeyevna, I think it is time you discovered what happens when your challenges are accepted," he murmured, turning her to face the bed. . . .

"Sweet heaven!" Sophie moaned some considerable time later collapsing onto her stomach as her knees gave way beneath her. "If that is what happens when my challenges are accepted, I shall have to make a practice of issuing them more frequently."

Too breathless for the moment to respond verbally, Adam tapped her bottom with his fingertips. They lay in the shaft of moonlight from the porthole until the sweat had dried on their bodies. Sophie, shivering in the sudden chill, reached down for the sheet twisted beneath her, but Adam forestalled her, turning her body as he disentangled the covers, drawing them over her. Lazily, one finger flicked her nipple as he covered her breast, his hand squeezing the soft globe.

"Oh, don't do that!" Sophie winced, covering his hand with her own.

"Did I hurt you, sweet?" Remorsefully, Adam sat up. "I did not mean to be ungentle."

"You were not," she said. "It is just that I am a little tender at the moment. I expect it is the time of the month." A slow, cold sweat started on her body. Adam, unnoticing, lay down again beside her. Sophie stared up at the cabin ceiling, wrestling with her errant memory. When? She could not remember. She had never paid the slightest attention to that inevitable monthly inconvenience. It came when it came. Sweat trickled between her sore breasts, puddled in her navel. Queasiness, fatigue, no interest in wine, hunger . . . Holy Mother, she did not need Tanya to interpret the signs for her. Her body went rigid.

"Whatever is it?" Adam propped himself on one elbow. "You've gone as stiff as a board, Sophie." He smoothed her hair. "You're sweating, love. Do you not feel well?"

She licked her dry lips. "I am not ill exactly. I think . . . I think I am with child, Adam."

The stillness in his body was matched by the silence in the cabin. "But I thought you—"

"So did I," she interrupted. "It would seem that Paul's failure to sire an heir should perhaps be laid at his door rather than at those of his wives."

Adam sat up, his expression calm. "Do you suspect this, Sophie, or do you know it for a fact?"

"I know it," she said hopelessly. "But I did not know it until just this minute. I did not even suspect . . . although the signs . . . Oh, what are we going to do, Adam?"

"I expect your husband will be overjoyed," he said coolly, hiding his anguish.

"It cannot be Paul's child," she said, her voice flat. "He has come to my bed but once since he sent me away to Berkholzskoye, and he failed to . . ." She shrugged expressively.

Adam got out of bed, pulling his robe around him. It was

a piece of information that filled him with the most absurd pleasure, yet it was the least helpful fact in these desperate straits. He forced himself to think clearly. "How many weeks is it?"

Sophie shook her head in mortification. "I cannot remember. I know it is silly, but I just cannot remember."

Adam stared at her. "That is not so much silly, Sophie, as downright careless. All women keep track of these matters."

"How do you know they do?" She could hear the defensive sullenness in her voice.

"I have four older sisters," he said shortly. "They treated me as part of the furniture most of the time. I heard many things."

"Well, I am not like all women." She turned her face to the wall.

"No, you are not." He sat on the bed beside her, rubbing her back gently. "You must try to remember, however. It is vitally important. Was it before you came to Kiev?"

"Yes, I think so."

Adam closed his eyes on his exasperation. "You must do better than think, Sophie."

She had been in Kiev six weeks. After a minute, she nodded definitely. "It has not come upon me since I arrived in Kiev."

Adam sighed. "Let us try to get a little closer. Was it before the wolf hunt?" Then his face cleared. "Actually, I can answer that for you. Do you remember how angry I was when you jumped that ravine during the hunt?"

Sophie turned around to face him, her expression puzzled. "Yes, but what has that . . . ? Ahh . . . It was that night, of course. You decided to forgive me, only I was indisposed." For a moment, she smiled at the memory as if forgetting why it had been prompted.

"That was the end of January," Adam said. "It is now the beginning of April. We have until perhaps July before your condition will become too obvious to be concealed beneath your gowns, however loose."

"What are you suggesting?" She lay looking up into his

face, which revealed nothing but the countenance of a man accustomed to making plans, to dealing with crises, doing both those things. In a way it was comforting, but in another way dismaying that he should not evince an emotional reaction to this disaster.

Abruptly, Adam stood up, striding to the porthole, where he stood looking out at the land sliding past beneath the moonglow. Of all the tragic ironies of fate. The woman he loved was bearing his child, a child he could never acknowledge as his own. And his wife had carried another man's child that she would have had her husband acknowledge as his own.

"There is only one solution, Sophie." He spoke out into the night so that she had to sit up, concentrating in order to hear him. "It is a common problem, and the solution is as common. You must remain at court until your condition cannot be concealed, then you must petition the empress for permission to retire to Berkholzskoye for a spell. If necessary, you will tell her the truth. She will not deny you the right to . . . to cover up your error." He shrugged, his dry tone masking the terrible bleakness. "She was obliged to do the same during her own marriage. You will deliver the child, who will then be established with some family on the estate. The child, for its own protection, will grow up in ignorance of its parentage, but it will be well provided for."

He swung back to the room, but his face was in shadow. "It is fortunate that your husband will be little in your company during this journey. At Kiev, on the return journey, you will petition the empress. Since Prince Dmitriev will not be welcomed at Berkholzskoye, there is every reason to hope that he need never discover the truth. After the birth, you will return to St. Petersburg as if nothing had happened."

Sophie touched her stomach, wave after wave of desolation washing through her until she thought she would drown in its blackness. "We must give up our child?"

"There is no alternative," he rasped.

"When we reach the Crimea, it would be simple enough surely to slip over the frontier into Turkey," she whispered.

"And do what?" he demanded harshly. "Outlawed adulterers with neither family nor fortune, wandering the Ottoman Empire at the mercy of every Turkish bandit . . . Oh, Sophie, be realistic."

Her head bowed, the thick hair falling forward, baring the supple column of her neck. Adam crossed the cabin, bending to kiss the fragile, curving pillar. "We have at least until June, sweetheart. There is a place in Potemkin's wonderland for us. Let us enjoy the present and face the future when it comes."

In a world where happiness was so ephemeral, could be snatched from one with such violence, it would be a criminal waste to sully what one had with what would be. She raised her head, reaching over her shoulder to stroke his face.

"We will live in Potemkin's illusions then, love, and welcome the substitute for reality."

As the galleys glided in stately procession down the Dnieper, everything conspired to ensure that reality was suspended as they all became lost in the prince's dreamland. The air was filled with music from the orchestras playing on the decks. Flags fluttered gaily in the spring breezes. On the banks a continuous pageant was played out before the spellbound audience. A troop of Cossack horsemen would suddenly appear, charging out of the desert, wild and warlike on their magnificent steeds, performing before their empress and her guests the most amazing equestrian feats that utterly entranced Sophie.

"I wish I could join them," she said wistfully to Adam as they leaned against the rail. "On Khan, I could do all of those things just as well."

Adam, who had seen exactly what she could accomplish on the back of her Cossack stallion, did not disagree. "Why do you not suggest to Potemkin that when they appear again, they should have a warlike woman in their midst? I am sure he can provide the costume."

"Do you think I could?" Eagerly, she looked up at him. "Oh, you are teasing me."

"No, surely not!" he exclaimed, wishing he could tuck a wind-whipped lock of her hair under her hat, that he could kiss the tip of that straight nose, could . . .

"Just look at that pretty village." Sophie, unaware of his wishful musings, had turned again to the rail. Brightly painted houses clustered among gardens brilliant with flowers. Peasants, smiling and waving, their clothes sturdy, clean, not a rag to be seen, worked in their gardens or drove goats and cows along the straight white road disappearing into the steppe.

"Do you think those houses are more than a painted façade?" The Prince de Ligne appeared at the rail beside Sophie. He shook his head in amazement. "Do you really think they have inhabitants, Princess?"

"The Russian peasant is not in general so well clothed and housed, your excellency," she said with a sigh. "But I do not think we are supposed to view Russia in its truth."

"That road was laid last night," Adam told them with the authority of a member of Potemkin's staff. "The crews worked all night to create the village, its gardens, and its road."

"Just to be displayed for as long as it takes this fleet to pass," broke in the Comte de Ségur. "It is a mirage Potemkin has created. A mirage to the glory of his empress."

"But we are none of us impervious to its charm," Sophie pointed out with absolute truth.

"No, indeed not." The Prussian envoy shook his head once more in amazement. "It is to be transported out of time, out of place." He laughed. "We are a part of Cleopatra's fleet; the czarina is a modern queen of Egypt."

Potemkin had certainly succeeded in his aim, Adam reflected, looking out at the grandeur of the flower-strewn steppes, the brilliant sky, the whole magnificence of this wild landscape. The prince had intended to impress this bevy of distinguished foreigners with the overwhelming majesty of Russia, and the majesty of her empress. They might not be deceived by Potemkin's illusions, but they could not fail to be impressed, something that would be communicated to their governments.

A twitter of pipes came across the water. Glancing down, Sophie saw a launch being rowed to the galley. Resplendent in his braided uniform and plumed hat sat her husband, the only passenger. Instinctively, she moved away from Adam's side. The company of the Prince de Ligne and the Comte de Ségur was unexceptionable; indeed, to ensure their entertainment and comfort was a part of her duties. In the manner of a hunted animal seeking protective covering, she stepped between the two ambassadors, beginning an animated discussion on the music presently enlivening the air around them.

Prince Paul Dmitriev stepped onto the galley amid the ceremony accorded a man of his rank. His cane was tucked beneath his arm, his buttons shone in the sun, the plume of his hat waved gracefully in the breeze. His cold, pale blue eyes fell upon his wife.

"Madame." He stepped toward her, took her hand, and deliberately kissed her cheek in husbandly greeting. "I have sadly neglected you, I fear, but duty must come before pleasure."

"And you are ever dutiful, Paul," Sophie said.

Adam clenched his fists. Surely, Sophie could not be underestimating her husband, not after what he had done to her, and tried to do to her? She would simply madden him further with the quickness of her retorts. It was a quickness that came naturally to her, he knew. But it was lunacy to sharpen her wits on such a one as Paul Dmitriev.

The general's thin smile flickered. "There is no duty that I will fail to perform, my dear wife. By whatever means are necessary."

The menacing reminder of that duty he intended performing when the world returned to normal brought the sick fear again; but she was quite safe here, under the bright blue sky in Potemkin's fairy tale, Adam beside her, the two ambassadors smiling benignly, hearing nothing out of the ordinary in the exchange. She was quite safe . . . here . . . for the moment. Her hand drifted to her belly.

Chapter 16

"Do you notice anything at all out of the ordinary about Sophia Alexeyevna, Grisha?" Catherine frowned, leaning back in her chair late one evening in her cabin, with its twin beds. The favorite was at the moment playing cards with some of his fellow guardsmen in the library, an activity smiled upon by his imperial mistress. His absence provided his elders with the opportunity for intimate discussion.

"She is in love," Potemkin declared unequivocally. "That faraway radiance cannot be explained in any other way."

"But with whom?" Catherine tapped her fingers on the arm of her chair. "Both the Prince de Ligne and the Comte de Ségur are much in her company, but she could not be so foolish as to attempt dalliance in such fields."

"They do not outrank the princess," Potemkin pointed out gently.

"No, of course not. That is not the issue." Impatience tinged the czarina's generally calm tones; she took a long drink from the glass of hot water that served as her habitual nightcap. "But Prince Dmitriev is not the kind to look upon a little adventuring by his wife with equanimity. We cannot afford a scandal involving foreign ambassadors."

"It will perhaps be advisable to keep the general occupied," mused Potemkin. "Until we can discover who is the most fortunate of men."

Catherine smiled. "Do I detect a note of envy, Grisha?"

"I fear so." The prince sighed heavily, but his eye gleamed.

"Fortunately, there is no shortage of youth and beauty, so one can find consolation for dashed hopes."

"Well, you must keep the husband as far from his wife as possible. I will have a talk with her. . . . Ah, Sasha. Did you win?" All smiles, the empress turned to the just-opened door, where lounged Alexander Mamonov, somewhat the worse for drink, his red uniform jacket unbuttoned at the neck.

"Alas, no, Madame," he said, hiccuping, then met a piercing stare from Potemkin. The prince had put Monsieur Redcoat in the czarina's bed and could as easily remove him. Alcohol tended to inhibit vigor, and Her Imperial Majesty demanded an excess of vigor from her young men. Potemkin would not countenance a slipping in performance.

"I will leave you, Madame." Potemkin bowed over Catherine's hand, kissing her fingers, and if in either of their breasts rose the powerful memories of kisses they had shared, of the excessive vigors of their erotic love, joined so many years ago, it was a secret they kept from the young man struggling to prepare himself for the night's duties lying ahead.

A puzzled Sophie left the czarina's cabin the next morning. She had just been subjected to a gentle, yet most skillful interrogation, and she did not know why. The empress had inquired into her health, into her habits, into the friends she had made on board, into the amount of time she spent with her husband. She had asked Sophie's opinion of all the distinguished guests on board, and those pleasantly smiling eyes had not missed a nuance of expression on Sophie's face as she had answered frankly. Yes, she did find the French and Prussian envoys particularly good company, but then so did the empress, did she not? It would be difficult not to be amused by such cultivated, witty gentlemen. The czarina had been obliged to agree with her lady-in-waiting's seemingly unimpeachable objectivity.

Sophie had been dismissed after an hour, having no idea whether the czarina had discovered whatever it was she wished to discover. It was most unnerving, particularly when one *was* harboring a particularly weighty secret. Could the czarina possibly suspect the lover, the pregnancy? No, there was not a hint of the latter about face or form, and she and Adam were far too careful for suspicion.

Another cloud hung over her horizon, however. They would reach Kaidak on the morrow, where the Prince of Prussia would join the grand tour. Paul's primary duty would be completed then. Presumably he would have more time to spend at the social functions that made up the daily round of shipboard life. He would be in his wife's company as much as he chose.

That quiver of fear ran up her spine again. He never lost an opportunity to remind her of the temporary nature of her present refuge. In company, he talked openly of his intention to spend some time on his country estate when this journey was completed. The cold blue eyes would rest upon her in mocking derision, as if he could see through the indifferent facade to the terror beneath. Alone, imprisoned in the country mansion with only serfs, locked in their own terrified obedience, for witness, she would be defenseless against a cruelty that she knew acknowledged no limits. And if he were to discover her pregnancy . . . dear God, the images such a prospect conjured were too appalling to contemplate. Supposing she could not persuade the empress to grant her permission to go to Berkholzskoye? The empress's permission would override any contrary order of her husband's, but what if Catherine would not grant even the few months of rustication necessary to accomplish the secret birth of the child she carried?

That night Sophie did not respond to the tapping on the partition. Plagued as she was with the horrific fancies of an imagination already exacerbated by the emotional upheavals of pregnancy, she knew that tonight she could not behave with Adam as if only the present illusion was important. It would not relieve the fears to share them, and it would add most dreadfully to Adam's anxieties, which he tried so manfully to keep from her.

Next door, Adam frowningly contemplated the thin, utterly

uncommunicative piece of wood. He had been occupied all
day with Potemkin and preparations for tomorrow's arrival in
Kaidak. A glimpse of Sophie at dinner was all that had been
afforded him; it was not a glimpse that had done much for
his peace of mind. She had looked wan, abstracted, quite
without her usual glow. Was she asleep now? He stared at
the partition as if it would dissolve before his eyes. It did not,
but he was convinced that Sophie was lying wide awake on
the other side.

His mouth took a grim turn. The narrow passage outside
the cabin door was deserted, and he slipped out of his cabin
and into the one next door with no more disturbance than a
shadow. The mound on the bed stirred as he closed the door.

"You are not asleep," he stated, padding soft-footed to
the bed. "Do not play games with me, Sophie. I don't have
the patience for them."

Sophie opened her eyes, wondering why he sounded so
annoyed. "I do not feel like making love."

"Then we will not," he said matter-of-factly. "Was that
why you would not answer me when I knocked?" When she
did not reply, he sat on the bed, catching her chin between
finger and thumb, turning her face toward him. "I trust that
was not the reason, Sophia Alexeyevna. I am not some client
in a whorehouse."

Color flooded the pale cheeks. The dark eyes sparked anger. "How could you say something like that?"

"Was it the reason?"

"No, of course it was not." She sighed. "Why are you so
annoyed?"

"Because something is troubling you, has been all day,
unless I much mistake the matter, and you would exclude
me. Now sit up and tell me all about it, before I become
extremely annoyed."

"I wonder what that would be like," Sophie murmured, a
thoughtful gleam in her eye.

"You are about to find out."

It was banter, but there was a base of gravity. Sophie sat
up, pushing her hair away from her face. "I suppose it is just

that we are about to reach Kaidak and this magical voyage will be over. It makes me gloomy.'' It was half the truth, at least.

"But from Kaidak we will be crossing your beloved steppes,'' Adam said. "Sleeping in tents beneath the stars. Come, sweetheart, it is exactly the sort of thing you love.''

"Carriages,'' Sophie said glumly. "Carriages and Paul. He will not be so occupied once Prince Joseph joins us.''

Adam frowned, wondering which of the two concerns was causing the greatest anxiety. "I'm sure you will be able to ride most of the way, if you explain your malady to the empress,'' he said. "And where you may not, you may travel in an open carriage. It will not be so bad.'' Seeing that she looked a little more cheerful, he said, "I do not know about your husband. I have not seen anyone's orders for the next stage of the trip. But you remain with the imperial suite, and he remains with the working officers. It will be no different from Kiev.''

"I suppose so.'' Sophie sighed, her head dropping to his shoulder. "Hold me, love. I feel all weak and vulnerable, as if I've shed a skin.''

"Then take mine,'' he said gently, sliding into bed beside her, wrapping her tightly against his body. "All I have is yours, sweet love, blood, bone, and sinew.''

Two days later, the party, augmented by Joseph II of Prussia, left the galleys and took to the steppes. Sophie, mounted on a neat, spirited mare as the procession set out, felt her heart lift on a surge of joy. Gliding down the river in the spring sun had been wonderful, but nothing could compare with being on horseback, even if she was obliged to ride sidesaddle. The czarina had presented not the least difficulty when told of her lady-in-waiting's distressing weakness when it came to wheeled travel, merely telling her that she should not ride far from the imperial carriage.

Prince Dmitriev was not so accommodating, however. At the sight of his wife on a caracolling horse, laughing with pleasure, he thundered up to her on his own steed. "What is this? Why are you riding?"

"I have the czarina's permission," she said, trying to make her voice conciliatory. "She understands that I suffer acutely from travel sickness."

"I will not have you riding like some hoyden when the rest of Her Majesty's suite are traveling decently in carriages," he said with icy fury.

"I do not ride like a hoyden," Sophie said mutinously, although she knew she should not. Her husband's hand tightened around his riding whip and her heart jumped. But the general was a master of control.

"My dear, I am sure you must understand that it is not seemly. I will speak with the czarina." Wheeling his horse, he rode to the imperial carriage.

Utterly dismayed, Sophie sat her horse. Would he persuade Catherine that a husband's wishes were owed precedence over the mere megrims of the wife?

"You look as if you have lost a fortune, Sophia Alexeyevna." Prince Potemkin, bubbling with exuberance at the sight of his beautifully organized caravan, rode over to her. "Come, I will not have sad faces on such a day. It is not to be permitted. I command a smile."

Sophie offered a wan attempt. "Indeed, Prince, I would oblige you if I could, but I fear my husband is going to compel me to travel in a carriage."

"How should that be? I understood you do not travel well in such fashion," declared Potemkin, his eye gleaming fiercely.

"My husband does not consider riding to be seemly," she murmured, lowering her eyes.

"Never heard such nonsense!" Potemkin galloped off in the path of General Dmitriev.

Sophie could only sit and wait, chewing her lip. If Paul were overruled, his fury would exceed all bounds, but it would simply be added to the list of offenses for which he intended she should pay in full measure. At this point, she would rather store up hell for later than endure the present torment of a carriage.

The caravan began to move forward. Neither Potemkin nor Paul had reappeared, so Sophie encouraged the mare into a long-strided walk. It was very decorous, she thought, really most boring, tedious in the extreme. Her knees pressed the mare's sides. She broke into a trot. It was a little better, but not much. Sophie's eyes skimmed from side to side. The carriages were rumbling along the road, behind them trailing the baggage train, which stretched to the horizon. She was surrounded by horsemen, officers mainly, and one or two of the imperial guests who preferred the activity to sedentary travel. No one seemed to be taking the least notice of her; ahead lay the glorious emptiness of the steppe; beneath her she could feel the mare's eagerness, the speed and power she was reining in. What possible harm could it do?

Three minutes later, Adam, riding with Potemkin at the head of the caravan, heard the thunder of hooves, felt the air whistle past as a dapple-gray flash shot by.

"Holy Mother!" exclaimed Potemkin. "That's Princess Dmitrievna. . . . What a magnificent seat she has." He clicked his tongue against his teeth admiringly. "But I do not think her husband will appreciate such a flight." He chuckled.

Adam, white-faced, could barely keep his voice steady. "Perhaps I should go after her, Prince. The czarina might also be displeased."

Potemkin nodded. "Yes, I daresay you are right. Catch her if you can."

Adam put his horse to the gallop. This time she was not riding the unbeatable Khan, and his own mount was a match for any ordinary beast.

Sophie, hearing the hooves behind her, looked over her shoulder. She waved a hand at him, then urged the mare to greater speed, inviting her pursuer to a race. Adam swore every oath he knew, desperately touching his horse's flanks with his spurs. Unused to such an unkind prod, however lightly administered, his mount sprang forward, drawing level with the mare, who was beginning to tire. Sophie turned laughing to Adam as she eased back on the reins, then the laugh died on her face, faded from her eyes.

"You are completely devoid of the most basic common sense!" Adam exclaimed. "How dare you ride neck or nothing in your condition!"

"What condition?" Sophie said, having completely forgotten anything but the wondrous joy of her gallop. Then comprehension dawned. "Oh," she said. "But why should it matter? I am not about to be thrown."

Adam sent heavenward a swift prayer for strength and restraint, while contemplating a variety of ways of relieving his feelings.

"Oh, dear," Sophie said, having little difficulty reading the white face and blazing eyes. "I think you are about to murder me and bury my body on the steppe."

"Something like that," he said tightly.

"I cannot help feeling that that would be even more detrimental to my condition," she murmured pensively, regarding him through her eyelashes.

"It may strike you as strange, but I do not find this in the least amusing," Adam said, a chill in his voice strong enough to strike to the marrow of her bones.

It would be clearly politic to withdraw. "No," Sophie said humbly, hanging her head. "It was a joke in very poor taste. It was just so exhilarating after being cooped up for so long."

In silence, Adam swung his horse back the way they had come. Sophie followed, keeping a few paces behind him, wondering how long it would be before the ice melted. His wife was supposed to have died in a riding accident while carrying a child. The remembrance served to dampen her exhilaration, to produce an uncomfortable prickle of remorse for her flippancy.

They returned to the caravan, slowly winding its way across the steppe. Prince Potemkin, glancing at Sophie's subdued expression, then at his colonel's grimness, guessed that Count Danilevski had subjected the errant princess to the well-known rough edge of his tongue. Thoroughly deserved, thought the prince, deciding to leave well enough alone.

"You would be well advised, Princess, to take up your position with the imperial carriage," Count Danilevski said in the same Arctic tones.

"Yes, Count," replied the princess meekly.

She trotted off and Potemkin chuckled. "Were you harsh, Adam?"

"No more than necessary," the count said shortly. "If her husband witnessed such an indecorous display, he would be justified in insisting she travel in a carriage."

"Well, it is unlikely that Prince Dmitriev will be overseeing his wife's behavior for a while." Potemkin peered into the shimmering distance. "He is going ahead to Bakhchisarai to ensure that the Tatars are prepared to welcome their sovereign with all due ceremony and respect." Potemkin rubbed his chin thoughtfully. "Her Imperial Majesty insists upon entering the Crimea without the escort of Russian troops. She is convinced that if she trusts in the loyalty of the Tatars, she will receive it. It is but four years since the Khan yielded to Russian governorship. I trust Her Majesty's instincts are as true as always, but just in case I thought an advance force, arriving in peace, of course, might be a wise precaution."

Adam made the right noises in response to this confidence, but it required some effort to concentrate. His anger with Sophie dropped miraculously from him. In the absence of Dmitriev, the freedom of the steppes would truly be theirs. Sophie would be relieved of the niggling anxiety that he guessed occasionally hovered on the edge of panic; he would be free to contrive the scenarios for their loving in a spirit of play and adventure, liberated from the shadowy tentacles of a vengeful husband.

An hour later, Sophie, riding decorously beside the imperial carriage, engaged in conversation with the English ambassador, Lord Fitzherbert, who had also chosen to ride, became aware of a large troop of cavalry coming up from the rear of the caravan. At their head rode General, Prince Paul Dmitriev. He came over to her.

"I must bid you farewell, Sophia Alexeyevna. We will be reunited in Bakhchisarai."

Her heart leaped in her breast; she lowered her eyelashes, knowing the spark of excitement would shine from her eyes. "Do you go on a military exercise, Paul?"

"I go to ensure a peaceful reception for the empress," he said, the pomposity of his tone failing to disguise his pride in such a mission. He gestured to the troop of cavalry. "A show of strength should be sufficient to ensure compliance, but we are prepared should more be necessary."

"I do commend you, Paul," Sophie said demurely, conscious of the British ambassador beside her. "It is a mission for which you are supremely fitted." She turned to Lord Fitzherbert with an affected shudder. "The Tatars are such a violent, unpredictable race, sir, and they have only recently been made subject to Her Imperial Majesty. It would not be extraordinary if there were to be some demonstrations of disaffection."

"Indeed not," agreed His Lordship, eyeing the magnificent general and his troop. "You have some experience in the Crimea, I understand, General Dmitriev."

"A certain amount." Paul bowed in acknowledgment. "I fought with the field marshal during the annexation and have dealt with several insurrections since."

"Then our reception is in good hands," the Englishman said politely. With courteous delicacy, he urged his mount forward, leaving the general and his wife to make their farewells in a degree of privacy.

"Enjoy your riding, my dear," Paul said softly. "It is not a pleasure you will have for much longer." He rode away from her without waiting for a response. That clammy miasma settled over her, spoiling what should have been a moment of triumphant joy. She was wondering if she dared ride up to the head of the caravan to engage Count Danilevski in an unexceptionably neutral conversation that might serve to warm the temperature a little and dissipate her unease, when Lord Fitzherbert dropped back beside her. She returned to her duties.

In late afternoon the caravan halted. The passengers descended from their carriages to wander the green, flowery land. The sun had lost some of its earlier power, and the air was fresh with the scent of grass and flowers. Soon woodsmoke rose from braziers, then the heavy aromas of roasting meat. Samovars bubbled, servants ran from group to group, while crews put up the city of tents that would accommodate the enormous party. The tents of the distinguished guests were elaborate structures, richly decorated with silver braid and precious stones that winked in the dusk as the sun disappeared beyond the horizon.

Sophie found herself assigned to a tent with two other members of the suite. It was not unexpected, but she could not help wrinkling her nose at the inconvenience. No husband, but two chaperones! However, Count Danilevski had made no attempt to exchange so much as a glance with her since the contretemps that morning, so she was obliged, in some disgruntlement, to assume that pardon had not yet been granted. He presumably knew that Paul had left the procession, so it was to be hoped it would not be withheld overlong.

Dressed for dinner, she made her way to the czarina's tent, easily identified by the crown and two-headed eagle surmounting the jewel-bedecked canvas structure. Catherine's sleeping area was separated from a large reception room by a heavy tapestry. The reception area was furnished as if it were a salon in Czarskoye Selo, the summer palace outside St. Petersburg: chairs, divans, ottomans, rich rugs that covered the ground, filling the air with the scent of crushed flowers. Lamps glowed in elegant silver holders. Lackeys passed trays of champagne and vodka, olives, salt fish, and pickles.

Sophie joined the circle around the empress, her eyes skimming the throng for a sign of Adam even as she smiled, talked, gingerly sipped champagne. She felt him come up behind her. The little hairs on the back of her neck lifted. He brushed against her as he bowed to Catherine, who greeted him affably.

"May I procure you a glass of fruit syrup, Princess Dmitrievna? I have noticed you prefer it to champagne." He spoke softly as he turned from the magic circle around Catherine.

"It is kind of you to offer, Count, but I am not really in need of either." Her eyes questioned with a degree of anxiety.

"I do not know what is to be done with you, Sophia Alexeyevna," he said in the barest whisper, but the gray eyes sparked amusement and she relaxed with relief. "I understand your husband is gone to Bakhchisarai." He spoke casually, for all to hear.

"Yes, to ensure that all goes smoothly. It is a task for which he is most suited."

Talking in this manner, they managed to extricate themselves from the press quite naturally. Sophie fanned herself vigorously. "It is very hot, is it not, Count?"

He gave her a sharp glance as if to satisfy himself that her remark was merely a ploy to get them to the door and not indicative of genuine distress. But her color was normal, her smile steady. "A breath of air," he suggested, gesturing to the tent opening.

They stood for a moment looking out on the amazing sight of a canvas city imposed upon the wilderness. "Follow the north star," Adam instructed in a voice that rose and fell in normal cadences as if he were saying nothing out of the ordinary. "There is a grove of trees. You will find me there."

"When?" Her voice dropped involuntarily.

"Whenever you are able to leave your tent without remark." His voice did not alter, and Sophie realized that the experienced conspirator recognized that words would not be noticed in the melee, whereas surreptitious attitudes and whispers might draw attention. She had not thought of Adam as an experienced conspirator. Perhaps it was just a skill growing naturally out of a military training.

Her own skills at extricating herself from her tent fellows were not well honed, she found. The empress had chosen carefully. Thinking to provide Princess Dmitrievna with congenial company of her own age, she had assigned gossipy Natalia Saltykova and the more gentle, sweet-tempered

Countess Lomonsova to her tent. In the choice of Natalia, the czarina had an ulterior motive. The gossip missed little and was most conveniently indiscreet; the slightest prompting let loose the prattle like water from a dam. If Sophia Alexeyevna could be induced to confide in her friends, the czarina would hear what she needed to know.

As they prepared for bed, Sophie wondered fancifully whether Natalia would fade into thin air if she ever stopped talking. The ceaseless chatter pouring forth from a rosebud mouth seemed to define the person. She was just words, no substance at all. It seemed impossible that sleep would put an end to the flow, which was serving to put Sophie to sleep very effectively. She could hardly keep her eyes open as the words washed over her in the soft gloom. The exertions of the day took their toll, the fresh night air soothed and relaxed . . .

She woke with a jerk, wondering what had penetrated her doze. It was the silence, blissful silence disturbed only by the deep, rhythmic breathing of her companions. It was too dark inside the tent to see the time. She slid out of bed, reached for her cloak, slipped from the tent to stand in the moon-bright, star-bright silver night. Her watch said two o'clock. Was Adam still waiting for her? Drawing the cloak tightly around her, she ran on bare feet across the grass, following the north star. The grove of trees stood out in the boundless, dark expanse beneath the brilliant, shimmering sky. The grass prickled beneath her feet as she ran, filled with anxious expectation. Would he still be waiting?

He stood, a darker shadow in the shadows of the trees. Gasping, she ran into his arms, laughing and apologizing in the same breath, lifting her face for his kiss. "I fell asleep. I do not know how I could have done so. Unless it is that Natalia's chatter is as soporific as laudanum."

"I am glad you slept." He pushed her hood away from her hair, running his hands through the silken chestnut-brown mane, drawing it over her shoulders, a concentrated smile playing over his mouth. "I would not have you unrested."

"Have you been waiting forever?" Her eyes held his, soft with promise yet sparkly with excitement.

"An eternity," he replied. "Let us go farther onto the steppe." Taking her hand, he led her out of the trees' shadow, into the milky light. "It is as if one is inhabiting another world," he said softly. "Look over there."

"A caravan of camels," Sophie said, watching the stately shapes plodding, necks swaying, outlined against the horizon. "I used to lie in bed on summer nights listening to the shouts of the drivers as they passed by Berkholzskoye." She smiled up at Adam. "Such romance, I used to think. A magic world embodying all sorts of things that I could only feel as vague yearnings, delicious stirrings that I did not understand and couldn't describe." She laughed. "Fortunately, for had I attempted to tell Tanya about such mysterious sensations she would have muttered about indigestion and dosed me with sulphur and molasses!"

"And do you feel those mysterious sensations now?" He touched her face with a finger.

"Oh, yes," Sophie said. "But I understand them now."

Adam unfastened her cloak, spreading it upon the ground. "What a wanton creature you are," he murmured. "To come out on the steppe in your nightgown."

"I did not think there was much point in dressing," she replied with that crooked, quizzical smile. "Since I did not expect to remain dressed for very long."

"Shameless one!" He drew her down, leaning over her, hands braced on either side of her body. "I have a fantasy I would like to enact."

"Oh." Her eyes sparkled responsively. "Can we both play?"

"Well," he drawled, trailing a kiss down the bridge of her nose. "Your role is somewhat passive in this particular fantasy."

"Tell."

Thoughtfully, he stretched out a hand, picking a violet from the steppe, then a daisy. He threaded them into her hair. "I

am going to plant you with flowers," he murmured, "everywhere on your body."

Sophie shivered deliciously. "Everywhere?"

"Everywhere . . . very slowly."

Her body quivered, moistened, burned. Her breath came
swift through parted lips; her eyes glowed luminous. She was
suffused with desire, mastered by passion, lost in the image
of erotic promise. The balm of the night air laved her skin as
he drew her nightgown up her body, her limbs spread wide
upon the cloak as she lay, a sacrifice to the gods of love and
lust, bathed in starlight to be grafted with the delicate, fragrant beauty of the steppe.

The stars were fading, a pink tinge hovering in the sky,
when the night of love drew to its inevitable close. "Hurry,
sweetheart," Adam said on a note of urgency, drawing her
upright. "It is later than it should be."

Sophie tucked her hair beneath her hood. "No one can tell
that I have only my nightgown on. A dawn stroll will not
seem too extraordinary in this fairyland, should we be seen."

He glanced down at her feet with a rueful chuckle. "Barefoot, Sophie?"

She curled her toes into the grass. "I like to feel the dews
upon my feet. It is a perfectly reasonable explanation for one
who has the steppes in her blood."

"I am not sure I would be convinced," he said. "We must
not be seen together, though." He hurried her through the
grass to the grove of trees, pausing there for a last kiss before
sending her on ahead, approaching the canvas city himself
from a different direction.

It was too late for such a precaution, however, although
neither of them was aware of it. Prince Potemkin, restless in
the dawn, his energetic mind seething with plans and pros-
pects, had also left his bed before the night was done. Whispers, a soft laugh unmistakably rich with pleasures received
and imparted, reached him in the still air. Curious to see who
was so clearly enjoying the sensual delights to which he was
no stranger himself, he cautiously approached the sounds. A
small hillock offered concealment, and from its shelter he

identified the voices of Princess Dmitrievna and Count Danilevski.

Delicately he withdrew, voyeurism not being one of his
pleasures, and went off to report to the empress this most
satisfactory answer to the puzzle of Sophia Alexeyevna.

Chapter 17

It was a most satisfactory answer, Catherine reflected, leaning back in her carriage, allowing her eyes to close in the afternoon's warmth. Her companions in the vehicle discreetly turned away from the drowsy little old lady whose breath came through the slack, toothless mouth in short puffs. Most satisfactory . . .

Satisfied and happy with a lover, Sophia Alexeyevna would put a good face on her marriage and there would be no more talk of annulments and rustications. Adam Danilevski was a perfect choice. Unencumbered himself, he reduced the tangles usual in such liaisons by at least one strand. Of course, Dmitriev must be kept in ignorance. He was not the stuff of which complaisant husbands are made, and court scandals were really most unpleasant. Grisha would ensure his absence for most of this journey; once back in St. Petersburg ·. . . well, that was in another world, to be thought about when the magic was over. It was to be hoped she did not conceive, though. . . . However, she had not done so in all these months. . . . The czarina's head fell forward onto her breast. The little puffs took on a certain resonance.

To her amazement, Sophie found that she was never again assigned a tent fellow. True, her shelter was not as lavishly furnished or decorated as others; it was small, but the luxury of privacy had to be paid for. As they journeyed into the Crimea, she continued to ride in pleasant and varied company. Frequently, Prince Potemkin would invite her to join him at the head of the caravan, and she would find herself in the company of Count Danilevski; at other times she rode beside the czarina's carriage in the company of one or more of the ambassadors. Everything seemed designed for the fur-therance of her pleasure, for the easy accomplishment of in-timacy. When in questioning wonder, she expressed this to Adam he simply nodded, a slight smile tugging at the corners of his beautiful mouth.

"What is funny?" They were a half day's ride from Bakh-chisarai, and Sophie was beginning to feel the first hint of oppression fogging the cloudless serenity of the last days.

"I think," Adam said slowly, "that we have had a few cherubs on our side recently."

"Cherubs? Whatever can you mean?" Despite the hover-ing despondency, she could not help laughing at such a choice of word.

He looked mysterious. "You do not need to know, and I can only guess. Let us simply be thankful."

Sophie began to protest, then subsided with a gasp as they crested a rise and saw galloping toward them an army of Tatars dressed with such magnificence it quite took her breath away, armed with such seriousness it brought her heart into her mouth. "A reception committee or a repulsing army?" mused Adam. "The latter would hardly be surprising. We've imposed Christian officialdom on Islam, overshadowed their minarets with our churches."

"Invaded their streets with unveiled women," Sophie added somberly, watching the glittering, warlike army ap-proaching. "They despise women, they detest Christianity, why should they bow beneath the yoke of a Christian woman—even such a one as Catherine?"

"Because she trusts them to do so," Adam said. "Watch."

The splendid cavalcade of warriors surrounded the impe-rial carriage, where sat Catherine and the Prince of Prussia. Not a Russian fighting man was in sight, only officers in full ceremonial regalia.

"They could carry Their Majesties off to Constantinople, and no one could stop them." Sophie choked, half amused at the idea, half horrified. "Can you imagine what entertainment His Highness, Abdul Hamid would derive from such prisoners? Just think of the czarina in Abdul Hamid's harem!'' Sophie was assailed by a fit of giggles at the appalling irreverence of the thought.

''I'd rather not,'' Adam said dryly. ''But I do not think such a thing is about to happen. Her Imperial Majesty has simply been accorded a worthy escort for the empress of the erstwhile subjects of the Crimean Khanate.''

The imperial cortege and its escort entered the city of Bakhchisarai: a city of white houses dozing beneath the benediction of the southern sun, silver-leaved olive trees, the fragrance of jasmine and roses filling the air from gardens lushly burgeoning.

Sophie gazed, marveling, from the glories of the lavender-hued mountains to the crisp, jade green of the sea. ''Such bounty, Adam.''

He smiled his agreement, but made no other response. Somewhere in this city was to be found General, Prince Paul Dmitriev. Adam glanced sideways at Sophie.

''Perhaps it would be as well if you were not at my side,'' she said, perfectly attuned to his thoughts. ''I will drop back to find some quite innocent company.''

The city's inhabitants evinced indifference to the invading procession, turning their backs upon the splendor as if it had nothing to do with them. It was one form of self-defense, Sophie reflected. When a proud nation was humbled in such fashion, apparent apathy could tarnish the glitter of the invader.

They arrived at the palace of the dethroned Khan to be transported into the land of the Thousand and One Nights. This southern palace bore no resemblance to the grand habitations of Catherine's northern capitals. Here were orange and pomegranate trees, softly plashing fountains in fragrant courtyards, marble walls and tiled floors. Cashmeres and silks upholstered the divans and ottomans, rugs from Persia and Turkey lay in careless, scattered profusion, and the soft sea breezes wafted through arched windows, across deep balconies.

If this was the culmination of Potemkin's fairy-tale journey, he could not have chosen better. Sophie wandered, wide-eyed, through salons and courtyards, the incessant excitable babble of Natalia Saltykova at her shoulder. The urge to tell her to hold her tongue for just one minute that she might absorb what she was seeing became almost irresistible. The words were on her tongue when she heard a familiar, precise clicking of booted feet across the tiled floor. It took her back to the dining room in St. Petersburg, when she would sit in her chair waiting for the clock to strike two and her husband's measured stride to sound from the hall.

"Ah, my dear wife, you have had a pleasant journey, I trust?" He bowed, hat in hand, pale eyes derisive, as if he could hear the speeding of her heart—a reaction to fearful memory rather than to the present, but nonetheless powerful.

"Very pleasant, thank you, Paul." She curtsied to her husband, gave him her hand, moved her mouth into a smile shape. "You accomplished your mission most successfully, it would seem. The czarina's reception was magnificent."

"Did you imagine I might not succeed?"

She shook her head, saying truthfully, "No, I never imagined such a thing."

"Permit me to show you around the palace." He offered her his arm, inclined his head to the bevy of young women with his wife. "You will excuse me, mesdames, if I take my wife away from you for a short spell."

Sophie laid her hand upon her husband's arm, telling herself she was still safe. He could frighten her, but he could not harm her, not here . . . not now . . . not yet. Again, her other hand went surreptitiously to her belly, a soft curve invisible beneath the copious folds of her riding skirt.

With the appearance of complete affability, Prince Dmitriev escorted his wife through the palace of the Khan, imparting the knowledge he had acquired during the weeks of his stay. "The Tatars exhibit the most admirable understanding of a woman's function in the world and of her worth," he remarked casually, leading her through a series of opulent salons. "This was the prince's harem. Here, he kept his women secure from the eyes of all but themselves. A Mohammedan woman has but two tasks: to minister to her lord's pleasure and to be fruitful.'' The blue eyes rested upon his wife. "Should a woman fail to perform in either task she is expendable . . . not worth the protection, shelter, means of subsistence granted by her master.''

"There is no need to labor the point, Paul.'' Sophie could see little value in pretending to believe they were having an ordinary conversation.

His smile flickered thinly. "Of course, in some cases certain efforts are made to encourage a . . . a recalcitrant, shall we say, to conform. Generally,'' he continued pensively, "such efforts prove most successful.'' He laid a hand over Sophie's, resting nerveless upon his arm. "We will try again, Sophia Alexeyevna. I have learned much from the followers of the Prophet.''

Sophie wondered if perhaps her husband had become unhinged under the temperate skies of this southern clime. Had he become infected with the barbarous attitudes and customs of a people who had pillaged and enslaved whole populations as they enslaved the entire female sex? It occurred to her that Paul was ripe for such an infection; such beliefs and behavior would find rich growing ground in a mind already dedicated to the complete dominance of any soul unfortunate enough to be in the least dependent upon him. It was a singularly uncomforting reflection.

"This is your chamber.'' Paul gestured toward an arched doorway, beyond which lay a small sleeping chamber overlooking an inner courtyard. Sophie obeyed the invitation to enter, followed by her husband, who closed the door softly behind him.

"Now,'' he said, seating himself upon an upholstered divan. "Let us see if such an environment cannot produce a beneficial effect in you, my cold, barren, unworthy wife.'' The pale gaze pinned her to the spot. "Let us see if you cannot kindle at least a flicker of desire in my breast. You see, I do not find you in the least appealing. But I think that is because you do not try hard enough. Would you be good enough to undress for me?''

Sophie wondered if she had really heard the polite request.

She could feel a scream building deep inside her. But what good would that do? There was nothing out of the ordinary about a husband and wife enjoying a little privacy after a separation. Would he notice anything untoward about her body? Her waist was a little thicker, her breasts heavier, but her height masked these changes. If he was not looking for them, he would not see them.

The calculations raced at breakneck speed through her fevered brain. If he was going to force himself upon her, she would endure it as she had done in the past. Slowly, she shrugged out of her jacket and began to unfasten the buttons of her blouse.

A knock at the door stilled her fingers. A spasm of annoyance crossed Paul's face as he bade the knocker enter. Sophie turned away to the window, looking down on the courtyard as she refastened her shirt.

"Prince Potemkin is holding a council, General, Prince Dmitriev," a young, breathless voice was saying. "I am bidden to request your presence."

A reprieve, but for how long?

Paul, all thoughts of his wife departed under the press of duty, was flaying the young cornet for the unsoldierly bearing that would have him present himself to a superior officer breathless and sweaty. Sophie felt compassion for the lad as the general's tongue stripped him of every vestige of dignity, but she was human enough to be grateful for the diversion. The cornet unwisely attempted to defend himself on the grounds that the general had been hard to find and his message urgent. Dmitriev's cane whacked down upon the lad's shoulder with bruising force. Sophie winced, but kept her eyes on the courtyard beneath the window.

"I will come to you after you retire," her husband was saying in clipped accents. "We will continue then." The door clicked shut behind him.

Sophie let out her breath on a long exhalation of relief. Another knock produced Maria, come to unpack her mistress's belongings. Since Paul's departure at Kaidak, Sophie had loftily dispensed with the maid's more intimate services, thus ensuring that Maria was in no position to notice any physical changes in her mistress. The serf, well aware of how little favor she found in the princess's eyes, had shown no surprise at being relegated to the basic duties of wardrobe mistress. Since the prince was not there to give her contrary orders, she had no choice but to obey Sophia Alexeyevna. If she was surprised that laundering of the princess's undergarments was accomplished by a young girl in Countess Lomonsova's service, she appeared to accept it with the blind resignation of her kind.

Leaving Maria to her task, Sophie went quickly to the czarina's apartments. Here all was bustle as the empress settled into her palace, and the Grand Mistress, now that the journeying was over for the time being, set to with customary dedication to impose order and routine upon the court.

"Do you care to stroll through the gardens, Princess?" The Prince de Ligne bowed. "I am afraid that if I do not remove myself, Countess Shuvalova will assign me some task."

"Come now, Your Excellency, the Grand Mistress would never be guilty of such a gross breach of etiquette," said Sophie, laughing. "But I would love to take a walk, in order that *I* should not be assigned some irksome duty."

"Sophia Alexeyevna."

At the czarina's calm summons, Sophie shrugged ruefully. "I spoke too soon. Excuse me, Prince." She crossed to where the empress was seated at a table examining the reports that reached her daily from every corner of the empire. It mattered not whether she was under a tent on the open steppe, drifting down the Dnieper in a galley, or taking up residence in the palace of the Khan, the government was wherever Catherine was, and the business of government continued.

She looked at her lady-in-waiting thoughtfully. "I trust you will not be too disappointed, Princess, but I am afraid I have need of your husband's services in a matter that will take him from your side again." The joyful flash in the dark eyes was swiftly extinguished, but not before the empress saw it. She smiled to herself, thinking indulgently of how pleasant it was to facilitate the paths of love. "He will be leaving before night-fall for the Sublime Porte, bearing my message for the Sultan."

"It would be a poor wife, Madame, who could fail to be pleased by such an honor for her husband," Sophie said, curtsying.

Duplicitous baggage, Catherine thought tolerantly. "You will continue to bear the French, Prussian, and British envoys company, Princess. It is a duty you perform well."

"It is hardly a duty, Madame." She curtsied again. "May I have leave to accompany the Prince de Ligne on a stroll about the gardens?"

Catherine waved her away, and she returned to the prince, unable to keep the spring from her step or the light that shone more lustrously than usual from her eyes. There would be no conjugal visit to her sleeping chamber this night or for many nights to come.

"What do you think of this magical palace, Princess?" the Prussian envoy inquired as they walked down tiled corridors open onto courtyards lush with vegetation, the heavy scents of tropical flowers hanging in the air.

"That it is a house of fantasy," Sophie replied.

The prince laughed. "I must show you the apartments assigned to the Comte de Ségur and myself. They are such voluptuous chambers it would be impossible not to indulge in fantasy. Ah, there is Count Danilevski." He greeted the count, who was coming toward them across the courtyard. "I was just telling Princess Dmitrievna about the voluptuous chambers we are allocated. Is not yours in the same part of the palace?"

"In the harem," Adam said with a slight smile. "And you choose an accurately descriptive word, Your Excellency. May I join you on your walk?"

"Please do, Count," Sophie said. "The prince maintains that in such surroundings all fantasies are like to come to life. Do you agree with him?"

"We talk only of voluptuous daydreams, you understand," said the prince with a smile. "I venture to suggest that the one universal male conceit is in the forefront of many a mind in this place.''

"And may a woman inquire what this universal fantasy might be?'' asked Sophie, looking up at the prince with a mischievous smile.

"I do not know," mused the prince, glancing across at the count. "What do you think, Count Danilevski? Should we enlighten the lady?''

Sophie looked from one man to the other. Adam's eyes held a secretive gleam, and a tiny smile played over his mouth. "It is to own a woman, Princess," he said. "Body and soul.''

"Is it?'' Sophie directed the startled question at the prince, who laughed.

"Indeed, it is. This possession need not be of a permanent nature, you understand. In fact, it is best if it is ephemeral; but it must be total for the duration of the fantasy."

"How very Mohammedan of you all," Sophie declared.

"Ah, no!'' Adam held up a forefinger. "Not quite, because you see, for the illusion to be entirely successful, the woman must be a wholehearted participant. She must derive from her role a pleasure to match that of her partner's. Is that not so, Your Excellency?''

"Exactly so," laughed the prince. "Now, see . . ." With a grand gesture, he flung open a door upon a vast chamber with delicate mosaics on the tiled floor, gleaming marble walls, a cushioned divan running around the entire perimeter. In the center played a fountain falling into a marble-tiled bowl. A greenish light filled the room, produced by the thick vegetation screening the windows from prying eyes. "Fantasy land! What a waste to sleep alone in such a chamber."

"You are similarly endowed, Count?'' Sophie's eyebrows lifted.

"I will show you.''

The idea took shape, grew, delicious and outrageous. Why ever not? In a way, it would serve to exorcise the soft-spoken menace of her talk with Paul, a secret defiance of his beliefs and precepts. Excusing herself from her escorts, she made her way back to her own modest chamber. It could not be hard to find what she wanted in the city markets. A light cloak and veiled hat would hopefully ensure that she caused no offense to the city's inhabitants, although the fact that she was one of the infidel foreign invaders would be recognized immediately. But she would not be at risk of assault if she did not offend.

In ten minutes, Sophia Alexeyevna was hurrying through the city streets, where the warmth of late afternoon still clung, but the shadows were lengthening and men stood in doorways, taking the air, idly chatting. The women she saw were heavily veiled and burdened, staggering to the wells for water, laboring under pots and baskets filled from the markets. There was no standing around in leisured gossip for them, although, in a square, where a spring bubbled in a stone basin, a group of swathed, dark-clad women were doing laundry, scrubbing with stones, their voices rising in the evening air like starlings returning to their nests.

Sophie found what she wanted in a dim little shop behind a bead curtain. No words passed between herself and the wizened old man; they communicated in gestures, Sophie interpreting through her veil.

She entered the palace gardens through a side gate set in the high stone wall, hurrying across the grass beneath laurel and orange trees, her bundles concealed beneath her cloak. In her chamber, she found a pale Maria.

"His Highness, madame . . ." she stammered, "came looking for you. I said I didn't know—"

"No, of course you did not. You cannot be expected to know things I do not tell you," Sophie interrupted briskly. "Did he say why he wished to see me?"

"I understand he is going away," Maria said, a little sulky at the brusqueness that seemed to discount the serf's fear that her lack of information about her mistress would earn some penalty. "He came to bid you farewell, I expect."

"You may go," Sophie said coldly. Once the door had closed on the sniffing maid, she buried her bundle at the bottom of the cedar chest, where were placed her undergar-

ments and nightclothes in neat, fragrant piles. Perhaps, like
a dutiful wife, she should hurry to see if her husband had
already left on his envoy's mission, bidding him a tearful
farewell should she happen to be in time to do so. Her lip
curled sardonically, but she left the chamber, making her way
to the great square in front of the palace.

A troop of cavalry were gathered, their horses pawing the
paving stones. Paul was standing at the bottom of the steps
leading into the palace in discussion with Potemkin.

"I am in time to bid you farewell, Paul," Sophie said
pleasantly, coming down the steps. "Maria said you had been
looking for me. I was with the Prince de Ligne, on the czarina's instructions." Not so much a lie as a manipulation of
timing, she reflected comfortably.

"It is such a shame that you must be separated again,"
Potemkin said, his eye gleaming at Sophie. "But for such a
delicate mission as this one, only your husband would do."

He knows, Sophie thought, the illuminating discovery making her want to laugh out loud. Was Potemkin the cherub Adam
had referred to? Such an unlikely-looking cherub! Her eyes
danced, and laughter trembled on her lip. Oh, but Prince Potemkin was a powerful friend! Dropping her eyes hastily, she
turned to her husband with formal words of farewell. He bowed
coldly, mounted, and the troop clattered out of the square.

"A word of advice, Sophia Alexeyevna." Potemkin turned
back to the palace, speaking casually over his shoulder. "If
one sleepwalks, it is always wise to wake from one's trance
well before dawn."

"How long will my husband's mission last, Prince?" Sophie, recognizing that the advice required no response, kept
pace with him up the steps, asking her so natural question.

"I do not imagine Prince Dmitriev will be rejoining our
little excursion," Potemkin said airily. "When his mission
to the Porte is completed, he will return directly to St. Petersburg."

Oh, *such* a powerful friend! Sophie hugged her joy, and
the last lingering tatters of oppression drifted from her, so
many feathers in the wind. Paul would not be around when

she asked Catherine for permission to retire to Berkholzskoye for a spell. She would have her baby, safe in her own home, the home that would become the child's. Tanya Feodorovna would care for it.

For the first time, she allowed herself to think of the life in her belly as existing outside herself. She could make certain the child grew up secure, healthy, loved, in the home that had nurtured its mother. Even if she must deny herself parentage, she could make sure her child did not suffer. And there were still weeks and weeks before any more decisions must be made, any further action taken. Weeks and weeks of unhindered loving. And tonight . . . well, tonight she had something very special planned.

A yellow moon hung heavy in the luminous purple sky. The four officers sauntering through the palace gardens were in a reflective mood, each one touched by the exotic strangeness of their surroundings, the sense that in the very air they breathed existed almost tangible memories of erotic encounters taken place at a time long past between couples long gone, taken place amid the fountains and the jasmine where they strolled, entranced aliens.

"I've no desire to seek my bed yet awhile," said one of the officers, tilting his head to look up at the sky. "I am full of the strangest yearnings."

"An excess of suckling pig, Ivan!" said Adam Danilevski, chuckling. "It sits heavy on the stomach."

"You're no romantic," protested the major, slapping his friend's shoulder. "It is something in the air. Can you not feel it?"

"I have an exceptional vodka in my chamber," Adam replied. "It is a fine cure for indigestion."

Ivan sighed. "If that is all to be offered on such a night, then I daresay one must lower one's expectations."

Laughing, the group turned through an archway into the palace, making their way to the former harem and Adam's chamber.

Adam opened the door. They all stood for a minute absorbing the atmosphere—a languid sensuality flowed through the room, illuminated by the soft golden glow of oil lamps, scented with the bowls of jasmine and roses spilling in every corner. It flowed from a still figure, veiled in delicate, diaphanous gauzes, seated cross-legged upon a cushion on the floor at the foot of the divan.

"Do I dream?" murmured one of the men on a note of awe. "Adam, is she real?"

"Oh, yes," Adam said softly, recovering his breath. "Quite real. Come in, gentlemen, into my own Arabian night."

The figure on the cushion rose fluidly, glided across the room, a waft of rose and white gauze. Only her eyes were visible above her veil; outlined with khol, almond-shaped, they glowed deeply luminous in the dim golden light of the room. Her hands opened in a gesture of greeting, of invitation, and she moved toward the divan circling the room.

Mesmerized, the four men sat, sinking into the opulent comfort of cushions, their eyes riveted on the silent figure whose body beneath the translucent flowing tunic and wide-legged trousers, caught tight at the ankle, glimmered in tantalizing curves of pearl-pink and ivory.

"Where did you find her?" Ivan whispered, returning slowly to his senses.

"I bought her," Adam said, his eyes narrowed. "From a camel driver." The slightest quiver shook the slender frame as she brought a tray of vodka glasses over to the divan. Kneeling, she presented the tray to each man in turn, her eyes demurely lowered.

"Can we see her face?" Colonel Oblonsky reached a hand to touch the bent head.

"No," Adam replied, stretching lazily. "She is mine, gentlemen, and only I may look upon her."

"You dog, Danilevski!" exclaimed the fourth member of the group. "In a single afternoon you have created your own paradise."

Adam merely smiled with a hint of complacence. His boots were being removed by the kneeling figure, whose skillful fingers massaged each stockinged foot as she slipped its covering free. Rising again, she wafted across the room, returning with a pair of silk-lined slippers, which she eased upon his feet. Adam's eyes closed for a moment as he breathed deeply of the mingled fragrances in the chamber, of the jasmine twisted in the dark hair now so close to his chest as her fingers began to unbutton his braided tunic.

Stirred almost as much as if they were the recipients of these attentions, the others watched as if hypnotized.

"What is her name?" Ivan asked, his voice a little unsteady.

"Seraphina," Adam replied promptly, sitting up so that she could remove his unbuttoned tunic. "And she was *very* expensive." Her fingers were busy with his shirt buttons now, and he laid his hand over hers. "I think perhaps that is far enough for the moment." Her head bowed in instant acknowledgment; standing up, she fetched his brocade dressing gown, maneuvering his arms into the long sleeves while he lay back, moving a little only when absolutely necessary.

"Does she talk?" asked Colonel Oblonsky, loosening the top button of his own tunic.

"In the company of men she speaks only the language of love," replied Adam, resting his head against the back of the divan. Delicate fingers were massaging his temples, his eyelids, and when he looked into the luminous dark eyes so close to his he read a passion to match his own, her soul, her self, lost in the dream she was creating for them both. They were not Sophie's eyes, they were Seraphina's. He allowed his hands to drift, barely touching, over her body as she bent over him. The warmth of her skin beneath the translucent covering, the way she leaned into the caress, lending herself as if she had no other existence outside that bounded by his hands, destroyed his last hold on the world beyond the illusion.

"I do not wish to appear inhospitable—" he murmured.

Seraphina, a cloud of gauze, billowed to the door, opening it for them, bowing low as the three officers went out, their eyes lingering hungrily on the figure, head meekly lowered, hands clasped, body graceful, concealed yet not concealed, the very embodiment of fantasy in this chamber fragrant with the promise of untold delight.

"Come here," Adam commanded softly as the door closed. Sitting up, he drew her between his knees, unfastening her veil, before pushing his hands up beneath the loose tunic, cupping her breasts, running a fingertip over her ribs, dipping into her navel. "Put your hands on top of your head." When she obeyed instantly, he loosened the drawstring at her waist. The gauzy trousers rustled to her ankles. For long minutes, his hand roamed at will while she stood before him, his to do with as he wished, immobile except for the rapid rise and fall of her bosom. Then he released her, and lay back again in invitation and demand.

Seraphina stepped backward, kicking away the garment clinging to her ankles, before returning to her interrupted task. She undressed him with all the delicate skill of one trained to the task, making each removal an act of loving service, bringing him to aching arousal. Throughout, she said not a word, allowing her hands and eyes to speak for her. Barefoot, wearing nothing but the tunic skimming her hips, she moved across the chamber while he lay back on the divan, almost febrile with desire, drifting in the trancelike languor that accompanies fever. He watched her bend over a brazier in the corner of the room, the ivory curve of her backside gleaming in the lamplight, and his chest tightened, his loins throbbed. She picked up the copper jug heating on the brazier, pouring its contents into a deep bowl, which she brought over to the divan, a smile curving her mouth.

Rose petals floated on the surface of the water in the bowl. She dipped a soft cloth into the water, drawing it, scented with roses, down his body. Adam lay back on the divan, wondering for a bare second who belonged to whom in this fantasy. Kneeling at his feet, she began to massage oil into his warmed, softened skin, starting with his toes, before crawling slowly up his body, a frown of concentration between her brows. Stretching lazily downward, he caught the hem of her tunic and drew it up to her waist, giving him an uninterrupted view of the soft roundness of her bottom as she progressed upward. Her eyes lifted from her task, met his in a question: Was this pleasuring him, or did he want something else from her?

"Do not stop," he directed, linking his hands behind his head. "I merely wished to improve the landscape."

Lost in the art of giving pleasure, in the possession through homage of another's body, Seraphina wandered in her own Arabian night, where passion grew, insidious amid the rich scents of arousal, the lush fragrance of the flowers of love, the whispering fountain, the golden lamplight. She was formless, consisting only of pleasure centers, of nerve centers stimulated to the point where bliss hovered on the brink of pain. When the time came for her to give herself into his possession, to move as he bade her, to position herself as the hands dictated, she slipped off the edge of the universe into the rose-tinted, golden-hued world where ecstasy was the only sensation; and it was infinite.

"Adam?"

"Mmmm?" Indolently, he rolled over to look down at her. It was the first time she had spoken since he had walked into his chamber with his friends, a loving lifetime ago. He brushed a lock of hair from her breast. "Is the fantasy over then?"

She smiled. "I have not the strength to endure another such."

"No," he agreed, lying down beside her. "Such extremity of pleasure is not to be borne too often. Which is perhaps fortunate." He chuckled. "What a mistress of invention you are."

"I am not the only one with a creative imagination." She sat up suddenly, a spark of indignation in the dark eyes. "How could you have said you bought me from a *camel driver*?"

Adam grinned. "I thought, on the spur of the moment, it was remarkably quick-witted. It was not as if I was expecting to find one of love's slaves waiting for me. How I am to hold my head up in the regiment again, I don't know."

"Oh, rubbish!" Sophie declared. "Did you not see how they envied you?"

"I suppose in keeping with true Turkish hospitality, I should have offered to share you," he mused.

"Was I a skilled and obedient slave?" Her eyes dancing, she kissed his mouth.

Adam groaned. "Beyond my wildest dreams. So much so that I cannot find it in me to be angry with you for the risk you took." He struggled up, leaning against the cushioned back of the divan. "I will not even ask how you acquired the props for your little play, because I am certain I will not enjoy the answer."

"I took every precaution," she assured him seriously.

"I am sure you believe you did," he said with a mock sigh. "You are reckless beyond permission, Sophia Alexeyevna."

"I thought you said you were not going to be vexed," she protested. "It is most ungrateful of you."

"Ah, no, never that! You must absolve me of ingratitude, sweetheart." Sighing, he swung off the divan. "It is time you returned to your own bed, before the world wakes."

Sophie yawned languidly. "I do not see why it should matter anymore. Prince Potemkin knows . . ." She stopped, seeing the look on Adam's face. "All right, it does matter. I am going." She slipped on her gauzy costume again. "No one will recognize me in this, anyway."

Adam drew her against his length, slipping his hands inside the trousers, grasping her buttocks firmly. "Do not ever again say it does not matter. Just because Dmitriev is absent does not mean you can behave as if he does not exist. Do you understand me, Sophie?" When she gave a rueful nod, he kissed her in hard farewell. "Off you go." His hand slapped her bare skin as he turned her to the door. She skipped through it with a mock indignant ouch and did not see his face where for a moment hopeless frustration etched deep lines, darkened the gray eyes with something like despair.

Chapter 18

"How long do you think you would like to remain at Berkholzskoye, Princess?" The czarina regarded her lady-in-waiting with kindly, yet speculative, eyes.

The June sun was hot, pouring in through the palace windows standing open to the River Dnieper where the water life of Kiev was continuing with customary bustle.

"Four or five months, Madame," replied Sophie. "I could be certain to return to St. Petersburg by early December, if you desire it."

"That will depend upon your husband, I would think." Catherine played with her quill pen, turning it between her hands. Sophia Alexeyevna showed little sign of her pregnancy. Her loose Russian caftan of pale blue cambric concealed any thickening beneath. There was a serenity about her face, though, a hint of roundness softening those previously definite features, an inner tranquillity revealed in her eyes.

What a crying shame things had had to turn out in this way, reflected the empress. Had Adam Danilevski presented himself as a suitor for the hand of the Golitskova, there would have been no possible objection. The princess could have made her choice between Dmitriev or the count with the czarina's blessing. Instead, they were in this tangle. Of course, it was a perfectly common tangle, she thought pragmatically, and the young woman and her lover seemed perfectly capable of dealing with it without undue fuss.

"We will inform Prince Dmitriev that we granted you leave of absence from court until December to visit your grandfather.

Should you wish to remain in the country throughout the winter, assuming your husband does not object, then you have our permission to do so.''

Sophie curtsied deeply. ''Madame, I shall be eternally grateful for your consideration.''

The empress nodded in brisk agreement. ''Yes, but then we accept that these things do happen. They must just be tidied up neatly.''

Relieved, Sophie left the imperial presence, wondering when the czarina had first guessed at her pregnancy. She had not been obliged to take Catherine into her confidence when making her request. The reason for it seemed to have been understood already. But was her secret known only to Prince Potemkin and the empress? No one had given any indication of knowledge, no covert looks, none of the sly innuendos that usually accompanied such discoveries; but gossip was the staff of life in this court. It seemed almost impossible that such a piece of scandal should have slipped past the scandalmongers. Still, there was little point constructing causes for anxiety when the major concern was now dealt with. She would dispatch a messenger to Berkholzskoye, asking her grandfather to send Boris Mikhailov and Khan to Kiev. On Khan, she could be home within a day.

Adam, however, did not see the advantages in this plan when she imparted it to him that afternoon in the hunting cottage on the riverbank. ''If you send such instructions to Prince Golitskov, I will ensure that he receives a message from me countermanding them,'' he announced flatly. ''You will not ride fifty versts on that stallion in your customary flamboyant fashion. Is that understood?''

''And I suppose you would have me jolted in a carriage, vomiting every half mile!'' she returned. ''I am quite capable of riding!''

''I did not say you were not.'' He spoke with the assured calm of one confident his will would prevail. ''You must be a little more considering of your condition, Sophie sweet. You were dancing until all hours last night, after spending the day sailing on the river in the heat of summer. It is not sensible.''

"But I feel perfectly well." She smiled, taking his hand. "Do not mollycoddle me, Adam. I am strong as a horse."

"Oh, yes," He nodded gravely. "Strong as a horse, but you can't endure the sight of blood without swooning, or the motion of a carriage—"

"Oh, that is unfair!" she broke in. "Everyone has some weaknesses." She tilted her head, regarding him quizzically. "I do not know what your weaknesses are, though."

"You," he said quietly. "You are my greatest weakness, and it is such an Achilles heel that I could not survive with more than that one."

There was nothing to be said. They tried—oh, how they tried—to forget the future, to pretend that they were not locked into an insoluble maze; but all the imperial indulgence in the world could not alter the facts.

"How am I to journey to Berkholzskoye in a manner that will satisfy you?" Sophie asked, reverting to the original topic because there was nothing to be said on the other one.

"With my escort, on a mount of my choosing," he replied promptly. "By which I mean a staid, broad-backed animal with an easy gait and not the slightest inclination to take the bit between its teeth."

Sophie opened her mouth in laughing protest at this appalling prospect, then realized what he had said first. "With your escort? How?"

His smile broadened, and she saw what she had only been half aware of before. He was bursting with some news, his complacent satisfaction visible in every expressive line of his face. "I am sent on a diplomatic mission to Warsaw," he informed her. "To leave immediately."

"And Berkholzskoye is not far out of your way." She laughed delightedly.

"Better than that," he said. "I have permission to accomplish *any* family business that might appear imperative whenever it can be fitted in with my mission, as long as I have rejoined my regiment in St. Petersburg by the first of next year."

Sophie crept into his arms, only now recognizing how fearful she had been. "You will be with me."

"Yes, love, I will be with you." Tenderly, he stroked her hair and cheek, holding her as if he had known all along what this would mean to her. In fact, he had known, tormented as he himself had been at the thought that he would not be able to be with her when she gave birth to their child. "I will take you to Berkholzskoye, leave you there while I go to Warsaw, and be back by your name day."

September 17 was her name day, the feast of St. Sophia. He would be back with her in ample time. Tears clung to her eye-lashes, spilled to glisten on her cheek. "I cannot describe how happy that makes me." She lifted his hand to her wet cheek.

"You do not have to, love," he replied softly. "Because I know how happy it makes me."

There was a moment of silent communion, then Sophie said in a different tone, "About this horse, Adam—"

"Staid, broad-backed, and sluggish," he reiterated firmly. "And we will spend one night upon the road."

"Tyrant!" Then her eyes gleamed. "We could spend the night at the post house where we stayed when you took such shame-less advantage of an innocent maid."

"A wild-tempered, hard-riding, fast-shooting Cossack woman," he corrected remorselessly, slipping easily into the relaxed, joking humor necessary to dispel an emotional out-pouring that would do neither of them any good.

Sophie's good humor was sorely tried, however, when she saw the horse Adam had selected for her journey. He had meant exactly what he had said. "No," she declared. "I will not ride it, Adam. It does not deserve the name 'horse.' It belongs to some other species."

"He is a comfortable ride," Adam replied, imperturbable. "I grant you he is not pretty, but he is solid."

"Solid!" Her lip curled in disdain. "He is solidified!"

"Nevertheless, my love, you are going to ride him and no other."

"But I will be so embarrassed! What will Boris Mikhailov say?"

"When he knows your condition, he will commend my choice. Allow me to assist you."

It was fortunately very early in the morning, and there were only serfs in the stables to bear witness to the discussion. "I do not see why your wife's riding accident should make you assume that all pregnant women are at risk on a horse," Sophie declared crossly, and without thought.

Adam froze; the earth seemed to catch its breath in its ordained orbit of the sun. "What do you mean?"

"I beg your pardon." Sophie forced herself to look him in the eye. "I did not mean to speak out of turn."

He shrugged, saying in cold dismissal, "I had thought you too sensible to pay attention to the babblings of the little Saltykova and her like."

A confusion of guilt, self-consciousness, and embarrassment flooded her, and with it the angry protest that she had no reason to feel so. She had done nothing to be ashamed of, said nothing to be embarrassed by. "You said yourself that Eva died in an accident." She gathered up the reins of her stolid mount. "It is true I heard tell it was a riding accident."

"And you heard, also, that she was with child." His voice bit into the summer morning. "I imagine you also heard that the child could not have been mine."

It was unbearable, here in the sunny stable yard, with her own child, Adam's child, quickening within her, unbearable to hear the pain masked by the cold, dispassionate contempt in his voice. The contempt was for himself, which made it so much harder to hear. Sophie searched for something to say that would diffuse this, but there was nothing. If she reminded him that pregnancy was simply a consequence of the infidelity he had known about anyway, and should not therefore be seen as an added cross to bear, she would be painting their own picture in the vivid colors of the truth that they kept locked inside themselves.

In silence, she placed her foot in the stirrup, swinging upward onto the horse's broad back with no more than the slightest diminution in her customary agility. In the same silence, Adam mounted and they moved out of the yard, joined at the gate by the six serfs from Adam's personal retinue who were to provide armed escort.

After about ten minutes, Adam, in the most natural tone imaginable, drew her attention to a hawk, hovering immobile against the brilliant blue sky, just the tip of its wings fluttering to keep it balanced, poised over whatever prey it had spied in the long grass. It dived, plummeting through the morning air, the embodiment of violent death, sleek, contained, every feather and sinew part of the beauteous weapon that was itself.

"I never tire of watching them," Sophie said.

"I know." Smiling, he leaned over, tipping her chin to kiss the corner of her mouth. As he straightened again, he said cheerfully, "If you were riding Khan, I would never have been able to do that, so there are compensations."

Subject closed, Sophie thought. Closed but unresolved. Oh, well, she gave a mental shrug. They had enough problems without her digging into a past he wished kept buried.

They spent that night at the same post house, ate what Sophie swore was the identical chicken stew, drank klukva, and walked in the milky Nordic night in quiet memory of the kiss that had set them upon a path of joy, of growth, of fear, and of futility.

The next afternoon, the reed-thatched roofs of Berkholzskoye appeared. "Boris Mikhailov taught me to ride before I could walk," Sophie said, squirming uncomfortably in her saddle. "I think I would prefer to walk now. I have my pride, Adam."

"Too much of it," he retorted. "Your mount is of no importance. You still ride him as if he were a Cossack stallion, and that is all that is going to interest Boris Mikhailov."

Old Prince Golitskov was taking the evening air in the rose garden when a young lad came breathlessly with the news that riders were approaching down the poplar avenue. Hope set the prince's gnarled hands trembling slightly. It was not inconceivable that it should be Sophie. He had heard that the empress's suite was returned to Kiev from the Crimea and was taking a short respite before continuing to St. Petersburg. He hastened, as fast as his rheumatics would permit, to the front of the house.

"Holy Mother, *petite*!" he exclaimed as the cavalcade appeared on the gravel sweep before the house. "Whatever are you riding?"

"I told you, Adam," Sophie exclaimed, almost tumbling

from the broad back in her anxiety. "Oh, *Grandpère*, I have missed you so. Are you well?"

Golitskov embraced his granddaughter for a long moment, feeling the change in her before standing back, regarding her with an all-seeing eye. "I am quite well, Sophie. And you?"

"Perfectly well," she replied, "except for bruised pride after riding that excuse for horseflesh."

Adam dismounted. "Prince." The two men clasped hands.

"I bid you welcome, Adam." They exchanged a smiling look that spoke volumes.

"Oh, here is Boris." Gathering up her skirts, Sophie flew across the gravel to hug the giant figure. "How is Khan? I cannot wait to—"

"Sophia Alexeyevna!" Adam broke in sharply. "Don't you so much as think of throwing your leg across that beast's back!"

"You talk such nonsense!" she exclaimed in exasperation. "Khan is as gentle as a lamb. Is he not, Boris?"

Pulling at his beard, the muzhik looked at his princess with the wise eyes that missed nothing. "Khan's many things, Princess," he pronounced, customarily laconic. "But that's not one of them."

Sophie's face fell ludicrously. "I had counted on you, Boris Mikhailov."

The muzhik merely smiled, crossing to greet Adam, who took his hand. "Does my eyes good to look upon you, Count."

"And mine to see you, Boris Mikhailov."

"Let us go inside," Golitskov said. "You'll be glad of a glass, Adam, I daresay."

Sophie was about to announce that on this occasion she also would not look with disfavor upon such a thing when a loud shriek of joy came from the door and Tanya Feodorovna, in a flurry of calico skirts, came rushing out. "Sophia Alexeyevna, by all the saints! Let me look at you." After kissing her soundly on both cheeks, she stood back to do just that. Then she nodded briskly. "Home's the best place for you for a while. No more of this gallivanting. Just you come upstairs and I'll make you a tisane. Been riding all day, if I know you."

"But I am not in the least fatigued, Tanya," Sophie protested as she was swept willy-nilly into the house.

Golitskov chuckled. "She'll be in good hands now." He looked sharply at Adam. "When?"

"October," Adam replied.

"Dmitriev?"

"Has no idea."

"You trust."

"Yes, I trust."

"Well, you can tell me the details and what you plan over a glass or two, preferably before Sophia Alexeyevna rejoins us. While she's under this roof, I'll not have her concerning herself with anything but what touches her most nearly. A serene pregnancy tends to make for an easier birth, as the women will tell you." With this piece of wisdom, Golitskov ushered his guest into the library, closing the door firmly behind them.

Adam felt the weight of anxiety lifted as he shared his burden. In this house, Sophie would be nurtured and sheltered; he could leave her without undue fear while he journeyed to Warsaw, and he would return in plenty of time for the birth. What would happen after that . . . What would happen after that would happen.

He left two days later. Sophie rode with him down the avenue to the boundaries of the estate. "God go with you," she said quietly. "Come back safe."

"Look for me before your name day," he replied, stroking her hand. "And, Sophie . . ."—a fleeting smile skimmed his lips—"promise me that you will do as you are told by those who know about these matters."

"My choices these days tend to be somewhat limited," she replied with an answering smile. "Tanya has become like a wolf with a single cub." She looked into the gray eyes for a long minute, touching his soul with her own, before saying softly, "Go now. I have never been able to abide farewells."

He raised her hand to his lips before turning his horse and cantering off down the white, winding road across the steppe.

* * *

General, Prince Paul Dmitriev left the Sublime Porte and the Sultan's lavish hospitality in June. His instructions were to proceed directly to St. Petersburg, where the empress was expected to return by July. The court would disperse during the hot month of August, retreating to their country palaces along the Gulf of Finland. Paul Dmitriev also intended to go into the country, to his estate at Kaluga. As he journeyed across the Crimea, across the steppes under the summer sun, his mind was pleasantly occupied. He had enjoyed his stay in the Ottoman court, had enjoyed particularly the attentions of several young girls given to him for the duration of his visit as part of the Sultan's hospitality.

With all the enthusiasm of a dedicated scholar, he had learned all he could about the Turkish way of life and had found it most congenial. In all but religion, the domestic attitudes and customs prevalent within the Ottoman Empire matched those of many a noble Russian landowner. Polygamy was not legal in Russia, of course, but many a Russian had his own harem of female serfs. Mohammedans carried their domestic hierarchies into government; it would be inconceivable for a woman to hold a position of any power outside that of the harem, and within the harem her power was only over women and was dependent upon how well she pleased her master.

Russia was not so consistent when it came to man's dominion over woman. While it was absolute within the family structure, powerful women, as ruthless in the pursuit of that power as any man, were far from unknown in the political history of that country. Paul Dmitriev, while he would never utter a word of criticism of his empress and would never consider disobeying an imperial command, preferred to consider the presence of a woman on the throne of Russia as an aberration, one hopefully to be concluded on the death of the present empress and the accession of her son.

The image of his barren wife, never far from the forefront of his mind, rose clear before him; accompanying the image was the cold satisfaction that the moment was not now far off when he would be able to exact the penalty for the slights, the defiance, the near-unendurable frustration that somehow she had deprived him of his revenge against the Golitskovs. But he would have that revenge now. In the seclusion of Kaluga, far from imperial eyes, he would teach Sophia Alexeyevna the ways of the Sublime Porte.

On his arrival in St. Petersburg he presented himself immediately to the Winter Palace, where the court was but newly returned and was making preparation for its removal to Czarskoye Selo for August. A disconsolate air hung over those who now found themselves back on the ground, their fairy circle broken, their journey of illusion passed into history.

Catherine greeted her general affably, complimented him on his diplomacy with the Sultan, thanked him generously for his assistance. Then she told him that his wife had desired to visit her grandfather when they passed through Kiev.

"I gave her permission to be gone from us until December, Prince." The czarina smiled her toothless smile. "I would have no objection if she wished to wait out the winter at Berkholzskoye, but, of course, that is for you to decide."

"You are most generous to my wife, Madame." The general bowed, concealing the violent surge of rage at being yet again balked. It was as if there was some conspiracy against him. "I do not think, however, that I will be able to tolerate a separation through the winter."

"Then you must write and acquaint your wife of your decision," said the empress blandly. "She will accept her wifely duty without demur."

"I trust so," returned the prince, a hint of acid in his voice.

The czarina's gaze cooled. "Thank you, Prince," she said, turning back to the papers on her desk, making clear his dismissal.

Four months. He had waited many years for the right combination of circumstances. He could wait another four months.

A strange thing happened after Adam's departure. Sophie, usually so vital and outgoing, seemed to turn in upon herself, communing silently and constantly with the life burgeoning within. Her body, as if responding to the removal of the need for concealment, grew round in its fruitfulness. The dark eyes contained a serene smile, and she moved with measured pace, graceful as always, but with a smoothness to her step instead of the spring of the past.

Golitskov found her an abstracted companion, and whenever he attempted to broach the subject of selecting a family for the unborn, she looked at him as if he spoke a language she did not understand and changed the topic. It did not bode well, he thought with some apprehension, but she would have Adam, who, if anybody could, would be able to help her through the dire necessity of maternal separation.

Throughout the heat of August, she sat beneath the trees with a busily sewing Tanya, or walked slowly by the river. It was as if her mind were emptied of all fear, all memory, all thoughts of the future, and she grew round and tranquil in her waiting, surrounded by women who preserved her peace with their own knowledge of the processes by which body and mind prepare themselves for the delivery and nurturing of a new life.

It was late on a night in early September when Adam returned to Berkholzskoye. For the last few miles he had not been able to contain the surging panic that something had gone amiss in the weeks of his absence, that he would find Sophie . . . Images of Eva plagued him. Eva bleeding, so much blood, so red, so impossible to staunch. Her face graying as the blood ran from her, pooling beneath her. In all his years of soldiering he did not think he had seen so much blood spilling from one body. . . .

The house gleamed in the distance, pale in the moonlight. He touched spur to his horse, in the dread conviction that ahead lay only despair and horror. So vivid was his certainty that when Gregory, drawing back the bolts on the great front door, greeted him calmly he could not believe the watchman's statement that all was well with everyone in the house.

"Adam! I thought when I heard such tempestuous hoofbeats beneath my window that it must be you." Prince Golitskov, in dressing gown and nightcap, came down the stairs. "Come into the library. Gregory shall find you some supper. I am sure Anna will have left a tasty dish or two in the pantry." Nodding pleasantly, he led the way down the stone-flagged corridor.

"Sophie . . . ?" Adam said, his haste and alarm sounding in the one-word question.

"She is very well," the old prince reassured him. "I must say, I shall be glad of your company. The house has come to resemble a *gynaeceum* in recent weeks; I feel an interloper most of the time." He laughed, but he was not entirely humorous. "I am surprised Sophie did not hear your arrival, but she retires early these days." He poured vodka for his guest.

"That is not like her." Adam tossed off the contents of his glass and refilled it.

Golitskov smiled. "You will find her somewhat different. The prospect of motherhood brings such changes, I have noticed. The tyranny of the womb, you might call it."

Adam looked uncomprehending. "But she is quite well?"

The prince nodded. "Yes, but I have some fears, nevertheless." He looked down into the empty grate, while Adam waited in growing, apprehensive impatience. "I do not think she will find it easy to part with the child," Golitskov said finally. "If she cannot bring herself to do so, then she and the babe must flee her husband's vengeance."

"Must flee Russia then," Adam said slowly. "Once I wished her to do that. Now I do not know how I could bear it." His face twisted in that anguished helplessness. "If I were to leave Russia, I would stand convicted of treason and desertion, you know that, Prince. My estates would be confiscated, my mother left destitute, my family disgraced. How can I visit such a punishment upon the innocent?"

"You cannot," Golitskov said firmly. "It is not going to be asked of you, either by Sophie or myself. I wished only to prepare you. If anyone can reconcile Sophie, then you will be able to."

Gregory entered the library with a platter of smoked fish, black bread, and pickled beetroot. "This do you, lord?"

"Amply, thank you. . . . Do not let me keep you up, Prince."

"I will bear you company if you wish it." The old man looked shrewdly at him. "Unless you've a mind to be alone with your thoughts."

Adam sighed, shaking his head. "I have been alone with them too long on the journey from Warsaw. Plagued with fears, with premonitions." He speared a forkful of smoked sturgeon. "Perhaps the tyranny of the womb has a long reach."

Golitskov laughed. "Eat and you will feel better. It is only natural you should have been worried when you were away, but Sophie is strong and healthy, and Tanya is an expert midwife. All will be well, you will see."

It was an hour later when Adam, carrying his candle, entered the bedchamber in the west wing. The wind soughed softly, rustling the curtains at the open window, filling the room with the fresh night scents of the steppes. Shielding the candle with his hand, he stood by the bed. She was asleep on her side, her cheek pillowed on her hand. The candlelight caught the chestnut tints in the dark hair massed upon the pillow, threw into relief the rich sable crescents of her eyelashes resting upon her cheek. So peaceful, he thought, as his love flowed sweet, banishing fear.

Undressing swiftly, he blew out the candle before sliding into bed beside her, relaxing luxuriously into the body warmth beneath the quilted coverlet.

"Adam." Her voice came soft and sleepy in the moonglow. "Am I still dreaming, or is it really you this time?"

"Really me, sweetheart." Sliding an arm beneath her, he rolled her into his embrace. "Have you dreamed of me every night?"

"Every night," she averred, running her fingers over his chest in gentle rediscovery. "I have missed you most dreadfully."

"You have grown most dreadfully," he teased, caressing the hard mound of her belly. His hand jumped involuntarily, and he laughed in wonder. "It kicked me."

"It kicks *me* all the time," she grumbled in mock complaint. "Are you ever going to kiss me?"

"I'm thinking about it," he murmured consideringly. "I'm trying to work out how to circumvent the lump."

"Then allow me to show you." Hitching herself upon her elbows, she leaned over him, bringing her smiling mouth to his. "See, it is quite simple."

"So it is." His hand slipped beneath the shining curtain of her hair to palm her scalp, to draw her mouth down to his again for a more thorough demonstration.

"I would like to make love," Sophie announced, running the tip of her tongue over his lips. "Or are you too tired after your journey? Oh, no, you are not too tired, it seems."

"Not in the least." Gently turning her onto her side, facing away from him, he pushed up her nightgown, fitting his body to hers. One hand stroking softly over her belly matched the soft stroking within as he tenderly took her into the verdant valley of release, afterward holding her against him until the first jubilant cockcrow woke them and, with mischief in her eye and a resurgence of her old energy, Sophie demanded a repetition.

Adam's return broke her self-absorption, much to Golitskov's relief. He had been much afraid that increased introspection would only make more certain her refusal to follow the sensible course once the child was born. Adam denied her the opportunity to brood. He walked with her, talked with her, fished the streams with her, played cards in the garden in the autumn sun, exacting severe penalties for her cheating, none of which did the least good, and patiently he waited for her to bring up the subject of the baby's future. She never did. Every time the words formed on his own lips, they died as he saw her joy in her pregnancy and he thought of the ordeal she must face to bring the child into the world. Condemning himself for cowardice, yet unable to face this responsibility now, he let the matter drift.

Sophie's name day dawned green and golden. She was as excited as she always was on this day that was all her own. Last year it had gone all but unremarked, Prince Dmitriev not being in the mood to indulge his wife, but this year she was surrounded by people whose only object was to ensure a perfect celebration in Sophia Alexeyevna's honor.

According to the tradition of her earliest childhood, the day was declared a holiday and all members of the estate and the village were invited to the celebration. They would pay their respects to the saint's namesake, filing through the hall, some of them bearing little gifts that they would present to Sophie, standing at the foot of the stairs to greet them. The feasting that followed would take place in the great barn, with tables spilling out into the courtyard. Beer and vodka would flow unchecked from morning until the last reveler had collapsed. Boar and suckling pig, goat, oxen, and whole sheep were roasted over pits, and Anna, with every woman on the estate, was busy for days beforehand creating the delicacies, the cakes and jellies, pickles and breads that would be piled upon the long, groaning trestle tables.

After breakfast, Adam, smiling mysteriously, disappeared, refusing to answer Sophie's importunate questions as to his destination.

"Is it my present?" she demanded. "Oh, tell me, Adam!"

"Now, what makes you think it could have anything to do with a present?" he mused.

'Oh, you know very well! Because it is my name day, of course. Everyone else has given me a present."

"Then you cannot possibly need another."

"Sophie, stop pestering," Prince Golitskov reproved through his laughter. "You do not *ask* for presents, surely you know that."

"Was she always like this?" Adam inquired in a tone of mild curiosity.

"Oh, much worse," Golitskov told him. "Maturity has sobered her considerably."

"Good God!" Adam cast his eyes heavenward. "You would describe *this* exhibition as maturity?"

"Oh, you are both impossible!" Sophie declared, marching to the dining room door. "You are supposed to be kind to me on my name day. I am going to see how matters are progressing in the kitchen."

Leaving them both laughing, she went off to immerse herself in the masterminding of the various complexities attendant upon a production of this magnitude. Emerging from the kitchen an hour later, she went into the hall, where an army of serfs was busily hanging decorations, others coming in from the gardens, arms filled with foliage and flowers.

"Oh, no, do not put those there!" Sophie hurried up the stairs to where a lad, perched on a ladder at the head of the staircase, was arranging a wreath of dark green laurel leaves around a picture. "It looks positively funereal," she said, beckoning him down. "I will put these instead." "These" were field poppies with heavy scarlet heads. A drowsy, languorous flower of brilliant hue, it was one of Sophie's favorites.

She was halfway up the ladder, her arms brimming with poppies, when Adam walked through the front door into the hall. The buzz of voices, tapping hammers, laughter, faded into the distance as he saw her poised so precariously at the head of the stairs, her belly pushing against her skirt, scarlet flowing from her arms.

He dropped the saddle of fine tooled leather, inlaid with gold, beaded with ivory: a saddle fit for a Cossack stallion and a Cossack woman on her name day. He flung himself up the stairs, his gray eyes pinpricks of fury in his whitened face. "Get off there! You reckless, mindless fool! What are you trying to do?" He pulled her off the ladder. She staggered slightly, off balance, staring stunned at this outburst. She put out a hand to steady herself against him. Holding her, heedless of the shocked faces drifting in and out of his blurred vision, he shook her. "Are you trying to kill yourself? How dare you behave with such criminal negligence—"

"Adam!" It was Prince Golitskov's voice, cutting sharply through the tirade. Summoned by an alarmed servant, he mounted the stairs rapidly. "Get a grip on yourself, man!"

Sophie was no more than a limp rag under his hands; as his grip slackened, her knees buckled and she slid gasping to the ground, her skirt billowing around her. She looked up at him, incredulous, wounded to the core of her being. "Why?"

Adam took a deep, shuddering breath. "You are nearly nine months pregnant and you climb a ladder that is perched precariously at the head of a flight of stairs," he articulated slowly. "I have never come across such stupidity!" His eyes filled with pain, and he passed his hand over them as if to wipe out the image. . . . He had put out his hand and she had fallen, rolled over, her body thudding sickeningly on each step, her cry hoarse in the silent house. He had hurtled after her, but she had tumbled to the bottom, inert, crooked like a child's discarded doll . . . and then the bleeding had begun.

Grimly, Sophie seized the banister rail, pulling herself to her feet. Her grandfather cupped her elbow, assisting her. She moved her hand in dismissal, her eyes on Adam. She knew that haunted expression. It was the one he bore when he looked upon one of those bad moments in the past. She had thought them exorcised, but obviously this one had escaped the light of day.

"Let us go for a walk in the sunshine," she said, her voice steadier than her knees, which were still wobbling in the most inconvenient fashion. "Come." She held out her hand imperatively as she put her foot on the top step.

His eyes snapped into focus. This was Sophie, pale and resolute, hand outstretched. He became aware of Prince Golitskov's grave stare, of the wide-eyed circle of serfs, looking at him with the fearful hostility one might evince toward a mad dog.

"Come," Sophie repeated, a hint of steel in her voice. "I'll not be shaken like a rat in a terrier's mouth without explanation. Particularly not on my name day. Take my hand, my knees are wobbly."

Adam looked down the shallow sweep of stairs. The front door stood open, a broad road of yellow sunlight stretching from the door to the bottom of the staircase. He stepped toward her, took her hand. Her fingers closed over his and she remained standing, solid and steady on the top step.

They walked hand in hand down the stairs between phalanxes of questioning eyes, across the hall and out into the sunshine. A whisper rustled behind them, swelled to a babble. Prince Golitskov, leaving his household to the freedom of speculation and the luxury of gossip, returned to his library.

Outside, they walked in silence through the bustle of party preparations until they reached Sophie's rose garden. At the stone sundial, she stopped. "How did Eva die?"

"She fell down the stairs," Adam replied, looking past Sophie toward the dove cote in the corner of the garden. "I put out my hand . . . to steady her . . . I think to steady her." The words came slowly as if torn from his soul, as, for the first time, he articulated the fear—the fear that in his anger and the rawness of his wounds, when she had stood laughing at his old-fashioned outrage, her belly swollen with another man's child, the hand he had put out to steady her as she swayed in her laughter at the head of the stairs had pushed instead.

"The child slipped from her body in blood," he finished on a sob of anguish. "There was nothing anyone could do. It just went on until she was drained." He gripped the stone sundial with both hands, his knuckles white. "We were in Moscow. The court was at St. Petersburg. It was said only that she died as a result of an accident. The rest was assumed and I could see no reason to enlighten the gossips with the truth."

"The truth that you murdered your wife in a fit of jealous rage? Or the truth that she slipped and fell?" Sophie laid her hands over his as they continued to grip the stone. "You did not push her, Adam."

"How can you know that if I do not?"

"Because I know *you*," she replied with firm conviction. "I know you as I know myself, as I know this child that grows within me. We share parts of each other, and I *know* that however great your anger, however raw your wounds, you could not harm anyone in that way. It would be like . . . like Boris Mikhailov wantonly destroying a horse! Oh, maybe that sounds an absurd comparison! But it is a question of what is totally foreign to one's nature, of what it is impossible for someone to do, whatever the provocation." Suddenly seizing his wrist, she tugged him around to face her. "You know you did not do it."

"But I wanted to," he said quietly.

Sophie nodded. "It is the guilt of wanting to, not that of the doing, that has tormented you."

"Will you tell me she deserved it?"

Sophie shook her head. "No, no one deserves to die in such a manner."

She looked into his face, watching as the hard lines of anguish dissolved, as tears stood out in his eyes. Taking his hand, she drew him down with her to the grass, cradling his head upon her bosom, upon the shelf of her belly, fruitful with his child.

Chapter 19

"What do you mean, 'with child'? Answer me, woman!"

"She is, lord, I swear to it." Sobbing, sniveling, the petrified Maria fell to her knees before the towering fury of her master. The bearer of evil tidings, she bowed her head before his limitless wrath, knowing that had she kept such information from him, her suffering would have been magnified a hundredfold. Only the truth could provide adequate excuse for the fact that she was no longer in the princess's employ, coldly dismissed in Kiev, sent back to St. Petersburg to report failure to her lord, who did not tolerate failure. Maria was supposed to keep watch on the princess at all times. She was no longer doing so, but the blame must be laid at another's door. "She wouldn't let me serve her after we left the boat, lord, but I knew."

"How?" The word cut through the drear air in the mausoleum that was the Dmitriev palace in St. Petersburg.

Maria trembled violently, almost unable to speak. Would her negligence be held the cause for the princess's infidelity? "There were signs, lord, on the boat. The princess wasn't always well, sickly . . ." She hung her head, playing with her apron. "Also, lord, since she arrived in Kiev, she did not have . . . have . . . her time did not come upon her," she finished wretchedly. "Then she would not let me launder her clothes . . . so I would not remark . . . but I talked to the laundry maid of Countess Lomonsova, who did the princess's washing, lord. She said there were no . . . no signs of . . ."

"I understand you quite well!" interrupted the prince, directing a vicious kick at the kneeling figure. "Your orders were to keep the princess under your eye and report to me anything . . . *anything*, you hear me . . . that struck you as out of the ordinary. Why did you not tell me of your suspicions earlier?" He kicked her again, and Maria cringed, moaning with fear.

"Please, lord, I did not think anything of it until she sent me away at Kiev and went off with the count—"

"Count? What count?"

"Why . . . why the Polish count, lord, the one who used to come here so much—"

Adam Danilevski! Dmitriev wheeled away from the kneeling, whimpering Maria, who remained, still whimpering, still kneeling, in the middle of the carpet.

"The count was her escort," Maria said. "The empress sent him with her to her grandfather."

"Did you ever remark any closeness between the count and your mistress?"

"No, lord." Maria confessed to this further dereliction miserably. "Perhaps it is not him—"

"Idiot!" the prince shouted, swinging back at her. "How would you know whether it was or not? Who did the princess spend time with?"

"Countess Lomonsova—" She fell forward, clutching her ear, sobbing under a backhanded clout.

"Not women!"

"The French count, lord, the Prussian prince, lord—"

"Who else?" Dmitriev knew full well that his wife would not have been indulging in a liaison with either of the ambassadors. The czarina would never have permitted it. But she had permitted this. The appalling humiliation of the truth engulfed him. He had been duped by the empress, laughed at behind his back, sent away so that *his* wife could paddle palms with some . . . could conceive a bastard! Not his rightful heir, but a bastard! His barren wife had conceived. . . . Rage more ferocious than any he had experienced before swept him in waves, each one more violent than the last. The

Golitskovs had defeated him, routed him utterly with this final, ultimate humiliation.

Maria was still blubbering at his feet as she tried to find an acceptable answer to the question, but Sophia Alexeyevna had never been seen in any man's particular company.

"Oh, get out of here!" He kicked at her once more. "Don't let me see your face again if you want to keep the skin on your back!" The serf stumbled to her feet and fled the room.

The identity of the lover could wait. The scalding human fury vanished, leaving in its wake an inhuman iciness. He would be revenged upon his faithless wife in the traditional fashion. The severity of the vengeance might be deplored, but it could not be denied him, not even by the czarina, not when the evidence of adultery was there for all to see. Sophia Alexeyevna would suffer every minute of the rest of her hopefully long life; and his own life would be daily enriched by the knowledge of her suffering.

It was the end of September when Prince Dmitriev set off with a sizable armed force of his own serfs. Unencumbered, on horseback, they would accomplish the journey to Berkholzskoye in three weeks.

Sophie slipped out of bed in the darkness, padding barefoot to the window. It was the night of the fourteenth of October. A winter-promising wind came howling from the steppes. The night sky was for once overcast, its star-brilliance doused.

"What is it?" Adam spoke sleepily from the bed, frowning at the white shadow by the window. "Can you not sleep, love?"

She turned, smiling slightly. "I do not know what it is . . . strange sensations . . . a surging energy as if I must be up and out, striding the steppe." She shrugged. "It's nothing. Go back to sleep."

Adam sat up. "Shall I fetch Tanya?"

"Good heavens, no! It is nothing, I told you. Just a peculiar feeling."

"I will fetch her." He swung his legs to the floor, but Sophie forestalled him.

"Let her sleep, Adam. It is not time yet."

He stared at her face, pale in the gloom. "But it soon will be?"

She shrugged again, touching her mounded stomach. "Perhaps." She came toward him. "Go back to bed. I will just sit on the window seat until I feel sleepy again."

"How can I sleep when you are keeping vigil?" But he did as she asked, sensing that it was what she really wanted. Much to his later chagrin, sleep returned to him almost instantaneously. Soon his deep, rhythmic breathing was the only sound in the bedchamber, lulling Sophie as she sat, her forehead pressed to the cool casement, staring out at the shadows, the scudding clouds, the occasional glimmer of a star momentarily revealed.

She was still sitting there when the first pale streaks of dawn showed in the east. Adam, waking, got quietly out of bed, coming over to the window. "You are chilled, sweet," he said. "Come back to bed now, just until you get warm."

He had the sense that she was in some way withdrawing from her surroundings. It frightened him, yet it awed him, too. Something was happening to her in which he could have no part. But she allowed him to lead her back to bed, to hold her close until she was warmed again. He felt her first sudden, sharp indrawing of breath and was out of bed, pulling on his robe before Sophie realized.

"Where are you going?"

"To fetch Tanya. The baby is coming."

Sophie laughed gently. "It is too soon to fetch her, Adam love. Nothing is going to happen for hours yet."

He looked at her, bewildered. "How can you know?"

"I just do."

"But I felt you—"

"It was just a twinge," she broke in. "If you are going to be in such a state until this is over, you will be a wreck." She was still laughing at him, and he began to feel as if he had strayed into a world where the landscape was uncharted territory and the customs were known only to the few.

"I am still fetching her," he declared, as if to assert his right to an independent judgment.

He returned in five minutes with a clucking Tanya, nightcap askew on her sleep-tumbled hair, shuffling in her slippers. "By all the saints!" she declared, seeing Sophie quite calm in bed. "I expected to find you delivered already!" She shook her head at Adam. "First babies are never in a hurry, lord." Bending over Sophie, she pulled aside the covers, laying her hand on her mistress's abdomen. "How bad are the pains?"

"Just an occasional twinge," Sophie said. "I told him not to wake you."

Tanya tut-tutted reassuringly. "I was awake, dear. It's always hard for the men, particularly the first time."

"Well, *I* am going to get up," Sophie announced. "I see no reason to lie here counting twinges."

"But she can't get up! Tanya Feodorovna, will you please establish some order!" exclaimed Adam.

"Let her do what feels best, lord," Tanya said soothingly. "She's the best judge of that. You go off in your dressing room and stop fretting."

Sophie chuckled at Adam's expression of rebellious discomfiture. "Oh, do go," she said. "You are making me nervous."

That drove him from the room, and she stood up, watched closely by Tanya. Suddenly, she put out a hand to grasp the bedpost. "Perhaps I won't get dressed just yet, Tanya."

"I'll fetch you up some breakfast. You'll need your strength." The woman bustled out, leaving Sophie still holding the bedpost. She let go tentatively, wondering how afraid she really was. Her mother had died going through this; there was the woman in the village whose baby had been pulled from her in pieces; there was . . . No! She forced herself to close out the images. Thousands of women had yearly pregnancies and came unscathed through childbirth, many of them without the skilled care and experienced attention Sophie would have.

"What can I do?" Adam spoke from the door to his dressing room. He was dressed, but his expression was haggard.

"Love, there is nothing anybody can do at the moment." She came over to him, putting her arms around his neck. "Just knowing that you are here is enough."

"You go off downstairs and keep the prince company," Tanya ordered, coming in again with a breakfast tray. "I'll call you if you're needed. Eat hearty and keep your strength up."

Sophie laughed. "That is Tanya's prescription for all ills." She broke off, a spasm crossing her face.

Tanya pushed Adam to the door. "Just you go downstairs and have your breakfast with the prince, lord."

Adam obeyed reluctantly, but he could not see what alternative he had. He was clearly not wanted. In the dining room, he found Prince Golitskov, always an early riser.

"So it's begun," he greeted Adam without preamble. "Anna's in such a state of excitement she overboiled the eggs and scalded the milk for coffee. But I daresay we'll have to put up with it. If I tell her to do it again, the results will be the same. Well, sit down, man . . . sit down. . . . You're not the one having the baby."

"I only wish I were," Adam said dismally, pouring coffee. "They sent me away as if I were some grubby schoolboy interfering in adult affairs."

Golitskov laughed. "We'll go riding after breakfast."

Adam looked horrified at the suggestion. "I could not possibly leave the house."

Golitskov shrugged. "Please yourself. Let's hope it's over before dinner, else we'll be on short commons, I fear. Nothing's going to get done today."

Adam wondered if this grumbling indifference was a front to conceal the prince's real anxiety and to diffuse Adam's own. He sent a searching glance across the table at his companion. The prince looked up. "Dammit, Adam! I cannot bear to think of her enduring this."

"Her mother—" Adam began, expressing the core of his dread.

"Sophia Ivanova was a different kind of woman," Golitskov said with instant comprehension. "An ethereal creature, made more of air than of flesh and blood. No, that should not concern you."

"I think, perhaps, I will go upstairs again." Adam tossed his napkin down beside his plate of uneaten food.

The bedchamber was filled with women, stripping the bed, drawing back the hangings, placing cauldrons of water on the newly kindled fire. One of them was knotting a bedsheet to the bedpost at the foot of the bed and chills ran down his spine. Sophie was walking up and down the room, her face pale but calm.

"Sophie, surely you should be lying down." He took her hand.

"I prefer to walk." She let her hand lie in his. "Will you read to me while I walk?"

"Sweet heaven, anything." He was overwhelmed with relief at the idea that he might be of service.

"Montaigne," she said. "I always find him tranquil."

For two hours Adam read aloud from Montaigne's essays as Sophie paced steadily around the room. He tried to continue reading, to keep his voice even, whenever she stopped and held on to whatever piece of furniture was handy, but there came the time when a soft moan escaped her, and his voice faltered.

Tanya, who had been sitting quietly sewing, moved swiftly toward her. "Hold tight," she said, rubbing her back as she hunched forward.

"It's over." Sophie straightened. "Go on, Adam."

He started again, but after a couple of sentences he realized she was no longer concentrating on the words. Her face was drawn tight, her features etched in stark relief, the dark eyes filled with pain.

"You'd best leave now, lord." Tanya took Sophie's arm. "Let's put you to bed, dearie."

Adam watched helplessly as Sophie crept into bed. Her

moan became a cry. Tanya pushed the knotted bedsheet into her hands and Adam fled, unable to bear the prospect of her pain.

All afternoon it went on. Women ran up and down the stairs in the hushed house. Men spoke in whispers as they went about their business, and every now and again a scream would shiver through the house and everyone would stop, breath suspended. In the library, Adam and the prince drank vodka, but it brought not even a spurious ease.

"Something must be wrong," Adam gasped in the middle of the afternoon. "It cannot be continuing for all this time!" He ran from the library, up the stairs, entering the birthing chamber. "What is wrong?"

Tanya straightened from the bed, a lavender-soaked cloth in her hand, and spoke soothingly to him. "Why, nothing's wrong, lord. Whatever makes you think such a thing?"

He came over to the bed, staring aghast at the face on the pillow. Her eyes were closed and he wondered for a dreadful minute if she were already dead, so deathly pale was her sweat-beaded face, so limp and dank with sweat the hair on the pillow. Then her eyes opened. Amazingly, she smiled. "It does seem to take an unconscionably long time."

"I will never forgive myself," he whispered, kneeling beside the bed, taking her hand between both his. "To cause you so much suffering."

"What a great piece of nonsense," she scolded, then gripped his hand with a strength he could not believe she possessed as the pain wracked her anew. She made no sound though and, when the agony receded, sank limply back upon the pillow as if drained of all strength.

"How long must she endure?" Adam demanded of Tanya, who was again bathing Sophie's forehead with lavender water.

"Not much longer," she said calmly. "It's all going beautifully, lord. The child is coming headfirst. It's just that the head is a little large."

So cool and matter-of-fact she was! The image of the baby's head, too large for the slender body locked in its elemental struggle, filled his brain. It was his fault the child's head was too large. His mother always told him how large his own had been.

"Adam!" Sophie's voice was barely a whisper, but the urgency could not be mistaken. "Give me your hand."

She gripped with that same superhuman strength, but something different was happening. He looked in amazement. Her eyes were again closed, but her face was contorted with effort, not pain, now, the veins in her neck standing out against the ivory skin. Tanya moved to the foot of the bed, throwing back the covers. One of the other women hefted a cauldron of boiling water off the fire, placed a fresh kettle upon the trivet.

"Push again, Sophia Alexeyevna." The calm instruction came from the foot of the bed. Sophie's hand still gripped Adam's, but it was as if she did not know what she was holding. He was transfixed by the extraordinary transcendent beauty of her face, which reflected the effortful labors of her body, lending his hand to the struggle with a sense of joy that he could participate even in this small way.

There came the moment when a sleek, dark head appeared between her thighs. He held his breath, suspended in wonder at the eternal miracle. A piercing wail filled the room, and Sophie's hand went limp in his.

"Well, what a lusty lad," Tanya declared a second or two later with undisguised satisfaction. "Crying before he's even out in the world."

"A boy?" whispered Sophie.

"A fine boy." Tanya placed the naked, blood-streaked scrap of humanity in her arms.

Adam looked down at his son, wondering if more could ever be added to the sum of human happiness. He touched a tiny hand, wrinkled like an old man's.

"Sasha," Sophie said softly. "Do you like the name, Adam?"

Alexander, Sasha in diminutive. "Yes, I think it suits him," Adam said solemnly.

"Now, lord, you go down and tell the prince he has a fine,

healthy great-grandson," Tanya instructed, taking the baby from Sophie. "There's more work to be done here. You can come back when the princess is comfortable."

Thus dismissed, Adam bent to kiss Sophie's damp brow, running his fingers through the lank strands of hair. "I have never seen you more beautiful or more radiant."

"She'll be more beautiful still if you'll let me get at her," Tanya scolded, pushing him away from the bed. "Get along with you now. Men in the birthing chamber! I've never heard of such a thing."

Adam walked on air out of the room filled with its own joyful bustle. At the foot of the staircase stood Prince Golitskov, his expression a mask of apprehension.

"I have a son," Adam said dreamily as he came down the stairs. "I have a son, Prince."

Golitskov embraced him with tears in his eyes. "And the mother?"

"Radiant," Adam said in the same tone of bemused wonder. "After enduring so much, she is radiant. Such strength women have, Prince."

Enough to endure maternal separation from the child so newly separated from her body? wondered the prince. "Come, we shall celebrate. I have been keeping a superb claret for just such an occasion."

In any other circumstances, the birth of a Golitskov great-grandson would be heralded with the pealing of bells for leagues around. For a week, barrels of wine and beer would stand on every street corner, in every courtyard, replenished when they were emptied. Thanks would be given in every church, and neighbors between here and Kiev would come bearing congratulations.

But not for this great-grandchild, thought Golitskov with sorrow in his heart. Not for this illegitimate son of a Polish count and a Russian princess, whose birth must be kept a Berkholzskoye secret, preserved from the outside world.

Chapter 20

"Katya Novikova is a strong, healthy girl, Princess. She will make a fine wet nurse." Tanya Feodorovna smoothed the patchwork quilt on Sophie's bed a shade nervously.

"But I have told you, there is no need for a wet nurse," Sophie said tranquilly. "I have more than enough milk for this little one." She smiled down at the babe in her arms. A shock of spiky black hair crowned the still slightly misshapen head nestled against her breast. His eyes were closed as he suckled greedily, one tiny hand clenched in a fist against the succoring breast.

"Oh, dear," sighed Tanya. "You must be sensible, Sophia Alexeyevna. The longer you suckle the child yourself, the harder it will be for you."

Sophie looked at her blankly. "To do what?"

Tanya sighed again, more heavily, and left the room. In the library she found the babe's father and great-grandfather, both of them in earnest conversation. "I do not know what's to happen," she stated without preamble. "It is usual for a newly delivered mother to have some strange fancies for a few days, but Sophia Alexeyevna does not seem to be considering what is to be done. She behaves with the child as if they are in a world of their own. If there were a sign of fever I would understand."

"There is none?" asked Adam sharply, the dread spectre of puerperal fever never far from his mind these days.

"Bless your heart, no, lord," assured Tanya comfortingly. "The princess will be up and about in a day or two." She dusted a corner of the table with her apron, shaking her head. "But what is to be done? I've found a good wet nurse in Katya No-

314

vikova, but the princess will have none of it . . . says she has more than enough milk herself, as if that was the point!''

"Perhaps we should both talk with her." Golitskov heaved himself from his chair. "This cowardly procrastination is not going to help.''

Adam nodded, giving the old man his arm. They went slowly upstairs to the west wing. Sophie's chamber was bright with jugs of autumn foliage. A fire crackled merrily, and buttery sunshine filled the casement.

"I was hoping for a visit," she said, moving the baby to her other breast. "Your son has a hearty appetite, love." She held out her hand to Adam. "Come and see. He is amazingly like you.''

Adam could not fight the joy and pride he felt in this child of his loins. "My head is a better shape," he laughingly protested, tenderly touching the soft, pulsing spot on the child's crown where the bone was not yet formed.

Prince Golitskov moved closer to the fire, warming his rheumatic hands. Adam was as absorbed in his fatherhood as Sophie in her motherhood. Love was responsible for more tragic tangles than such a supposedly soft and productive emotion had any business to be! He turned to the lost couple at the bed.

"Sophia Alexeyevna, you are going to have to make some decisions.''

The harshness in his voice startled Sophie. "What do you mean, *Grandpère*?''

"Have your wits gone begging?" he said. "You know you cannot acknowledge the child as your own. The longer you continue to suckle him, the more devastating it will be for you.''

"Your grandfather is right, sweetheart." Adam spoke with difficulty. "Let him be put to the wet nurse.''

"No!" She exploded with a violence that startled the child, whose mouth opened on a protesting wail. "Hush," she soothed, holding him against her shoulder, rubbing his back gently. "I do not know that I will have to go back to St. Petersburg." But she did know it. Paul would not let her slip away again. She took a deep, steadying breath. "For as long as I may, I will mother my child.''

"Sophie, as soon as you are able to travel, I will arrange for you and the child to go into France.'' Golitskov spoke decisively. ''You will be well provided for, out of your husband's reach.''

Sophie looked at Adam. Slowly, she shook her head. ''I cannot do that.''

''It is that or you must surrender the child.'' The hard choice, implacable, dropped like stone.

''I do not have to surrender him yet,'' she said in a small, broken voice. ''Not yet, not until I must.''

''Sophie, you must go into France.'' Adam, in his own anguish, said the only thing possible. ''I will come—''

''No,'' she interrupted quietly. ''If you abandoned your family you would never forgive yourself, and I will not live with that burden. I will not go alone because I would never have news of you and I cannot live in such a desert. I will accept my destiny, here. Sasha will not suffer, I know that. I can endure my own affliction, but I will not hasten it. I would have what I may while I may.''

Defeated, Prince Golitskov silently left the room.

''At least let us make some plans, sweet love.'' Adam sat on the bed. ''Let me hold him.''

She placed Sasha in his arms and he gazed in wonder at the bright blue button eyes, the snub nose; he examined each perfect miniature finger and toe, while his son blinked his unfocused eyes and yawned.

''The czarina gave me permission to stay here until the spring, if my husband permitted it,'' Sophie said. ''Paul has not communicated with me. If he waits until the onset of winter before sending for me, I may, in good conscience, refuse to make the journey until spring. The empress will stand my friend in such an instance.'' She sat back against her piled-up pillows. ''I am not concerned, Adam. It is already the middle of October. Paul would have to send for me by the end of the month. I have a feeling he is not going to do so.'' Smiling, she leaned forward, tickling the babe's stomach. ''Do not wear such a long face, love. Anything could happen between now and the spring.''

Adam tried to fall in with this mood of happy insouciance. But he could not dispel his foreboding, could not discount the feeling that Sophie was deliberately adopting a policy of self-deception as shield against the harsh truths that in the deepest recesses of her soul she acknowledged.

In Kiev, General, Prince Paul Dmitriev was obliged to halt for several days. He needed to purchase and equip two carriages; three of his escort were sick of a fever and the horses needed reshoeing. But he was prepared to bide his time. Sophia Alexeyevna was going nowhere and could be left to enjoy her delusion of safety. Its violent shattering would be all the more devastating the longer she had enjoyed it.

A spy sent hotfoot to Berkholzskoye returned with the information that Princess Dmitrievna was said to have given birth to a healthy son.

Further questioning elicited the interesting information that a Polish count was staying at Berkholzskoye as guest of Prince Golitskov.

The inhabitants of the Wild Lands kept their own counsel, Dmitriev reflected sourly. Only by going to Berkholzskoye and ferreting out the information for oneself could one discover scandals that anywhere else would be shouted from the rooftops. Here in Kiev, a mere fifty versts away, no rumor of shameful happenings on the Golitskov estates was bruited. If he had not heard of her faithlessness from Maria, he would never have known.

But he had her now, helpless in her unknowing, waiting to receive the entirely legitimate vengeance of the deceived husband.

"Why so restless, Adam?" Sophie, curled in a big wing chair by the bedchamber fire, shook her head in mock amazement. "You were the one who said restfulness was the quality to be most admired in a woman. Here am I, perfectly reposed and contented, and you cannot sit still for a minute."

Adam bent over the back of the chair and kissed her. "You do appear to have undergone some remarkable transformation," he teased. "To tell the truth, love, I am trying to summon up the courage to ask your permission to go hunting."

Sophie laughed. "You absurd creature! Why should you need my leave?"

He looked rueful. "I feel guilty about abandoning you. But Boris Mikhailov tells me that there is a pack of wolves terrorizing the village of Talma."

"And you would go hunt them down." She smiled wistfully, her eyes going to the casement, where the day blustered, cold and bright. "I wish I could come. I have not been hunting this age."

"You know you cannot, which is why I will not go," he declared with resolution.

"No, you must! I insist, Adam. Just because I am still so ridiculously lethargic does not give me the right to tie you to my bedside. I do not know why it should be taking so long for me to recover my strength," she added, a mite disconsolately.

"It has not been much above a week, love," Adam reminded her.

Sophie sighed. "I suppose so. It is just that I am not accustomed to feeling enfeebled." A wail from the crib in the corner of the chamber brought her to her feet in a most unfeeble fashion. "Ah, *mon petit*, are you hungry again?" She bent over the crib, lifting the infant, kissing the firm, warm roundness of his baby cheeks. "Go with Boris, Adam. I have much to occupy me with a woman's work for the moment."

He smiled tenderly. "Indeed, it does seem so. We will not be gone more than three days."

"You will be gone until you have hunted down every last wolf in the pack," she said with mock sternness. "Do not pretend otherwise to salve your conscience." She sat down in the chair again, opening her bodice for the hungrily nuzzling babe.

That shadow of foreboding darkened his vision as he looked at the picture they presented—such perfect contentment could only tempt an unkind fate. It would take but the slightest touch to shatter the picture into myriad fragments of grief and loss. Resolutely, he put such futile ponderings from him, bending to kiss the top of her head, to stroke his son's cheek with a fingertip. "I will get my things together, then, if you are sure you will not be lonely."

"I shall miss you, but I have *Grandpère*." Her eyes danced mischievously. "*He* does not become unpleasant when I cheat at cards."

"Perhaps if he had been a little more unpleasant in the past, he might have cured you of such a deplorable habit," Adam declared, going into his dressing room. "Do you know where the bootboy put my hunting boots?"

"Are they not in the rack?"

"Ah, yes, I have them." The eagerness in his voice made her smile, although it was a smile tinged with envy. She could well empathize with such enthusiastic anticipation. A few days on horseback engaged in a battle of cunning and wits with a pack of wily wolves was a heady prospect, particularly after such a sedentary week of bedside occupations.

She went downstairs to see them off, waving from the open front door as the group—Adam, Boris Mikhailov, and four serfs to act as gun bearers—trotted down the drive.

"Such a long face," Prince Golitskov gently chided. "Next time, you will be able to go."

Gregory closed the door on the chilly afternoon as they turned back into the house. A curious dank emptiness seemed to hang in the air, and Sophie shivered involuntarily. It was absurd to feel so bereft, so . . . so defenseless, just because Adam had gone hunting.

It was dusk when the party of horsemen, two empty carriages bowling behind them, turned onto the avenue of poplars leading to the mansion. They rode in silence under the bare trees, over the mud-deep earth that in summer was a dustbowl. At their head, Prince Dmitriev bore an expression that would have been familiar to his soldiers. It was the anticipatory satisfaction of one about to accomplish a mission of duty—regardless of cost.

The mansion stood closed against the night. He signaled to one of his men, who dismounted and began to hammer on the great iron knocker. Casements flew open, startled faces peering down at the small army, threatening upon the gravel sweep. Within, Prince Golitskov came slowly into the hall, one hand held to his breast, where ugly premonition blossomed. Yet no one whose business was illegitimate would hammer so peremptorily upon the door. Sophie, the child in her arms, rushed to the head of the stairs, staring wide-eyed into the hall below as Gregory, at a sign from the prince, pulled back the bolts.

General, Prince Paul Dmitriev stepped into the hall. He saw his wife first, hair tumbled about her shoulders, dressed casually in a loose print gown, a child clutched to her bosom. For a long moment, the cold blue eyes absorbed the sight while she stood impaled by his menace. Then he turned to the old man, who tottered slightly.

"I am come for my wife," Prince Dmitriev said in his cold, dispassionate fashion. "Do not attempt to prevent me. You do not have the right, and a man is entitled to take charge of his adulterous wife."

Prince Golitskov recovered himself. He stepped forward. "Prince Dmitriev, I will not allow you to remove Sophia Alexeyevna from my roof. The treatment she has received from you in the past—"

"She is my wife!" hissed Dmitriev in the same low voice. "Much though I may regret it, it is so, and I will have a husband's vengeance for her infidelity and her bastard."

"No!" Golitskov, in appalled horror at the mire of hatred and venom revealed by this speech, raised a hand in protest. There was a flash of steel. Slowly, he crumpled to the ground, blood spreading untidily across his shoulder.

"You have killed him!" Sophie, heedless of even the child she held in her arms, flew down the stairs, dropping on her knees beside the still, ghost-pale figure of the old man.

"It is a shoulder wound. He will not die of it," her husband told her carelessly. "You!" He beckoned to Anna, who stood moaning and wringing her hands. "Tend to your master!" He caught Sophie by the hair, jerking her upright. "Get upstairs to your chamber with your bastard, whore!"

Stumbling under the force of his push, she caught the child convulsively against her with one hand, putting out her other to grasp the banister. He shoved her again, his knuckles digging into her back, and she staggered up the stairs, biting her lip to keep the moans of fear from escaping.

Tanya Feodorovna, with a loud cry of outrage, sprang from

a doorway in the upper hall. She dropped to the ground, felled by an almighty blow to the side of the head from Dmitriev's fist.

Dear God, Sophie prayed in silent repetition. Do not let him hurt the child. I do not mind what he does to me, but do not let him harm the child. She fell into her bedchamber under another violent push. He stood looking down at her as she crouched on her knees, one hand supporting herself on the floor, the child cradled against her with the other. He read her terror. Contempt filled his eyes, overlaid with a deep satisfaction.

"Finally, my dear, we come to a reckoning. You are a whore, my adulterous wife." With a sudden movement, he bent, snatching the baby from her, pushing her backward as he did so, causing her to lose her balance.

"No!" She scrambled to her feet, her eyes wild, her hair swirling around her as she grabbed for the child. Paul struck her with the back of his hand, and she reeled. His signet ring had cut into her lip, but she barely noticed the sticky warmth of blood on her chin. She sprang at him again, and this time the blow brought her back to her knees, sobbing with pain and terror.

"Stay where you are and listen to me," he said in the same cold tone. The baby in his hands set up a piteous wailing, and Sophie could hear her voice pleading through her own sobs. "Be quiet!" he said, and she fell despairingly silent.

"I will take this bastard as mine." So cold, so deadly cold, as if snakes' venom ran in his veins. "He will grow up as my heir, but he will abhor the name of his mother. He will suffer through his growing, and he will know to lay that suffering at the door of the whore who gave him life."

Sophie began to shake uncontrollably as the diabolical words pierced her like a rapier of ice. The child's wails increased in volume, and the milk flooded into her breasts in response.

Dmitriev swore a vile oath. Striding to the door, he bellowed and one of his men came running. "Take the brat!" He almost threw the squawling infant at the man. "Find some woman to act as wet nurse. She will come with us to St. Petersburg."

"Yes, lord." The man took the red, screaming, soggy bundle and bore him off.

As her son's wails grew fainter, Sophie huddled over her ach-

ing breasts, now spilling nourishment for the child torn from
her. She was drained of all strength, muscle and sinew liquified,
her mind retreating from this hellish nightmare, as if, by so
doing, it would go away and she would wake up.

"Get up!" Seizing her hair again, he yanked her to her feet.
Her scalp burned; her face stung from the blows. "Where is
Danilevski?"

She shook her head, and he jerked her head back by the hair
and hit her again. "Where is he?"

"I do not know," she croaked between her swollen, bleeding
lips. "He went to Mogilev." She did not know why she lied,
except for the vague hope that if Paul could not put Adam definitely on the scene, he would have no evidence that he was the
guilty lover. Without evidence, he could not injure him.

"Then I must postpone dealing with him." Dmitriev shrugged
carelessly. "It does not matter, for the moment." He looked
coldly into her face as if he were examining some repellent creature of a different species. "As for you, my faithless wife—"

"Why? Why would you have me to wife?" The question
interrupted him. It was the question that had haunted her since
their wedding night, when he had made it so mortifyingly clear
that she disappointed him and she had not known why. The
disappointment had become loathing, and she still had not
known what she could have done to inspire such an extremity
of distaste. He was looking at her now with that same disgust
he had so often evinced in the past. Facing the end of all that
meant happiness, she could ask the question with a curious indifference. The answer did not really matter, but she might as
well go to her death with the riddle solved. "Why did you woo
me and wed me, Paul, when you knew I did not please you?"

His laugh dripped acid. "No, you did not please me from the
moment I laid eyes on you—bold, brazen, indecorous, with
none of your mother's delicacy and beauty. I had expected to
wed Sophia Ivanova's daughter—"

"Why?" she asked again, interest kindling despite her throbbing face, her burning scalp, her bereft soul.

The pale eyes looked at her, yet did not seem to see her. "I
wanted your mother, and I would have had her but for you, who

killed her." His gaze focused on her again. "I thought to have the daughter in her stead." He jerked back on her hair again. "And look what I possessed!" So vicious was his tone that she flinched in the expectation of another blow. "An unappealing, unfaithful whore!"

"Kill me," she said. "You have taken my child, what more can you do to me?"

A slight gleam enlivened the ice-blue stare. "Oh, I have not begun yet. I will have my revenge on the Golitskovs through you. You will live a very long life, I trust." Another jerk on her hair brought tears flowing from her eyes. "I repudiate you," he spat. "As is my right with an unfaithful wife, one who has born a bastard. You will enter the Convent of the Assumption as a penitent." For a second that ghastly gleam in the cold eyes flared with fanatical satisfaction. "You will enter as a penitent whore, with your head shaved, barefoot, and with the stripes of the lash upon your back. These instructions together with details of the crime for which you are repudiated shall be given to the superiors at the convent." His thin smile flickered. "You will live long to pay for your crime, Sophia Alexeyevna, and for the humiliations visited upon me by your parents. And you will do so in a pitiless climate—the convent has a harsh and unforgiving regime dedicated to the redemption of sinners through prayer and penance." A poisonous satisfaction laced every carefully articulated word.

Sophie barely heard him. Her fate held no interest for her, not beside the monstrous life he planned for her child. To grow up in that mausoleum, to grow under the hatred borne him by this vicious despot . . . And there would be no way to stop him. If he declared the child his own, his heir, his generosity would be applauded. He would repudiate the wife, as was his right in the eyes of the Church and of the law, but would care for the innocent child. It was a diabolical vengeance. As she had paid and would continue to pay for the supposed injuries her parents had inflicted upon Paul Dmitriev, so would her son pay for his mother's crimes, and every day she lived she would be tormented by her knowledge of the life her son would be enduring.

Her lack of response to this description of her punishment penetrated his cold dispassion, and a tide of rage swept hotly through him. "Perhaps you do not fully understand what I am saying." His eyes darted around the room, fell upon the scissors on the dresser. Dragging her by the hair, he crossed to the dresser. "I will start what the monks will finish, then maybe you will begin to understand."

Before she could realize what was happening, he began to hack at her hair. She stood staring, disbelieving, into the mirror as the rich, dark locks fell to her shoulders, to the floor in luxuriant, chestnut-tinted profusion. That same fanatical light shone in his eyes as he hacked down to the scalp, pulling agonizingly as he did so. Tears poured down her cheeks, mingling with the blood from her split lip, but her mutilated image was blurred now in the mirror as she seemed to enter some dark world of her own. Her knees buckled, but he held her up by what little hair she had left, before flinging her facedown across the bed. Her hands were wrenched behind her. The roughness of rope bound her wrists so tight she had cried out before she could stifle the sound in the quilt.

The door clicked shut on his departure, the sound of the iron key turning. Sophie lay, trying to gather some strength, just enough to enable her to turn over. But when she did so, the cramping in her arms as she lay upon them was agonizing, and not all the will in the world would force her muscles to make the complicated maneuvers necessary to bring her to her feet without the use of her hands. With a sob, she rolled again onto her belly.

All night she lay, having no idea what was happening in the rest of the house; whether her grandfather lived, whether her child slept in a stranger's arms; whether Tanya had recovered consciousness. The general's army had taken over the house, and all at Berkholzskoye knew that this was the princess's husband, who had the perfect right to remove his wife if he so chose. In the absence of any leadership of their own, they bowed to the invader's rule.

At dawn the door opened again with the same lack of emotion with which it had been closed. "I trust you slept well," came the cold voice above her. He turned her over, pulling her into a sitting position. "It is time for you to begin your journey. Stand up."

Sophie did so. She had lost all sensation in her arms, could feel milk leaking from her breasts, staining her bodice. Her face was stiff with dried tears and blood, aching with bruises.

He looked at her with an expression of ineffable disgust before flinging a cloak around her, pushing her ahead of him out of the room, down the stairs, and out of the house. She saw not one familiar face, only her husband's men, stone-faced, staring ahead. Two carriages stood on the sweep. Beside one she saw a peasant woman wrapped in a black shawl. In her arms was a bundle.

"Sasha!" Sophie stumbled, unbalanced by her bound hands, toward the woman, but her husband pulled her back.

"You have had your last sight of your bastard!" He propelled her toward the other carriage. She was bundled inside to fall crouching upon the floor. The door slammed shut and she dragged herself, slowly, painfully, onto the seat. A whip cracked, and the vehicle moved forward, jolting on the rough road. Soon, the inevitable nausea would come to plague her. But what did it matter?

During the long reaches of the night she had accepted her fate. In her weakness, acceptance came readily. It offered some kind of comfort, for to fight would bring only renewed agony of the mind and the body. There was no hope of rescue. Her destination would be known to no one. By the time Adam returned to Berkholzskoye, she would be long gone. The wife's seducer could hardly demand explanation or satisfaction from the husband whose actions were entirely legitimate. And he would be able to do nothing for his son. He could not claim him as his son, and Paul would keep the boy immured, far from the eyes of the world, as he wreaked his vengeance.

She had nothing left. Paul had stripped her of the last vestiges of human dignity, and she felt herself no longer human, just some befouled and tattered piece of flotsam that had for a while held her head up upon the earth. She had enjoyed the sun; she had loved; she had given birth. Her eyes closed as she slipped into the peaceful world of memory.

Chapter 21

Adam felt the first prickle of foreboding at dawn. Frowning, he tried to rationalize the uncomfortable feeling. He had felt it before where Sophie was concerned, but without cause. Shrugging, he mounted his horse. It had something to do with the fetters of love. They bound so securely that to be apart from her caused these occasional panicky flutters.

They were following wolf spoors, clear in the night frost still lingering on the steppe, when an icy shaft, as powerful as if it had corporeal substance, dug deep into his breast. He gasped as if with pain, and Boris Mikhailov, riding at his side, looked over in sharp-eyed concern.

"What is it, Count?"

"I do not know," Adam said. A cold sweat bathed his body. "But something is badly amiss, Boris."

"With Sophia Alexeyevna?" The muzhik asked the question, although he did not need Adam's affirmative nod.

"Tell me I am being fanciful, if you will, but I feel it," Adam said slowly.

"I'll not tell you you're being fanciful," Boris replied. "Such knowledge is hard to explain, but it is frequently correct. We can be back at Berkholzskoye in six hours."

They rode hard, reaching the poplar avenue at noon. Adam had said not a word, his face drawn in grim lines, his mouth set, his eyes looking inward as he urged his mount to yet greater effort. Boris, in the same silence, kept pace with him, their four-man escort trailing.

The silence on the estate was eerie. Not a sound of hammer or saw, not a sight of gardener or stable hand. It was an estate of the dead. The two men, dread made manifest, spurred their flagging mounts.

"In the name of pity!" Adam hauled back on the reins as something caught his eye, fluttering among the thick trees lining the avenue. Hanging by his hands from a low branch was Gregory, the watchman, his back torn by the knout.

Boris was already off his horse, running, knife in hand, to the still figure. He cut him down, laying him gently on the ground, feeling for the carotid artery. "He's alive, Count. But frozen, as if he's been out here for hours."

"Dmitriev," Adam said.

"It bears his mark." The giant muzhik hoisted the inert body of the watchman across his shoulder. "Take my horse, Count. I'll be better on foot."

Adam nodded, set his horse to the gallop. He arrived on the gravel sweep where the mansion stood, blind and closed, shrouded in desolation. He flung himself from his horse. The front door swung open as he laid his hand upon the knocker. Sick with dread, he stepped into the hall. There was no sound, no sign of life. Lifting his head, he opened his lungs in a bellow that would have raised the dead.

It brought Anna, creeping from the kitchen, ghastly, shrunken, clutching her apron to her face. "Oh, lord, it is you," she said, and began to weep soundlessly.

"Where is Prince Golitskov?" Adam did not ask where Sophie was. He knew she was not here.

"In his bed, lord. He's sore wounded. When Gregory tried to stop them . . . they . . ."

"Yes, I know," he said, touching her shoulder. "Boris is bringing Gregory to the house. Please see to his tending, Anna."

"He is not dead?" A flicker of hope, that indication of life, showed in the old eyes. "We did not know where to find him . . . after . . . after they had gone."

Adam understood the despairing apathy of shock. He nodded. "Boris says he is not dead, but he'll need much nursing." Leaving the woman, he took the stairs two at a time, bursting into the prince's bedchamber. Tanya Feodorovna cried out with fright, springing to her feet from her kneeling position by the bed. Then she saw who it was and fell back to her knees, sobbing.

"Hush now, Tanya." He lifted her, saw the livid bruise on her temple. "Dmitriev did this?"

She nodded, struggling to regain her composure. "And ran the prince through the shoulder with his sword."

Adam stepped over to the bed. Golitskov was lying pale and clean and still beneath the sheet, a waxen form with a thick white bandage padding out his nightshirt at the shoulder. He looked too frail to live, Adam thought, but he could see that he did. "How severe is his wound?"

"On a younger man, lord, it would be of less concern," Tanya said, seeming to recover her competence by the minute. "But with the Holy Mother's help, if it be God's will, he will live."

"And Sophia Alexeyevna?" He could hardly bring himself to ask, so great was his terror of the answer.

Tanya shook her head. "He took her, lord . . . her and the baby, with one of the women from the farm for wet nurse. In carriages they went. Old Peter saw them from the attic window. The princess in one, the baby and the nurse in the other. We were kept locked in the kitchen until they left. No one saw her, lord . . . not after he took her upstairs . . . except for Peter from the window. Shut up in a carriage she was, lord. She can't abide carriages, lord." The tears flowed in a river, and she buried her head in her apron. "Why would he take the child from her?"

"Why would he not?" Adam asked rhetorically, more to himself than to Tanya. "I shall be gone within the hour. If the prince wakes before then, send for me." Leaving the chamber, he ran down the stairs, noting on the periphery of his awareness that the house had come to life again, the pall lifted, as if, with his arrival, the energy of hope had vanquished the stunned trance.

Boris was in the hall. "The prince?"

"Tanya is not despairing," Adam replied, but a shadow

hung in his eyes. "He is an old man, Boris, to endure such shock and loss of blood."

Boris Mikhailov's face hardened. It was an expression that was not to soften for many days. "I've sent two men into the village to discover if they can the direction the general took."

Adam nodded his approval. "We'll need fresh horses."

Prince Golitskov came back to the world fleetingly before they left. His tired eyes looked into the hard, resolute face of a man who had imagined the worst and put it from him. "I was expecting you," the prince said in a thread of a voice. "I knew you would know. You must free her from him."

"I will do so," Adam promised, taking one gnarled hand between his. "And I will bring her back to you . . . and my son."

Golitskov's head moved on the pillow in a faint gesture of acceptance, then his eyes closed again.

"Let me come with you, lord." Tanya put her hand on Adam's arm in urgent appeal. "She will need me after . . ."

"I cannot take you, Tanya," he said gently, covering her hand with his own. "We must ride hard. You will slow us down." Tanya bowed her head, turning back to her patient.

Out on the gravel sweep, Boris Mikhailov waited with two fresh, strong mounts. Adam came out, and as he walked over, men appeared from the house, from the trees; men, walking firmly, staves in their hands, some with firearms, some with knives. There must be twenty of them, Adam thought, for a moment bemused. They ranged themselves behind the horses without a word spoken.

"They have known Sophia Alexeyevna since I brought her here, a babe no older than your son," Boris said softly. "They are come to fight for their lord."

"Then mount them!" Adam said. "We will take such an army against Dmitriev!"

"I will arm them, also. It will not delay us long." Boris went amongst the men, who followed him to the stables. Within half an hour Adam looked upon his army and was as satisfied with his motley crew as if they had been an immac-

ulate, highly trained and disciplined regiment of the Imperial
Guard. Purpose and determination stood out on every face,
and they held themselves erect on the assortment of sturdy
mounts Boris had selected. To a man, they evinced the dedication of those who believed in the cause for which they
would fight. It was that dedication that made a trustworthy
and effective fighting force, as Adam well knew, much more
than the harshest of military discipline and the endless drill-
ing so favored by General Dmitriev and his like.

He urged his mount down the avenue, and his small force
followed. By concentrating only on the task ahead, the elimi-
nation of Dmitriev, Adam was able to keep at bay the nightmare
images that would interfere with his planning. There was no
point in concerning himself with Sophie's fate at the moment.
She was suffering that fate and would continue to do so until
her husband's tyranny was overthrown in the only way possible.

They took the Kiev road, as instructed by one of the villagers
who had seen the dawn cavalcade with its two coaches. They
had been traveling fast, the informant told them. Six horses to
each carriage and they were driving them hard. For a second,
the picture of Sophie tortured by nausea, jolted in the ill-sprung
vehicle swaying violently at speed over the rutted road to Kiev,
filled his mind. She was not yet recovered from the birth, still
bleeding, so much of her strength going into the production of
milk for the child. How could she endure?

Boris Mikhailov had no difficulty reading his companion's
mind. "They have an eight-hour start, Count. If they stop for
the night, we'll come up with them soon enough. If they
continue, we will catch them by midnight."

"They will have to change horses," Adam said. "We will
keep track of them through the post houses."

They fed and watered her as if she were an animal, Sophie
thought dully, whenever she troubled to think. She became
aware that at some point in the afternoon the carriage in
which she was traveling had veered off the Kiev road, sepa-
rating itself from the main party. There were still four outriders and the coachman with her as they swayed over a

miserable cart track across the steppe, and occasionally one of the men would come into the carriage, hold water to her lips, offer her bread and sausage. She turned her head away from the food. The less she had in her belly, the less she was likely to vomit, and even through her hopeless trance, she recognized that that humiliation she could not endure, bound and captive as she was.

They unfastened her hands and allowed her to seek privacy behind a bush when the need became imperative, but she was never unbound long enough for sensation to return fully to her arms and hands, although she recognized that they did not tie her as tightly as had Paul. No expression enlivened the flat peasant faces as they performed these tasks. Neither pity nor cruelty showed in their eyes. They were simply serfs obeying the orders of a master who could not be disobeyed.

Darkness fell, and the carriage continued to sway and jolt. They stopped to change horses, but the curtains were pulled across the windows so she could not see out, and, more important perhaps, no one could see in. Obviously, this journey would not stop until her destination was reached. How long she would remain in this limbo she could not begin to guess. Her head pounded with such agony she wept, and tears fell undried because she could not use her hands, and the milk leaked from her spurned, swollen breasts.

Adam rode through the night, through Kiev, and onto the road that led to St. Petersburg. Inquiries at post houses elicited the information that horses had been changed several times for one carriage and a mounted escort of some fifteen men. A description of General Dmitriev brought nods of recognition. Someone said a baby had been heard crying from the carriage.

Adam's chin sank onto his chest. They were following Dmitriev and the child, and they must continue to do so, but every verst they traveled took them farther from Sophie. They could not discover exactly when one of the carriages had split from the main party, although they knew it had happened before Kiev. That meant that Sophie's destination lay across the steppes toward Siberia. Dmitriev could not be intending such a barbarous destination! But Adam knew absolutely that he could.

"Count!" Boris's voice spoke with soft urgency in the dark.

Adam, who had been half asleep in the manner of an experienced campaigner, came to instant awareness. "What is it?"

"They are about three versts ahead of us," Boris told him. "The scout has just returned."

Adam frowned, his mind crystal clear as energy surged through him at the prospect of action, the closeness of their quarry. Not wishing to come upon Dmitriev suddenly, he had been sending scouts ahead, riding parallel to the road, screened by trees and bushes, for the last three hours. "How many of them exactly?"

"Sixteen, counting the coachman."

"How armed?"

"Swords and pistols."

"Let us all do a little scouting, Boris. I've a mind for an ambush," Adam said thoughtfully. "I think Prince Dmitriev and his band of villains are going to run into a band of even greater brigands."

Striking out across country so as to be sure they were invisible from the winding road gleaming white in the moonlight, the group rode fast. Once Adam was certain that they would have overtaken their quarry, they took to the road again, searching for a likely spot to stage an ambush.

Finally they came to a stretch where the road dipped between rocky outcrops. The cover was scanty but the best they were going to find, Adam decided. He looked up at the sky. "It will be dawn in an hour, Boris Mikhailov. I'd have this over before the light of day."

The muzhik nodded. "Don't want any stray travelers running into us. Not as if the general's doing anything he shouldn't."

Adam gave vent to a short, bleak laugh. "No, the wrongdoing is all on the other side, Boris."

"In principle," agreed the other. "But I've always favored practice over principle. You going to see to the dispositions?"

Adam could not help a smile at this laconic pragmatism so

typical of Boris Mikhailov. He was the most reassuring companion in a crisis. The men were waiting quietly on the road, relaxed and calm, confident in their commander, committed to their cause. They received their orders in intelligent silence and dispersed behind the rocks. The horses were tethered in the trees beyond the ambush site, out of sight of anyone entering the gully. Those men most experienced with firearms were positioned at the entrance to the ambush and its exit. Only one immutable order had been given. No one was to fire upon General Dmitriev.

Dmitriev ignored the knowledge that his men were fatigued almost to the limit of endurance. If he could endure, then so could they. He would allow a halt once the sun was well up, but night travel was too hazardous for rest periods. Besides, while they kept moving, the screams of the brat were less noticeable. The minute they stopped, the dreadful wailing filled the air, unsettling the men with its note of helpless, hopeless, unfocused distress. The woman said the child refused the breast, or if he took it would turn away from it within seconds, howling with frustration. Dmitriev, who knew nothing of these things, wondered acidly if peasant milk had a coarseness to it, noticeably unpleasant to a child who had suckled only a princess's breast. The reflection did nothing to sweeten his mood.

Ahead, the moonlight sparked off quartz-seamed rock on either side of the road. A warning prickle ran down the soldier's back. For several hundred yards they would be traversing something resembling a gully. The night was quiet, except for the hoot of an owl, the howl of a wolf, the whistle of the ice-tipped wind. It was a well-traveled road, but few would be abroad at night, except perhaps in the summer, when it would be light as day and warm. Late autumn was not the season to encourage brigands in the pursuit of their trade. However, Dmitriev was an experienced soldier who knew the value of caution. He ordered his men to close ranks, to take out their firearms.

They rode into the gully. Dmitriev was instantly aware that

something was amiss. His head swiveled from side to side, but he could see nothing, yet he knew eyes were upon them. He gave the order to increase speed, and just as the cavalcade reached the center of the gully all hell broke loose. The night was lit with gunpowder flashes, deafened by pistol reports, as men seemed to pour from the rocks hemming them in behind and ahead.

Confusion reigned as his own men returned the fire. Swords scraped out of sheaths; horses, unaccustomed to battle and alarmed by the cracks and flashes, reared up, unseating riders who found themselves tangled up in flailing hooves. Gunsmoke hung heavy in the air, making identification difficult so that Dmitriev's men in their confusion found themselves occasionally slashing at each other.

Dmitriev assumed they were under attack from brigands. It was an assumption that died when he recognized a giant muzhik, wielding a mighty sword with grim effect. Men, if they did not fall beneath the sword, fell back before the power and resolution of the swordsman.

"Boris Mikhailov!" Dmitriev whispered savagely, taking careful aim at the large target. Then the gun fell from his hand as a knife pressed into his back.

"Where is she?" Adam Danilevski's voice rustled in the prince's ear. The knife pressed deeper, drawing blood.

Dmitriev was no coward, but the sensation of a knife in his back, a knife wielded by a man the general knew from the depths of his soul would use it without compunction, was more terrifying than anything he could imagine. He called "To me!" but all his men were occupied with their own private battles. They were outnumbered, they were trapped, and they had been surprised.

The knife cut and the prince choked. "Where have you sent her, Dmitriev?"

"She is a whore!" the prince spat through his terror, then cried out as the knife cut again, then again, ripping through his coat. He could make no move to defend himself without the knife's penetrating further. "To me!" he called again.

This time his cry was heard. A man, pistol at the ready,

came running. A shot rang out and he fell. Boris Mikhailov slashed his way toward Adam and the prince. "Where have you sent her?" The inexorable question came again. Blood trickled warmly down Dmitriev's back. At his front stood the giant muzhik, gaze implacable as he placed the blade of his sword flat against the prince's throat.

"Answer the question, Prince."

"To the Convent of the Assumption at Orenburg." The admission came through saliva-flecked lips as Dmitriev struggled with fear, humiliation, and rage. "I will see you hang for this, Danilevski!"

"I don't think so." Adam withdrew the knife, wiping the blood upon the prince's coat. Somehow he managed to keep hidden his surge of nearly uncontrollable rage and terrifying fear at the knowledge of the destination Dmitriev had chosen for Sophie. Images of the barren, tortured existence to which she had been condemned writhed in his mind, and for a few seconds he could not speak. Then he said in an almost bored tone, "Boris Mikhailov has a score to settle, I believe."

Dmitriev looked into the eyes of the man he had once condemned to cruel death, and he read his own death there.

"There are many reckonings to be met, Prince," Boris said slowly. "I do not know how you were responsible for the death of my friend and master, the young Prince Golitskov, but I know that you were." Dmitriev's pallor grew ghastly. "As you were, in the same way, responsible for the death of Sophia Ivanova. You sent Sophia Alexeyevna away, intending that she should meet her death upon the road. You left Gregory hanging after torture for the cold and the crows. I do not yet know what you have done to Sophia Alexeyevna this time, but I will add it to the reckoning nevertheless. Prince Golitskov lies sore wounded at your hands. Even if I forgive the harm you have done to me, Prince Dmitriev, there is enough there to warrant your execution."

"I will not die at the hands of a serf!" He turned his head against the flat blade, outrage at such final degradation mingling with appeal as he looked at Adam, who, an aristocrat himself, would surely understand the impossibility of such an end.

Adam turned on his heel and walked away toward the carriage. Order was emerging gradually from the chaos of the battlefield. Dmitriev's men, those left standing, were huddled against the rocks, under the steady-eyed guard of two of the Golitskov men. "How many of our own are injured?"

"Just two, lord," was the answer. "They're being attended to over by the carriage. No deaths, neither."

Adam nodded and continued to the carriage. Into the semisilence came a shrill wailing. He opened the carriage door, peering into the dim interior. A woman moaning in fear sat huddled in the corner. From her arms came the squalls of Adam's son.

"You're quite safe," he said gently to the woman. "Cease your moaning and give me my son."

"Oh, lord, here he is. Quite unhurt." The words tumbled anxiously from her as she held out her bundle. "But he will not take the breast, lord. I cannot soothe him."

"That does not surprise me in the least." Adam stepped backward into the gray light of dawn, feeling some measure of peace come upon him as he retrieved this precious part of his little family so violently torn asunder. Sasha, as if responding to familiar arms, ceased crying and lay hiccuping in his father's arms. Adam wondered how he was to feed the child during the desperate ride ahead and placed his face against the drenched, distraught infant's.

"He'll take milk on a rag until we reach his mother, Count." Boris, as usual an accurate reader of Adam's thoughts, spoke softly. "I did it with his mother on just such a journey when she was younger even than he."

Adam rested the child against his shoulder, rubbing his back until the hiccups died down. "Is it done, Boris Mikhailov?"

"It is done," replied the muzhik.

"Then there is nothing to keep us here. Send the woman back to Berkholzskoye with our men."

"And those?" Boris gestured disdainfully toward the prisoners gazing around the littered gully with morose and fearful incomprehension.

"Turn them loose. As far as they know, they have been the victims of a brigand attack. Their master is dead. With luck, they may strike lucky and find a better one. I don't see them plodding on to St. Petersburg, somehow." Adam opened the leather pouch at his belt, drawing out a handful of rubles. "Give them this; let them fight it out among them. I would have more sympathy if I did not know that one of them had used the knout on Gregory."

"We take the road to Orenburg?"

"Yes, but we will cut across country. I know this area well, Boris. It is coming into the territory of my own home, Mogilev. If we retrace our steps to beyond Kiev and take the Siberian road they would themselves have taken, we will be over a day behind them. If we go across country, it will be rougher riding, but we will join the Siberian road farther along. With luck, we should not then be far behind them. Maybe even ahead of them." He turned impatiently to his horse. "It is not much traveled, that road. We shall get information of their passing easily enough." Holding the child tightly, he swung up. Not many people chose to journey into Siberia, particularly at this season. But it was to be presumed that Dmitriev intended her to arrive this time, so adequate preparation would have been made, and they would stop frequently to change the team.

They reached a post house within an hour, and Boris explained their needs with the knowledge acquired so many years ago. The postman's wife, clucking energetically, produced goat's milk and a clean rag. Adam, seating himself in front of the fire, squashed his desperate need to continue the journey without respite and set himself patiently to satisfy his infant son's ferocious appetite.

For some reason, the babe who had rejected the peasant woman's breast showed no reluctance when held safe in familiar arms to suck upon the rag. The tears dried miraculously, and the pale cheeks pinkened as the rhythmic sucking soothed and satisfied. It seemed to Adam almost as if Sasha grew round and content again before his eyes.

"Poor little mite's soaking wet," the postman's wife declared. "You'd best change his clothes before you go on again, lord." Whatever she might think of the extraordinary circumstance of a lord mothering a baby in her post house, she said nothing. It was not her place to notice, let alone comment.

Sasha had not been ill-provided for on his journey, and Boris had brought the bundle from the carriage. Fed, washed, and in clean clothes, the baby fell asleep and stayed so, exhausted by his earlier desperation, for nearly six hours, during which they rode, barely talking, pushing their horses over the steppe until they discerned the barely discernible cart track that constituted the road to Siberia.

The noonday sun was bright, warming the air a little. They stopped to rest the horses, feed and change the now-fretful baby, and eat the food provided by the postman's wife. Adam looked along the track. "The question is, Boris, are we ahead of them or behind them?"

"Behind," Boris said with confidence. On receiving a raised, questioning eyebrow, he said, "They had orders to drive day and night, changing the team whenever they could so they were always fresh. There are four of them, and the coachman."

"You gleaned this valuable information from one of Dmitriev's men?"

Boris nodded and said nothing more. He would not tell the count that Sophia Alexeyevna was cruelly bound, that her escort had orders that she was to remain so until they reached their destination. The escort were also under orders to ensure that she reached the convent alive, although her condition was immaterial.

"Then let us go. We will change the horses at the next farm."

They rode through the afternoon, exchanging their own exhausted mounts for two nags who were at least fresh. The farmer who cheerfully provided the exchange informed them that a coach and outriders had passed some three hours earlier. Generous payment ensured good care for their horses until their return and bought more milk for Sasha, and black bread, cheese, and beer for themselves.

With the certain knowledge that he was now within a hand's grasp of Sophie, Adam curbed his hideous imaginings, forced himself to eat and to tend the baby patiently, experience having taught him that any attempt to hurry over his care for the child produced wails and restlessness, which in turn led to what Boris diagnosed sagely as an attack of wind.

On the road again, though, Adam could not conceal his agitation. No less anxious, Boris kept his own counsel. A few wispy clouds became massed cumulus crowding the sun, then obscuring it. The first drops of rain plopped, huge and wet upon the track ahead. Adam swore, drawing his cloak more tightly over the baby. The track twisted, turned, and ahead of them moved a coach with four outriders, cloaks turned up against the dash of raindrops.

Adam drew in his breath, exhaled on a deep sigh. "Shall we join forces with our fellow travelers, Boris?"

"I am sure they will be glad of our company," returned his companion. "It might be best to leave the babe, though."

Adam searched the roadside. "If Moses could be hidden in the bullrushes, I see no reason why Sasha should not find a temporary cradle beneath a blackberry bush." He dismounted, carried the well-wrapped, sleeping child to the shelter of a flourishing bramble, and gently laid him down.

"Let us make an end of this business." He remounted, his voice curt, edged now with the fear of what he would find in the carriage. Dmitriev could have done anything to her during the long hours of that night at Berkholzskoye.

"How do you want to do this, Count?"

"I think we simply ride up with them. Exchange a few civilities. They will not be expecting pursuit, how should they? I would avoid further bloodshed if we can."

Boris nodded. They caught up with the carriage and horsemen, and found their easy greetings returned monosyllabically. Chatty inquiries as to destination produced grunts, mutters.

Adam casually moved his mount sideways so he flanked the riders. Boris did the same on the other side. Both drew their pistols simultaneously, aiming at the head of the nearside rider on either side.

"I suggest we stop here," Adam said politely. "You will come to no harm. My interest is with your prisoner."

The four men looked stunned. They had not been prepared for this—a courteous aristocrat on the Siberian road intent on rescue of that silent woman who already looked as if she was no longer of this world. Brigands they knew to look out for . . . but these two were not brigands.

"What do you want with us, lord?" The lead rider stammered, his hand creeping to his pistol. A shot singed his cuff and his hand fell back. He stared in disbelief at the scorch on his sleeve.

"Just that you throw your weapons down and move to the side of the track, where my companion here will keep a friendly eye upon you," Adam said, wondering how long he could keep this iron curb upon his muscles, straining toward the carriage. Why had she not heard his voice? Why had she not looked out, showing at least minimal interest in the fact that the carriage had halted?

But he could not drop his own guard until he was sure that Boris had them all in charge. The coachman came off the box, the escorts off their horses under the threatening muzzle of a pistol, and they were all herded to the side of the road, where Boris deftly tied them together with a rope that had been coiled on his saddle. It wasn't so much the count's pistols that ensured quivering obedience from the five men; it was the look in the giant's eye.

Adam flung open the carriage door. For a moment his heart stilled in his breast. Then, as if he were some other person, someone not bound by the fetters of indissoluble love to the inert, beaten woman huddled in the corner, he climbed into the vehicle, closing the door behind him. Sitting on the padded seat beside her, he lifted her upright. He saw her wrists, but the words he hurled at God and the devil never broke from his lips. Instead, very, very gently he drew his knife from his belt and with the utmost care severed the rope that bit deep into the swollen flesh.

The rage in his heart was great enough to feed the fires of hell as he lifted her onto his knee, cradling her, looking down at her bruised, battered face, stroking her mutilated scalp. "Sophie," he whispered. "Wake up now, sweetheart."

She was neither asleep nor unconscious, merely inhabiting a world where spiritual and physical agony could not touch her. For a while she fought the return demanded by the familiar voice of love. Why should she trust in chimera?

"Sophie." He kissed her mouth, a feather touch that could not exacerbate her hurts. "It is safe to wake up, sweetheart."

"Sasha?" she said, quite clearly.

"He is here, love, safe and sound. Open your eyes."

The dark eyes opened in response to the plea. She tried to smile and winced. But he saw the awareness return to her, the life reentering her eyes. "Is my husband dead?"

"Yes."

Her eyes closed again, but this time not in retreat. When she opened them again, Sophia Alexeyevna was in full possession of her senses. "I hurt so," she said. "Except for my arms and hands." She looked down at her hands where they lay in her lap as if they did not belong to her. "I cannot feel them."

"You will," he said confidently. "You were not bound in that manner long enough to lose the use of them." But by the time they reached the convent in Siberia she would have been crippled for life. He put that thought from him forever. "I am going to take you to Mogilev now. We are closer to there than to Berkholzskoye." He was massaging her hands as he talked. "My mother is perhaps a poor substitute for Tanya Feodorovna, but she is kind and skilled at nursing."

"*Grandpère* . . . ?"

"He will live," Adam said, continuing with his chafing. "The wound has weakened him, but he did not look willing to give up the ghost yet a while." It was the hardest thing imaginable to smile, but he managed it.

There was a rap on the door and Boris's head appeared in the carriage window. Without losing his hold on Sophie, Adam leaned sideways to open the door. "Thought the princess might be glad of the child," Boris said. "Seems to be hungry again."

Adam took the baby, placing him in Sophie's lap. Her face was transfigured with joyous relief. "I have ached to feed him," she said softly. "Unbutton my gown, Adam. I cannot quite make my hands move properly yet."

He did so, then lifted the baby, who gave a little sobbing

gurgle as he found what he had been missing. Adam placed Sophie's arms around the child, and she nodded. "I can hold him now." A deep silence of renewal filled the narrow space. Adam held them both, willing the vengefulness from him. It was over now, and to dwell upon the images of what might have been could only destroy the peace to which they now had a right.

"Whatever will your mother think?" Sophie asked suddenly, moving the baby to her other breast. It was a fumbling movement, but she managed it without assistance. "How can you possibly appear without warning with such . . . such extraordinary appendages? I do not need a looking glass to know what I must look like."

"I cannot imagine what she will think," he said, and this time the smile was easier. "Thinking is not one of her great strengths. But she is not given to judging, either. She is a serene and accepting woman who will welcome the woman who is to be my wife from the vast well of loving warmth with which she is blessed."

"Boris must go to *Grandpère*—"

"He will do so, and as soon as your grandfather is fit to travel, then he will come to Mogilev for the wedding."

"But should we not be married from Berkholzskoye?"

Adam groaned. "Sweetheart, I really think the place is immaterial."

"I daresay you are right. And I should meet your mother. It would be most discourteous, otherwise."

Yes," he agreed solemnly. "And I am very sorry for the indignity, sweetheart, but you are going to have to ride before me to Mogilev."

"Is there not a spare horse?" The dark eyes looked aghast.

"No," he said placidly. "And even if there were, you are not strong enough."

"I can think of worse excuses for being cuddled." Sophie capitulated with a miraculous lightheartedness. When one had been given back one's life and one's love, everything else paled beside such gifts.

Epilogue

"Is it a good idea for him to eat worms?" Adam said in a tone of mild inquiry. He strolled down the garden basking in a soft April sun.

"I didn't realize he was *eating* them." Sophie sat back on her heels, regarding Sasha, who, with the concentrated dedication of a six-month-old, was crawling in her wake, picking out squiggly worms from the earth newly turned by her trowel. "I thought he was just trying to hold on to them."

"The route from hand to mouth is immutable," Adam reminded her with a grin. In confirmation, the baby abruptly thumped onto his padded bottom and stuffed a fat, dirt-filled fist into his mouth.

"I do not suppose it will hurt him. It's all God's good earth," Sophie said easily, returning to her weeding. "And he will only howl if we try to stop him."

Adam sat on a low stone bench, stretching his long legs with a luxurious sigh. "Do you think he is a trifle spoiled, Sophie?"

She looked over her shoulder at Adam in surprise. "Of course he is. All babies should be spoiled, Tanya says. I was, and it never did me any harm."

Adam's eyes narrowed against the sun as he drawled, lazily provocative, "I seem to recall one or two occasions when I have taken issue with that conclusion."

Sophie threw a handful of earth at him, and Sasha, with a gleeful gurgle, offered his own imitative effort.

"You are a most irresponsible parent," Adam declared

343

severely, brushing dirt from his sleeve. "You set the most appalling examples."

Sophie chuckled, shuffling on her knees across the grass to where he sat. "Like this, I suppose." Resting her forearms on his lap, she reached up to kiss his mouth.

Her hair, still short, but thick and luxuriant, smelled of sunshine, her skin of lavender and the good, rich earth caught beneath her fingernails. Cupping her face between his hands, he drank deeply of her fragrant sweetness, rejoicing in the very fact of his wife.

"Oh, dear, Sophie, Sasha is eating worms!" The vague tones of the elder Countess Danilevska broke into the charmed circle as she glided in stately fashion down the path toward them, her hoop setting her turquoise silk skirts swaying, the breeze fluttering the ribbons on her lace cap.

"I know, *chère madame*." Still on her knees, Sophie turned to smile at the woman who had welcomed without question the bruised and battered piece of human wreckage her son had brought to her six months earlier. She had taken her prospective Russian daughter-in-law to her ample bosom, looked vaguely surprised at being told that her grandson, so clearly her son's child, was known as Prince Alexander Dmitriev, although for reasons not vouchsafed he did not bear a patronymic, and proceeded to forget all the oddities attendant upon her son's choice of wife. She had welcomed the arrival of a rather irascible Prince Golitskov, a weeping but clearly competent Tanya Feodorovna, a giant muzhik, and a Cossack stallion who had terrified her own stable hands. She had arranged the wedding, very simply dealt with any niggling objections to those arrangements expressed by the old prince by ignoring them while offering smiles and vodka; and had the immeasurable joy of seeing her beloved son obviously married in love.

"I wonder if it is good for him," she now said, examining her grubby grandson, who was beaming his one-toothed beam proudly through his dirt. "What would Tanya Feodorovna say?"

"That what goes in has to come out," Sophie promptly replied. "*Méchant!*" Springing to her feet, she swooped on the child, lifting him into the air so that he squealed and kicked his chubby legs gleefully.

"Have you told Sophie about the imperial messenger, Adam?" the countess asked.

"I was about to do so, *Maman*, but Sasha's gastronomic predilections distracted me," Adam replied.

Sophie stiffened, glancing at her husband, unable to hide the flash of anxiety in her eyes. "A letter from the czarina?"

"Give me the baby, *ma chère*. I will take him to Tanya Feodorovna to be cleaned up." Her mother-in-law took Sasha from her. "His great-grandfather has been asking for him, but he won't welcome him as dirty as he is." Tickling the child's stomach so that he shrieked with laughter, she bore him off toward the long, low house.

"*Grandpère* is anxious to return to Berkholzskoye," Sophie said absently. "I would wish to accompany him. We could perhaps spend the summer there, if your mother does not mind." Her voice caught. "What does the empress say?"

Adam patted the bench beside him, reaching into his breast pocket with his other hand. He drew out two documents, both bearing the imperial seal. "There is one for you, also."

Sophie sat down and took the document. "Every time I have received one of these it has spelled disaster," she said slowly. "I cannot help it, Adam, but I feel sick. Will you open it for me?"

"Let me tell you what was in mine first," he said. "Then maybe you will not feel so sick." He unfolded it carefully, then laid it on his lap, looking over the garden as if he knew the contents of the letter by heart. He smiled ruefully. "I am first roundly scolded for not presenting myself in St. Petersburg by the first of the year as the empress had instructed. Then I am thanked for my report on my mission to Warsaw." Bending, he picked a crocus peeping through the grass at his feet. He threaded it into the rich, dark head leaning against his shoulder. "I seem to remember some other occasion with flowers . . ." he mused.

Sophie choked with laughter despite her anxiety. "Yes, you proved a most skilled gardener! Now do not keep me in suspense. You have not reached the important bits yet."

"My request to resign my commission in the Preobrazhensky regiment is granted." Sophie gave a whoop of joy. "Although with some reluctance," Adam continued. "Her Imperial Majesty, while recognizing that I now have other responsibilities, ones that would inevitably interfere with the single-minded dedication of a career officer, requests that I hold myself ready to serve my country in the event of war."

Sophie shivered. "I suppose such a stipulation was only to be expected."

"Of course it was," he replied briskly, dismissing the caveat as of no further importance. "Finally, Her Imperial Majesty grants me permission to retire to my family estates for eight months of the year. For the four-month period from the end of November to the end of March I am to bring my wife and family to court."

"Four months!" Sophie groaned. "I suppose I will survive."

"Sophia Alexeyevna, you ungrateful monster!" exclaimed Adam. "Do you not realize how indulgent the czarina has been?"

"I want it all," Sophie said, sighing.

"Spoiled brat! Open your letter now."

Her fingers shook slightly, although she knew now that her own communication could contain nothing too dreadful. She read it through silently, then leaned back, looking up into the spring-silver foliage of a willow tree. Fingers of sunlight massaged her eyelids, and a great peace filled her.

"Well?" Adam demanded. "Are you also castigated?"

"Only mildly," Sophie said. "For not waiting the correct mourning period before remarrying. I am, however, commended for having committed that indiscretion discreetly, if you see what I mean." Adam nodded. "She says that Prince Alexander Dmitriev is recognized as heir to the estates of General, Prince Paul Dmitriev, his father. The unfortunate circumstances of the general's death at the hands of brigands are much lamented by the czarina, who writes that brigands remain one of her empire's greatest scourges."

They sat silent in the afternoon sun, while the final shadow was lifted from the little world of happiness they had inhabited the last months. The stain of illegitimacy would not touch their son, who would inherit the vast Dmitriev fortune that had been augmented by his mother's.

"The empress who rules with a knout in one hand and the scale of justice in the other," Adam observed.

"She has a softness for lovers," Sophie said, turning her head against his shoulder, lifting a hand to caress the strong profile, to linger upon that beautiful, smiling mouth. "Could we have done anything, love, to alter the course of this? Sometimes I have wondered if we could have done something . . . said something . . . that would have averted . . . Oh, I do not know what I am trying to say."

Adam caught her chin. "I know what you are trying to say. And the answer is no. We could have prevented nothing. Dmitriev had his own agenda, the empress had hers, and for a while we were caught in them both. Caught, until . . ." Smiling, he touched her lips with his finger.

" 'I will a round unvarnish'd tale deliver of my whole course of love; what drugs, what charms, what conjuration, and what mighty magic.' "

Sophie frowned for a second, then she began to laugh. " 'A maiden never bold; of spirit so still and quiet, that her motion blush'd at herself.' Adam, I will not play Desdemona to your Othello! It would be an appalling piece of miscasting."

"I had forgotten the rest of the speech," Adam confessed through his answering laughter. Then his laughter died abruptly. "And I will never play Othello to your Desdemona, my love."

"You will never have cause," she said. Suddenly her eyes danced mischievously, dispelling the moment of gravity. "Not that Othello did, either."

There was a short silence, then, with quiet deliberation, she said, "I can promise that you will never have to play Adam to my Eva. The past is behind: yours, mine, and ours. All such matters are abolished by imperial decree!" Jumping to her feet, she seized his hands, pulling him up with her. "Come, I would ride Khan in celebration."

Adam planted his hands on his hips, saying slowly and with emphasis, "You would do *what* in celebration?"

"A slip of the tongue," Sophie said hastily.

JANE FEATHER

JANE FEATHER was born in Cairo, Egypt, and grew up in the New Forest, in the south of England. She was trained as a social worker and—after moving with her husband and three children to New Jersey in 1978—pursued her career in psychiatric social work. She started writing after she moved with her family to Washington, D.C., in 1981. Five contemporary romances were followed by two Regencies and several historical romances, including *Chase The Dawn* and *Heart's Folly*, both available from Avon Books.